LADY BEAUCHAMP'S PROPOSAL

SCANDALOUS REGENCY WIDOWS, BOOK ONE

AMY ROSE BENNETT

D1452439

COPYRIGHT

Lady Beauchamp's Proposal

Copyright © 2014 Amy Rose Bennett
First Edition Publication: August 2014
Second Edition Publication: September 2015
Third Edition Ebook Publication: April 2023
Third Edition Print Publication: July 2023

Third Edition Editor: Emily EK Murdoch
Cover Artist: Erin Dameron-Hill

ISBN Print Book: 978-0-9954283-3-1

PRAISE FOR AMY ROSE BENNETT

"Amy Rose Bennett is a fresh new voice in historical romance with a flair for historical atmosphere."

— ANNE GRACIE FOR *HOW TO CATCH A WICKED VISCOUNT*

"Amy Rose Bennett is a charming new voice in historical romance."

— ANNA CAMPBELL FOR *HOW TO CATCH A WICKED VISCOUNT*

"A sweet and spicy read full of sly wit and rich with delicious details that pull the reader into the scene. A delightful confection of ballroom banter and bedroom seduction."

— SALLY MACKENZIE, *USA TODAY* BESTSELLER FOR *HOW TO CATCH A WICKED VISCOUNT*

"The perfect blend of sexiness and humor... Amy Rose Bennett has created a lush, vibrant love story, her characters sharing a fabulous sensual chemistry that fairly scorches the page."

— CHRISTINA BRITTON, AWARD-WINNING AUTHOR FOR *UP ALL NIGHT WITH A GOOD DUKE*

ABOUT LADY BEAUCHAMP'S PROPOSAL...

A runaway countess finds love when she least expects it...but she can't hide from her past forever.

Elizabeth, Lady Beauchamp, fears for her life. When she discovers her dissolute and long-estranged husband has syphilis—and he wants to beget an heir no matter the cost— she flees to a remote part of Scotland to begin a new life as the widowed governess, Mrs. Beth Eliott at Eilean Tor Castle.

When Mrs. Eliott unexpectedly arrives on his doorstep, the reclusive and recently widowed Marquess of Rothsburgh is both irritated and intrigued. No longer in need of a governess —his young daughter now resides with his sister's family in Edinburgh—he proposes the beautiful widow fill a position of a different kind...

Torn between staying true to her marriage vows and her wanton attraction to the devilishly handsome marquess, Elizabeth struggles against the temptation to become his mistress. But living a lie is not easy when you have fallen in love. And secrets always have a way of coming out...

DEDICATION

For Richard... I love you.

PROLOGUE

Harcourt House, London
September 1815

E lizabeth Harcourt, Lady Beauchamp, sat before her cherrywood dressing table, determinedly brushing her hair with slow methodical strokes, trying in vain to relax. The simple routine always used to be soothing. A balm to her taut nerves.

But not anymore.

Especially not tonight.

The longcase clock in the hall outside suddenly heralded the hour. Midnight.

With a shaky sigh, Elizabeth placed the brush upon the silver tray and glanced at her candle-lit reflection. A grave young woman stared back at her. Shadows as dark as bruises marred the pale skin beneath her gray eyes. She was so tired. And so anxious, she felt as brittle as a dried-out birch twig that was going to snap at any moment.

But she couldn't break now. All going well, in six hours she would be gone from here in a hired hackney cab that was scheduled to arrive in the mews behind the servants' entrance where her traveling trunk had been carefully stowed. Despite her fatigue, she doubted that she would be able to sleep at all between now and then.

There was too much at stake.

The unexpected sound of her bedroom door opening made her start. In the dark shadows behind her, the reflection of her husband's tall, lean frame appeared. He paused on the threshold and by the way he leaned against the door frame, it was obvious that he was drunk—not an unusual circumstance for this time of night. Elizabeth knew that he'd probably spent the best part of the evening at his club or some gaming hell.

But what *was* unusual and caused her heart to hammer against her breast was the fact that he had come to her room at all.

Hugh hadn't entered her bedchamber for more than a year.

She tried to read his expression, judge his mood. Desperately tried to fathom what could have prompted this unexpected nocturnal visitation. But Hugh's blue eyes, indeed the sculpted planes of his entire face, were hidden in shadow.

"Elizabeth." Pushing away from the door he prowled toward her bed, then with a heavy sigh, sank onto the pale blue silk counterpane. The lingering odor of port and stale cigar smoke assailed her. Even though Elizabeth's stomach cramped with fear, she forced herself to remain still as she watched and waited. It made no sense at all that Hugh had come to her instead of seeking out the more titillating company of his latest mistress or a prostitute in a high-class bawdy house—his usual custom at this late hour.

Unless... Does he know what I have planned?

Despite her rising panic, Elizabeth was suddenly struck by the realization that her husband was uncharacteristically maudlin. Turning to face him, she was acutely conscious of the fact that she only wore a thin, white cotton night rail. Although it buttoned all the way to her throat and had long sleeves, she felt vulnerable. Exposed. It bothered her that her feet were bare.

But she couldn't afford to show any weakness.

"Are you all right, my lord?" she asked carefully, forcing the words past her tight, dry throat. It seemed safer than asking: What do you want? Or: Are you here to stop me leaving you?

She hoped to God he hadn't uncovered her secret. She must tread carefully. Her life depended upon it.

His gaze traveled over her, but quickly returned to her face. Grimacing, he then ran a hand through his golden blond hair, ruffling it into messy spikes. At the age of twenty-eight, he still looked boyishly handsome, although Elizabeth had long since ceased to think of him in that way.

"To be honest, I don't know," he replied at last.

Honest. That was a word that Elizabeth no longer associated with her husband, Hugh de Lancey Harcourt, the Earl of Beauchamp. Strangely enough, she did believe him tonight. He was in a peculiar mood indeed.

The silence between them stretched. Surely he could hear her frantic heartbeat. She was unsure what to say or do next. She just wanted him to leave.

Please, God, make him leave.

He started to speak again, his words slightly slurred. "It has been a long time since I... Since we..." His gaze dropped to her chest where her breasts were well concealed beneath her chaste night attire.

Elizabeth noted that he couldn't bring himself to complete the thought. Perhaps he was going to say, "Since I fucked you," or, "Since we made love." The latter statement would have been grossly inaccurate, of course. In three years of marriage, Elizabeth did not believe that they had ever truly made love.

Though what he had intended to say mattered little. What mattered was, it was not like Hugh to be inarticulate, or melancholy, or in her room. His behavior was troubling. And it disturbed her that she could not predict what he would do next.

Elizabeth didn't know what to do either. Terror trickled an icy trail down her spine and rendered her mute. All she knew was that regardless of his mood, she could not let him touch her. If he did, she would be damned just as much as he was.

Hugh didn't seem to notice her petrified silence. Perhaps he was distracted by his own personal demons. She knew all too well that he had many. But there was one in particular that plagued her. The words of the letter her husband's lover sent to her a mere fortnight ago had tainted Elizabeth's mind as surely and insidiously as the contagion Hugh now undoubtedly carried.

Your husband has the great pox, my lady.

Elizabeth did not doubt the veracity of the writer, anonymous though she was. She had already seen traces of the telltale sore on the ring finger of Hugh's left hand. The lesion was so inflamed, he no longer wore his favorite sapphire-set signet ring. Dr. Morton had called the sore a "chancre" after she'd described it to him.

She could not see it now because Hugh still had his gloves on.

Her husband drew in a deep breath. "I've been thinking..." he began then trailed off as if the attempt to clarify where this out of the ordinary encounter was heading was a struggle for him. "Elizabeth..." He at last met her gaze. "I think it is time that I got you with child."

Elizabeth stifled a gasp and somehow managed to stay upright. Her hands gripped the sides of her velvet covered seat. Surely he jested.

But no, he was deadly serious. He took off his gloves and removed the sapphire pin from his cravat. Even though he was a few feet away, she could see the mark of the pox—the chancre.

Didn't he know that he had the disease? How could he not know?

Elizabeth suspected he must know yet did not care. And what scared her most at this particular moment was that she believed he was fully capable of acting with depraved indifference toward her. He had always been selfish. It obviously mattered little to him that he would be exposing her to the infection in the attempt to conceive an heir. Dr. Morton had warned her that any child resulting from their union would also be inflicted with the pox and Elizabeth could not countenance such a diabolical act.

She had to get away, now more than ever. If only she could make it through the next few hours without Hugh touching her.

Strange to think she'd once longed for his touch...

As Hugh stood and moved toward her, she summoned what she hoped was a convincing smile. "As you wish, my lord." Her voice was husky, but not with desire. She prayed he couldn't discern the difference.

He laid a hand upon her shoulder. His touch was hot, heavy.

Deadly.

She smiled up at him. "Hugh, it has been such a long time, and clearly you have taken me by surprise. I feel at a...disadvantage. If you would indulge me, I would like to change into something more...pleasing to the eye. I know how you loathe these night rails."

Hugh's eyes locked with hers. Speculation, perhaps even interest flared in the deep blue depths. A corner of his wide mouth lifted in a sensual smile. "Of course, my lady."

He brushed the pale curtain of her hair aside and when he dropped a hot, open-mouthed kiss onto her neck, she struggled to suppress a shudder. She couldn't even recall the last time he'd kissed her. He hadn't even kissed her goodbye before he left for Belgium to serve in Wellington's army in April. It was now September. She swallowed and dredged up her voice again. "Give me a few minutes. I will come to you in your room."

He drew back. She could clearly see his erection, pushing impatiently against the fall of his navy-blue silk breeches.

"I look forward to it, my dear," he said with another slow smile.

Then, thank the Lord, he left.

Elizabeth didn't have much time. Opening the top drawer of her dresser, she retrieved her household keys before slipping out of the door into the hallway. She didn't bother to close it. She was afraid Hugh would hear it.

Picking up the hem of her night rail, she rushed away, grateful that the plush Aubusson carpet deadened her footfalls.

Where to hide, where to hide? That was the question. She headed for the servants' quarters. She knew there was a spare bedroom. One of the footmen had left their service just recently.

By the time she reached the fourth floor, she was breathless. She paused for a moment, trying to control her ragged gasps. It wouldn't do to wake the servants. She recalled that the vacant room was at the beginning of the corridor, adjacent to the landing where she now stood.

Fumbling, she pulled out her keys, trying to find the right one. The only light she had to work by was a frail shaft of moonlight that spilled through a small window at the head of the stairs.

A door slammed. Hugh was coming. She tried key after key, her shaking fingers making the metal rattle in the lock. Someone would hear her. She brutally choked back a sob. Then mercifully a key slid in and turned easily, tumbling the lock. She pushed open the door, offering a silent prayer of thanks to their butler that it did not squeak. Jenkins was worth his weight in gold.

Shutting the door as silently as she could, she then locked it again from the inside. It was so dark, she could hardly see at all. But there seemed to be a closet on the opposite side of the small, barely furnished chamber. She swiftly skirted the narrow single bed and tried to open the door, her sweaty palms slipping on the handle. *No, no, no.* It was locked and there was no key.

"Elizabeth!"

Hugh sounded closer. Too close. She could hear his heavy footsteps on the stairs.

How had he tracked her so easily? Swallowing down a wave of nausea, she glanced about the room. Aside from the closet, the bed and a wooden chair, there was no other furniture. But there were floor length curtains partly drawn across a small window to the left of the bed. She slipped behind the dusty, moth-eaten fabric and waited, barely breathing. Trembling.

And then she heard it. The doorhandle rattled slightly. She bit her lip to stop herself crying out.

Please, for the love of God, go away. Leave me be. Don't come in, don't come in...

CHAPTER 1

Aberdeenshire, Scotland
Two weeks later...

P*lease, for the love of God, go away. Leave me be. Don't come in, don't come in...*

"Wake ye up, madam. You are havin' a bad dream."

Elizabeth's eyes flew open and somehow she swallowed the scream threatening to escape her throat. One of her fellow travelers, Mrs. MacKenzie, was shaking her by the shoulder, but when the woman saw Elizabeth had awakened, she quickly released her grip.

"Humph." The older woman sat back down on the opposite carriage seat. A deep frown of concern—or perhaps it was disapproval—creased her brow. The rest of the carriage's occupants were obviously embarrassed by the situation. Mrs. MacKenzie's husband—a middle-aged gentleman who'd introduced himself as the vicar of Kintore at the commencement of their journey—studied the toes of his muddy boots with great interest, and Miss MacKenzie, the couple's daughter, promptly looked out the window when Elizabeth glanced her way.

Elizabeth cleared her throat and addressed the glowering Mrs. MacKenzie. "I'm sorry to have...discommoded you all," she said, aiming for grave sincerity but sadly missing the mark given that her voice was husky with sleep and barely contained emotion. The remnants of her nightmare still clouded her brain, making it difficult to focus. Indeed, she felt as though she was still hidden behind dusty curtains, in fear for her life in her former home in London, not being jostled about in a mail coach in the wilds of Scotland.

With a decided effort, Elizabeth strove to calm her breathing and slow her racing pulse as she reassured herself that she was safe. She suddenly wondered if she'd cried out. She had a strong suspicion that she must have, given the strained atmosphere in the carriage.

Mrs. MacKenzie nodded slightly in acknowledgement of Elizabeth's apology. "You say ye are a governess," she said stiffly, her disbelief evident. It was more a query than a statement.

"Yes, I am," Elizabeth replied, steadily holding Mrs. MacKenzie's gaze. "But it is very much a new endeavor for me. You see, I lost my husband in the Battle of Waterloo and given my situation, I must now make my own way in the world."

She was surprised how easily the lie rolled off her tongue. She had never been one to lie, and truly hated being forced into carrying out such a grand deception. But sadly, her use of deceit was a necessary evil. She needed to accept that she would have to employ subterfuge for the rest of her life in order to have any life at all. She had become Mrs. Beth Eliott, widow of a British infantry officer, forced to seek employment as a governess in the far reaches of Scotland.

The Countess of Beauchamp, Elizabeth Harcourt, was no more.

Hugh must never find me.

Mrs. MacKenzie had the good grace to look suitably mortified. "Och, I'm so verra sorry, my dear. No wonder ye have nightmares. I do hope you find yer new occupation a rewardin' one. Why, there must be hundreds of poor creatures like you across the whole country with no real income to speak of. It is a verra sad time for so many, despite Wellington's victory. My condolences to ye, madam."

Elizabeth inclined her head. "Thank you."

She knew only too well the desperate straits the many wives of fallen British soldiers found themselves in when their husbands had failed to return home. Indeed, up until a fortnight ago, she had been one of the patronesses of the London-based Widows of Waterloo Trust, a charity that she and several of her friends had established shortly after the campaign abroad had ended.

It did not sit well with Elizabeth that she had abused her privileged position in the Trust. She had effectively stolen a governess's post that could have been offered to another woman who had lost her husband and no longer had a source of income.

But then, Elizabeth was also desperate.

Even though Hugh was as rich as Croesus, he controlled the purse strings. She had barely any pin money and certainly no personal fortune to speak of. And with no immediate family left on this earth to help—her parents, Lord and Lady Lydenhurst, had passed away shortly after she'd wed Hugh—Elizabeth needed to disappear, to become someone else. A woman of independent means. She just prayed that come Judgment Day, she would be forgiven for her duplicity.

The travelers all lapsed into silence again. Elizabeth, or Beth as she now styled herself, looked out of the carriage window at the desolate scenery. They were traveling along a fairly decent road that ran parallel with the rocky coastline.

Under a lowering gray sky, sheer cliffs fell away to great piles of tumbled boulders and shingle-strewn coves. Like the mail coach, the seagrass, whin bushes and purple heather clinging to the clifftops were being buffeted by a strong gale blowing straight off the North Sea. The wind would be cold and astringent with brine, of that she had no doubt.

Elizabeth glanced at the small silver pocket watch pinned to her black widow's weeds. It was mid-afternoon. The small mail coach had left the coastal town of Montrose at first light so she estimated it wouldn't be long before they reached her destination: the village of Torhaven and God-willing, her new place of employment and residence, Eilean Tor Castle.

Leaning forward a little, Elizabeth squinted at a narrow rocky promontory in the far distance. She could just discern the gray bulk of a medieval fortress and wondered if it was Eilean Tor. Its name fitted its appearance exactly, if that were the case. The castle looked to be a great rocky pile on a headland that could almost be an island. Waves crashed against the cliffs upon which it sat, sending great plumes of spray into the air around it.

It was isolated. Inhospitable.

It was perfect.

Now she just had to convince Eilean Tor's master, the Marquess of Rothsburgh, that he required her services.

Elizabeth sighed and rested her head back against the squabs, stretching her stiff back and limbs. She was so very tired. Her flight from London had begun two weeks ago, and since then, she had been traveling constantly on stage coaches, privately hired post-chaises, and mail coaches from dawn until dusk, taking a circuitous route northward that would be hard to track.

She had already suffered the same nightmare about Hugh's pursuit of her through their London home several times during her journey, but until this afternoon, the dream had only come when she had been alone at the dead of night. The long days of travel and weeks of poor sleep were obviously taking their toll if she was falling asleep heavily enough to dream on public conveyances.

If only the nightmare would dissipate when she awoke.

It had started innocuously enough a month ago with the arrival of a letter. Elizabeth had barely noticed the creased and travel-stained parchment in amongst the pile of other pristine invitations and letters on the silver salver that Jenkins brought into her when she was partaking in her first cup of tea at breakfast. Strange how something so inconspicuous could be so noxious.

Now the words of the letter had taken root in Elizabeth's brain like a canker.

Dear Lady Beauchamp,

You won't believe me, but I write this missive with the best of intentions. It is not out of a malicious wish to inflict pain, or out of spite that I share this certain knowledge with you, but out of a sense of moral decency; although I will freely admit, that is an attribute that I have never possessed, up until this point in my life.

You see, I have been your husband's mistress for quite some time now. But I beg you not to cast away this letter until I have stated what I need to say—your life may depend upon it.

Your husband has the great pox, my lady. Or in some circles it is known as the grandgore. But the name of this disease does not really matter; the result will be the same in the end if one is so afflicted—death.

*You ask how do I know this to be true? It is because I now
have the pox. After an encounter with your husband
several months ago, I developed sores, ulcerous craters on
my body. And now I have a rash and worse. But I will
not describe the rest of the symptoms of this terrible
malady to you as I am sure you do not care to know
about the afflictions of your husband's mistress.*

*Suffice it to say, I am absolutely certain that it was your
husband, Lord Beauchamp, who infected me. Indeed,
there was evidence of the pox on his body at the time of
our very last encounter—an ulcer on the ring finger of
his left hand was the most prominent mark.*

*However, I did not know of its import until it was too
late. I pray that it is not too late for you.*

Of course, Elizabeth had not wanted to believe her
husband's mistress. Instead, she had wanted desperately to
believe that the anonymous writer—although she claimed
otherwise—had only written to Elizabeth out of malice and
spite. But then she had noticed that her husband did indeed
sport the incriminating mark of the disease. She'd spotted the
angry, red ulcerated patch on his finger when he had eventually joined her for breakfast later that very morning.

Her eyes had fixed on his left hand as soon as he'd entered
the room. She'd watched his ring finger with something akin
to morbid fascination as he'd buttered his toast, picked up his
teacup and turned the pages of his newspaper. He hadn't even
noticed her unusual fixation or her barely contained distress,
which was not unsurprising. He hardly noticed anything
about her at all most days.

She'd had no clear idea of what action she would take that
morning. She realized now that she must have been in a degree

of shock. It wasn't until Jenkins had inquired after her well-being as he'd replaced her cold pot of tea with a fresh one, that the idea of seeking a medical opinion had entered her dazed mind.

Somehow, Elizabeth had scraped together what could pass for a normal voice. "Hugh...I am going to ask Dr. Morton to call on me this morning... And I wondered..."

Hugh continued to read. His article was obviously more engaging than his wife.

She started again. "I noticed...the mark on your finger..."

He flicked her a glance over the pages. "It's nothing." He resumed reading.

"Are you certain? It looks—"

He lowered the paper. His eyes narrowed on her, his gaze cold. Hard. Like bright blue ice. "I told you. It's nothing."

"But—"

"For God's sake, Elizabeth, I don't need you to carp on at me like a fishwife." He threw the newspaper down on the table, his mouth a hard line. And he walked out.

That's when Elizabeth knew that she would have to leave. Even before Dr. Morton had confirmed her worst fears and had warned her about the dangers of sharing any kind of intimacy ever again with her husband.

Intimacy. That was something she had never shared with Hugh. Even though she no longer loved her husband—it was hard to love someone who proclaimed you to be as dull as yesterday's broadsheets—it still hurt that the charming, golden-haired Adonis she'd married had turned out be such a false idol. He'd wooed her, wed her, bed her for a month or so, then promptly ignored her for the most part. And she'd never understood why.

The solution to Elizabeth's dilemma had come unexpectedly the very day that she'd received the incriminating letter. After Dr. Morton had departed Harcourt House, Jenkins had asked if she still required the carriage to attend the monthly Widows of Waterloo Trust meeting that afternoon at two o'clock. She'd completely forgotten about the appointment and had seriously contemplated not going, given her ongoing distress. But in the end, she had decided that focusing her energies on alleviating the problems of other women in more desperate circumstances than herself would help to take her mind off her own situation.

It had turned out to be a fortuitous decision. A chance remark made by a fellow committee member—the formidable bluestocking Lady Airlie—about the perennially vacant governess's position within the Marquess of Rothsburgh's household in Scotland, had planted the seed of an idea to make good her own escape. Thank heavens the woman had a clarion-like voice because it was that alone that caught Elizabeth's attention and had drawn her out of her distracted state.

"It's such a shame that we cannot seem to help my dear friend, Helena, Lady Maxwell, find a governess for her niece," Lady Airlie had said to her neighbor Lady Talbot. "The letter I received from her just yesterday indicated that her brother, the Marquess of Rothsburgh, lost his wife recently under tragic circumstances. I don't know the precise details, but I believe there was a terrible accident at their home in Scotland. Apparently, Lady Rothsburgh had been trying for some time before her death to secure a reliable English governess for their five-year-old daughter, but the applicants either turned out to be unsuitable or were unwilling to travel so far."

Lady Talbot had nodded sagely. "I understand the marquess's seat of Eilean Tor Castle is terribly remote. It would be a lonely existence, I should imagine, to be so far removed from society. And from what I've heard, the marquess is quite the misanthrope."

"Yes, indeed," Lady Airlie agreed. "Helena remarked that she thinks her brother scares the poor gels off. A pity—we could have recommended one of our widows if it wasn't such an unappealing position."

Unappealing or not, it was a better prospect than contracting syphilis...

As the carriage jolted over a rough patch on the coastal road, Elizabeth unconsciously tightened her hold on her reticule that contained her self-penned letter of reference. Trying to ignore the nervous churning of her stomach, she prayed that she could convince Lord Rothsburgh that she was the very woman he needed for the post. If the man did indeed turn out to be a misanthrope, it might actually work in her favor. A man who shunned the company of others would probably leave her alone to get on with the business of educating his daughter. Yes, the less attention she received, the better.

Looking out the window again, Elizabeth could see the carriage was slowly negotiating a steeply winding road down to the small seaside village of Torhaven. The village consisted of a meager cluster of squat stone buildings that clung like limpets to the shoreline below whin-covered hills and towering cliffs of slate colored rock. She had lost sight of Eilean Tor. The headland upon which it sat was obscured by a gigantic, rocky outcrop that jutted into the roiling sea and overshadowed the northern edge of the cove and village. She could not see a single living creature.

Even though the weather had deteriorated—it had started to rain—Elizabeth was relieved to have at last reached her destination. She was longing to quit the cramped, stuffy interior of the carriage so she could breathe the fresh sea air and stretch her aching muscles. Today in particular, she felt much older than her twenty-four years. Indeed, she felt weary beyond measure. She felt like an old woman.

She hoped the village inn where she would shortly be deposited had a decent room for hire. She needed to change out of her travel-stained clothes and freshen up in general to ensure she made a good impression on Lord Rothsburgh when she presented herself for interview. An interview that was completely unsolicited.

To quash her anxiety, Elizabeth had already rehearsed in her mind everything she would say to persuade the marquess that she was up to the task of developing his young daughter's intellectual, artistic, and musical skills. In her humble opinion, five years old was a tad young to begin formal lessons, but she certainly wasn't going to dissuade Lord Rothsburgh from engaging a governess.

Elizabeth couldn't, no *wouldn't* contemplate the idea that she would be turned away.

CHAPTER 2

"I'm verra sorry, ma'am but I canna hire oot a room to ye."
Elizabeth stood in the dimly lit taproom of The Black Barnacle Inn—the place where the mail coach had deposited her and her trunk only minutes ago—and stared at the innkeeper, not wanting to believe what he had just told her. A tall, thin man with stooping shoulders, a craggy countenance and sandy-red hair, he looked none too pleased to see her. Indeed, his pale blue eyes regarded her with something akin to suspicion, perhaps even dislike.

Ignoring his less than welcoming manner, she summoned her most polite smile. "Are you certain, Mr...."

"Geddes," he supplied. "I assure ye, it is the case."

Elizabeth fought down a wave of frustration. This wouldn't do at all. How could she approach Lord Rothsburgh looking as rumpled as a pile of dirty laundry? "But surely you can't be full," she ventured again, forcing herself to maintain her smile. "The village seems to be so quiet..."

Mr. Geddes grunted. "No' a question if there's a room. It's more the case we havna the staff to take care of ye—" He broke off and coughed, a great hacking sound that shook his whole body and left him breathless.

When the fit was over, he fixed his watering eyes on her. "There has been a terrible ague...in the village this past fortnight, ma'am...an' several older folk have even died, ye ken. There isna anybody, aside from myself an' my son Seamus, to look after things here."

Elizabeth raised a gloved hand to her throat. "Oh heavens, I'm so sorry, Mr. Geddes," she said with heartfelt sincerity. "And you are clearly not well either. But I'm afraid that I have not arranged anywhere else to stay. Would there be a private dining room or parlor that I could hire for a few hours until I can make alternative arrangements?"

If she could secure the governess's position this afternoon, perhaps she could ask Lord Rothsburgh to accommodate her within the servants' quarters at the castle.

Mr. Geddes shook his head. "There is only this room, ma'am. Torhaven doesna get many visitors, ye ken, an' The Black Barnacle is only a small inn. We dinna have any private rooms because we havna the custom."

"Oh, I see..." Elizabeth sighed and cast her eyes about the taproom. Despite the strong smell of peat smoke, hops and some sort of fishy stew, it was a clean, pleasant enough room. It would have to do for the moment. "Then perhaps, if it isn't too much trouble, might I take a seat by the fire for a while? I have traveled all the way from London, you see, and find I am a trifle weary."

Mr. Geddes's eyes narrowed on her. "A Londoner you say. Wha' on earth have ye come all the way here fer, if ye dinna mind my askin'?"

Elizabeth swallowed. Her throat felt dry and scratchy, and she really wanted nothing more than to sit down and have a cup of tea. Nevertheless, she had nothing to lose by answering the innkeeper's question. Perhaps she could even glean some additional intelligence about the mysterious marquess. She was already taking a huge risk approaching Lord Rothsburgh when the man would still be in deep mourning for the marchioness. She certainly hoped that neither he nor his daughter had taken ill as well. It would be reprehensible if she turned up on the marquess's doorstep unannounced in such an unfortunate circumstance.

"I've come to apply for the governess's position at Eilean Tor Castle," she said then blushed when Mr. Geddes threw back his head and laughed. However, he quickly succumbed to a coughing fit again that left him gasping.

"I don't understand, Mr. Geddes," she said, her brow furrowing with confusion.

"Och...it's just tha'...there have been so many young English lasses tha' have tried oot fer the job of nursemaid and governess. I canna believe there's another one. But by all means, Miss..."

"Mrs. Eliott. As in the Lowlander spelling," she supplied with an inclination of her head. She had chosen the alias simply because it had been her mother's maiden name. But if it helped her to gain some ground with the taciturn and quite possibly anti-English Mr. Geddes, then all the better.

"Och, ye wed a Lowlander, did ye? So yer no' just a Sassenach. Well, take a seat by all means. An' I s'pose ye'll be wantin' a cup of tea as well?"

"If it's not too much trouble..."

"Och. It's no trouble." The man's craggy face twisted into what might have passed for a smile. "But I think ye will have need of somethin' a wee bit stronger afore ye face Lord Rothsburgh. Are ye sure I canna bring you a wee dram of whisky or sherry?"

In the face of Mr. Geddes wry amusement, Elizabeth suddenly feared that the marquess *was* really going to live up to his churlish reputation. Not that it would make her change her course of action. She would just have to work harder to win the unsociable nobleman over. At least it didn't sound as if he had contracted the ague.

"No thank you, Mr. Geddes. Just the tea will be sufficient," Elizabeth replied then smiled again at the innkeeper. She would need to exercise her charm a little more on him—not that it had really helped her thus far. But she needed a way to get to the castle. "I'm afraid I need to ask you for another favor, sir. As I cannot stay here, perhaps I could ask you or your son to take me and my luggage to Eilean Tor, when I am done taking tea? Of course, I will pay you well for your trouble on such an inclement afternoon."

Again Mr. Geddes seemed amused at her expense. "I'm verra sorry, Mrs. Eliott, but I canna take you. Our cart has a broken axle, an' neither me nor Seamus have been up to fixin' it of late. Besides, the tide is still high, an' the causeway across to the castle will be too dangerous fer anyone to cross fer another hour. Ye will have to wait a wee while yet."

Elizabeth closed her eyes for a moment, trying to push down another surge of exasperation. Since she had arrived at Torhaven, nothing was going smoothly. She prayed this wasn't a bad omen. But because she had come so far, these few last obstacles would not stop her from succeeding. She just needed to summon her patience.

Drawing a deep breath, she looked squarely at Mr. Geddes. "I had not realized that Eilean Tor was on an island. Would it be possible to hire a horse to cross the causeway when the tide goes out? I do not fancy walking there in this weather."

Mr. Geddes nodded. "Och, aye, ma'am. We can do tha' fer you. It is only aboot a quarter of a mile across the causeway once you get over the Tor. An' verra safe once the tide is far enough oot. Dinna worry. Auld Fern, our pony, will get ye there safely enough."

Once Mr. Geddes quit the room to prepare her tea, Elizabeth sank onto one of the chairs before the fire. She suddenly felt very cold beneath her traveling cloak, woolen spencer and gown, and was grateful for the warmth emanating from the embers of glowing peat. She supposed the chill sea air and her damp boots weren't helping matters—she'd accidentally trodden in a puddle in the inn yard before she'd entered the Black Barnacle. Part of her wished that thick flannel drawers were *de rigueur*.

She removed her black chip bonnet and tugged off her kid leather gloves. The tips of her pale fingers looked almost blue from the cold. She chafed her hands together then held them toward the smoky fire. Her silver wedding band, which she now wore on her right ring finger, caught the fire's glow. It didn't feel right to remove it. Even though it wasn't safe to live with Hugh as his true wife anymore, she was still married.

How bleak to think that she would probably never marry again.

At least I'm already used to feeling alone.

Much to her chagrin, her eyes suddenly brimmed with tears, but she hastily brushed them away when Mr. Geddes returned with her tea. Self-indulgent weeping wasn't going to help. She needed to stay strong.

The brew that Mr. Geddes had poured for her was weak, but Elizabeth didn't mind. She wrapped her chilled fingers around the cup and found comfort as the warm liquid slid down her dry throat. It wasn't long before the tea and the fire warmed her right through. In fact, she'd begun to feel quite hot and perspiration prickled down her spine.

Putting aside her tea, Elizabeth rose and crossed to one of the grimy, salt-encrusted windows.

The rain had grown heavier and the rocky promontory— the Tor as Mr. Geddes had called it— was now obscured by low clouds that had rolled in off the sea. She shivered. She really didn't want to go out in this weather. She would be soaked to the skin before she even left the inn yard.

Not only that, it also suddenly struck Elizabeth how wild and close the crashing breakers were. Every now and again, a shot of spray hit a windowpane, making it rattle. She wasn't entirely certain that she wouldn't be swept into the North Sea as she crossed to Eilean Tor.

But there seemed to be no other alternative open to her. She would just have to grin and bear it.

Perhaps looking wet and bedraggled might even work in her favor when she arrived at the castle, for surely the marquess would take pity on her and let her inside. She hoped to God he wasn't entirely heartless.

Elizabeth had just finished her tea, and was in the process of donning her bonnet and gloves again, when Mr. Geddes came back to announce that Auld Fern was saddled and ready to go.

"Do you think if I waited a while longer that the rain might ease, Mr. Geddes?" she asked without any real hope of a positive response.

"I dinna think so, Mrs. Eliott. It could rain fer days, ye ken. An' now would be the best time to leave afore the tide turns again an' it grows dark."

Resigning herself to the fact she was going to get wet, Elizabeth paid the innkeeper for his tea and the hire of the pony. It was arranged that Auld Fern would be returned to The Black Barnacle the following day—all going well with her interview. She trusted one of the castle staff would be able to help her out in that regard. She would also send word to Mr. Geddes on how and when to forward her trunk.

Once all was settled, she collected up her reticule. Then, squaring her shoulders, she marched out into the rain. There was no turning back.

CHAPTER 3

E lizabeth clung to Auld Fern's sturdy back as the old gray
pony trudged steadfastly down to the causeway. Even
though she was an experienced rider, it took all her strength to
maintain her seat as a strong gale ripped at her bonnet and
cloak with icy fingers, and flung stinging rain and spray into
her face. Indeed, the roar of the wind and sea, and the biting
cold were so relentless, it wasn't long before Elizabeth was
drenched and shivering uncontrollably.

So much for her plan to arrive on the marquess's doorstep,
refreshed and composed.

Although the distance from Torhaven to this point was
only half a mile, it had taken her the best part of a half hour to
get this far because of the rugged terrain and foul conditions.
She gritted her teeth to keep them from chattering and
narrowed her eyes against the elements to examine the
causeway below. Thank God she was almost there.

The path ahead slid down to a wide cobbled road that
arced out to sea before winding up the steep headland to
where Eilean Tor sat. Stark and formidable, the fortress's great
rounded keep and towering crenelated battlements dominated

the horizon. It would be completely cut off from the mainland at high tide, the wild North Sea creating a natural, deadly moat.

Strangely, Elizabeth felt relieved, rather than daunted. It was as if she had journeyed to the ends of the earth. Hugh would never find her here.

Fortunately, the tide was indeed out; Mr. Geddes had been correct in that regard. The surface of the causeway was slick with rain but it seemed to be well-raised above sea-level. Jagged boulders had been piled up along the edges of the road, creating an additional barrier against the churning gray water. Spray shot up into the air when the occasional large wave broke against the side of the causeway, but none appeared to break over the edge.

Reassuring herself that she would be perfectly safe, Elizabeth kicked the pony into a trot, keen to negotiate the last quarter of a mile that lay between her and her destination.

The sea sucked and hissed at the sides of the causeway as she urged Auld Fern along. She was amazed that the marquess thought to raise his young daughter in such a forbidding place. It must be a lonely and austere existence for a child who had so recently lost her mother. Her heart went out to the little girl she was yet to meet.

She suddenly recalled Lady Airlie's comment that Lady Rothsburgh had met her end through accidental death at the family home. Had the marchioness died here at Eilean Tor? The place certainly appeared dangerous enough, given its situation. An air of tragedy seemed to hang about its very walls like the wreaths of torn mist that scudded by.

Thankfully, Elizabeth gained the other side of the causeway without event, and it wasn't long before Auld Fern was carrying her beneath the raised portcullis into the deeply shadowed courtyard beyond. Elizabeth scanned the castle's many windows and apertures but all of them—whether they were archer's slits, murder holes, or arched mullioned windows—were dark. There was not a single glimmer of light from within. Eilean Tor appeared completely deserted.

Quelling a wave of unease—Elizabeth prayed the castle wasn't as uninhabited as it appeared—she reined in Auld Fern and slipped from the pony's back. She was momentarily surprised by how weak she felt—her legs shook, and her knees nearly buckled beneath her. She held onto the saddle for a few moments until she felt steadier and then turned around, looking for any kind of entrance to the castle's interior.

As it was, the main door was easy to locate. A massive wooden structure, hinged and studded with iron, it was shaded by an elaborately carved stone portico in the center of the keep. Elizabeth looped Auld Fern's reins to a ring in one of the walls of the barbican passage, and then after retrieving her precious reticule from the saddlebag, she crossed the stone flagged courtyard toward the door. Although she was soaked, at least her letter of reference would be dry.

Nearly there, Elizabeth. There was a set of wide stairs before the entrance—only three in total—but the stone was treacherously slippery with rain and moss. She lifted her sodden skirts as she negotiated them, a ragged sigh of relief escaping her frozen lips when she at last gained the shelter of the portico. Although there was barely any light, she managed to make out a large, heavy iron knocker in the center of the door. She raised a shaking hand and hammered.

And waited. Minutes passed, but there was not a sound or stirring of life anywhere. Her already dry throat suddenly felt raw and constricted. She would not cry. There would be someone within. Surely Mr. Geddes would have told her if the marquess was *not* in residence.

She raised the knocker again and struck it hard, three more times. Again she waited, but to no avail. Hot tears pricked the back of her eyelids.

Don't be such a baby. There had to be another entrance, for deliveries and the servants. And there must be stables as well. She would just have to look about until she found someone. She turned around and her elbow brushed against something —a thick rope hung to the right of the door—a bellpull.

Cursing herself for her lack of observation, Elizabeth grasped the rope with both hands and pulled hard. An enormous clanging immediately started up, and she was forced to cover her ears—it was loud enough to wake the very dead. She decided that if that cacophony didn't raise anyone's attention, nothing would.

At last, she heard the unmistakable sound of bolts being pulled back, and then the door was thrown wide. A bright lantern was thrust toward her face, blinding her. She raised a hand to her eyes in a futile attempt to shield them and squinted upward. An extremely tall man was holding the lantern aloft. She could discern little else about him as the intense light in her eyes obscured her vision.

"What do you want, woman?" The man's voice was a low growl.

Elizabeth drew a deep breath and summoned her most imperious voice. She had come so far and would not be cowed by an obnoxious servant. "I seek an audience with Lord Rothsburgh. Is your master at home?"

"What the deuce for?"

She immediately bristled at the insolence in the man's tone. "I'd have a care to mind your tongue, sir. And lower that lantern. You're hurting my eyes."

The light was immediately lowered, and Elizabeth was able to see a little more of the man who seemed to be filling up the whole doorway. He must have been at least six foot four, with black hair that fell across one eye. She also noted that he was informally dressed in a loose white cambric shirt that was open at the neck, black breeches, and boots. The marquess obviously had low standards when it came to fitting out his staff in proper livery.

"Well, aren't you going to invite me in?" she demanded.

The man—she assumed he was some sort of sloppy butler or footman—let out a snort of laughter. "What on earth for?"

She scowled and drew herself up, raising her chin. She would not be laughed at by the hired help. "I understand there is a vacancy for a governess. I've come to offer my services to Lord Rothsburgh."

"Have you indeed?" There was still an annoying undercurrent of laughter in the man's voice. Nevertheless, he stepped aside and made a grand sweeping gesture with his free hand. "Then by all means, come in."

Elizabeth picked up her skirts and started to step forward when the toe of her boot caught on an unevenly laid flagstone on the threshold. With an unladylike squeal she pitched forward toward the floor...until she was deftly caught about the waist by the vulgar butler.

With a gasp of half-shock, half-embarrassment she found her midriff was bent across his muscular forearm, whilst her side was crushed roughly against his wide chest. One of her hands had involuntarily fisted into the linen sleeve of his shirt where underneath she could detect the bulk of a sizeable, iron-hard bicep.

The scent of the man flooded her senses—warm male, whisky, and the tantalizing scent of exotically rich soap. It reminded her of sandalwood, leather, and a spicy note she couldn't quite place. Perhaps it was cloves.

She took all of this in within the instant that she was suspended above the floor before the man righted her. Her cheeks flaming, she took a step away. "I'm so sorry, sir. How clumsy of me. And I've made you all wet...Mr...."

The man's arm lingered across her waist. Perhaps he thought she would fall again. She noticed he had dark eyes; his gaze traveled over her face, studying her. She must look a sight.

"James," he said, his eyes holding hers. In the dim light she couldn't work out if they were dark brown or black.

Elizabeth was taken aback by the intensity of his stare and let go of his sleeve. She was relieved when he also dropped his arm. "Well, Mr. James," she said, hoping she didn't sound as breathless as she felt. "Thank you for preventing me from making more a fool of myself than I have done so already. Perhaps if you could ring for your master—"

Mr. James interrupted her. "How did you get here?" he fired at her, eyes narrowed.

"Why, Mr. Geddes from the inn lent me a pony. She's tethered in the barbican passage."

"What, Auld Fern?"

"Why, yes—"

"Devil take it, woman—"

"Really, Mr. James, I must protest that you keep calling me that. My name is Mrs. Beth Eliott."

He stared down at her, a look of disdainful incredulity on his face. She was suddenly struck by the fact that he was handsome underneath his shabby façade. "Well, Mrs. Eliott, are you insane? You must be if you rode that hack of a pony across the causeway in this weather. Bloody Geddes should be flogged."

Elizabeth bristled again at the man's use of foul language. "Well, perhaps I am mad," she snapped. "But I'd rather be that, than just plain rude."

Mr. James ran a hand through his unruly black hair in a gesture of resigned exasperation. "Humph. My apologies. I'm afraid we don't receive many visitors here, Mrs. Eliott, so perhaps my manners are a bit rusty. But seeing as you've made it this far, you'd best come in all the way." A glint of mischief sparked in his dark eyes. "Mind your step now."

She shot him what she hoped was a venomous look, then proceeded past him into the hall.

And froze. The space ahead of her was dark and cavernous. The lantern held by Mr. James revealed glimpses of a wide area of stone-flagged floor that disappeared into dark corners, and a high vaulted ceiling that was filled with flickering shadows. The steel of ancient weaponry mounted on stone walls glimmered dully, and a suit of armor stared blindly at her from a wall recess. Elizabeth was unsure in which direction she should turn. It struck her anew how dark and apparently devoid of life the castle was.

"This way, Mrs. Eliott." Perhaps sensing her uncertainty, Mr. James strode past her.

Elizabeth picked up her skirts again and followed him with careful haste. Within a few moments she could see they were heading for a wide stone staircase that swept upward into darkness. She followed Mr. James, trying her best to keep up with his long-legged stride. But her legs were trembling, and her heart and head were pounding by the time she gained the top of the stairs. She paused for a moment, her hand on the carved stone balustrade, fighting a sudden wave of dizziness.

Mr. James turned back. The lantern cast strange shadows over the angular planes of his face, giving him a distinctly saturnine expression. She shivered.

"Are you all right, madam?"

She nodded. "I think so... I have traveled such a long way. Perhaps I am a little fatigued... That is all."

Mr. James cocked an eyebrow. "Well, if you're sure. It's not much farther." He then turned and continued on down the corridor without glancing back.

Elizabeth hurried to keep up but was relieved that the footman-cum-butler was as good as his word. Within a short space of time, he ushered her into another vast room that appeared to be a library. She paused on the threshold, astounded by the magnificent proportions and opulence of the room. She hadn't expected such grandeur considering the starkness of the Great Hall—the sections she had been able to see at any rate.

A large fire roared in an enormous fireplace that was surrounded by a black marble mantelpiece, elaborately carved with fluted columns, scrollwork, and motifs of all manner of wild creatures—lions, stags, and eagles. On a sumptuous Turkish carpet before the hearth lay two massive deerhounds. They blinked at her sleepily before lowering their heads back onto their paws, clearly disinterested in her arrival.

The room was relatively well-lit with strategically placed lamps and wrought-iron candelabra that held clusters of fat, beeswax candles. By their light, Elizabeth could see that the library had two levels. Towering bookshelves covered two of the walls on the lower level where she had entered, whilst the upper level was comprised of shelves entirely. Heavy, Jacobean-style side tables in dark oak and armchairs upholstered in dark brown leather or gold and burgundy damask were strategically arranged around the hearth and other places about the room.

Directly opposite the doorway was a solid oak desk, also elaborately carved. A tapestry of a hunting scene hung directly behind it. On either side of the desk, thick curtains of burgundy velvet framed wide, arched mullioned windows that were set in deeply recessed embrasures. All Elizabeth could see beyond the diamond-shaped panes at this moment was inky blackness, although she could just detect the muted pounding of waves. She imagined that during the day, the windows would look out across the sea.

Mr. James marched in and placed the lamp on the desk, then turned to scowl at her. "Why are you hovering there? You're not afraid of the dogs, are you? The last governess that was here—Miss Lark, I think her name was, or maybe it was Miss Goose—turned tail and ran when she saw them."

Steadfastly refusing to rise to this man's bait again, Elizabeth willed herself not to scowl back. "N-Not at all Mr. James. I quite like d-dogs. It's just that I am still soaking wet, and I do not think Lord Rothsburgh would appreciate it if I drenched his f-fine carpets."

"Nonsense. You're obviously freezing." He moved across the room to a leather settee by the fire, and held up a blanket of green, dark blue, and black patterned tartan. "Why don't you remove your bonnet and cloak then sit before the fire with something warm and dry around you? I swear you are turning blue as we speak."

Elizabeth gritted her teeth to stop them chattering and undid the bonnet's ribbons at her throat before removing her cloak. She dropped both water-logged items onto the flags outside the library door, then with as much dignity as she could muster, crossed to the hearth and took the proffered blanket. She was, to her dismay, icily cold and shivering uncontrollably.

Mr. James frowned at her. "Sit down, Mrs. Eliott. I will fetch you some tea and summon the marquess. He won't be long."

She placed her reticule beside her and perched on the edge of the settee before wrapping the blanket about her shoulders. "Th-Thank you."

"You're welcome."

As soon as the library door snicked shut, Elizabeth let herself relax against the back of the chair. Heavens, she felt decidedly unwell. Her head throbbed and her throat felt raw. She was ill, there was no denying it. But how in God's name was she to sway the marquess when she looked like a bedraggled cat and could barely sit upright?

She reached for her reticule and retrieved her reference, relieved to find it was relatively dry. She would just have to let the words of The Right Honorable, Countess of Beauchamp, impress Lord Rothsburgh. The way she currently looked and felt, she would be lucky if the marquess didn't toss her out onto the doorstep.

Long minutes passed in which Elizabeth fought the urge to sink into the welcoming arms of sleep. Surprisingly, one of the deerhounds stood, stretched his rangy body, and then came and placed his large shaggy head on her lap. She stroked one of his silky ears, and the hound let out a contented sigh. *If only Lord Rothsburgh could be so easily pleased.*

"Mrs. Eliott."

Elizabeth opened her eyes to find Mr. James had returned. He was placing a tea tray onto the low table beside her.

"Oh, I'm sorry. I seem to have drifted off," she said, forcing herself to sit upright. She dropped the blanket from her shoulders as she had begun to feel decidedly warm. A bead of perspiration trickled between her shoulder blades. "Is Lord Rothsburgh coming?"

Mr. James cocked an eyebrow and smiled. "Yes. In fact, he's already here."

Elizabeth glanced about the room. There was no one else in the library besides herself and Mr. James. It was then that she noticed the butler was wearing a superbly tailored coat of black superfine with a neatly tied cravat at his throat.

Pure, undiluted horror swept over her.

"Oh, no." She couldn't believe she had been so stupid. How could she not have realized that Mr. James was in fact James Huntly, the sixth Marquess of Rothsburgh? She had researched his lineage in Debrett's Baronetage and Peerage before she'd left London. Her heart in her mouth and cold dismay gripping her belly, she forced herself to stand, then dropped into a deep curtsy. "Lord Rothsburgh. I'm so deeply sorry for my lack of—"

"Don't be silly, Mrs. Eliott," interrupted the marquess.

"How were you to know that I, Lord Rothsburgh, would answer the door? Now sit back down before you fall down."

Elizabeth subsided onto the settee again, her cheeks burning. In her wildest imaginings, she could not have envisaged anything as nightmarish as this. "I...I don't know what to say, my lord," she said. "Please forgive my presumption—"

"Mrs. Eliott, I think I preferred it when you were rude to me." Lord Rothsburgh smiled at her, a decided spark of amusement in his dark brown eyes. He bent over the tea tray and deftly poured her a steaming cup. "How do you take your tea?"

"A little milk. No sugar thank you," she replied meekly as she removed her gloves.

Lord Rothsburgh handed her a cup and saucer of the finest bone china—the pattern was Wedgwood if she wasn't mistaken. She took a sip and closed her eyes, savoring the soothing liquid. She could have sworn that the tea was a smoky Lapsang Souchong, her favorite blend.

"I can see you have made friends with Rosencrantz."

Elizabeth opened her eyes and looked down. The deerhound, which had been resting his head on her knee earlier, was now lying at her feet, his head on her boots. She smiled then glanced over to where Lord Rothsburgh sat in a leather wing chair opposite her.

"Guildenstern, I take it, obviously prefers your company, my lord." The other deerhound had moved over to his master's side, his head on the marquess's lap.

"More fool him," replied Lord Rothsburgh, his dark gaze roaming over her.

Elizabeth felt her already feverish cheeks grow hotter, and she glanced toward the dog at her feet. A misanthrope she could deal with, but a darkly handsome voluptuary? She had not anticipated the marquess would be such a man, which was quite short-sighted, really. Men of his class often lived a hedonistic lifestyle.

She should know, considering she was married to one of the worst offenders.

But perhaps Lord Rothsburgh was only testing her mettle, to see if she was made of sterner stuff than her predecessors. Despite her throbbing head and raw throat, she would just have to show the marquess that she was not some withering violet.

She looked up to find that the marquess was still watching her. He'd stretched back in his chair. His long muscular legs, encased in form-fitting breeches, were extended out before him, his booted feet crossed at the ankle. He was the personification of the arrogant, indolently graceful aristocrat. In one long fingered hand he held a glass of amber-colored liquor—whisky perhaps.

Noticing the direction of her gaze, he raised the glass and took a sizeable sip. "Would you like some?" he asked, arching a black-winged eyebrow. His voice was low and soft, like velvet.

Elizabeth swallowed. "No thank you, my lord." Her voice emerged as a husky croak. She took another quick sip of tea, then placed the cup and saucer on the table. They rattled faintly against each other. She was shivering again, and she could feel a sheen of cold perspiration on her brow. Banter was all well and good, but she needed to get down to business to secure her position as governess.

She reached for her reference and offered it to the marquess. "P-Perhaps we could speak about the governess's p-post, Lord Rothsburgh," she said, although she inwardly cursed her chattering teeth. It made her sound nervous. "This is my letter of reference from the C-Countess of B-Beauchamp."

Lord Rothsburgh leaned forward and took the letter from

her, frowning. "Are you sure you are all right, Mrs. Eliott? You look a little flushed."

She shrugged. "I think I must have caught a chill, my lord. I will be f-fine."

He sat back, his dark eyes lingering on her a moment longer before he turned over the folded piece of parchment and broke the wax seal. "This is from Lady Beauchamp, you say?"

"Yes. She is one of the p-patronesses of the Widows of Waterloo Trust, my lord. It is a charity that aims to f-find paid, decent work for wives who have lost their husbands at Waterloo and n-no longer have a source of income."

Lord Rothsburgh sought her gaze. His eyes were somber. "Then I'm sorry for your loss, Mrs. Eliott."

Elizabeth inclined her head in acknowledgement of the condolence yet felt herself blushing a little more—if that was at all physically possible. Although she had uttered the lie about her situation with relative ease, once spoken it was as if a bitter taste still lingered in her mouth.

The marquess returned to perusing her reference. "You come highly recommended," he said thoughtfully when he had finished reading it. He put the letter aside and fixed his gaze on her again. "Although given Lady Beauchamp is tied to that first-class bounder, Hugh Harcourt, the Earl of Beauchamp, her recommendation isn't worth much. Only a fool would have married a right royal prick like that."

Elizabeth gasped. He knew Hugh, but he obviously didn't know her. She quickly scanned her mind for any memory of having met Lord Rothsburgh before, but she could not find one. Her real identity was safe.

But even though what he had just said about Hugh was accurate, his comments about her true self—Lady Beauchamp —still stung. That meant her reference was worthless. Lord Rothsburgh had dismissed her well-chosen words outright.

And it was not as though her claims about Mrs. Beth Eliott were an entire fabrication. She did truly possess the personal qualities and attainments delineated within the letter. She *was* suitable governess material. And she did really want and need the work.

Elizabeth sat dumbfounded, searching for some sort of argument that would convince this mercurial man she was the right person to teach his daughter. But nothing came to mind.

She raised a shaking hand to her fevered brow and pushed a damp lock of hair out of her eyes. "I...I don't know what to say, Lord Rothsburgh." There was a hard lump in her throat and her eyes were suddenly misty. She bit her lip and willed herself not to cry. It had been a mistake to come here. Perhaps she was the fool the marquess thought she was.

She couldn't stay. Perhaps the tide was still low enough for her to return to Torhaven. She could beg Mr. Geddes for a room—she would pay of course. "It's probably best if I go then, my lord." She stood abruptly and the room swayed before her eyes.

"Mrs. Eliott..."

Her name was the last thing she heard before blackness descended.

CHAPTER 4

"Mrs. Eliott...Christ."

Rothsburgh leapt to his feet but he wasn't fast enough to catch the crumpling form of the beautiful widow. She sprawled face down across the rug before him.

Rosencrantz whined and nuzzled at her head. Rothsburgh fell to his knees and after shooing away the hound, he gently turned the woman onto her side. She was out cold.

He felt for a pulse at her neck—it was strong—and he noted her breathing was slightly shallow yet steady. As he had already suspected, she was burning up with fever. Her smooth, alabaster skin was unnaturally hot beneath his fingers and there was perspiration across her brow. There was no doubt in his mind that she had contracted the dreadful ague that had recently plagued this corner of Aberdeenshire.

He sighed heavily. She would be decidedly ill for another three or four days until the fever broke. Then she would develop a debilitating cough that would last for another week or more. That meant he would be responsible for her care for at least another fortnight.

How ironic, considering that after the death of his faithless wife only six weeks ago, he'd sworn that he would never let another female who wasn't family or a clanswoman under his employ cross his threshold again.

Confounded woman. This was the last thing he needed. He should never have let Mrs. Eliott through the door in the first place.

The ague had arrived with devastating impact in Torhaven about a fortnight ago and most of the staff at Eilean Tor had succumbed to it as well. In fact, the castle's housekeeper Mrs. Barrie, the wife of the gamekeeper, had sadly passed away.

Rothsburgh thanked all the angels in heaven that his sister Helena had taken his daughter, Annabelle, to Edinburgh a month ago, well before the pestilence had arrived. He was one of the few who had not contracted the illness. God only knew why.

He ordered Rosencrantz and Guildenstern to stay at the edge of the hearthrug, and then crossed the room to ring for Roberts, his butler-cum-valet. He was reluctant to do so. The man still had a fearsome cough, as did his wife, the castle's cook. In fact, Rothsburgh had ordered both of them to retire early this evening to assist with their recuperation. But he would need the good man's help to open up and ready one of the guest rooms in the wing where his own suite of rooms was located.

Roberts appeared in good time and took the news of the unexpected arrival of Mrs. Eliott in his customary stride. The man was loyal to a fault and truly unflappable.

Once he'd quit the library, Rothsburgh returned to Mrs. Eliott. Beth. She had not moved at all. He bent down and easily lifted her into his arms. He had already noted when he'd first opened the door to her that she was of medium height and very slender. In fact, she barely weighed anything at all. Indeed, he suspected that half the weight he carried was sodden wool.

Looking down at her, he noticed that her head had lolled back at an awkward angle, so he adjusted her position until she was better cradled in his arms with her head resting against his shoulder. She murmured slightly and her eyelids fluttered open for a second before she subsided into oblivion again.

He couldn't resist the temptation to study her face for a moment. Even though she was in a feverish, disheveled state, he was helplessly arrested by her delicate beauty.

She had the face of an angel.

He guessed she was in her early twenties. In his opinion, she was far too young to be a destitute widow. She should be enjoying life to the full, instead of searching for work in the middle of nowhere. But as he well knew, life was hardly ever fair.

He suspected she had blond hair, although it was so wet, it was difficult to tell the exact shade. Whatever hairstyle she had previously arranged it into had largely collapsed. Nevertheless, he could tell it was luxuriously thick. It curled damply in natural waves about her cheeks and across her forehead. Long, surprisingly dark eyelashes fanned over her flushed cheeks, and although hidden from his view now, he also knew she had large gray eyes. The irises were a clear, silver-gray, rimmed with a darker gray. He'd registered their exceptional shade during her interview, such as it was.

His eyes drifted lower to her rose-pink lips, now slightly parted as she breathed softly against his neck. Her lower lip was quite full, even sinfully full he thought, when compared to the rest of her angelic fairness. It pouted in such a way that he had to suppress the sudden, dangerous urge to suck the tantalizing curve into his mouth and kiss her.

Cursing himself for being both a cad and the worst kind of fool—it had been a long time since he'd been so captivated by a woman's physical beauty—he roused himself from his unashamed perusal and strode out into the hall, and then up the stairs to the east wing.

Faint light spilled from one of the open doors. Roberts had obviously got the fire going and set the candles alight. Entering the room, he found the butler turning down the bedclothes. Nearby was a pile of fresh towels and additional blankets. There was also a bowl and ewer filled with fresh water, warming by the fire.

"Can I get ye anything else, milord?" asked Roberts. His voice was strained and slightly breathless. Rothsburgh could see that he was trying very hard to suppress a fit of coughing. The butler was not a young man by any means and still sick as a dog.

"No, that will be all, Roberts. I'll take care of things from here."

"Weel, if ye are sure, milord—" Roberts covered his mouth as he at last succumbed to the urge to cough.

Rothsburgh gave him a mock frown. "Go, man, and get back to bed. Don't make me come and tuck you in."

Roberts bowed his thanks and swiftly left the room, closing the door behind him. Rothsburgh wasn't sure if the subsequent barking sound coming from the corridor was coughing, laughter, or both.

He crossed the room to the large four-poster bed, and gently laid the young widow upon the exposed sheets. She did not make a sound. He straightened and then crossed his arms, staring down at her. What he needed to do—which was to get her warm and dry—would be difficult without her being conscious. He wished to God the woman would wake up.

He placed a hand on her shoulder and shook her gently. "Mrs. Eliott. Beth. Open your eyes. Can you hear me?" She didn't stir at all. He squeezed one of her hands. Her fingers were hot and clammy at the same time.

A glint of something silver caught his eye. Lifting her right hand, he noticed a wedding band. It was a delicately wrought piece—an intricate filigree design—and quite beautiful. He didn't miss the significance of her wearing it on her right ring finger. Mrs. Eliott obviously still honored the memory of her husband. She'd intimated he'd perished at Waterloo so he would have died three months ago. She would still be in deep mourning.

A cynical smile quirked the corner of his mouth. He, on the other hand, barely grieved for Isabelle, even though her death was recent. But then, his love for her had died long ago. Indeed, he didn't even know where Isabelle's gold wedding band was. Even sadder was the realization that he didn't really care. How could he, when Isabelle had hardly ever worn it? Like holding to her marriage vows, the ring had obviously meant little to her.

He brushed his thumb across Beth's silver wedding ring and tried to rouse her again by calling her name. Her eyelids did not flicker in the slightest.

Hell and damnation. He was going to have to undress her himself.

Aside from the butler's wife, Mrs. Roberts, who was currently indisposed, there were no other female servants at Eilean Tor. After Isabelle's death, her lady's maid had secured another position, and the nursemaid who looked after Annabelle had gone with his daughter to Edinburgh. The few maids from the village who Mrs. Roberts saw fit to employ within the kitchen were all currently in Torhaven caring for their own sick families, or they were unwell themselves.

She's sick and unconscious, man—just bloody get on with it. He'd fought at Waterloo himself for Christ's sake. Why should he hesitate when it came to carrying out such a simple task? Hadn't he undressed women hundreds of times? He knew what to do—could do it with his eyes closed in fact. But the difference was, the women had always been awake and willing.

Sighing heavily in resignation, Rothsburgh moved down to the end of the bed and unlaced Mrs. Eliott's black ankle boots, before tugging them off. Despite his best intentions not to pay attention to particular details about her, he noticed that beneath her fine silk stockings, she had small, delicate feet and slender ankles. Blowing out another exasperated breath, he placed her boots by the hearth to dry, and then returned to sit next to her.

"Mrs. Eliott... Beth, wake up."

Still, there was no response.

Now comes the hardest part—taking off her dress and undergarments. He couldn't help but smile ruefully at himself for his choice of words, because despite his best efforts, *his* recalcitrant part was growing exactly that—hard as a bloody rock. At least Mrs. Eliott wouldn't notice.

Gritting his teeth, he set about undoing the jet buttons of her black woolen spencer. He eased her forward, trying to ignore the feel of her breath against his cheek as he slid the jacket off. Whilst he was not overly *au fait* with the fashions of the day, he noticed that her clothes were well-cut and of high quality. She also possessed a silver pocket watch.

Interesting. Perhaps her husband had been an officer. She must have had a little money at some point. He guessed she must hail from the middle-classes. That would also explain her perfect enunciation and genteel accomplishments, although not so much her brusque manner. He smiled, recalling the flash of her silver-gray eyes when she'd stood up to his deliberate taunting. She had spirit, he'd give her that much.

He cast his eyes over the bodice of her traveling dress, more black wool, trimmed about the modest neckline with black lace. No buttons. The gown obviously did up at the back. As gently as he could, he rolled her onto her side, then quickly released the small jet fastenings. As each one slid open, he exposed her fine linen shift and lightly boned stays that also laced down the back.

He'd been right when he'd assumed that she was slender. Perhaps she was even a little too thin. He could clearly see the outline of her elegant spine and her small waist as he unlaced her stays. However, as he rolled her back then gently eased off the garments, he was surprised to see that she had quite an ample bust, despite her slimness. Through her wet shift, he couldn't help but notice that her breasts were perfectly rounded, and her peaked nipples were a dusky pink beneath the flimsy, transparent fabric. He swallowed and returned his gaze to her face, suddenly feeling as guilty as a youth caught spying through a keyhole at a woman attending to her toilette.

But she was still asleep, thank God. He was as randy as a stallion, his balls in sheer agony. And he hadn't even taken off her wet shift.

To distract himself, he picked up her discarded clothes and draped them over a chair before the fire. Turning back was a mistake. Perhaps she'd moved—he wasn't sure—but her shift had rucked up revealing long, slender thighs. Christ, he would come before he'd even finished the job. There was no doubt about it, he was a wicked devil. He shouldn't feel this way, but his unruly body seemed to have a mind of its own.

It suddenly occurred to him that he had nothing to dress her in once all of her wet things were removed. He couldn't leave her naked. Swearing under his breath, he returned to the bed and pulled the covers over her. He would have to hunt for something for her to wear.

Rothsburgh left the room and strode down the corridor to his own bedchamber. On entering, he immediately noticed that Roberts had thoughtfully ignited the fire and candles before retiring as instructed. He made straight for the sideboard and poured himself a double whisky before tossing it back in one gulp. He knew he shouldn't drink too much but,

God in heaven, he needed something to douse the fire in his loins before he returned to Mrs. Eliott.

He poured himself another dram. Whilst sipping this one, he racked his brains to think of some garment he could easily procure to preserve a little of the widow's dignity, and his own sanity. He assumed the blasted woman had luggage—she'd probably been forced to leave it at The Black Barnacle. Of course, her things could be retrieved tomorrow, but that wasn't going to help him tonight. Isabelle's clothing had all been disposed of by his sister. And he could hardly go knocking on Roberts's door to request one of his wife's night rails.

He downed the last mouthful of whisky and realized that he would just have to dress her in one of his nightshirts for the time being. It was better than nothing. Marginally.

Feeling slightly more in control of his baser urges, he snatched up one of his shirts and retraced his steps to the guest room. Beth—although he should try to think of her as Mrs. Eliott—had managed to kick off the covers and she had started shivering again. It was imperative that he finish what he'd started.

Clenching his jaw and focusing on the practicalities of the task at hand rather than the beautiful body being laid bare, Rothsburgh deftly pulled off Beth's shift, before pulling his nightshirt over her head and guiding her limp arms through the sleeves. Then and only then did he remove her stockings.

Breathing a sigh of relief, he went over to the basin and dampened a washcloth to bathe the widow's flushed face. She was murmuring in her sleep now. Her brow was creased and she tossed her head a little. Perhaps she was having a bad dream.

He knew all about bad dreams, both real and imagined.

He returned to her side, but he couldn't make out the

words. "Beth," he said softly, placing the cloth on her forehead. "You're quite safe."

"Please...leave me be," she whispered.

"It's all right, Beth. No one will harm you." Rothsburgh didn't know if she could hear him, but he wanted to ease her distress. He pushed a strand of hair away from the corner of her mouth, wondering who had frightened her so badly.

He prayed it wasn't him.

Surprisingly, she rolled her cheek onto his hand and stilled. He even thought he could detect the curve of a faint smile on her lips. So maybe it wasn't him. He suddenly felt inordinately pleased that his voice and touch seemed to soothe her.

Tread carefully, Rothsburgh. She may look like the embodiment of heaven, but caring for her, like any woman, will only lead you into hell.

You've already been there, and you can never afford to go back again.

～

"Please, for the love of God, go away..."

Rothsburgh sat bolt upright in the armchair besides Beth's bed, all senses on high alert. In the dim light of the banked fire, he could just make out Beth tossing beneath the gold damask counterpane. Her nightmare had come back again. It was the third night he'd spent by her bed. And this was the third time she'd had the dream.

He reached out and touched her hand as he had done each time before. "Beth, hush now, lass. It's all right. You're safe."

She instantly became quiet, and her breathing grew less ragged. He had no idea why he was able to dispel the nightmare. Nevertheless, he was pleased that something so simple seemed to ease her inner, if not her physical, turmoil.

For him, the only way to prevent the visions of the blood-soaked and gore-strewn battlefields of Belgium parading through his head every night was to imbibe enough wine and whisky to knock him into a dreamless stupor. Not healthy nor wise, he knew, but sometimes it was the only thing that would help him to sleep.

He sighed and subsided back into the armchair where he'd been dozing prior to Beth's outcry. Not for the first time he wondered whom she entreated to leave her alone. Her husband? But why would she still wear her wedding ring—a symbol of devotion and affection—if he had been the abusive type? It didn't make sense if that was the case. But then she could just as easily be dreaming about a stern parent figure, a combative sibling, even an over-zealous teacher from her childhood.

Speculating in the dead of night wasn't going to get him anywhere and besides, was it really any of his business? And would she even tell him, a virtual stranger, what troubled her if he asked? He sighed and closed his eyes.

Probably not.

He yawned. Christ, he was tired. After three nights keeping a bedside vigil, he wanted nothing more than to lie down and try to get some sleep. He opened his eyes and looked longingly at the space beside Beth. Would she even notice if he stretched out beside her for a few hours? She had been barely conscious for the last three days and nights. The problem was, even though she might not be aware of him, his body would certainly be aware of her.

Indeed, since she'd arrived, he seemed to be in a perpetual state of fever himself. It took only a soft breath sighing from her full pouting lips, or the sight of her slender ankles and elegant bare feet to send the blood pounding through his veins straight to his cock. How would he be, lying beside her with his balls aching with wanting her? He probably wouldn't get a wink of sleep.

But then again, perhaps exhaustion would just win out. And he'd never know unless he tried. Tired of his fruitless, internal debate, he quietly pulled off his boots and then eased himself onto the bed, very carefully avoiding any contact with her, tempting though it was to take her hand in his again. She didn't stir at all.

He closed his eyes, content to listen to the soft rhythm of her breathing. He had been wrong. For once his desire for the oblivion of sleep was greater than his physical desire for Mrs. Beth Eliott. At last, he felt his tension starting to ebb away...

CHAPTER 5

By slow degrees, Elizabeth became aware of herself again. Her mouth was dry, her throat was painful, her entire body ached. There was a dull, insistent throb somewhere in the vicinity of her left temple, and she instinctively knew it would hurt to open her eyes. Wherever she was, it was dark, although she sensed a fire burning somewhere near. There was a faint glow against her eyelids, and she heard the soft ashy crumble of a log disintegrating. Somehow, she knew that she was safe.

Grimacing, she swallowed and arched her stiff back. Even though she was still drowsy, she was aware that she was lying on her side in a large comfortable bed. Except her cheek was resting against something incongruously hard, as was one of her legs. She drew in a breath and was suddenly overwhelmed with the scent of warm male and rich, spicy soap. Cloves and sandalwood...musk.

Oh, no. Elizabeth's eyes flew open and her heart seized as the shocking reality of her situation penetrated her foggy brain. *I'm curled up in bed with Lord Rothsburgh!*

She gasped, and immediately pushed herself away from his

body as horrified confusion seized her. The marquess was fast asleep, but that hardly mattered. *This was wrong, so wrong.* But how on earth had this situation come to pass? That within a fortnight of leaving Hugh, she'd ended up in another man's bed?

She cast her mind back, desperately trying to recall what had happened to her. She clearly remembered talking with the marquess in the library and then his scathing appraisal of her reference. Hadn't she tried to leave? Then there was no clear memory of anything much at all...until now.

She knew she had been ill—in fact, given the way she felt, she still was. But for how long? And why was she in bed with Lord Rothsburgh?

Carefully, slowly, she rolled away from his large, disturbingly masculine form and gently pushed herself upright. She was wearing one of her own night rails, and Lord Rothsburgh was clothed as well, albeit somewhat informally. His loose linen shirt had partially rucked up around his waist revealing a tantalizing glimpse of a taut abdomen, and a thin line of dark hair that disappeared into buff nankeen trousers.

Cheeks burning, Elizabeth's eyes drifted lower and she noticed his long feet were bare. Their mutual state of *dishabille* and current situation suggested they had perhaps engaged in sexual congress. However, although her body ached and she felt spent, she could not detect any of the usual sensations associated with having taken part in such an act. She didn't think that the marquess had taken advantage of her in her weakened state.

And sick or not, surely she would remember having intimate relations with someone as overpoweringly male as Lord Rothsburgh.

Feeling slightly breathless, she tore her gaze away from him to look around the room. They were in a spacious, well-appointed bedchamber with a high vaulted ceiling. The bed they shared was a large four-poster, curtained with swathes of rich amber velvet. A golden damask counterpane and fine cotton sheets were crumpled at the end of the bed as if she or Lord Rothsburgh had kicked them away.

Despite the grand proportions of the room, it was warm enough. As she'd suspected, a fire burnt low in the substantial ivory marble fireplace opposite the foot of the bed. It gave off a soft glow and illuminated the rest of the furniture that was elegant enough to grace a French boudoir. A delicately carved walnut dresser and wardrobe stood against the stone walls. A chaise longue upholstered in ivory brocade was positioned before the hearth, and a matching armchair sat nearby on her side of the bed.

Her gaze skittered across the room to a pair of windows. Faint light seeped in around the edges of the drawn amber velvet curtains, but it was impossible to tell if it was morning or afternoon. She thought she could hear the sea.

She also spied her traveling trunk in a dark corner beside the armchair. *When on earth did that arrive?* Her clothes spilled out of the top, as if the contents had been hastily rummaged through. A large shawl of pale, gray cashmere was uppermost in the pile.

Trying hard not to disturb the marquess, Elizabeth slowly moved toward the edge of the bed, swung her feet over and stood up. The room tipped with a sickening lurch, and she was forced to steady herself against one of the carved walnut bedposts before she took the few steps to her trunk. Never before had she felt so unwell. It was highly disturbing to say the least.

With shaking hands, she pulled her shawl around herself and sank into the armchair, tucking her cold bare feet up beneath the hem of her night rail. A brief glance back toward the bed confirmed that Lord Rothsburgh was still asleep. *Thank heavens.*

She felt like she could breathe again.

One thing she needed right now was time. Time to gather her wits before she spoke with the marquess about what had happened. And more importantly, what would happen next. How could she even consider working here after waking up in bed with him? She was not fit to play the part of the upright governess when for all intents and purposes it now appeared she was a woman of ill-repute.

She released a shaky sigh and clasped her arms more tightly about herself, trying to recollect any detail, no matter how small, about her lost hours. She suddenly wondered where all the other servants were. When she had first arrived, it had seemed as if she and Lord Rothsburgh were the sole inhabitants of this vast, lonely place. But then an image of another, older woman with gray hair suddenly materialized in her mind's eye—she was a servant, Elizabeth was sure of it. She had a vague memory of the woman bathing her brow, holding a glass of water to her lips and assisting her to use the privy. Yes. She knew there was a garderobe through the door to the right of the bed and the older woman had helped her to get there.

But clearly it hadn't just been the older woman who had cared for her...

Elizabeth's gaze drifted over to the bed again. Lord Rothsburgh was sleeping peacefully. For a moment she worried that he had also been struck down with the ague, but she could see no signs of fever or restlessness. He was lying on his back, one arm tucked behind his head, while the other lay relaxed at his side. She was struck again by how tall the man was. And how muscular. She didn't mean to, but she couldn't help but compare him to Hugh. Her husband was also tall and lean, but in a coltish way, whereas Lord Rothsburgh appeared to be broader and harder—a man who was obviously accustomed to physical exertion. He was certainly not an indolent nobleman.

Her gaze roamed over his wide shoulders, his bulging upper arms that were barely contained by his linen sleeves, and the broad plane of his chest that she now knew from experience was as unyielding as rock. Her eyes then wandered lower to where his shirt was still rumpled up around his lean hips, and her breath caught in her throat.

The man had a rampant erection.

Oh, my Lord. Blushing furiously, Elizabeth ripped her gaze away from the tented fabric at his groin and glanced at his face. Thankfully he was still fast asleep. At least he wouldn't know she had seen him in such an unguarded state.

Stop looking at him, Elizabeth. But it seemed her eyes wouldn't obey her. A strange nervous curiosity held her in its grip. Regardless of the danger—the marquess might wake at any moment and catch her out—and the certain knowledge that what she did was wrong, she couldn't seem to resist the temptation to continue her blatant study.

Despite his body's obvious physical prowess, and ruggedly handsome looks, Lord Rothsburgh appeared strangely vulnerable in sleep. But when he was awake... Raven-haired and almost olive-skinned, Elizabeth couldn't decide whether the marquess reminded her more of a wicked pirate or even Lucifer himself. She already knew that even a fleeting glance of his brown-black eyes was enough to put her to the blush.

Yes, for all his apparent softness now, Lord Rothsburgh was dangerous indeed. Frowning, she continued to trace over his features, trying to ascertain why just looking at him made her heart beat as wildly as that of a silly young girl. Of course, it couldn't be his high slashing cheekbones, his straight blade of a nose, and wide, firmly sculpted mouth. Or the wing of sleep-ruffled black hair that perpetually flopped across his brow, making her fingers itch to push it out of his eyes.

It most certainly couldn't be the fact that he badly needed a shave. His lean, square jaw was so shadowed with dark stubble, she could only just make out the slight indentation in his chin. She clenched her hands into fists. No, she wouldn't think about what his smooth jaw would feel like under her fingertips after he'd used a razor.

What on earth was wrong with her? Maybe the fever had addled her brain.

Just at that moment, Lord Rothsburgh began to stir. Elizabeth started guiltily and turned her gaze to the fire. Out of the corner of her eye, she noticed that he rolled to his side and one of his arms reached toward the side of the bed where she had been.

"Beth..." he murmured sleepily. His use of her Christian name was telling. It implied an intimacy between them that she knew nothing about. How much had he been involved in her care? It was frustrating in the extreme that she couldn't remember.

His hand ran over the sheets and then he opened his dark eyes. "Beth?" He quickly pushed himself up to a sitting position, looking around the room—for her.

His eyes quickly came to rest upon her, and he smiled sleepily. She was surprised that it seemed to be in genuine pleasure. "Beth...I mean, Mrs. Eliott. You're up. How are you feeling?"

"I've been better." Her voice emerged as a hoarse rasp. It hurt to talk.

Lord Rothsburgh frowned and immediately got up from the bed. She was grateful that his loose shirt now concealed his inopportune arousal, especially when he poured her a glass of water from a jug on the nightstand and brought it over to her.

"Here, drink this, Be—Mrs. Eliott."

She dutifully took the glass, taking care not to brush her fingers against his, and took a much-needed drink. After a few painful sips she paused.

"Razor-blade throat?" he asked.

"Very much so," she croaked.

"You don't have to talk." To her surprise, he suddenly reached out and tenderly felt her brow. "At least your fever has broken," he said with a smile, his gaze wandering over her face.

As if to belie his pronouncement, Elizabeth felt her whole face heat with a scalding blush. She couldn't bear the marquess's close scrutiny and gentle touch. It was a stark reminder that Hugh had never touched her with care or kindness. Her heart was pounding so hard inside her chest, surely Lord Rothsburgh must hear it and suspect how affected she was by him. His raw masculine beauty was difficult to deal with even at a distance. This closeness was too much.

To break the moment, she suddenly thrust the glass toward him. "I've had enough. Thank you."

He quirked an eyebrow then to her relief, he moved away to replace the glass on the nightstand. Then he sat on the edge of the bed directly opposite her, a thoughtful expression in his eyes.

He'd said she didn't need to talk but she had to. She needed to find out exactly what had happened, and perhaps even more importantly, she needed to work out what she would do next.

But first she needed to convey her thankfulness to the marquess for taking her in—before she lost her nerve. She drew in a shaky breath and met his eyes. "I'm at a loss as to what to say, Lord Rothsburgh, other than I'm so sorry to have inconvenienced you—"

He snorted. "What nonsense, Mrs. Eliott. You really don't need to apologize. It's not as if you contracted the ague intentionally."

She frowned. "Nevertheless, my lord, I feel I must apologize for having put you and your staff out at such a difficult time. My arrival on your doorstep was without invitation. That, in and of itself, was presumptuous of me to say the least.

And then to force such a burden of care upon you... Whatever you say, my lord, I feel compelled to express my gratitude. I am in your debt."

Lord Rothsburgh inclined his head. "Your thanks is duly noted, Mrs. Eliott. But I must insist there is no indebtedness on your part."

She nodded. His words were reassuring but she still felt awkward beyond imagining. And flustered. She supposed that being clothed only in a shawl and night rail in front of a very casually dressed Lord Rothsburgh wasn't helping matters. Nevertheless, she needed to broach the next difficult topic on her mind.

Dredging up her courage, she spoke again. "Thank you for your graciousness. However, I must say, my lord, that I am more than a bit troubled by the circumstances which I find myself in."

He raised a quizzical eyebrow.

She gestured at herself, and then toward him and the rest of the room. "This seems...highly inappropriate...to say the least."

Lord Rothsburgh shook his head, his wide mouth tilting into a wry smile. He rested his forearms on his thighs and looked up at her. "You've been gravely ill, Mrs. Eliott, and you're worried about propriety?"

She blushed in flustered indignation. "Well, yes... When I woke up...you and I were... I'm sure you know what I mean."

The marquess's eyes had grown darker, his gaze more intense as she spoke. "I can assure you that your virtue, for want of a better way to put it, is intact," he said with grave sincerity. "I apologize that I...fell asleep on the job, so to speak."

Elizabeth's cheeks were burning now. "I'm afraid I don't recall much..."

"I'm not surprised. You've been barely conscious for three days."

"Three days?" Elizabeth was aghast. She had indeed been ill. Her mind reeled at the implications, and despite the marquess's assurances to the contrary, she certainly did owe him more than mere gratitude.

Lord Rothsburgh watched her steadily. "I can see that you are shocked. And as you have perhaps already surmised, I have taken part in a great deal of your care—out of necessity, not by design I assure you. Mrs. Roberts, Eilean Tor's cook, assisted when she was able. Unfortunately, she is still recovering from the ague also. And as all the other female servants have been similarly indisposed, and are not currently at the castle, I thought it best that I attend you. There really was no one else."

Elizabeth swallowed and clutched her shawl more tightly about herself. This was far worse than she had thought. A maelstrom of questions whirled around her mind. Had Lord Rothsburgh removed her wet clothes? How much had he seen of her body? How had he touched her? How many times had she curled up against him in sleep? She glanced toward the garderobe. For heaven's sake, had he taken her to the privy?

"Oh...that must have been...arduous for you, my lord," she whispered.

He clasped his hands together and leaned forward, his arms still resting on his long muscular legs. His penetrating gaze locked with hers. "Please forgive me for mentioning it, but I was at Waterloo like your husband, Mrs. Eliott. Nothing really daunts me anymore after surviving that. Caring for you was not onerous at all." He smiled gently then. "Even helping you to the privy."

Mortification swept over Elizabeth in a great wave. She dropped her head, unable to look at Lord Rothsburgh any longer. Hardened soldier or not, he shouldn't have had to—

no, she didn't want to think about it. There was absolutely no way on earth that she could find employment here now, knowing the marquess had been her nursemaid. She couldn't endure it.

But where was she to go? What was she to do?

She raised a shaking hand and pushed her snarled hair away from her face. It felt like a matted bird's nest. What a sight she must look. Then she realized the marquess had probably seen her in a far worse state over the last few days. She closed her eyes, fighting the unexpected urge to cry.

"Beth, it's all right." Lord Rothsburgh's hand grasped one of hers. "I didn't mean to upset you. I'm a complete dolt with words sometimes. I speak too plainly."

Elizabeth opened her eyes. Lord Rothsburgh was kneeling before her. He was too close to her again, his dark brown eyes regarding her too softly. She was not used to such behavior from a man. She couldn't bear it. She must go.

She bit her lip hard and swallowed back the tears. "I'm just a bit...overwhelmed. Perhaps you could send Mrs. Roberts to help me when she is able, and then I will prepare to go. I've been too much trouble already. Do you know when the next mail coach comes?"

Lord Rothsburgh scowled. "Don't be ridiculous. You're not going anywhere. The disease has yet to run its full course. Your fever may have broken, but you will be as weak as a kitten for many more days to come. And then the cough will set in. It will be another week or so before you are up to even getting dressed." His expression then softened. "But I will send Mrs. Roberts to you later this morning and arrange for a bath to be sent up if you'd like."

Elizabeth nodded. "Yes, I would like that." She dropped her gaze to her lap where Lord Rothsburgh still held her right hand. His long tanned fingers completely covered her own pale ones, concealing her wedding ring. She felt small, frail and, oh, so weak in more ways than she cared to admit.

She determined that the sooner she recovered and found herself another position the better.

It seemed she had been doomed to fail at Eilean Tor before she'd even started.

~

Rothsburgh strode away from the guest room, cursing himself with every expletive he knew for being such a tactless blockhead. Rosencrantz and Guildenstern ran at his heels. At least they didn't mind foul language. He smiled ruefully as he entered the library. His dogs were about the only company he was fit to keep.

He made straight for the sideboard and poured himself a double whisky, before pacing to one of the bay windows that overlooked the North Sea to watch the sun rise. He couldn't believe he had managed to shock, wound, and embarrass Beth so badly in such a short space of time.

Waking up in her bed with a rampant erection had been the first of his blunders. He prayed that she hadn't noticed. But he was certain that she had.

He grimaced and took a decent sip of the whisky, hoping to dispel his own acute embarrassment. Christ, he hoped he hadn't reached for her in his sleep. She must think him the worst kind of lascivious beast. In fact, he was surprised she hadn't screamed blue murder and struck him over the head with the poker, just for finding him in her bed. It was probably no less than he deserved though, given that for once he hadn't been dreaming of hand-to-hand combat on the battlefield, but of action of an entirely different kind—with Beth. God help him, his cock was already starting to twitch again at the memory.

Of course, his second mistake had been to reveal how much of her care he'd administered. He should have realized that she would not react well to the idea of a man—a complete stranger—caring for her in such a personal way. But devil take him, what else could he have done given the circumstances?

He had anticipated that she would have periods of memory loss. Over the last three days and nights she'd done little more than toss and turn in a perpetual state of feverish sleep. There had been one or two times, however, when Beth had seemed partially aware of her surroundings. He'd obviously been wrong. When he'd told her that he'd been her main caregiver, she'd reacted with genuine shock, as if she hadn't any recollection of the last few days at all.

And then he'd gone and mentioned the bloody war. He'd only meant to reassure her that caring for her had not been testing or burdensome. Instead, all he'd done was completely humiliate her and tactlessly remind her of her husband's death, in one fell swoop.

Rothsburgh tossed back the whisky and then poured himself another. He'd had too many breakfasts like this. But then what did it matter, if he drank too much or at inappropriate times, when there was no one to naysay him? When no one cared?

Turning from the window, he threw himself into one of the leather wing chairs, and the hounds settled at his feet. He stared into the dead embers in the grate.

He'd often feared his soul was just as cold and dark. Until Beth had crossed his doorstep. Somehow she had reignited his long dormant soul and had set his heart beating again. He might be physically exhausted right now, but he also felt more alive, more energized than he could recall feeling for the longest time.

He must be mad. He barely knew the woman. The baser, masculine side of him suspected that it was pure animal attraction that had set him afire. Beth was beautiful, and despite the disheveled state in which she had arrived and her illness ravaged state now, he thought she was one of the loveliest women he'd ever laid eyes on. He hated to think how overcome he'd be when she was well and looking her best.

If he were honest with himself, he should also acknowledge that it was more than her looks that attracted him, little that he knew of her. He sensed spirit and a keen intelligence... and honor. Her adherence to the convention of wearing the staid garments associated with deep mourning, as well as her wedding ring, suggested she wished to pay due respect to her husband's memory. She possessed qualities he found both admirable and...refreshing.

This morning he'd also learned that she obviously valued her virtue, given her shocked reaction at finding him in her bed. But then, he'd also sensed a reluctant attraction to him if her shy sideways glances and her blushes were anything to go by. Perhaps she wasn't completely indifferent to him.

He sighed heavily. Not that it mattered. He really shouldn't be harboring any sort of interest in the woman, carnal or otherwise. Corrupting chaste widows was not his usual style. His mouth twisted into a mirthless smile as he leaned his head back against the headrest of the chair. Tumbling ready and willing courtesans was more to his taste. But even though he was a hardened reprobate to the very core, his own transgressions paled into insignificance when he compared them to the sins of his wife.

Isabelle.

Rothsburgh took another slug of whisky, trying to deaden the old pain. It had faded with time but invariably came back at unexpected moments like this, to stab him anew. Ironic that the pain of betrayal still hurt him more than the battle wounds —both physical and emotional—that he'd sustained at Waterloo. And to his shame, even the actual death of the woman herself.

But then, how could he be expected to mourn the death of a woman—a woman he had once loved beyond all reason—when she had turned out to be utterly faithless? When, with malice aforethought, she had brazenly tried to pass another man's bastard off as his own child within the first year of their marriage?

Of course, when he was newly wedded and in the first mad throes of love, he'd never envisaged that things would turn out so disastrously.

Lady Isabelle March had been as dazzling as any of the stars in heaven's firmament when he'd first met her during her second Season in London six years ago. Black-haired and gentian eyed, she'd had a sparkling wit and beauty beyond compare. She was always dressed in the height of fashion, rode like an Amazon through Hyde Park, and her dance card was always full. She also had an impeccable lineage. Her father, the Earl of Granthorpe, was extremely well off, and her maternal grandfather was a duke. She seemed to be a diamond of the first water. And after he'd first seen her, he'd been determined to win her.

Who'd have thought that she'd be such a wild hellion and completely lacking in principles?

He *had* heard the whispered warnings, of course. That despite Lady Isabelle's apparent suitability as a prospective wife for any nobleman, she was also rumored to be fickle with her attentions. Hence the lack of an engagement by the end of her debut Season.

Stupidly, blindly, he'd ignored all the speculation and gossip. He hadn't cared. The worldly, rakish, Marquess of Rothsburgh had been well and truly besotted by the incomparable Lady Isabelle. But he'd been nothing more than Isabelle's cuckold.

It had taken him a long time to crawl out of the black void of despair and disillusionment that Isabelle had flung him into. He'd learned to exist as a man who was really only half-alive and, up until three days ago, he had been relatively content to carry on that way. But now...perhaps Mrs. Beth Eliott had revived his long dead heart.

And he didn't like it one little bit.

Rothsburgh finished his whisky, then paced over to the bay windows again to watch the sun slowly ascend through scattered shreds of cloud over the perpetually cold, dark sea. The question was, what was Beth going to do now? That she needed to stay at Eilean Tor until she had completely recovered from her illness, was a foregone conclusion.

But after that...

There was no longer a governess's position here. He hated to think that Beth had traveled all this way in good faith, for nothing. She was clearly alone in the world and desperate.

He cast about in his mind, trying to think of friends or acquaintances of his that had children and required a teacher, but he could think of none. It was a shame that Lady Beauchamp's intelligence about the position was old. He supposed that Isabelle must have enlisted the services of the Widows of Waterloo Trust to try to secure a suitable applicant before her death. Perhaps he could enlist his sister's aid in finding Beth another situation. He certainly had no suitable position of an honorable nature to offer the young woman.

He doubted that she'd consent to becoming his mistress.

As much as he was loath to say farewell to Mrs. Eliott, he knew it would be for the best if she left this cursed place. For both their sakes.

CHAPTER 6

Much to her consternation, Elizabeth quickly discovered that Lord Rothsburgh's prognosis about her current state of malaise, and the expected rate of her recovery, was entirely accurate.

After he'd left her alone, the only activity she'd had the strength for was returning to bed, where she'd alternately dozed and worried over her future...until Mrs. Roberts had arrived with a pot of tea and a bowl of stodgy, salty porridge to "build up her strength." Elizabeth was dismayed to find that she barely had the energy to lift her spoon or her teacup. As much as it frustrated her, the grim reality was, she wasn't going anywhere for the next few days.

As promised, Lord Rothsburgh arranged a bath for her. Mrs. Roberts returned mid-morning and pulled the amber velvet curtains around the bed before the tub was discreetly set up by several—Elizabeth assumed—male servants. She felt grateful, but also a little self-conscious for such a luxury being bestowed when she was really nothing more than an interloper at the castle.

Mrs. Roberts, a gray-haired, stout woman with the type of

dour countenance that brooked no argument, shooed the men from the room before she drew open the curtains again. "It's verra good to see you are much better, Mrs. Eliott," the older woman commented as she ran her shrewd gaze over Elizabeth. "Would you like me to help ye with yer bath?"

Elizabeth politely declined the older woman's kind offer. "I'm sure you have enough to do, Mrs. Roberts, what with cooking all the meals here and hardly any staff to help. And from what I've discovered this morning, I have already claimed too much of your time. You must be exhausted."

The cook shrugged. "It doesna matter. There's no' many to feed at the moment. Wha' wi' Lady Annabelle now in Edinburgh wi' the master's sister—thank the Lord and sweet Jesus, the child left afore this wretched ague came to Eilean Tor—there's only Lord Rothsburgh left to cook anything special for. 'Tis only a wee bit o' work."

Elizabeth's breath caught in her chest as the import of what Mrs. Roberts had just said sank into her brain. *Lady Annabelle isn't here?* Surely she hadn't heard correctly.

Somehow, she managed to suck a quick shallow breath into her constricted lungs in order to speak. "Excuse me, Mrs. Roberts, but what did you just say about Lord Rothsburgh's daughter? She's in Edinburgh?"

Mrs. Roberts nodded. "Weel, yes. The poor wee mite has gone to live wi' Lady Maxwell and her husband, and their young children." The cook suddenly frowned and looked wary. "But perhaps I shouldna have said anything. 'Tis no' my place to discuss any matter to do wi' his lordship. Mr. Roberts is always tellin' me to watch my tongue."

Elizabeth's head suddenly buzzed with dizziness and nausea swirled in her belly. She was grateful she was still sitting in the bed as she didn't think her legs would support her. Why hadn't Lord Rothsburgh told her there was no governess's post here as soon as she'd arrived? No wonder he had laughed at her when she'd first announced her intentions on his doorstep. And then to go through the bizarre charade of pretending to be the butler before conducting a sham interview. It made no sense. Why was he playing these strange games with her? She didn't understand this man. No, not at all.

Elizabeth reached out and grasped the older woman's arm. "Please, Mrs. Roberts. It was not my intention to draw you into gossip. You are obviously a very loyal servant." She studied the cook's expression, trying to detect if there was any degree of suspicion or judgment hardening the woman's gaze. What on earth did Mrs. Roberts make of her?

It only just occurred to Elizabeth that her arrival must appear odd indeed if there was no longer the need for a governess here. So, what *had* the marquess told his staff about her? Surely they must know their master had been looking after her, attending to her every personal need... That he'd shared her bed.

Oh God. Do they think I am his mistress?

She couldn't bear it if Mrs. Roberts or the other staff thought she was some high-class harlot.

A whore.

Panic squeezed Elizabeth's chest, making her breathless. "It's just that...I'm a little confused...and I'm not sure what Lord Rothsburgh has told you about my...presence here, which I know must seem highly unusual. You see, I came here to apply for the governess's position..."

Understanding and perhaps compassion suddenly appeared in Mrs. Roberts eyes. "Och, Mrs. Eliott. Dinna worry aboot how things look." She patted Elizabeth's hand. "His lordship explained tha' there was a misunderstandin'— tha' yer London committee fer widows referred ye fer the job here, even though ye wasna needed. Such a shame too. Ye wouldha' suited her young ladyship verra well."

Elizabeth closed her eyes and breathed a sigh of relief. She wasn't convinced the staff wouldn't look askance at her because of Lord Rothsburgh's attentions during her illness. But at least they all knew why she had come here. Even though she was Mrs. Beth Eliott, she couldn't countenance the idea of being branded as a man's mistress, no matter how rich and titled that man was.

With a sinking heart, she realized her continued presence at Eilean Tor was more precarious than she'd originally thought. With no charge requiring a governess, she had no business being here at all. Her stomach began to churn again with a tumult of emotions: anger at Lord Rothsburgh's lack of honesty; acute embarrassment at the whole, strangely burdensome situation; and fear of what was to become of her.

She was going to have start afresh...again. And soon.

Fighting a wave of tears, she dismissed Mrs. Roberts with sincere thanks for her assistance before she shakily disrobed, and then climbed into the steaming bath. As the lavender scented vapors rose about her, she immediately felt a little calmer. It was reassuring to know she had a few days' grace to recover some of her strength and formulate a new plan of action for her future.

But even though she was grateful to the marquess for his continued care, she resolved to seek him out. No matter how unwell she felt, she would demand that he explain his perplexing actions thus far. She would not be able to rest until she did.

It was late afternoon when Elizabeth finally set forth from her sick bed in order to locate Lord Rothsburgh. She hadn't seen him since he'd quit her room earlier. Part of her was relieved that he hadn't returned given she'd still been abed, whilst another part of her was impatient to demand why he'd strung her along.

Indeed, it was her indignance alone that helped her to summon sufficient energy to don her least crushed set of widow's weeds, and to arrange her freshly washed and dried hair into a simple chignon. Even these simple actions left her breathless and shaking. She hated feeling so weak.

Emerging from her room, she found herself in a completely unfamiliar hallway. A thick Oriental runner extended the length of the polished wooden floor and absorbed the sound of her footsteps as she made her way down the long gallery toward a staircase. Richly colored tapestries and portraits of glowering men and woman in anti-quated dress—ancestors of the Huntly family line she supposed—were interspersed between tall arched windows that afforded glimpses of wind-lashed sea, and a horizon of pale, blue-gray sky.

Again, she was struck by the absolute isolation of this place. It was little wonder that the marquess had the reputa-tion for being a lone wolf given his place of residence.

He was definitely an enigma. Her conversational exchanges with him so far might have been limited, but she did not think he completely eschewed the company of others. He was unconventional in his behavior at times, and his moods seemed somewhat unpredictable, but he was certainly not the misanthrope Lady Airlie had deemed him.

So why was the marquess such a recluse? Elizabeth suddenly wondered if he was ever lonely.

She halted her thoughts right there. She would be on dangerous ground if she suddenly started to feel any sort of sympathy for the man. She already found him devilishly attractive in a physical sense. Cultivating any sort of tender feeling for him would be unwise indeed. She must always remember that she was married, and not a witless green girl.

More than anyone, she should know that she needed to keep her head.

She'd had her head turned before by a handsome man, and it had ended in disaster.

Elizabeth slowly descended the wide staircase, holding onto the stone banister for support—even this brief walk was making her feel heavy-chested and breathless—and noted a vaguely familiar set of double doors in carved oak ahead. She guessed she'd found the library. It was as good a place as any to search for Lord Rothsburgh. She certainly didn't have the stamina to look any farther afield for him, and she suspected it would be very easy to get lost within the environs of Eilean Tor.

Elizabeth slipped through the door—she had indeed gained the library—but it was deserted. Not even the deer-hounds, Rosencrantz and Guildenstern, lurked about the hearth. The grate contained logs that were yet unlit, as were the candles and lamps.

Contrary emotions assailed her again—she was relieved, yet oddly disappointed that Lord Rothsburgh wasn't present. She'd half expected him to be ensconced in one of the leather wing chairs, nonchalantly sipping a tumbler of whisky as he'd done on her first evening here. The evocative memory made her shiver—with either apprehension or feminine appreciation, she wasn't sure.

She just prayed she didn't lose her nerve before the marquess made an appearance.

Remember you're annoyed with him. And he owes you a decent explanation.

The clock on the black marble mantel suddenly proclaimed the hour to be four o'clock. The light was starting to fade, but it would be sufficient to read by while she waited. However, instead of choosing a book from the substantial collection of leather-bound volumes on display, Elizabeth was drawn across the room to the bay windows where a magnificent view of sea and sky beckoned to be admired.

Kneeling upon the brocade covered window seat, she looked down a plunging granite cliff face to where gray-green breakers exploded against slick, black rocks far below. A sudden wave of dizziness swept over her. Sitting back on her heels, she closed her eyes, waiting for the sensation of falling to ebb. She'd had no idea that Eilean Tor was situated on the very edge of the headland. It felt as if the whole castle was about to slip off the end of the world.

"Good God, Mrs. Eliott. What are you doing out of bed?"

Elizabeth's eyes flew open. Her back was to Lord Rothsburgh, but that didn't stop her from blushing at being caught in such an unladylike pose upon the window seat. Why did this man always seem to have the uncanny knack of catching her at a disadvantage?

As she hastily tried to turn around and get down from seat with as much decorum as possible, she felt his hand upon her arm.

"Allow me," he said, his touch and the warm baritone of his voice making her shiver. His hand steadied her as she slid one leg, then the other off the seat, and she was acutely aware that he was probably getting a good glimpse of her stocking-clad calves and ankles. Not that it really mattered. *He's probably already seen more of you than that, Elizabeth.*

"You didn't answer my question," he prompted, his hand still on her arm. His touch burned her even through the wool of her sleeve. She glanced up at his face to find his dark eyes studying her intently. Despite her resolve not to be affected by this man's physical attractiveness, Elizabeth realized it was hopeless as heat scorched her cheeks and her breathing became uneven.

Not able to return his searching gaze any longer, her gaze dropped to his freshly shaved jaw line and his beautifully sculpted mouth. It was a mistake because she immediately wondered what it would be like to be kissed by him. She closed her eyes and bit her lip.

No, no, no. Don't ever think it. You are a married woman. And the only reason the marquess is holding your arm is to make sure you don't trip over, or faint at his feet again.

Stupid, wicked Elizabeth.

Thank God, she would be gone from here within a week.

"I-I needed to speak with you, my lord," she said, annoyed with herself for sounding so obviously breathless and flustered. She took a step away and to her relief, Lord Rothsburgh's hand dropped from her arm.

He cocked a dark eyebrow. "Haven't you heard of ringing for the butler? You'll only delay your recovery, you know, if you try to do too much too soon."

"Of course I know how to summon the staff," she snapped back before she could stop herself. She should feel ashamed of her shrewish behavior. It was entirely inappropriate for someone of her assumed social status and current dependent situation. But in truth, she was relieved to be trading barbed comments with the marquess again. It helped her to maintain her distance. "I...just didn't want to be a bother."

Lord Rothsburgh didn't seem offended though. The corner of his wide mouth twitched with wry amusement. "You are not a bother at all, *my lady*."

Elizabeth paled at his teasing use of the honorific. She had come across as too imperious, too rude. She immediately felt contrite. "I apologize for my waspishness, Lord Rothsburgh. I am not usually so inclined. I think perhaps my ill humor is related to...my current indisposition in general."

"I'm sure that's the case." Amusement still tugged at the corner of the marquess's mouth. "And let me assure you that no offense has been taken. But would you please humor me and take a seat? You seem quite breathless and your continued rest is of paramount importance." He gestured toward the arrangement of chairs before the hearth where the hounds now sat. Rosencrantz thumped his tail when she glanced his way.

She smiled at the dog. Inviting as the wing chairs and the company of Rosencrantz looked, she wanted to retain a modicum of formality during her discussion with the marquess. She almost had to remind herself why she'd sought the man out to begin with. He had the alarming effect of scattering her thoughts into something as insubstantial as the shredded clouds drifting on the horizon over the sea.

"Perhaps we could sit...at your desk, my lord." The wide expanse of magnificently carved oak would provide a natural barrier between them, as well as create the atmosphere of decorum she was looking for.

He raised a quizzical eyebrow, but nevertheless inclined his head. "As you wish."

Elizabeth crossed to an oak Jacobean style chair before the desk, and sat as gracefully as she could, smoothing her skirts as she mentally prepared her thoughts. Lord Rothsburgh followed her, but instead of sitting behind the desk, he simply leaned in elegant negligence against it, not far from where she sat.

She straightaway lost her train of thought, all her senses focused on the way his long muscular legs, tightly encased in buckskin breeches, extended out beside her, and how he casually crossed his black Hussar boots at the ankle. Had he been riding? When he'd helped her from the window seat, she'd been too rattled at first, and then too exasperated to really notice what he'd been wearing.

She slanted a sideways look at him and confirmed her supposition. He was wearing a superbly cut, navy blue riding jacket of superfine over an ivory linen shirt with a simply tied cravat at his throat. His overlong black hair was hopelessly ruffled as though he'd been out in the wind.

He caught her gaze and raised his eyebrows, a faintly knowing smile playing about his lips. *Curse him*. He knew she'd been assessing his appearance. She sternly reminded herself that he was probably as vain as Hugh, and about as safe as Lucifer, the Great Tempter himself.

"Now, what is it that you wish to speak about, Mrs. Eliott?" the marquess prompted. As he crossed his arms over the broad expanse over his chest, he stared down at her, a hint of amusement still glinting in his dark eyes. "It must be of great import if it has prompted you to leave your sickbed to come in search of me."

Harnessing her wayward thoughts into some semblance of order by focusing on her annoyance with him, Elizabeth drew in a shaky breath to speak. "Yes, it is of great import. To me at any rate, considering it is about my whole future."

Understanding replaced the humor in his eyes. "Ah, I see." A muscle flickered in his jaw and he even looked a trifle guilty. But he held her gaze, waiting for her to continue.

Elizabeth swallowed past the rawness in her throat, trying to clear a sudden tickle. "Why did you not tell me that you no longer require a governess, Lord Rothsburgh?" she accused. To her chagrin, her voice had emerged as a hoarse croak which rather undermined the confident gravitas she'd been aiming for. But she wouldn't be deterred in her quest for an explanation. "I understand that your daughter, Lady Annabelle, now resides with your sister, Lady Maxwell in Edinburgh. Why did you let me...go through a farcical interview? I don't like games...my lord...especially when they involve my life." She stopped, too short of breath to continue, her eyes watering. The urge to cough was overwhelming. Damn the marquess for being right about the course of her illness. She threw him a furious glance as she tried to regroup and catch her breath.

He was watching her, concern etched across his features. "Can I get you some water, Be—Mrs. Eliott?" he asked quietly.

She nodded and accepted the glass gratefully when he returned from the drinks tray. After she'd taken a few sips, he moved to the other side of the desk and sat with his long fingers steepled beneath his chin. His dark, disconcerting gaze settled on her.

"What was I to do, Mrs. Eliott?" His deep voice contained a serious, almost bitter edge to it. "You arrive on my doorstep, wet and shivering, and frankly, I'm amazed you didn't get swept into the North Sea at the time you crossed. And believe me, I've had words with Mr. Geddes about that. So how could I turn you away at that point without hearing you out? Then, before I can enlighten you about the change in circumstances at Eilean Tor—your widow's committee obviously had erroneous intelligence—you promptly pass out. And up until this morning, you were hardly in a state to be informed about anything of consequence, or otherwise." His dark brown eyes suddenly softened as well as his tone. "Believe me, I have nothing but the best of intentions when it comes to your wellbeing. It is not my intent, nor has it ever been...to toy with you, so to speak."

Elizabeth inwardly conceded that he spoke sense, yet she was too tautly strung to let him off the hook entirely. "Yet... you let me assume you were the butler here when you answered the door. And you appeared to read my reference with due regard...until you saw who had written it. Tell me, Lord Rothsburgh, is it your habit to mock those with earnest intentions and sincere need?"

The marquess winced at this last accusation. "Mrs. Eliott, may I say without a hint of a lie that I never meant to patronize or ridicule you, and I am truly sorry if you feel that I have been less than hospitable or reasonable. I fully intended to discuss your circumstances with you, but I was waiting for an appropriate opportunity. It seems I have underestimated your degree of concern and tenacity."

Elizabeth studied his face and could only detect sincerity. His gaze was steady upon her. Perhaps she had been too hasty in judging his actions up until this point.

But what he had stated so far had not in any way eased her mind about what she was going to do once she left. He had only confirmed that there really *was* nothing here for her. Her continued unemployment and lack of prospects threatened to overwhelm her as surely as one of the breakers dashing against Eilean Tor's causeway at high tide.

She'd rather die than go back to Hugh.

She swallowed past a sudden lump in her throat and dropped her tear-misted gaze to her lap. She clasped her hands so tightly, her bones and knuckles stood out stark white beneath her pale skin. Her wedding band cut into her finger, reminding her of the painful reality of both Hugh's failure and her own in their travesty of a marriage. She knew Lord Rothsburgh still watched her. She could feel the weight of his gaze upon her like a physical touch.

She needed to speak, to break the tense silence, but for the moment words escaped her.

"Mrs. Eliott, I have a proposal for you."

Elizabeth looked up sharply, alert, her body stiff with tension. Lord Rothsburgh was leaning forward on the burgundy leather blotter of the desk, his large hands clasped together in an earnest gesture. The firm curves of his biceps were clearly visible beneath his jacket's sleeves. She forced herself to keep her eyes fixed on his.

Be careful, Elizabeth.

"It is entirely up to you whether you accept my offer or not," he continued in an almost matter-of-fact manner that belied the mischievous spark in his eyes. She wished she could keep up with this man's swift changes in mood. "Under no circumstance do I want you to feel obligated to take on this role. While it is entirely true that I no longer require a governess, I find that I have need of your services after all—when you are well, of course—and if you agree."

Although she willed herself not to, Elizabeth blushed hotly. Lord Rothsburgh was teasing her again. She should be shocked at his use of the word "services" and the inappropriate implication behind it. Instead, she was piqued.

She struggled to keep her tone neutral. "What do you mean, my lord? Please speak plainly. Although you just professed you do not play games, it seems you are doing exactly that."

His gaze grew darker, heavier. "Oh, my proposal is entirely serious, Mrs. Eliott. Lady Beauchamp's reference certainly sings your praises. It appears you have all manner of high attainments. And from what I have seen of you so far, you strike me as not only keenly intelligent, but also highly spirited, and well up to taking on any sort of task that you set your mind to."

Elizabeth fairly bristled with anger now. And the damned, irritating tickle was back in her throat. "I must insist that you stop...obfuscating, Lord Rothsburgh. What exactly is it that you want me to do?"

He paused and sighed, running a hand down his face. "On second thought..."

"Lord Rothsburgh!" She broke into a fit of uncontrolled coughing that robbed her voice and stole her breath.

The marquess was suddenly kneeling at her side, his hand alternately rubbing and patting her back. "Beth, I'm sorry. I was teasing you. I shouldn't have. Please forgive me."

When she regained enough breath to speak, she looked up to meet his gaze. His dark eyes were on level with hers, his brow creased with concern.

"You really are...the most frustrating man I have ever met," she gasped.

He smiled back at her. "No doubt."

~

Rothsburgh forced himself to remove his hand from Beth's back. Strange how within such a short space of time, it had become such an ingrained habit—this need to touch her. But now propriety dictated that he shouldn't.

When he'd entered the library and found Beth struggling to get down from the window seat, he hadn't thought twice about reaching for her arm to help her. Indeed, at this moment, he had to ruthlessly quell another impulse to reach forward and push a loose tendril of her soft blond hair away from her pale cheek. He realized that it felt more natural for him to have physical contact with her than not.

Even when he noticed that her breathing had started to settle into a semblance of a more normal rhythm, he still remained by her side. He didn't want to move away. He didn't want her to go either.

God, you are a hopeless case, Rothsburgh.

Despite his earlier resolution—the sooner Beth left Eilean Tor, the better it would be for both of them—the sight of her so desperate and on the verge of tears, had been his undoing. He couldn't turn her away when she apparently had nowhere else to go. The question was—would she accept his proposal when he stated it clearly? It was not something she had any previous experience of, and she may reject the idea outright.

But it was not as if he was going to propose that Beth become his mistress—as much as he was tempted to do so. He instinctively knew she was a moral creature, and even though her state of widowhood gave her the freedom to indulge in sensual pursuits outside of marriage, he doubted she would ever do so. He suspected she found him attractive, but for someone who so obviously valued respectability and honor, the pull of physical desire would probably never be enough to tempt her to embark on an affair, let alone become a paid courtesan.

Her affronted reaction to even his implied suggestion had been telling enough.

She was watching him warily again because he hadn't moved away. He didn't want her to feel uncomfortable, so with a sigh of resignation, he stood and then reclaimed the seat behind his desk. The unbidden image of her reclining half-naked across the burgundy leather blotter with her damnably severe widow's weeds pushed up around her waist as he pounded into her entered his mind. Christ Almighty, he needed to state his proposition before he asked her to be his mistress after all.

"How would you feel about filling the position of Eilean Tor's housekeeper, Mrs. Eliott?"

Beth blinked and then her clear gray eyes opened wider. She was clearly startled. "I...I don't know. I had not even considered applying for such work..." Her forehead dipped into a frown. "Your housekeeper—Mrs. Barrie?—she recently passed away from this ague, didn't she, my lord?"

"Yes, sadly she did," said Rothsburgh heavily. "Her husband is my gamekeeper. He lives on the estate, not far from Torhaven, on the edge of Blackhaven Wood. Mrs. Barrie had been on staff here for many years and...well, I hadn't thought to replace her so quickly. But now..." He paused. "Will you consider it, Mrs. Eliott?"

Beth's brow furrowed more deeply and she dropped her gaze. Rothsburgh wondered what she was thinking. With a jolt of surprise, he realized he was nervous about her response. "I imagine you would probably prefer to be employed as a governess," he continued. *Why wouldn't she look at him?* God, he hoped he wasn't making a mess of this. "But unfortunately, I do not know of anyone who is looking to secure one. I also thought of contacting my sister, Lady Maxwell, to ask for her support in finding another vacant governess's post. But as that may take a little time...well, perhaps you could stay on at Eilean Tor until something more to your liking came up. Would fifty pounds per quarter do for your salary?"

At last Beth raised her eyes. He was dismayed to see they were brimming with tears.

"Thank you, Lord Rothsburgh," she said with grave sincerity. "I will accept your most generous offer...but perhaps it would be better if you agreed to employ me for a trial period only, and for a lesser salary. I believe such a sum is unheard of for a housekeeper. Besides I...I have never worked in such a capacity before and...well, I'm afraid I may not be up to scratch."

"Nonsense. I can't imagine you *not* doing anything well. As for your salary, I'm sure your services are worth immeasurably more than what I initially offered. In fact, I think sixty pounds per quarter sounds more reasonable. And if it makes you feel better, I will agree to a trial. Shall we say three months? Starting from when you have fully recovered. And you must keep in mind that you are more than free to leave at any time within that period if you so choose. What do you say?"

He was pleased to see Beth was fairly flabbergasted. It was an offer too good to refuse. He was counting on it.

"I-I don't know what to say, Lord Rothsburgh."

He smiled at her. "You've already said yes, Mrs. Eliott. Why would you change your mind now?"

Because I'm throwing my lot in with the devil himself.

For the life of her, Elizabeth couldn't understand why Lord Rothsburgh would want to pay her so much. She had been responsible for the smooth running of Harcourt House in London as well as Scarwood Hall, Hugh's country estate in Gloucestershire, and knew exactly how much their staff had been paid. The sum Lord Rothsburgh offered her was outrageous. A housekeeper would be lucky to receive fifty pounds per year.

Unless he expects more from you than housekeeping.

Elizabeth gave herself a mental shake. Why would he? Hugh had never been particularly enamored of her, even at the beginning of their marriage. And later, not all. Why would Lord Rothsburgh be any different? Besides, he had just lost his wife. Elizabeth would be a ninnyhammer indeed to think he would be attracted to someone like her, especially when from the moment she'd arrived at Eilean Tor, he'd only ever seen her when she was bedraggled, bedridden with illness, or coughing up her lungs. Perhaps the wayward thought only occurred to her because he'd been teasing her earlier with his word games. And the fact that he was so strikingly handsome had stirred the long-buried feeling of desire within her.

Don't be a fool, Elizabeth. He would never be interested in someone like you. You couldn't even keep your husband interested.

She raised her chin and looked Lord Rothsburgh in the eye. She needed to accept that beggars couldn't be choosers. Besides, he'd just assured her that she could leave at any time. She really had no choice but to consent to his terms—ridiculous as they were.

"I find that I am overwhelmed by your magnanimous offer, my lord. And, if it so pleases you, I will abide by my agreement to enter into a trial period as Eilean Tor's housekeeper."

Lord Rothsburgh inclined his head and his mouth curved

with a thoroughly satisfied smile. "It pleases me greatly, Mrs. Eliott." He suddenly gave a mock frown. "Now that's settled, are you going to promise to behave and rest in your room until you are better?"

"Hmm, for the most part, yes. I cannot promise that I won't seek out the library again to perhaps borrow a book or two to while away the hours. If that is all right with you..."

"Of course. You must consider yourself my guest. And even after you take up your duties, I trust that you will always feel welcome here."

"Thank you, Lord Rothsburgh...for everything. You are too kind." The interview, such as it was, seemed to be over so Elizabeth rose from her seat and curtsied. The marquess had risen as well. When she looked up he was frowning.

"Such formalities are not necessary." He moved to her side of the desk. "In fact, let me escort you back to your room."

Before she could protest, the marquess reached for her hand and tucked it into the crook of his arm. He kept his hand over hers as if he was anticipating that she would try to escape. His fingers were warm and Elizabeth shivered as a strange, pleasurable heat suffused her entire body. She knew she should pull away, but it would seem ungracious to do so. Instead, she bowed her head and smiled faintly. At least her room wasn't far away. She was finding it wearying indeed to keep up the effort of continually suppressing her errant physical impulses.

"When you are sufficiently recovered, I will arrange a tour of Eilean Tor for you," Lord Rothsburgh said conversationally as they exited the library and proceeded to the stairs. "As you can see, the castle's living quarters are quite extensive. However, many sections are not in use and at some stage will require refurbishment..."

Elizabeth nodded, only half listening to the marquess's description of certain architectural and design features along the way. Her breathing had become effortful again and the urge to cough was back, stronger than ever. Half-way up the staircase, she dissolved into a paroxysm of coughing. If it hadn't been for Lord Rothsburgh holding onto her, she suspected she would have collapsed. The fit eventually eased, although her breathing was labored and her head spun with light-headedness.

"I will...be...all right...in a moment...my lord," she gasped, clinging to the marquess's arm.

"Mmm, I doubt that." Before she could draw another breath, he swept her up into his arms as if she weighed nothing at all. "You needn't bother protesting about what I'm doing," he said as he strode up the stairs. "Last time you told me you were fine, Mrs. Eliott, you promptly fainted a short time later. And I'd rather not risk you passing out on the staircase and breaking your neck."

Elizabeth meekly consented. She reasoned there was little else she could do given her less than able state. However, being pressed up against Lord Rothsburgh's formidable chest wasn't doing much to help calm her breathing or slow down her racing pulse. She was relieved beyond measure when they reached her room.

Once Lord Rothsburgh had installed her upon the chaise longue before the fireplace, he stepped back and retreated to the door. Even though he sought her gaze, he suddenly seemed distant, more formal somehow. She should be grateful for the respite from his overwhelming presence, but for some reason —and she didn't want to examine why—she felt vaguely crest-fallen that he wasn't going to linger a while longer.

"I'll have Roberts stop by to find out your reading prefer-ences. And remember to ring if you require anything else. I think it would be safer if you avoided the stairs for the time being." Lord Rothsburgh paused, looking uncharacteristically uncertain for a moment as if he was about to say something else, but had then changed his mind. Instead, he simply inclined his head politely. "I'll bid you a good evening then, Mrs. Eliott."

The door shut before she could bid him her own adieu.

It's better that he's gone, Elizabeth told herself as she stared at the oak paneling of the closed door. *Remember you're his housekeeper, nothing more.*

That is how it must be. Anything else was unconscionable.

CHAPTER 7

Six hours later, Rothsburgh found himself hovering outside Beth's closed bedroom door, Rosencrantz and Guildenstern at his heels. He wasn't sure what demon inside him had led him to her room. Earlier, when he'd determinedly left her here, he'd been adamant that he wouldn't return.

Yet here he was again.

It probably hadn't helped that he'd imbibed the best part of a bottle of claret and several drams of whisky. He grimaced and leaned his forehead against the smooth oak panel of the door. Beth had literally stumbled into his life only four nights ago, and now it seemed he couldn't pass a single evening without her. There was no denying it: he was a pathetic sap in more ways than one.

But whatever the reason that had brought him here, it hardly mattered now, especially when he could hear Beth coughing uncontrollably in the room beyond. Rosencrantz nudged his hand and whined. He looked down at the hound. "You're right, Rosencrantz. We can't walk away while she's in that state."

Rothsburgh knocked and waited until he thought he heard a faint invitation to enter. Opening the door, his gaze immediately found Beth. She was seated on the chaise longue, holding a shawl to her mouth. She was obviously trying to stifle her coughs.

Despite his concern, he waited in the doorway. He wanted to go to her aid, to rub her back as he'd done in the library this afternoon, but he sensed she would be disconcerted by his touch and suspicious of his motives—as she probably should be. So, he simply stood there until the fit eased before he spoke.

"Forgive me for visiting at such a late hour, Mrs. Eliott. It's just that...Rosencrantz missed your company," he said with a sheepish smile. He knew the excuse was weak, but he had little else to offer. "I'm surprised you didn't hear him whining at your door. He really is a tragic case."

Beth gave him a shaky smile in return. "Well...we can't have poor Rosencrantz pining away now, can we?" She stretched out her hand toward the hound and he immediately went to her side. Guildenstern followed and flopped down on the rug at her feet.

"I'm afraid both dogs spent a fair bit of time in your room while you were unwell. I hope you don't mind," Rothsburgh said, letting himself indulge in the simple pleasure of looking at Beth. He was pleased to see her beautiful blond hair was unbound, falling in a luxurious wave over one of her shoulders. Aside from a gray cashmere shawl, she wore only a pale blue silk robe over one of her simple, white cotton night rails. He tried to ignore the pang of disappointment within his chest when he saw her lovely ankles and feet were concealed by a thick woolen blanket.

"No, I don't mind. In fact, I'm rather fond of dogs." She stroked one of Rosencrantz's ears with her pale, elegant fingers. The hound had an almost beatific expression on his face.

Lucky Rosencrantz.

Rothsburgh pulled his gaze away from the rhythmic movement of her fingers lest his body betray how aroused he was becoming. He knew he shouldn't feel this way, given how exceedingly unwell the poor woman was, but it seemed he had no control over his body's reaction to her presence. So he remained where he was, hesitant to fully come into the room.

He noticed that she hadn't invited him to sit by her either.

As an awkward silence descended, he glanced about and noticed her supper tray on a nearby side table. Mrs. Roberts had sent up a smaller version of what he'd dined on earlier—a rich beef and red wine casserole with neeps and tatties—but it appeared Beth had barely touched the fare. She also hadn't drunk the dram of whisky he'd sent up with the meal to ease her coughing.

"It seems you haven't taken your medicine, Mrs. Eliott." He nodded toward the crystal glass of amber-hued liquid.

She looked up and grimaced. "I'm not much of a drinker when it comes to strong liquor, my lord."

"Nevertheless, I can highly recommend the *uisge beatha*—the water of life—for easing coughs. Even Mrs. Roberts swears by it."

"Hmm. I don't know whether I should believe you, Lord Rothsburgh." There was a sudden silvery glint of humor in the usually serious depths of Beth's eyes. "I think most ladies of good character would suspect that you were just trying to get them inebriated."

Taking her amusement as an encouraging sign—Rothsburgh felt like a gawking, inexperienced youth as he continued to linger in the doorway—he finally entered the room and sat in the chair opposite her.

"I wouldn't dare to do such an immoral thing," he said

with mock indignation. "What sort of gentleman do you take me for?"

She started to laugh. However, the sweet musical sound quickly dissolved into another bout of coughing. At the end of it, she was so breathless, she'd turned an alarming shade of blue around the mouth.

The severity of her condition concerned Rothsburgh greatly. He would have to send for Blackhaven's physician, Dr. Addison, to attend her again.

"On second thought, Mrs. Eliott, it would be remiss of me not to make you drink the whole dram." Taking the glass off the tray, he passed it to her. "Trust me. I promise it will help," he said gently. "Just take it slowly."

With a look of tired resignation, she nodded then took a few small sips, grimacing as she did so. Thankfully, her breathing started to grow less effortful and uneven with each passing moment.

She smiled weakly. "Thank you. You are quite correct. Who would have thought such a thing would work?"

"Och, we Scots are a verra canny lot," he said with a soft burr as he shot her a deliberately roguish grin. She immediately blushed. Good. She needed color in her cheeks.

But then she dropped her gaze. "My lord...I feel more than a little weary. Would you mind if I bid you goodnight?"

Damn. Disappointment welled within. He'd gone too far and had scared her off. But she was right. It was late and he really had no good reason to be here...other than to assuage his own less than honorable needs.

"Not at all, Mrs. Eliott." He rose and bowed. "Good night again. I trust that the whisky will help you to sleep." He clicked and Rosencrantz and Guildenstern followed him to the door.

"Good night then, my lord."

Resisting the urge to rake his gaze over her one last time,

Rothsburgh firmly closed the door and marched back to his room. He knew he shouldn't, but once in his own chamber, he downed another dram of whisky in an attempt to ease his aching need. Not only the ache of desire, but also an intense yearning for Beth's company.

Why did it only just occur to him how ill advised his offer of work had been? How the hell was he going to keep his distance from Beth, now that she had agreed to stay on as his housekeeper?

But perhaps she wouldn't stay for long. Hopefully, Helena would know of another governess's post, and Beth would leave before he gave into the urge to seduce her, or worse, fall in love with her. He was on treacherous ground indeed, and if he wasn't careful, he'd be lost just as surely as if he'd been caught by the tide on his own causeway.

He couldn't risk falling for anyone again, not after Isabelle.

There was only one thing for it: he needed to leave for Edinburgh at first light tomorrow, before the unthinkable happened.

"Lord Rothsburgh left fer Edinburgh first thing this mornin', Mrs. Eliott."

Mrs. Roberts had just delivered a breakfast tray to her room when Elizabeth had asked the servant where she might find the marquess. She wanted to discuss her duties as house-keeper in more detail with him at some stage during the day. Now she felt oddly deflated at the news. She wondered why he hadn't thought to mention his imminent departure last night when he'd paid her an unexpected visit. A visit that had been welcome and unsettling at the same time. She was more than a little bit reluctant to examine the strange feeling of emptiness that had filled her after he'd departed her room.

"Oh... I see." Elizabeth attempted to maintain a bland expression. "And did he say when he would return?"

"I'm no' sure. Per'aps a week, maybe two. It's hard to say wha' his lordship will do."

Elizabeth nodded. She should be pleased he'd gone to Edinburgh. He would undoubtedly be visiting his daughter. And perhaps he would speak to his sister about helping her to find a governess's position elsewhere. That could only be for the best.

She glanced at Mrs. Roberts who was busy uncovering the items on the breakfast tray. There was a pot of tea and another bowl of gray-looking porridge. Elizabeth knew she should eat. When she'd looked in the mirror this morning she'd been shocked to see how much weight she'd lost over the past few days, but she really had no appetite.

"Is the food no' to yer liking, Mrs. Eliott?" Mrs. Roberts asked. Elizabeth's lack of enthusiasm for the repast must have shown in her expression.

"It's absolutely fine. I just haven't been very hungry of late," she replied with a warm smile. She didn't want to offend the cook.

"Och. I ken wha' you mean. I didna want much of anythin' either when I was coughin' away." Mrs. Roberts's eyes narrowed, and she gave Elizabeth an appraising look. "But I have more meat on my old bones than you. Ye really do need to eat. An' the master said I must make sure ye have wha'ever takes yer fancy, so you dinna fade away to a shadow. I am happy to bring ye some baps, or a wee bit of toast if ye prefer. Or maybe some eggs an' kippers?"

Elizabeth smiled. "The porridge will be more than adequate, Mrs. Roberts. I don't want to be a bother." She started to eat the thick and slightly salty gruel. She didn't want to appear ungracious, especially now that she would be working alongside the cook and her husband. She wondered if

Lord Rothsburgh had informed the staff about her new appointment. She imagined it would take some time for everyone to adjust to her presence, especially since Mrs. Barrie had probably been housekeeper here for a long time, and her passing was so recent. Perhaps now would be a good time to test the waters in that regard.

She put down her spoon and caught the cook's gaze. "Actually, Mrs. Roberts, I was thinking that I would much prefer to take meals with you and the other staff...now that I am to be Eilean Tor's housekeeper."

Mrs. Roberts's sparse gray eyebrows dipped into a slight frown. "I am verra happy tha' you will be able to stay on as housekeeper, Mrs. Eliott. His lordship did tell us all about tha' afore he left. An' I would be pleased to have you dine wi' Mr. Roberts an' the rest of us at our kitchen table. But I'm afraid Lord Rothsburgh has ordered tha' ye are to have meals in yer room until yer cough has completely cleared up, which could be some days. You dinna want to hurry these things."

Elizabeth sighed. There was probably no point in trying to fight the marquess's well-intentioned decree, even in his absence. She would just have to accept Mr. and Mrs. Roberts' ministrations with good grace. She really didn't want to get them into trouble with their master for disobeying his orders.

Nevertheless, she really didn't think she could sit about languishing in this bedchamber—as luxurious as it was—for too long with nothing more to do than read novels or stare out the window at the sea.

In her former life as the Countess of Beauchamp, she was used to being busy and productive. What with organizing the smooth running of the households at Harcourt House and Scarwood Hall to meet Hugh's exacting expectations, attending meetings and fund-raising engagements associated with her charity work, keeping up with correspondence and paying the expected round of *tonnish* social calls, she rarely had a free moment. She knew that the sooner she started to take hold of the housekeeper's reins at Eilean Tor, the more satisfied she would be.

And it would keep her mind from dwelling on one darkly handsome and all too enigmatic marquess.

An idea occurred to Elizabeth as she looked over the breakfast tray and noticed there were two teacups. She wondered if the additional cup had been placed there by design or accident by the cook. Either way it hardly mattered.

"Mrs. Roberts, would you have time to join me in a cup of tea?" she asked. "As we will undoubtedly be working together, I would very much like to find out more about the running of Eilean Tor, and in what ways I can best contribute. I'm sure you would know better than anyone, all that is entailed."

The cook's habitually stern expression eased a little, and Elizabeth thought the woman almost smiled. "I willna say no to tha' at all, Mrs. Eliott. I just hope Mr. Roberts does no' catch us. He will be more than a wee bit jealous." She poured herself a cup then sat down in the armchair across from Elizabeth. "Now m'dear, what is it tha' you would like to ken?"

Rothsburgh stood by the set of French doors in the drawing room that overlooked the walled garden of his brother-in-law's Edinburgh townhouse, watching his daughter laughing with glee as her five-year old cousin, Charlie Latimer, Lord Adair, chased her around the parterres of flowers and neatly trimmed shrubs. The bright banner of her hair caught the late afternoon sunlight. Burnished to guinea gold, it was a painful reminder that Annabelle was not really his. Just like her mother had never been his.

"Even though she misses you, she has settled in quite well, James."

Rothsburgh turned and smiled fondly at his sister, Helena, Lady Maxwell. She stood beside him, studying him closely. He knew he must look thoroughly disreputable in his travel-stained clothes with his overly long hair curling over his collar, but he was in between valets and he hadn't wanted to waste time visiting his favorite barber in the High Street in the Old Town before he arrived.

"I'm pleased to hear it," he replied, then frowned. "Does she ask about her mother?"

Helena's brown eyes darkened with sadness. "Hardly at all. But from what you've already told me, that's not surprising given Annabelle never saw that much of Isabelle anyway. Her nursemaid—Miss MacFarlane—is excellent as, you would already know. And Annabelle seems to have taken to our governess, Miss Palmer, quite nicely." Her wide mouth curved into a smile as she watched her niece jump out from behind a hedge, making Charlie squeal. "Aside from having boundless energy, your daughter seems to have quite a curious mind. I think she will do well at her lessons."

"Good." He caught his sister's gaze. "I can't thank you enough, Helena, for taking her in," he said with grave sincerity. "Lord knows, I certainly haven't been in a fit state to take care of her adequately. It's such a relief to know the poor child has a proper family life now."

Helena grasped his arm and a fierce light sparked in her eyes. "James Huntly, I know you love Annabelle as if she were your own. So don't you dare blame yourself for Isabelle's neglect of her, or any of the other appalling choices that dreadful woman made. She was selfish through and through."

"I know." He sighed and ran a hand down his face. "I just wish that I had been there for Annabelle when Isabelle...when it all happened. It can't have been easy for my staff, what with their mistress dead and I... Well, I've been little more than an absentee father and landlord for the best part of this year."

"James, you were still in London, dealing with the aftermath of Waterloo when Isabelle died. I'm sure all your staff understands. It's not your fault, any of it. You must try to stop feeling guilty."

Rothsburgh gave his sister a wry smile. "You give me too much credit for being a good man, Helena. If you knew of the things I'd done..." He shook his head, thinking of all the times he had sought satisfaction outside of his marriage with mistresses. And worse. A vivid memory of the butchery he'd committed against Napoleon's troops at the battles of Quatre-Bras and Waterloo as he'd fought with the 92nd regiment of the Gordon Highlanders, flashed through his mind. He closed his eyes and pinched the bridge of his nose, trying to master the feelings of disgust and horror that always accompanied the recollection. "Believe me, you'd think differently, dear sister."

He felt Helena's hand on his arm again. "You *are* a good man, James. I know you. But I have a feeling we aren't talking about your marriage anymore. Tell me, are you still having nightmares about your time on the battlefield?"

"Not as often." Especially when he drank enough to plunge himself into a dreamless stupor. He dredged up a smile for Helena. He didn't want to alarm her with how troubled he really was. "But you'll be pleased to know that I've recently resigned my commission. And writing my memoirs, like you suggested, is helping."

As well as dreaming about making love to an angelically beautiful blond widow. Not that he could tell his sister that.

"Good." Helena smiled and patted his arm. "And I'm sure the whisky helps too." Her expression changed, becoming serious. "But remember, James, whatever you've done, you are a saint compared to Isabelle. I know you loved her at the beginning, whereas she..." Her lips pursed. "I don't like to speak ill of the dead, but I doubt she was ever capable of feeling such a fine emotion...even for Annabelle."

They watched the children play for a few minutes before Helena broke their companionable silence. Fixing her all too perceptive gaze on him again, she said, "Now tell me, James. Aside from reassuring yourself that Annabelle is all right, why have you really come to Edinburgh?"

CHAPTER 8

"Where would ye like the rosemary bush moved to, Mrs. Eliott?"

Elizabeth turned to Roberts and shielded her eyes against the bright glints of morning sunlight dancing on the deep blue surface of the sea behind him. There was barely a cloud in the sky, and for once, the wind had only a slight chill rather than a freezing edge to it. It was a rare, fine autumn day. A wonderful opportunity for gardening.

"Against the south wall, don't you think?" she suggested. "That way we can plant the bare-rooted roses against the north wall when we acquire some."

Roberts's deeply lined face creased into a smile. "Verra good, ma'am. I'll instruct Todd to start digging."

Elizabeth stood in Eilean Tor's much-neglected walled garden with the butler and one of the footmen. Rosencrantz leaned against her leg while somewhere beyond the wall, Guildenstern nosed about for rabbits to chase. The garden, which she had first noticed from her bedroom window over a week ago, lay on one of the few relatively sheltered and gentle slopes on the headland, just to the south of the castle's main wall. During her daily meetings with Mr. and Mrs. Roberts, she had discovered that it had been more than five years since there had been a gardener employed at the castle. And it showed.

On her initial inspection, Elizabeth had discovered the garden's dry-stone walls and slate paving were still relatively intact, but the garden beds had been hopelessly overrun with machair grass, weeds and thistles. Indeed, it had taken Mr. Todd, one of the young footmen, the better part of two days to clear the overgrowth.

Elizabeth hoped the marquess wouldn't mind that she had embarked on this project without his express permission. It had been ten days since he'd left Eilean Tor, and now that she was almost completely recovered from the ague—apart from the occasional cough at night—she had decided that she needed a task to keep herself busy until he returned.

Reviving the walled garden seemed like a worthwhile activity in the absence of any other direction from her employer. It helped that Mr. and Mrs. Roberts had oftentimes reassured her that the marquess would be very pleased to have a functioning castle garden once more.

Elizabeth had mapped out a tentative plan for the garden beds with Mrs. Roberts on the basis of what was most needed in the kitchen. As luck would have it, the cook had purchased packets of seeds for a good range of vegetables—carrots, turnips, onions, cabbages and potatoes—as well as herbs— mint, sage, parsley, sorrel and thyme—in the previous year, but she had never managed to have any of them planted.

"Her ladyship wasna interested in gardens, even when she was here," the cook had informed Elizabeth when they had first discussed the plan a week ago. "An' Lord Rothsburgh... Weel, he was often away with his Highland Regiment, or attending to business or estate matters. I didna like to bother him with somethin' as trivial as weeding an' such."

A gnarled rosemary bush was about the only useful plant that had managed to live on in the garden. As Todd carefully dug around its roots and jiggled the branches, the breeze carried the pungent scent of its leaves toward Elizabeth. She inhaled deeply, and was suddenly reminded of another strong, spicy scent. The heady scent of a man.

Lord Rothsburgh.

She closed her eyes and willed herself to banish the unbidden image of him lying asleep and aroused in her bed from her mind. Although she had been trying to ruthlessly bury her misplaced regard and wanton attraction for the marquess during his absence, it seemed she was fighting a losing battle. When she least expected it, wild, libidinous and altogether shameful imaginings tormented her. She had never experienced such feelings or thoughts before. She felt unsettled and strangely needy. Like a vixen on heat.

Lord Rothsburgh has offered you this post out of pity, nothing more, she sternly reminded herself. She also needed to remember that she was a married woman.

"Och, I do believe his lordship has come home," announced Roberts, startling Elizabeth out of her tumultuous reverie. "It's a good thing the tide's out. If ye dinna mind, Mrs. Eliott, I will leave ye, to attend to Lord Rothsburgh."

Elizabeth whirled around and looked toward the causeway. Sure enough, a fine black coach pulled by two pairs of fine grays barreled along the road toward Eilean Tor. At the pace they were setting, the marquess would be here within a few minutes. Rosencrantz and Guildenstern were already bounding up the hill toward the castle's courtyard.

"Of course, Roberts," she replied. "Todd and I will get on quite nicely." She was amazed her voice sounded normal even though her heart had kicked into an unsteady gallop.

Don't worry, Elizabeth. Lord Rothsburgh's sure to have

more pressing matters to attend to than inspecting his garden. Or seeing you.

Unless of course he had been able to find another governess's position for her. But it would be useless to speculate further. No doubt she would find out about any such possibilities when the marquess was good and ready to see her. Until then, it was best if she kept herself busy.

She took a deep breath and turned back to watch Todd finish releasing the rosemary bush from its bed of long-spent soil. Tomorrow, after the footman had replanted it, she would prune back its straggling branches. Perhaps Mrs. Roberts could dry the off cuts in the kitchen and use the leaves in her casseroles. And Elizabeth could always infuse a little oil with some of the leaves to run through the ends of her hair when they became dry—

"Mrs. Eliott. It's wonderful to see you up and about." Lord Rothsburgh's rich baritone carried easily to her on the sea breeze.

Elizabeth planted what she hoped was a pleasantly neutral smile on her face and turned around. And her breath caught in her throat.

Her memories of the marquess didn't do the man justice at all. Now, as he strode toward her up the slope, she realized she'd underestimated how tall and powerfully built he was. How devilishly handsome. He made her ache in ways she shouldn't.

And then before she could draw another breath, he was standing before her, while she was struck dumb like a silly debutante on her first foray into society. She dropped a quick curtsy while from somewhere behind her, she heard Todd greet his master.

The marquess acknowledged the footman before he turned his gaze back to her. He was but an arm's length away, dressed in snug-fitting, ivory-colored breeches that clung to the long lean muscles of his thighs, shiny Hussar boots, and a well-cut morning coat of black kerseymere. The wind picked up the black wing of hair that perpetually flopped over his brow. However, she also noticed that he'd had the back and sides cropped into a fashionable cut.

His dark gaze roamed over her face. As Elizabeth was facing into the sun, her black straw bonnet afforded her no protection from his keen scrutiny. To her consternation, she felt herself blushing.

"Roberts was right," he said softly as his mouth tipped into a smile. "You look very well, Mrs. Eliott. You have color in your cheeks."

"Thank you, my lord. I am much recovered, thanks to you and Mr. and Mrs. Roberts." She glanced away, frustrated with her inopportune physical reactions. She didn't want to make a fool of herself. "I trust your visit to Edinburgh was...rewarding."

"Yes...and no." The marquess moved slightly so that he was in her line of vision again. His large frame now shielded her eyes from the sun. "My daughter and my sister, Lady Maxwell, are well, as are the rest of my sister's family." He paused, his eyes seeking hers again before he spoke. "However, I'm afraid my sister isn't aware of any other vacant governess's positions at the moment. Of course, she will keep her ears and eyes open for any hint of an opportunity. But until then..." He gave her a crooked smile and shrugged a broad shoulder. "Well, I suppose you will just have to make do with us all at Eilean Tor."

He turned back toward the garden and placed a booted foot upon the stones of a nearby raised border, watching Todd as the lad turned over the soil in the bed intended for the root vegetables. "Roberts told me you were rejuvenating the garden."

Elizabeth couldn't see the marquess's face anymore, but

his tone of voice sounded equable enough. "Yes...I hope you don't mind, my lord. Mrs. Roberts already had the seeds on hand, so it hasn't made any difference to the household budget. And hopefully there will be a good yield of vegetables and herbs before winter arrives. I'd be happy to go through the plans with you, whenever you'd like. That is, if you're interested..." She almost bit her tongue to make herself stop babbling. She hated being inarticulate and awkward beyond measure. She slid a glance the marquess's way and found he'd turned back toward her. And he was smiling broadly.

He might be laughing at her, but at least he wasn't displeased with what she'd done. "I'd be very interested to see your plans," he said, taking a step closer. "Tell me, is gardening something you enjoy? I feel I know very little about you. Well, aside from what your reference states. I would like to know more."

"Yes...I do...enjoy gardening that is." Elizabeth paused. Was the marquess fishing for details of her life before she came here? But what could she say? She didn't want to make up false stories. But in talking about herself, she might accidentally betray some detail about who she really was.

Oh, she was walking on thin ice indeed.

Lord Rothsburgh was watching her, waiting for her to say something more. She summoned a slight smile that she hoped looked self-deprecating rather than nervous. "As for anything else about me...I suppose there's not much to tell that would be of any interest."

Lord Rothsburgh took another step closer—he was almost certainly too close now. Elizabeth was suddenly all too aware of his decidedly masculine, spicy scent, and she noticed a hint of dark stubble along his jaw line that he must have missed when shaving. She'd learned from Mrs. Roberts that unlike most men in his position, he didn't employ a valet. But then, Elizabeth was beginning to suspect the marquess wasn't like most noblemen in many regards.

His dark eyes fixed on hers. "Hmm. I beg to differ, Mrs. Eliott. I think you are very interesting indeed."

Elizabeth's cheeks flamed with a hot blush, and she dipped her head so that her bonnet shielded her face a little. Was Lord Rothsburgh flirting with her? No, he couldn't be. Hugh's voice suddenly sounded in her head. *You may be pretty, my dear wife, but you really are far too dull for words.*

Why would the rakish Lord Rothsburgh think any differently? He was obviously teasing her again for sport. It was hardly fair. Frustration and embarrassment rose swiftly. Even though it was unladylike to do so, Elizabeth bit her lip to stop herself accusing him of toying with her again. She must remember that housekeepers didn't argue with their employers.

Struggling to find something else to say, she lifted her gaze to Lord Rothsburgh's face once more. But he didn't seem to notice the heated expression in her eyes. His attention was completely focused on her mouth. He swayed toward her, and she sucked in a startled breath.

And then he paused.

Frowned and took a step back.

"Mrs. Eliott. Forgive me..." He ran a hand down his face, and then glanced toward Todd who was still busily tilling the soil. "I must go... An appointment in Blackhaven with my solicitor and steward."

As Lord Rothsburgh strode away from her, Elizabeth realized how truly immoral she was. Five minutes in his company and lust coursed through her veins, throbbed low in her belly. It didn't matter that he had teased her. Or that she might be as dull as Hugh had always proclaimed. Or that she was married.

In the moment Lord Rothsburgh had looked at her as if

he was about to kiss her, she had realized the awful truth about herself.

She had wanted him to.

~

His sister was wrong. He was no saint. He was a sinner to the depths of his dark soul. Why else would he attempt to seduce Beth in broad daylight in front of one of his footmen?

Rothsburgh set a fast pace as he stalked back to the castle, determined to put as much distance between him and Beth as possible. He had only been back a few minutes, and it seemed he couldn't control himself in her presence. Deliberately flirting with her was bad enough—he knew she disliked it when he teased her—but to actually go so far as attempting to kiss her?

She was his housekeeper, for God's sake.

The most beautiful housekeeper in Christendom.

Now that he'd seen her again, he suddenly realized what a waste it was for someone like her to be worrying about gardens, and menus, and linen inventories, or whatever the hell else it was that housekeepers occupied their time with. He should never have made her the foolish offer. He couldn't abide it. She was too beautiful, too refined and clever. Not for the first time he wondered about her life before she came here. Her husband, whoever he had been, had certainly been one lucky bastard.

It was time he faced the truth: he wanted her—more than he'd wanted any other woman before in his life. One look at her beautiful face in the clear light of day, and he had been overcome with a longing so strong it hurt. Ten days away from her had obviously done nothing to quell his physical desire. Nor his yearning for her smile, and the simple pleasure of her company. He hadn't lied when he'd told her that he wanted to learn more about her.

He wanted to know *everything* about her.

He passed Roberts in the Great Hall and ordered for his horse to be saddled before he raced to his room. He needed to get away from Eilean Tor before the tide came back in. Before he did something stupid like returning to the walled garden, dismissing Todd and ravishing Beth on the hillside until he lost himself in her, and she called out his name in ecstasy.

What the hell was he going to do? Christ, he was a mess.

When had this itch he needed to scratch become a full-blown, mad fever?

Once in his room, Rothsburgh resisted the urge to down a whisky or two, and instead began to change into his riding clothes. A good hard ride cross-country should help ease his rampant lust to some extent.

But it would only be a temporary respite. How was he going to deal with his urges tonight, and all the other nights when he sat alone in his library with only his dogs and a bottle of whisky for company? Or when he woke in the night shuddering with frustrated need as he spilled himself upon the sheets like an adolescent boy?

He tugged off his boots, and changed into buckskin breeches, steadfastly buttoning the placket over his half-aroused cock. He couldn't go on like this. He should have secured another mistress whilst he was in Edinburgh. But he just hadn't been able to summon the interest.

Ignoring the urge to examine the reason why that might be the case, he roughly pulled on his boots again, and then changed into a dark brown riding coat. As he loosened and retied his constrictive cravat into a less elaborate knot, he realized that perhaps his problem—his obsession with Beth—was largely due to the fact that he hadn't been with a woman since well before Waterloo. In fact, he'd farewelled his last mistress in

London some eight months ago, and he hadn't had sexual intercourse since.

Yes, that was what his problem was, the main source of his overwhelming frustration. It was that simple. He'd been too long without a woman. He wasn't falling in love with Beth. He was just randy as hell.

Crop in hand, Rothsburgh flung open his bedroom door then charged down the stairs, his dogs at his heels.

There was nothing else for it. He had to have Beth as his mistress.

Perhaps when he'd had his fill of her, the raging need inside him would be appeased. There would be sexual gratification—yes. Affection—most probably. But love? No, he wouldn't fall in love. He'd already learned an invaluable lesson long ago.

Love was for fools.

Once Rothsburgh had mounted his horse and exited the castle courtyard, he couldn't ignore the impulse to glance back at the small, isolated figure in black on the slope to the south of the keep. His mouth twisted into a ruthless smile. He didn't care that Isabelle was barely cold in her grave, just as he didn't care that Beth was still a widow in deep mourning.

Both hell and heaven be damned, he was going to seduce the chaste Mrs. Eliott.

Oh, he was a sinner indeed.

CHAPTER 9

"Lord Rothsburgh wants me to dine with him?" Elizabeth couldn't hide the note of incredulous shock from her voice as she stared at Mrs. Roberts who was putting the final touches to the marquess's first course of cream of oyster soup. It was about an hour until the staffs' dinner service, and she had come down to the kitchen to see if Mrs. Roberts required any additional assistance.

Mrs. Roberts shrugged. Her master's bizarre request didn't seem to bother her in the slightest. "Aye, Mrs. Eliott. He rang fer Mr. Roberts but a short time ago, an' asked tha' we pass on the message to you. His lordship says ye are to meet wi' him at seven sharp in the dining room."

"But...I don't understand. It seems highly unusual." What on earth would the rest of the staff think? Elizabeth doubted Mrs. Barrie had ever dined with the marquess.

They will think that you are his mistress...

She suddenly recalled how Lord Rothsburgh had looked this morning when it seemed he had been about to kiss her. She had tried all day to convince herself that she had been mistaken. Now, she wasn't so sure. His invitation—nay order —to join him for dinner was suspicious to say the least.

Her hands curled into fists. This wouldn't do. No, not all. Given that she now recognized her own hopeless attraction to the marquess, she feared that if he pressed her, she would succumb to temptation. She really shouldn't spend time alone with him.

But how could she refuse her employer?

The cook carefully ladled the soup into a silver tureen. "His lordship has a certain way aboot him, I'll give ye tha', Mrs. Eliott. But there's no naysayin' him. Once he's made his mind up aboot somethin', there's verra little ye can do to change it. It's best if ye just go along wi' whatever he says, if ye ken wha' I mean."

Elizabeth's face grew hot. It sounded as if Mrs. Roberts knew *exactly* what Lord Rothsburgh had in mind. Even more astonishing was the fact she seemed quite fatalistic about it. It suddenly occurred to Elizabeth that it really didn't matter if anything did or didn't happen between her and the marquess. The staff would assume the worst about her—that she *was* his bit on the side. The problem was, this newly awakened wanton creature within her almost wished she was.

Mrs. Roberts placed the lid on the tureen, and then glanced over at Elizabeth. Her eyes held a compassionate light. "Och, Mrs. Eliott. He willna bite, I swear it. He is probably just a wee bit lonely, that's all. We Highland folk are a no' as stuffy as most Sassenachs, so I wouldna fash yerself. If I were you, I'd just enjoy yer dinner. It will be much better than the mutton stew we are goin' to have."

Elizabeth offered a weak smile. Mrs. Roberts was obviously more perceptive than she had realized. And surprisingly nonjudgmental. At least where Lord Rothsburgh was concerned.

"Your cooking is wonderful, Mrs. Roberts," she offered. "I am sure I will enjoy every mouthful."

After excusing herself from the kitchen—it was already a quarter to seven—Elizabeth returned to her room to make a hasty change for dinner. Whatever Lord Rothsburgh's intentions, she couldn't very well wear the same widow's weeds she'd had on when she'd been grubbing about in the walled garden earlier today.

Of course, there was little to choose from in her wardrobe. In the end, she selected the only attire that seemed appropriate to wear to dinner with a marquess—a simple gown of midnight blue silk and a matching chiffon fichu that she could tuck into the bodice's sweeping neckline to provide a modicum of modesty.

Hurriedly smoothing her hair into a neater chignon, Elizabeth eyed her reflection fiercely.

Thou shalt not commit adultery, Lady Beauchamp.

Remember you are the wife of the Earl of Beauchamp—no matter your husband's own transgressions.

Satisfied that she had at last gained a tight control on her desire, if not her nerves, she quit her bedchamber and made her way to the dining room. She had no difficulty locating it as Roberts had given her a brief tour of Eilean Tor's main living quarters several days ago. She already knew it was another spacious apartment with a high-vaulted ceiling and wide windows that afforded magnificent sea views, just like the library.

When she entered, it was to find Lord Rothsburgh leaning against the gray and green-veined marble fireplace near the head of the vast mahogany dining table. He stared so intently into the leaping flames he did not seem to notice her at first.

How alone he seemed. Perhaps Mrs. Roberts was right—he had invited her to dine with him simply because he desired a little company. He was such a vital, charismatic man. Elizabeth wondered why he hadn't stayed in Edinburgh for longer. Surely there would be more in that bustling city that would rouse his interest. But then, he did have a well-known reputation for being reclusive. Perhaps this was just his way.

Steeling herself to remain quietly confident yet amiable, Elizabeth lifted her chin and took a few more steps into the room. On seeing her, Lord Rothsburgh immediately straightened and ran his dark gaze over her in obvious appreciation. "Good evening, Mrs. Eliott," he said as he bowed gracefully and quite unnecessarily. "Thank you for joining me. I must say the sunshine and sea air must agree with you. You are looking quite splendid."

She curtsied. "Thank you, my lord."

Lord Rothsburgh looked more than splendid himself, Elizabeth decided. He was dressed in the height of fashionable eveningwear—a black superfine evening jacket of superb cut was worn over a cream satin vest and ivory silk shirt. His cravat was arranged in such an elaborate style, even Hugh would have been envious.

Resisting the highly inappropriate desire to let her gaze wander lower to his tightly fitting breeches, Elizabeth kept her eyes on the marquess's handsome countenance as she took a few steps closer. "Although, I must admit," she added, "that I am more than a bit surprised by your very generous invitation to dine with you. You are most kind." If she could maintain a formal, business-like manner during dinner, she might yet survive the evening with her dignity and honor intact.

Lord Rothsburgh's mouth lifted into a slight smile. "Thank you. Although *I* must confess that it was not kindness that motivated me to extend the invitation—" He broke off and looked beyond her toward the door. "Ah, Roberts. Prompt as always."

So, what *had* motivated his invitation? Elizabeth supposed

she would find out in due course, but now was obviously not the time to pursue that particular topic.

Lord Rothsburgh held out a mahogany Hepplewhite chair for her before he took his own seat to her left, at the head of the table. The silence extended as Roberts and the young Mr. Todd proceeded to serve the soup course and what looked to be an excellent French Chablis. Despite the appealing smell of the soup, Elizabeth really didn't think she could eat at all.

Out of the corner of her eye, she was conscious of the marquess's quiet study of her, and she tried not to blush. She instead tried to concentrate on the exquisitely detailed tapestry that hung on the wall between the windows curtained in sage green velvet, directly opposite her. It depicted a very scantily clad Salome dancing with licentious abandon before Herod as his court looked on. To her annoyance, Lord Rothsburgh was smiling quite broadly now.

Despite Elizabeth's resolve not to blush, she found herself doing just that. "The tapestry. Is it Flemish?" she asked trying to deflect his attention away from her.

"You have a good eye, Mrs. Eliott. Yes, it is."

"It's...quite arresting." She really couldn't think of anything else to say.

Lord Rothsburgh's gaze remained on her. "Yes. I quite agree."

Oh my. Elizabeth's pulse began to skitter about, and her cheeks flamed even more. She was certain he wasn't referring to the tapestry. Her poise slipped even further when she noticed that both Roberts and Todd had quit the room—a most unusual situation, undoubtedly engineered by their master.

She suddenly felt like she was alone with a dangerously hungry lion in his den. Mrs. Roberts had assured her the marquess wouldn't bite. But by the way he was looking at her right now, she really wasn't convinced that he wouldn't.

Lord Rothsburgh raised his glass in a toast, and she reluctantly did the same. His dark eyes sought hers. "To new beginnings, Mrs. Eliott."

"Yes. To new beginnings, my lord." She was amazed her voice hadn't trembled. She dropped her gaze and took a tiny sip of the Chablis. She mustn't have too much. She needed to keep her wits about her.

"I hear you selected the dishes for this evening," Lord Rothsburgh remarked, picking up his silver soup spoon. "You really have the most excellent taste."

"Thank you." Elizabeth followed his lead and picked up her own spoon but hesitated before dipping it in her bowl. "I would have checked with you personally if dining *à la russe* was to your liking. And if the menu met with your approval. However, Roberts informed me that you were spending most of the afternoon in Blackhaven... I must admit that I am still finding my way in this new role. Perhaps, when it is convenient, I could discuss my duties with you in further detail. I really don't wish to disappoint."

Lord Rothsburgh frowned. "I seriously doubt that you would. But if it makes you feel any better, we shall indeed discuss my expectations of you tomorrow. And I shall also give you the grand tour that I promised." He then gestured impatiently toward her bowl. "Now I suggest you eat before your soup gets cold. It really is quite delicious."

Elizabeth nodded and proceeded to taste the creamy, rich, and slightly salty soup. The marquess was right. It was indeed delicious. She suddenly found she had quite an appetite, and despite her previous nervousness, she was able to finish the entire bowl.

She began to relax a little when she realized that the marquess really didn't seem to be about to launch himself across the table at her, but rather, was a most entertaining and convivial host. She found he was quite happy to talk about perfectly innocuous, but nevertheless interesting topics such as his recent trip to Edinburgh, as well as the fascinating history of his family and Clan Huntly, a sept of the much larger Gordon Clan.

Elizabeth was also quietly relieved that Lord Rothsburgh didn't pursue the topic of her own situation and background, given this morning he had seemed intent on discovering more about her. She had actually rehearsed what she would say in case he began to probe further, but for the moment, he seemed quite content to regale her with his own stories and amusing anecdotes.

The fish course—a delicate smoked trout mousse—followed by the main course of roast pheasant accompanied by a juniper and port wine sauce and roast root vegetables, were delivered at appropriate intervals, and served discreetly by Roberts and Todd. Lord Rothsburgh again proclaimed how inspired the menu was, and insisted she try a full-bodied claret with the pheasant.

"What do you think?" he asked, eyeing her intently over the rim of his glass.

She took a sip and closed her eyes, savoring the rich berry flavors, and dry yet silky smooth finish. Although she didn't drink wine or any other type of alcohol on a regular basis, she occasionally permitted herself a glass of fine red wine. And this was indeed fine. She opened her eyes and smiled at the marquess. "Very smooth with a hint of oak at the end, my lord. I think you have chosen well."

"Hmm. You seem to have quite a palate." Lord Rothsburgh's eyes had a speculative look in them, and with dawning horror, Elizabeth realized that she had been duped into revealing too much about herself. He was suspicious of her background.

How utterly, utterly stupid of me to have said such a thing.

How would a lowly governess or housekeeper know anything at all about the qualities of wine?

She took another quick sip, seeking to arm herself with a plausible explanation for her singular knowledge, all the while conscious that Lord Rothsburgh watched her closely. "My husband, George, was an officer...a lieutenant in fact, with the 28th Foot Regiment from Gloucestershire." She had decided to mention Hugh's regiment as it was the one she was most familiar with. She drew in a shaky breath and continued with the lie. "He...he quite enjoyed a good red wine on occasion. Claret was his particular favorite."

She hoped the marquess would interpret her apparent discomposure as a reluctance to talk about her supposedly deceased husband, rather than the fact she was in over her head in this dangerous game of subterfuge she was playing.

Lord Rothsburgh stroked the stem of his wine glass, drawing Elizabeth's attention to his long, well-shaped fingers. "Ah, I see. I suspected as much." He then threw her an almost apologetic smile. "I know it must pain you to talk of such things, but...well, to be perfectly honest, I find you quite an enigma. As I said this morning, you are indeed fascinating."

He smiled again and she saw the lion stir. He had been lying in wait the whole time, waiting for his chance to draw her out, to trick her into revealing things about herself that she didn't want to. He was far too clever.

He picked up his fork and knife. "Come, let us eat this fine fare before it too grows cold." Cutting off a sizeable piece of breast, he then forked it into his mouth with relish. Unlike herself, he clearly still had an appetite.

Elizabeth forced herself to take a bite of pheasant then swallow it down. However, her mind buzzed with so many anxious thoughts, she couldn't stomach any more. She suspected that Lord Rothsburgh had been a much higher-ranking officer with one of the Highland regiments, Perhaps the 92nd Gordon Highlanders. He couldn't possibly have known all of the subaltern officers who'd served in Wellington's army. So he wouldn't know that Lieutenant Eliott didn't really exist.

Slightly reassured that her fictitious self would continue to stand up to any further scrutiny, Elizabeth relaxed enough to continue eating.

Until Lord Rothsburgh spoke again. "The Gloucestershire Regiment. I do believe your benefactress's husband, Lord Beauchamp served with them."

Elizabeth almost choked on her second mouthful of pheasant. She hastily took an unladylike swig of her claret to clear her throat. How did the marquess know so much about Hugh when she had never even heard of Lord Rothsburgh until a month ago? Again, she scanned her mind for any memories of having encountered the marquess before she had come here, but she could find none.

She decided to risk making her own observation. "Really? I did not realize that." She kept her gaze fixed on her plate as with apparent nonchalance, she neatly sliced through a portion of roasted parsnip. "You do not appear to think much of Lord and Lady Beauchamp, my lord. I am still quite amazed that you wanted to employ me, given that my reference obviously meant very little to you."

Her barb struck home. Lord Rothsburgh grimaced and he shifted in his seat as though he was decidedly uncomfortable.

It served him right.

"Perhaps I was too hasty passing judgment on Lady Beauchamp," he said, his tone rueful. "It is true I do not think well of her husband, but as for her... I must confess, I have never met the poor woman."

He suddenly put down his knife and placed his large warm hand over hers. Startled, Elizabeth dropped her fork. Despite her earlier resolve not to react to Lord Rothsburgh in any way, her skin seemed to burn beneath his touch, and her heart began to race.

"Mrs. Eliott—Beth—I was wrong to say such things about your reference." There was an earnest, almost urgent edge to the marquess's voice. "I do truly believe you possess all of the skills and attributes so carefully detailed by Lady Beauchamp. And more. Please forgive me."

Elizabeth slid him a glance. Then found her gaze captured by his. The expression in the marquess's dark eyes was intense. She believed him to be sincere.

Unable to summon her voice, she inclined her head to acknowledge her acceptance of his apology. She was not used to such focused interest from a man. And he'd called her Beth again. Perhaps that explained why her pulse fluttered wildly. Surely he must feel it.

But Lord Rothsburgh seemed satisfied with her simple response. His wide mouth curved into a smile. "Good." He released her hand then relaxed back in his chair, his gaze lingering on her face. "So, Lady Beauchamp stated that you are quite an accomplished pianist. I should very much like to hear you play after dinner... If you would be so gracious."

"Yes, of course." Elizabeth placed her cutlery neatly upon her plate and glanced about the room. There was no pianoforte here. Indeed, during her brief exploration of Eilean Tor, she had not come across a pianoforte at all.

Lord Rothsburgh smiled and cocked an eyebrow. "There is a piano in the drawing room adjacent to here." He inclined his head toward a set of oak-paneled double doors on the far side of the room. "Would you like to see it?"

Elizabeth smiled with genuine pleasure. "Yes, I would indeed, my lord."

The marquess suddenly stood and seized the silver candelabra off the table in front of them. "Come then, Mrs. Eliott."

He offered her his arm. "Let me escort you. Your instrument awaits."

Bemused and at the same time disconcerted by the marquess's impulsive invitation, Elizabeth rose from her seat, and placed her hand on his muscular forearm. She loved to play the pianoforte—and was, in fact, quite good at it. Nevertheless, she suddenly felt an unaccountable surge of nerves as Lord Rothsburgh led her toward the drawing room.

After placing the candelabra on a nearby table, he unlatched the door and pushed it open to reveal a darkened chamber. Then he tucked Elizabeth's hand more firmly into the crook of his arm. It was almost as if he was still making sure that she wouldn't try to escape.

"You'll have to excuse the state of the room I'm afraid," he said softly as he retrieved the candles. "It hasn't been used in a while. I prefer my library."

Stepping across the threshold, Elizabeth could immediately see what the marquess meant. Every piece of furniture was shrouded in dustsheets like so many misshapen ghosts. The weak flickering light of the candles imbued the chamber with an eerie, other-worldly glow. She shivered.

Lord Rothsburgh must have felt the tremor of her hand. "I'm sorry there's no fire and it's so cold in here. Do you think you will be able to play by the light of the candles alone?"

She nodded. "Yes. The lighting, or lack thereof, won't be a problem." She knew she could play her favorite pieces with her eyes closed.

"Excellent." The marquess steered her toward one of the larger covered shapes, and after passing the candelabra to her, he pulled off the cloth with a flourish.

Elizabeth gasped. A beautiful mahogany pianoforte was revealed. It was not just an upright version like her own instrument at Harcourt House, but a sizeable grand style piano with an inlaid parquetry design of leaves, fruit, and flowers in paler shades of wood all over the lid. It was exquisite. "What a divine instrument," she breathed. She ran one of her hands across the smooth, gleaming wood before she tested one of the ivory keys. A note rang out, pure and clear. "Do you play, my lord?"

Lord Rothsburgh grinned back at her. "Only very badly." He pulled out the velvet-covered stool for her to sit upon. "It was tuned less than a year ago. Annabelle was learning to play. But I'm afraid she really didn't have the patience for it."

The marquess then took the candelabra and placed it on top of the pianoforte. His eyes were alight with expectation as he leaned against the instrument's side. "Play away, Mrs. Eliott. I'm dying to hear a good tune."

Aware that Lord Rothsburgh's attention was focused on her, Elizabeth sat as gracefully as she could. She prayed that she wouldn't disappoint. She closed her eyes and took a moment to decide what to play. A nocturne. That would do.

She reached forward and carefully placed her fingers on the keyboard, feeling for the notes she needed. And then she began to play. The cold dark room was suddenly filled with the hauntingly beautiful music that she loved so well. The melody rippled over her and through her like a gentle wave, transporting her away to another sphere of existence, to a place where she was at peace. As the last notes faded away, she sighed then opened her eyes to find Lord Rothsburgh staring at her in open-mouthed awe.

"Beth...I mean, Mrs. Eliott...that was utterly beautiful. You have a remarkable gift."

The marquess seized one of her hands and raised it to his firm, sculpted lips. The light kiss he glanced across her knuckles was the courtly kiss of a gentleman. Yet why did a shaft of heat shoot from Elizabeth's fingertips straight to her lower belly?

She knew exactly why.

She just didn't want to acknowledge the real reason.

Elizabeth's discomposure wasn't eased at all when a moment later, Lord Rothsburgh then raised his dark head to seek her gaze. "Thank you. I am honored that you played for me." His deep voice was like a soft caress in the darkness.

Elizabeth blushed deeply, hoping that it wouldn't show in the uncertain light. She was used to compliments about her playing. But not like this. The marquess's admiration—or was it some other emotion?—gleamed in the deep brown, almost black depths of his eyes.

Why didn't he let go of her hand? She couldn't bear it. He *was* as tempting as the Prince of Darkness himself.

"Thank you," she murmured. Her voice was husky, and so unlike her own, she almost didn't recognize it. "It was my pleasure."

Lord Rothsburgh's mouth curved into a slow smile. "No, the pleasure was all mine, Mrs. Eliott."

Oh no, oh no, oh no.

No, Elizabeth. You must not think of pleasure. Of any kind. Ever.

∼

The pleasure was all mine, Mrs. Eliott.

Damn. He had pressed her too far.

As soon as Rothsburgh had uttered the words, he'd seen panic flare in the soft gray of Beth's beautiful eyes. And as much as he wanted to drag her up into his arms and kiss her senseless right at this moment, he knew it was too soon. He needed to tread slowly, carefully, lest he frighten her off completely.

The sudden clatter of china and silverware being moved about in the next room broke the tense intimacy between them. Roberts and Todd were back, clearing the remnants of their main course away before serving dessert no doubt. He was not in the least bit hungry for food, however. He hungered only for Beth.

Beth had heard the servants as well. She glanced nervously toward the dining room door and with reluctance, Rothsburgh let go of her hand. He knew he had already pushed well past the boundaries of what was considered acceptable behavior between a master and his housekeeper, but he was counting on the fact his staff would be discreet.

They always had been, even when Isabelle had been at her worst.

But Beth wouldn't know that.

He picked up the candelabra and gestured toward the open door, smiling with what he hoped was mere politeness. "I believe dessert is served. I wonder what gastronomic delight you have in store for me this time."

Aside from Beth's positively brilliant skills as a pianist, her impeccable knowledge of food and wine was yet something else about her that astounded Rothsburgh. He'd managed to draw out of her that her husband had been a lieutenant, so he supposed she had attended her fair share of military formal dinners. That might explain why she knew how to plan a perfectly balanced *service à la russe*.

Still, her refined air, aristocratic bearing and accomplishments were the equivalent of any duchess in the realm. There was nothing middle-class about this young woman whatsoever, as far as Rothsburgh could see. Mrs. Eliott was a conundrum indeed.

The apple and blackberry pudding served with *crème anglaise* was delightful and the perfect end to the dinner. Rothsburgh was a man of simple tastes and Mrs. Roberts was an excellent cook. However, he rarely sat down to a full four-course meal in the dining room. A tray in the library was his usual habit.

But he'd wanted to begin his pursuit of Beth in this more

formal atmosphere. He sensed that the social mores associated with fine dining would provide an element of decorum that would help put her at ease.

He glanced at her as she discreetly licked a small crumb from her sinfully full bottom lip. Her tongue was stained ever so slightly from the blackberries and Rothsburgh fought to suppress a groan of frustration. He couldn't go on like this much longer. The woman was driving him mad with wanting.

Tomorrow he would take her on a tour around the castle. And he would insist she dine with him again. And play the piano. Perhaps he could even engage her in a game of chess. He was sure she was excellent at that too.

Slowly and surely, he would break down her resistance, until she was irrevocably his.

For his own sanity, Rothsburgh prayed it wouldn't take too long.

CHAPTER 10

E lizabeth awoke the next day feeling both tense and exhausted. She'd had the worst sleep imaginable. When she'd actually been able to get to sleep.

After she had retired to her bedchamber last night—Lord Rothsburgh had insisted that she retain the same one even though she'd offered to decamp to the servants' quarters— she'd tossed and turned well into the early hours of the morning. But it was not because she'd experienced her usual nightmare about Hugh. Instead, she'd been troubled all night by visions of a different man.

Lord Rothsburgh.

She hadn't been able to stop thinking about him. How he'd looked in her bed with an erection. How he'd almost kissed her by the walled garden. How his enigmatic eyes darkened with—dare she say the word even in her mind?—*desire* whenever he looked at her. His slow, heart-stopping smile. And the touch of his lips upon her hand.

She ached. Who would have thought that the boring, passionless Lady Beauchamp could ache with wanting? That wicked desire would be constantly simmering through her veins? It was wrong. It was depraved. But she couldn't help it.

Indeed, when Elizabeth had climbed into her bed last night, she had wanted to touch the hidden, most secret parts of herself to ease the needy pressure. But she hadn't been able to bring herself to do it. Surely such an act—to pleasure oneself whilst fantasizing about a man who wasn't one's husband—was adulterous.

Now, as she stared at herself in the mirror, she barely recognized the woman looking back at her. There were shadows under her gray eyes, and her mouth was set in a grim line.

She strongly suspected the marquess was trying to seduce her.

She had no idea what he saw in her. Hugh had never desired her very much, even at the start of their marriage. She had tried to please him as a wife should, but whatever she had done, it had never seemed enough. For the longest time she had believed that there had been something lacking within herself, something fundamentally wrong with her.

But now she wasn't so sure. She couldn't account for it, but she instinctively knew that Lord Rothsburgh wanted her. The worst, most shocking realization of all, was that she wanted him too.

It was time she faced the ugly truth. She was an adulteress. There was no denying that she had already committed adultery with the marquess over and over again in her mind, if not in actual deed. She knew she had. She sinned every time she even looked at him. Every time she thought of him. And that was constantly.

She couldn't continue on like this. But what could she do? What *should* she do?

The rational part of her brain told her to get dressed and pack her trunk and depart on the next mail coach for Edinburgh or Aberdeen before she damned herself to hell for being a shameless wanton. She would find another post. She was intelligent. She had a little money to sustain her for a few weeks, perhaps even a month if she lived frugally.

Elizabeth picked up her brush and began to ruthlessly tug at the knots in her hair. A sensible, virtuous woman would do that. And she had always been both of those things. But she had also been dead inside for such a long time. Hugh's callous disregard for her and their marriage vows had turned her into a pale ghost of her former self.

But Lord Rothsburgh—James—made her feel alive.

And she so wanted to live.

She placed her brush carefully back on the dresser and rose to select a gown for the day from the carved walnut wardrobe. Which one would it be? Her traveling gown of stiff black wool, or her lavender and pale gray striped silk that was suited for the period of half-mourning?

Elizabeth reached for the silk.

Lord Rothsburgh had requested that she meet with him mid-morning in the library so they could discuss her housekeeping duties before he took her on a guided tour around the castle.

Standing outside the door, Elizabeth now realized how superfluous this meeting would be. Nevertheless, she would show the marquess the suggested menu for his light luncheon and dinner today. And ask him a myriad of incon-sequential questions about such things as regimens for main-taining the smooth running of the household, staff management including the recruitment of several more maids to help with cleaning and kitchen duties, and the plans for the walled garden. Perhaps she could even ask him about reopening the drawing room. Even though it was presumptuous of her, she would dearly love to play that beautiful pianoforte again.

But while she discussed these things with him, she would be wondering the whole time when he might reveal his true intentions toward her.

Gripping the menu in one slightly damp palm, Elizabeth inhaled a deep breath, raised her other hand, and knocked. And nearly fell over when the marquess himself opened the door a moment later.

He smiled, looking her up and down. "Mrs. Eliott. I was just about to come looking for you."

"Oh, am I late?"

"No, not at all. It's just that it looks like the weather is about to take a turn for the worse, and I really did want to take you up to the battlements to admire the view. Do you have something warm to put over your gown? Lovely though it is, you'll freeze without a cloak or coat." He reached for her hand and noticed the menu. "What's this then?"

She offered it to him, and he ran his eyes over it briefly before grinning at her. "It looks wonderful, but I swear you are trying to fatten me up, Mrs. Eliott."

Elizabeth blushed. Just thinking about Lord Rothsburgh's lean and athletic looking body made her feel hot all over. But she couldn't imagine that he ever really had to be careful about what he ate.

"Oh...well..." she stammered. "Perhaps if I—"

"A tray in the library for luncheon and dinner this evening will be sufficient." He took her hand and tucked it into the crook of his arm before guiding her toward the stairs that led to the bedchambers. At the head of the stairs, they encountered Roberts, who had just emerged from Lord Rothsburgh's room.

"Roberts. Please pass this menu onto your wife. Tell her that I would like two trays sent up to the library at midday with"—he glanced at the menu again—"the *bouef en croûte*. Mrs. Eliott will be taking lunch with me today. We have a lot to discuss."

Roberts bowed, his expression completely neutral. Elizabeth was amazed at the older man's sang-froid. "Of course, milord. An' dinner?"

"Mrs. Eliott will be down later to go over the menu with Mrs. Roberts. But again, we will only require trays in the library." The marquess then turned to her. "And perhaps you might be so kind as to go down to the cellar with Roberts later to match a bottle of wine or two with whatever you choose for us to eat. Whatever you wish."

"Yes, my lord." Elizabeth was flabbergasted. He wanted to have both lunch and dinner with her again. Alone. And he obviously didn't care who knew. Despite her resolve earlier this morning to stay on at Eilean Tor, Elizabeth really didn't know if she could cope with Lord Rothsburgh's brazen interest in her being scrutinized by all and sundry on an ongoing basis.

Roberts, to his credit, simply bowed and menu in hand, took his leave.

Lord Rothsburgh started to propel Elizabeth down the hall once more.

"My lord," she said, hoping she didn't sound as breathless as she suddenly felt. "Whilst I am flattered that yet again you are showing me untold kindness, I am concerned that the rest of your staff will perhaps misconstrue the situation...and look upon me as—"

Lord Rothsburgh halted abruptly and Elizabeth almost stumbled, but he reached out and held her steady at the waist. He was looking at her intently. "Yes? As what?"

She felt warmth suffuse her cheeks. "An interloper perhaps, quite undeserving of your favor. I-I wouldn't want to create any discord. Or for my actions to be deemed...improper."

Lord Rothsburgh sighed and his mouth tilted into a gentle smile. "Mrs. Eliott. Or may I call you, Beth?" He didn't wait for her to acquiesce. "No one on my staff, from Mr. or Mrs. Roberts down to the scullery maid or stable lad, will look upon you with anything but the utmost respect. While I grant you that most masters would not cultivate such a close working relationship with their housekeeper, I think you should know that here at Eilean Tor, indeed in much of the Highlands, most clans-folk have a more—shall we say—liberal view of such matters. And I know my staff are loyal to a fault. They do not gossip. Rest assured, your reputation is safe."

So everyone would know about her unconventional relationship with the marquess. But no one would say anything. Could Elizabeth live with that while she resided here? Although the marquess obviously trusted his staff, she was sure some of them would privately censure her for her actions.

But did she really care about the reputation of the fictitious widow, Mrs. Beth Eliott, anymore? Now that something new and oh, so exhilarating was almost within her reach?

Lord Rothsburgh was watching her closely, his eyes focused on her mouth. She realized she was biting her bottom lip again. He must like it when she did that. The thought sent a decidedly illicit thrill through her, unlike anything she'd ever felt before. This uncharacteristically, naughty version of Elizabeth decided that she didn't care that she flirted with danger.

"I believe you," she said softly. "And to answer your earlier question, I don't mind if you call me Beth. In private." It had been her pet name as a child and she especially liked how it had sounded just now on Lord Rothsburgh's lips.

His brown eyes grew imperceptibly darker and yet softer at the same time. And something inside her, perhaps it was her heart, flipped over.

"All right then, Beth." His mouth lifted into that slow, easy smile again that made her ache for something more. "Now that's settled, let's fetch your cloak and then get up to the battlements while we still can."

"The view is magnificent, my lord. It's like being on the edge of the world."

Elizabeth peered out between one of the crenellated parapets on the north-eastern edge of the castle. She had to narrow her eyes against the strong gale that whipped around them and tore at her black wool cloak and hair with icy, briny fingers. But she didn't mind a bit. Not when Lord Rothsburgh stood beside her with his hand at the small of her back.

"Yes, I rather think so too." Lord Rothsburgh leaned in close to her to speak, perhaps so he didn't have to project his voice above the sound of wind and the waves crashing on the cliffs below. But then again perhaps not. Regardless of the reason, she could feel his warm breath against her cheek. And she liked it.

He pointed to the north. "Can you see the headland farther along the coast? Blackhaven is not too far beyond there. Although the shopping doesn't compare to Edinburgh, it's much better than what Torhaven has to offer. I would be happy to take you there next time I make a trip to see my solicitor, if you'd like."

Elizabeth stretched up a little to speak in his ear, and she caught the now all too familiar scent of his exotic soap. "That would be...most considerate, my lord." She was surprised that her voice sounded relatively normal given that at the same time she had spoken, she'd had to fight the sudden, uncharacteristic urge to place her lips against the distinct line of dark stubble on the edge of the marquess's jaw. He obviously had a habit of missing the same spot when shaving.

Shocked at the rate with which her brazen thoughts were increasing now that she'd seriously contemplated throwing all caution to the wind, Elizabeth determinedly returned her gaze to the seascape. If she wasn't careful, she'd be on her back beneath the marquess before the day was through.

But isn't that what you want, Elizabeth?

The unrelenting wind was churning the sea into choppy, white-capped waves, and she could see a bank of ominous, dark gray clouds looming closer to the shore. The unmistakable low growl of thunder carried across the water toward them.

Following her gaze, Lord Rothsburgh frowned. "It won't be long before that hits us." He took her hand and clasped it against his proffered forearm. "Walk with me to the western side? I'll be able to point out a few more points of interest before we need to beat a retreat."

"As you wish, my lord."

He led her to the west facing battlement and she was able to see Blackhaven Wood a mile or so to the north-west, as well as all of Lord Rothsburgh's other holdings that extended as far as the eye could see, and beyond. She suddenly realized how vast the estate was. The Marquess of Rothsburgh was undoubtedly a very rich and powerful man.

"When was the castle first built?" she asked after he had finished pointing out the very southern edge of Torhaven's cove that wasn't obscured by the Tor itself. He'd relinquished her hand at some point during the discussion, and she found it odd how in such a short space of time she had become so used to his touch that now she noticed its absence.

"The battlements and the main keep where the Great Hall is located were constructed by my ancestor, Sir Malcolm Huntly, in the fifteenth century. But various other descendants have added extensions and improvements over the years. In fact, the main apartments that adjoin the Great Hall were added in the sixteenth century by the first Marquess of Rothsburgh. My grandparents then set about modernizing the interiors of the rooms when my father was a boy. So, despite the great age of the place, it is quite comfortable to live at Eilean Tor, if one doesn't mind the isolation of course."

"I can see the causeway must have been a most effective moat in days gone by," Elizabeth observed. The tide was in, and the dark sea roiled angrily in the channel between the headland the castle sat upon and the Tor. "Though it must be very difficult when you need to get across but cannot."

Lord Rothsburgh shrugged. "One learns to live with it." He turned to face her, and she immediately noticed that his eyes held a deadly serious expression. "Promise me, Beth, that you will never attempt to go out on that causeway again unless you check with Roberts or myself about when it is safest to cross. And if you are not in my carriage, you must always take a decent mount from my stables. It can be a death trap at the wrong time in the wrong conditions."

"I promise," she replied just as gravely, unsure what had precipitated such a stern speech.

He nodded once. "Good." He sighed and ran a hand through his already hopelessly wind-ruffled hair. His gaze was now softer. "I apologize if I seem overly high-handed and protective, Beth. You see, it's just that my wife... Isabelle... She was swept off the causeway out to sea."

"Oh my God," Elizabeth gasped, her hand flying to her throat. She now understood why Lord Rothsburgh had been so cross with Mr. Geddes when she'd arrived here on the back of Auld Fern. The weather and the sea state had been atrocious that afternoon. "I mean...how terrible... I'm so sorry, my lord. I had no idea. I had heard there'd been an accident but... as to the exact nature of it..."

He cocked an eyebrow. "You heard my wife had died in an accident? From whom?"

Damn. She'd slipped up again. She really was a hopeless liar. But she couldn't very well reveal that her original source of information had been Lady Airlie from the Widows of Waterloo Trust. That would invite too many inconvenient questions.

"It wasn't your staff, I assure you," she replied whilst her mind frantically scrabbled about for another plausible response. "It was...when I first arrived in Torhaven. Perhaps Mr. Geddes mentioned it. I can't quite recall..."

Lord Rothsburgh nodded and then turned back to stare at the deadly waters still boiling around in the channel like a brew in a witch's cauldron. When he spoke again his voice was quieter, and she needed to lean closer to catch the words. "I was in London when I received word... I believe Isabelle had been missing for several days until her body washed up in a cove about a mile from here." He turned back to Elizabeth and ran his gaze over her face. "I apologize, Beth, if I've shocked you with my candor. As I've said before, I often speak without thinking."

She swallowed. "I don't know what to say, my lord, other than I'm so sorry for your loss. It is such a tragedy. And your daughter, Lady Annabelle—"

"Was here when it happened. It was eight weeks ago, to be precise. But Mrs. Roberts and her nurse, Miss McFarlane, took good care of her until my sister, Lady Maxwell, arrived. And then of course myself."

Eight weeks. Elizabeth's mind reeled in shock.

Lord Rothsburgh's wife had died only eight weeks ago.

Why, he had probably only arrived back at Eilean Tor within the last month.

Elizabeth reached out and gripped the rough, cold stones of the castle wall. What on earth was she doing here? She was indeed an intruder. How could she even be thinking about becoming Lord Rothsburgh's mistress? She'd been having improper—nay, positively shameless thoughts about a poor vulnerable man who was in the very initial stages of deepest mourning.

She must have misunderstood his intentions all along. He was lonely and grieving. That was all. She was nothing more than a silly, blind fool who obviously knew nothing about men.

"Beth. Are you all right?"

Somehow, Elizabeth focused her gaze back on the marquess.

Her employer.

"My lord...I really shouldn't be here if that is the case. You are so recently bereaved. I feel terrible... How insensitive of me to turn up like I did... I-I don't know what to say except I'm so, so sorry."

He seized her hand and pressed it between both of his. A spark of what she thought might be desperation was in his eyes. "Beth. No. Don't say that. It's quite all right. Believe me. I don't want you to go. Far from it."

She frowned and searched his eyes. "Are you certain, Lord Rothsburgh? My presence here...in your home. It doesn't seem right somehow, given the circumstances."

The marquess returned her gaze levelly. "It's perfectly all right, Beth. I should explain."

"You really don't need to—"

"Yes. I do." He sighed and his expression grew solemn. "This is going to sound dreadful, but my wife and I...we had grown apart a long time ago. Her death was tragic, yes. And I grieve for the fact that Annabelle no longer has a mother. But as for myself...I have regrets and I am deeply saddened, but I am not mortally grief-stricken. And as terrible as that sounds, that's the truth of the matter."

"Oh…" Elizabeth knew all about the distance that could develop between spouses over time. But despite her own experience of marriage, she couldn't deny that she was surprised by Lord Rothsburgh's disclosure.

She suddenly wondered if she would feel the same when Hugh died. Would there be only sadness and regret? But then, there was a difference between Lord Rothsburgh's situation and her own. She knew her husband was going to die.

She recalled her wedding vows. *In sickness and in health.* When the end came for Hugh, would she also feel guilty because she had effectively abandoned her husband to endure his fate alone? Perhaps in time, but right here and right now, she did not. She was certain that if she'd stayed with Hugh, an early and ignoble death would have been her fate also. Surely she didn't deserve that. She wouldn't feel guilty about saving her own life.

But there are other things you should feel guilty about.

A strong gust of wind suddenly howled through the crenellations and flung the first stinging drops of rain at them. Lord Rothsburgh grasped Elizabeth's hand and started to guide her back to the tower where the stairs were located. "It looks like it's time we went below and returned to the real world, Beth. Besides, I wouldn't want you to catch the ague again."

Following him along the ramparts, Elizabeth bent her head against the gathering tempest and was grateful when they began to descend the spiraling stairwell that led back to the Great Hall. Lord Rothsburgh had said they were returning to the real world.

But little did he know that in the real world, she was really Lady Beauchamp, the wife of someone he despised. A woman who'd seriously contemplated being unfaithful to her husband.

She prayed that Lord Rothsburgh would never find out.

∼

The rest of Elizabeth's afternoon passed in a relatively ordinary fashion—if one considered sharing lunch with a man as tempting as the devil himself to be ordinary. However, there was nothing devilish about the marquess's behavior. He had conducted himself in a perfectly gentlemanly manner the whole time she was in the library. Rosencrantz and Guildenstern had even played the part of canine chaperones.

She had discussed her plans for managing the staff and hiring two additional maids, as well as her ideas for the walled garden. All her proposals had met with Lord Rothsburgh's approval. She had even—although somewhat nervously—broached the subject of opening up the drawing room. Now that she knew the pianoforte was right next door, her fingers quite itched to play it.

To her relief, Lord Rothsburgh had been quite amenable to the suggestion, and so she had spent the best part of the afternoon with Todd and Maisie—one of the young maids who had recently returned to work—restoring the drawing room to its original splendor.

As Elizabeth helped to pull away and fold all the dustsheets, and arrange the placement of lamps and other ornaments around the room, she realized again what a fool she'd been in thinking the marquess had been trying to seduce her. The idea must have been a product of her over-active imagination. He was handsome and charismatic, undoubtedly, but after spending a completely uneventful, albeit pleasant few hours with him, it had become rapidly apparent that her shameful lust was, indeed, all one-sided.

By the time the mantel clock struck five, all had been arranged to her satisfaction. She dismissed Todd and Maisie and took one last look around. Not for the first time, she wondered why Lord Rothsburgh had closed up the room. She supposed that it might have something to do with his wife. But then again, perhaps now that he was a widower, he simply didn't feel the need to occupy such a large living space.

It really was a beautiful room. The fire and candles had been lit during the course of the afternoon to dispel the pervading gloom engendered by the incessant rain. The warm atmosphere was further enhanced by the sumptuous furnishings. Aside from the exquisite piano that was positioned by one of the bay windows, chairs upholstered in crimson brocade along with Adams-style mahogany tables were clustered around the similarly hued Turkish rug before the fire, whilst various other mahogany cabinets filled with all manner of eye-beckoning curios stood in strategic positions around the edges of the room.

Just as Elizabeth was turning to leave, she noticed a dust-sheet peeking out from underneath a tapestry that hung by the red marble fireplace. Maisie and Todd had obviously missed it, as had she. She gently nudged the tapestry to one side and noticed a large flat, rectangular item, possibly a mirror or painting resting against the oak-paneled wall. Curious, she lifted the dustsheet away to reveal a portrait of the most breathtakingly beautiful woman she had ever seen.

As soon as Elizabeth set eyes on the painting, she instinctively knew it was a likeness of the late Isabelle Huntly, the Marchioness of Rothsburgh. Lord Rothsburgh must have had the portrait removed after her death—perhaps because it evoked too many painful memories—but then he had forgotten to have it stored away.

The woman was depicted against a rather ordinarily rendered pastoral background, reminiscent of a typical Reynolds or Gainsborough painting. But then anything would look ordinary in comparison to such a sylph-like creature. She was simply dressed in a gauzy, almost transparent gown of white chiffon that clung to her slender curves, almost as if the fabric was slightly damp. Her hair was raven black and tumbled about her bare, elegant shoulders in abundant curls. Aside from a pair of pearl drop earrings, the only other adornment the woman wore was an ornate sapphire and pearl brooch pinned above her left breast. But it was the woman's eyes that one noticed the most. They were a startling blue— even more vividly blue than Hugh's, Elizabeth thought—and were fringed with long, curling black lashes. The marchioness looked out from the painting with an enigmatic expression, as if she were smiling to herself about something that was a secret.

She was mysterious and alluring.

She was everything Elizabeth wasn't.

A squall of rain hit one of the windows and Elizabeth jumped. She suddenly felt like she was sneaking a look at something that wasn't meant for her eyes. She quickly dropped the dustsheet back into place, and then after making sure it was tucked neatly behind the tapestry out of sight again, she hurriedly quit the room. She should put it out of her mind. It really wasn't any of her business.

When Elizabeth returned to her bedchamber to change for dinner, she caught a glimpse of her own wan face and nondescript gray eyes in the dressing-table mirror and sighed. It was abundantly clear that she was but a pale shadow compared to the sylvan Lady Rothsburgh. The marquess—a man who must be grieving the recent loss of his wife, despite his assertions to the contrary—would never be really interested in his all but destitute housekeeper. It was all for the best, really, because now she no longer needed to worry about being unfaithful.

Elizabeth sat and began to re-dress her hair. She should be relieved. She should be happy.

So why did disappointment settle over her like a cold, dark shroud?

CHAPTER 11

Rothsburgh sat alone before the fire in the library, a glass of whisky in hand, waiting for Beth to join him for dinner. Through the connecting door to the drawing room, he could see the results of her handiwork this afternoon. The chamber was just as beautiful as it had always been. It was a pity that it reminded him of too many things that were better left buried.

But perhaps, now that Beth was here, there would be an opportunity to create new memories. And he rather thought that she already had. The way she had looked as she'd played that poignant nocturne last night—with her eyes closed and her mouth curved into a rapturous smile—it was like watching and listening to an angel.

An angel with a sinfully pouting bottom lip that he couldn't wait to kiss.

Rothsburgh sipped his whisky, hoping the fiery liquid would calm the building anticipation within him. And more surprisingly, nerves.

He was certain that Beth detected the simmering tension between them, and that she was aware of his intent. Indeed, this morning she had seemed more than accepting of the touch of his hand at her back, his voice at her ear. She had even willingly conceded to his use of her Christian name. Rothsburgh had been heartened by the increasing familiarity between them...right up until the moment he had mentioned his wife.

Beth's subsequent offer to leave straightaway had alarmed him no end, but he couldn't, *wouldn't* let her go. He had obviously shocked her with his revelations, and as a result he had been more circumspect with her for the rest of the day. Because he also suspected that she was still nervous about the other servants' opinion of her, he'd behaved with the utmost decorum, especially when Roberts or anyone else made an appearance. As long as he and Beth didn't openly flaunt their affair, he could count on his staffs' discretion. He was their master and Clan Chief, and they would never show him anything less than absolute loyalty.

Rothsburgh lifted his whisky glass and grimaced. For once, the *uisge beatha* wasn't dispelling his tension. The truth was, he needed Beth. It was that simple. It was definitely time to ask her to be his mistress. And if all went well, by tonight's end, she wouldn't just be greeting him by his first name. She would be crying it to the heavens.

The library door clicked and he sat up straighter.

Beth.

She hovered at the edge of the room, and he immediately noticed she'd reverted back to the more somber style of dress associated with full mourning. As his gaze raked over her, he lamented the fact that her lovely figure was hidden beneath a severely cut gown of black bombazine. There might be a sprinkling of jet beads around the square neckline but they in no way relieved the dress's austerity. Beth had also pulled her blond hair back into a tight, high bun of some sort. His fingers immediately itched to let it down.

As for Beth's expression, she looked wary, but also defeated somehow. Something was definitely wrong. There was some change within her, but casting his mind back over the events of the afternoon, Rothsburgh couldn't fathom what could have precipitated such a dramatic shift in her mood.

Unless she was having second thoughts again because of their earlier discussion about Isabelle... Could that be the problem? Whatever it was, he was determined to find out. Nothing, or no one, would stand in his way.

"My lord," she murmured as she dipped into a stiff curtsy.

"Mrs. Eliott," he returned. He raised his glass. "Care to join me in a wee dram?" He knew she would decline, but he wanted to rattle her, to shake her out of this strangely subdued state she was in. Why, she wouldn't even come into the room.

"No thank you, my lord."

Rothsburgh frowned. Clearly some other sort of action was required. He stood and placed his half-finished whisky on the side table, then moved toward her. She stayed perfectly still, but as he advanced, he noticed she blushed and the pace of her breathing increased. Good. Despite her reversion to the guise of chaste widow, it seemed she wasn't completely indifferent to him. He caught her hand and placed a gentle kiss on her fingertips, watching her face all the while.

He was gratified to see her eyes widen, and he heard her draw in a quick breath.

Struck with sudden inspiration, he smiled. "Come now, Beth. Show me what you can do with these clever fingers."

Elizabeth sat with her so-called clever fingers resting on the keys of the pianoforte as the last notes of Mozart's Piano Sonata No.

11 rang out. In the ensuing silence all she could hear was the lash of wind and rain against the windowpanes. Why didn't Lord Rothsburgh speak? Perhaps the piece wasn't to his liking.

She raised her eyes from the keyboard and chanced a look at him. The dark-eyed voluptuary was back. He was leaning against the pianoforte beside her, wearing nothing but a white linen shirt, open at the neck, form-fitting black breeches and top boots. His informal state of dress brought to mind the first time she had met him. And he was still just as utterly mesmerizing.

Elizabeth clasped her hands together and cast her gaze downward. Ever since she had entered the library, she had sensed a change in the marquess. The gentleman she had spent the best part of the morning and early afternoon with had vanished, to be replaced by the man who made her tremble and blush and think about all manner of sinful things. Forbidden things.

She toyed with her silver wedding band and berated herself as she had done before in her room. *Wake up, Elizabeth. Lord Rothsburgh is grieving. He is lonely. He is your employer. You are married and have nothing to offer him.*

But the words meant nothing when she could feel his gaze upon her, and she wanted him so badly it hurt.

She suddenly felt Lord Rothsburgh's hand on her shoulder. Despite her earlier resolve, her traitorous body was reacting of its own accord. The touch of his fingers seared the bare skin along the neckline of her gown, and her heart began to hammer wildly against her ribs.

"Beth...tell me what's wrong."

She raised her eyes to his dark, penetrating stare. *What on earth can I say that won't be a lie?* "I—"

He slid onto the piano seat beside her, his thigh pressing against hers through the stiff fabric of her skirts. He was half turned toward her, his wide chest within inches of her shoulder.

"Beth." His voice was a whispered caress against her ear, making her shiver.

She should go.

"Beth, do you have any idea how beautiful you are?"

Not as beautiful as your late wife. Her gaze slid involuntarily to the tapestry where Lady Rothsburgh's portrait lay hidden. *Get up, Elizabeth. Go. Before he—*

Too late.

Lord Rothsburgh reached out and tilted her face toward his own. "You have the looks of an angel," he whispered, his gaze roaming over her features. "Everything about you is beautiful... Your hair." He leaned forward and pressed his lips against her temple. "Your cheek." Again, another feather-light kiss upon her skin. "Your neck." He bent and placed his firm, warm mouth against the sensitive flesh between her ear and jaw, and a bolt of heat shot through Elizabeth all the way to the juncture between her thighs. She sucked in a sharp breath, drawing in the intoxicating scent of the marquess's skin, then pressed a shaking hand to his linen shirtfront, unsure if she meant to push him away, or draw him closer.

Heaven help her. She couldn't resist this slow deliberate assault upon her senses.

"Your lips." Lord Rothsburgh's mouth hovered over hers for a moment. "Especially your lips."

And then he kissed her. And it was unlike anything Elizabeth had ever known before. All rational thought fled as his mouth slid over hers with tormenting, delicious slowness, his tongue gently pushing against the seam of her lips, demanding access. And she couldn't refuse. With a moan she parted for him, wanting him to taste her, wanting to taste him in return.

She swept her tongue against his, and he groaned deeply in his throat. Lifting his head for an instant, he drew in a ragged breath before he claimed her mouth a second time, sucking her lower lip between his. She gasped at the decadently sinful sensation, and taking advantage of her parted lips, he thrust his tongue into her again, boldly, blatantly exploring her. He speared one of his hands into her hair whilst the other seized her shoulder and dragged her closer, his mouth moving with an urgency that made her blood pound and her head spin.

She was falling. She was swept away.

She was an adulteress. And for once she didn't care.

"Milord. Dinner is served."

Elizabeth jerked away, her eyes frantically darting to the door leading to the library.

Oh God. Roberts is here.

Lord Rothsburgh closed his eyes and a muscle worked in his cheek. "Thank you, Roberts," he called. He fixed his gaze back on her, his eyes black and burning. "Don't think for a minute that you are going to escape answering my earlier question, Beth, about what is bothering you. I think it's time we both spoke plainly, don't you?"

Still reeling from the aftereffects of that most earth-shattering kiss, and the shock of being almost discovered, Elizabeth could do nothing but stare at the marquess, who sat with one hand still cradling her head, and the other behind her shoulder. Beneath her own hand she could feel the hard plane of his chest rapidly rising and falling with each breath he took, and with a jolt of surprise, she realized that he was still grappling to control his own response to their kiss.

But he didn't seem to mind the fact she was insensible. His expression softened and he tucked a strand of her dislodged hair behind her ear. "But perhaps we should dine first." He stood and with a bow, offered his arm. "Would you care to join me for dinner, Mrs. Eliott?"

Elizabeth placed her trembling hand on his forearm, and somewhat shakily, rose to her feet. She didn't think she would be able to eat or drink a thing. Not when she knew what was coming. Nevertheless, she let Lord Rothsburgh lead her through to take a seat at the small oak dining setting that had been set up to one side of the library fire.

They were alone again. Roberts, and perhaps Todd, had come and gone, and she had the feeling that they would not make an appearance again unless summoned by the marquess. She attempted a bite or two of the fillet of venison that Mrs. Roberts had prepared so beautifully, but within a short space of time, she realized she had no appetite for it. Her nerves were too tautly stretched, her stomach too filled with butterflies. Against her better judgment she picked up her wine glass instead and took a sizeable sip of the Burgundy. All the while, she was aware that Lord Rothsburgh watched her.

"Not hungry, Beth?"

She attempted a smile and met his eyes at last. "Not really." She glanced at his plate and noticed he hadn't eaten much either. "And you?"

He smiled slowly and his gaze dropped to her lips. "Not for venison."

Oh, dear Lord. She rather suspected the time for plain speaking had arrived.

Lord Rothsburgh pushed his plate aside and leaned forward in his chair. His gaze fixed unwaveringly on her face. "Beth, you do not seem yourself this evening. Ever since you walked in, you have seemed—and please forgive me for my bluntness—both disheartened and guarded. And you were not so earlier today. I find myself confused and concerned that I have done something during the course of the day that has upset you. I had thought that you and I...that *we* were becoming closer. I know you must sense the connection between us. And because of that, I hope you feel that you can be honest with me. Especially after our kiss." He paused then reached forward, laying his warm hand upon her arm.

"Please tell me what is wrong. I cannot stand seeing you this way."

Elizabeth closed her eyes and tried to assemble her roiling thoughts. There were so many things that were wrong. But what could she possibly say to this man? *I want you, but I'm married. I know you want me, but you shouldn't.*

She didn't want to lie, not to him, not after the kiss they had shared.

But she had to. She couldn't let him know about Hugh. Remaining Mrs. Beth Eliott was the only way she could ensure her safety. It was the only way she could stay. And even though it was wrong, part of her wanted to stay more than anything.

She felt like she was being torn in two...and perhaps she was.

The heavy silence between them stretched, and she was suddenly conscious of the storm that raged beyond the windows along with the thundering crash of breakers against the cliffs below.

"Beth?"

She drew a steadying breath and forced herself to look at Lord Rothsburgh again. There was one thing that bothered her that she could reveal. "When I was in the drawing room today, I discovered a portrait of a woman that had been placed behind one of the tapestries," she said, watching the marquess's far-too-handsome face. "I know I probably shouldn't even be asking this, but is it a likeness of your wife, my lord?"

The muscles around Lord Rothsburgh's eyes pulled imperceptibly tighter, and Elizabeth thought she saw a momentary flash of pain in his dark gaze. "Yes, it is. It should have been stored away by now. I shall get Roberts to see to it first thing tomorrow."

So, she had been right. Lord Rothsburgh was still grieving. That meant he was still very vulnerable. He was only trying to seek solace with her to ease his pain. Any way she looked at the situation, her conscience howled at her to go.

"Your wife, she was very beautiful," Elizabeth said softly. Lord Rothsburgh had called her beautiful too—an angel— right before he'd kissed her, but she didn't quite believe him. It really shouldn't matter, but for some silly and wholly feminine reason, she knew deep down that it did.

The marquess's hand slid down her arm to cover her hand. Her skin tingled beneath the touch of his bare palm.

"Believe me, Beth," he said gravely. "Appearances can be deceiving. I meant what I said earlier today. Isabelle and I... Well, let me just say that by the end of our six year marriage, she no longer wore my wedding ring." He looked down at her hand, and his fingers lightly brushed her own wedding band. "Not like you."

Elizabeth's breath caught in her throat. *No, not like me.* He was right. Appearances could be deceiving. Everything Lord Rothsburgh knew about her was entirely fabricated. And the weight of her dishonesty was so heavy, it felt like she was being crushed.

She tried to pull her hand away, but Lord Rothsburgh caught it and lifted it to his lips. He kissed each fingertip gently, then turned her hand over and placed his mouth on the sensitive flesh on the inside of her wrist.

Elizabeth gasped at the utterly decadent sensation. She couldn't think clearly. She couldn't breathe. She was drowning beneath the rising tide of her own desire.

Lord Rothsburgh raised his gaze to her face. His eyes fairly smoldered and she couldn't look away. When he spoke, his voice was husky with need. "Beth, I have a proposition for you. I know you have only been recently bereaved yourself. And you are free to reject me outright."

She knew what he was going to ask her, even before he uttered the words. He mustn't say the words. A kiss was one thing. But anything more? Now the moment was upon her, she didn't think she could go through with it.

She dragged in a much-needed breath. "Lord Rothsburgh—"

"Beth, please hear me out."

Elizabeth was astonished at the raw urgency in the marquess's voice and he held onto her hand so tightly, she didn't think she could pull away even if she wanted to.

"I know this is sudden, but try as I might, I can't stop thinking about you," he continued in that same turbulent, almost desperate tone. "Since you came here, since you literally fell into my arms, I find that I can think of nothing else but having you back there. I can't let you continue on as my housekeeper. Beth, I want you to be my mistress."

Oh God.

Elizabeth wrenched her hand away then pushed to her feet and stepped back from the table. Her mind, her conscience, her better self screamed at her to flee.

Her blood, her pounding heart, her entire body urged her to stay, to fling herself into Lord Rothsburgh's arms and never let him go.

"Beth?" Lord Rothsburgh stood and took a step toward her. She backed away and his face fell. He looked haunted. Stricken. "I'm sorry, Beth," he whispered. "I've shocked you."

"Yes." Her breath was coming in short, ragged gasps. "I-I just need some air... I need to think." She took another step back, and then another.

And then she turned and fled.

Elizabeth didn't stop until she reached her bedchamber. She shut the door and sank to the floor. Her legs were shaking and she realized she was crying. She felt so unlike herself, it was as if she didn't know who she was anymore.

What, in God's name, am I going to do?

The sensible, sane thing to do would be to pack her trunk and leave here first thing tomorrow morning, as soon as the tide was safely out. As she should have done this morning.

But she didn't feel sensible, or the least bit sane. She felt as if she'd broken into a thousand pieces. The image of Lord Rothsburgh's tortured expression when she'd rejected him, kept entering her mind. So did the memory of his heart-stopping, bone-melting kiss. She had never, ever been kissed like that before. And probably never would again.

How could she walk away from that?

But she must.

Elizabeth pushed herself up and brushed the tears from her eyes. Crying wouldn't do her any good. She must be strong. She would endure this setback because there really was no other choice.

Elizabeth crossed to the wardrobe and began to remove and neatly fold her gowns before placing them into her traveling trunk. She could do this. See, it was easy. She'd only been here a fortnight and a few days. She would soon forget about the too handsome, too charismatic, too tempting Lord Rothsburgh and his kisses.

I'm such a hopeless liar, even to myself.

Elizabeth dropped the gown she'd been folding onto the pile in the trunk and stared at her right hand. Her wedding band glimmered dully. What she suddenly couldn't work out was why she kept lying to herself that her marriage to Hugh mattered at all? She had truly loved Hugh at the start, and had tried so hard to make it work, but he had forsaken her and their marriage vows long ago. So why was she still trying so hard to remain faithful to a man who had never valued her love or commitment in the first place, and had broken his own promises to her countless times? A man who would have care-lessly infected her with a deadly disease?

She had no idea.

Before she could stop herself, she slid off the ring and dropped it into her trunk. Then she turned to go back to the library.

As she traversed the hall and descended the stairs, her foot-steps quickened. She was being reckless. She was being wicked. This new shameless Elizabeth—the woman who no longer wore a wedding ring—decided that she didn't care that what she was doing was dangerous, not when she was standing on the brink of something that promised to be the most profound experience that she would probably ever have.

Perhaps she would be damned, but right here, right now she was willing to risk all for the chance to have something that she'd always been denied—the physical fulfillment of her desire. She suddenly knew who she wanted to be.

Not Elizabeth, the Countess of Beauchamp.

Not Mrs. Beth Eliott.

She would be Lord Rothsburgh's mistress.

After Beth had fled from the library—from him— Rothsburgh had taken the bottle of Burgundy and his glass over to his chair by the fire with the intention of getting as drunk as humanly possible. Anything to drown his frustration and anguish at Beth's rejection. She'd declared that she'd needed air, time to think, but he knew she'd only said those things out of desperation so she could leave. She wouldn't be back.

He'd shocked her. In fact, he'd made a complete hash of everything. Come morning, Rothsburgh suspected Beth would be packed and waiting to cross the causeway at the earliest opportunity to go back to Torhaven in order to catch the mail coach to Edinburgh or Aberdeen. He'd make sure that his man of business paid her for her first quarter. No, to hell with that paltry amount—he'd pay her a six-month wage. She would need some funds to sustain herself until she found another situation. A better situation. At least one where her employer didn't proposition her to become his mistress.

How had he got it all so wrong?

Because you are an arrogant, selfish brute, that's why. He'd thought to reduce a lovely, virtuous woman into something less than she deserved to be—a means of relieving his tension. An entertaining diversion. And now she was gone.

Rothsburgh didn't want to think of it or how much it bothered him that he'd treated her so shabbily. He especially didn't want to think about the kiss he'd stolen from her. A kiss that had shaken him to his very core and had left him craving so much more.

But there would be no more kisses.

There would be no more Beth at all.

He'd perhaps made his way through two-thirds of the Burgundy when he heard the door to the library open, then shut. Even though he'd instructed Roberts not to bother coming back to clear the dinner trays, sometimes the man couldn't help himself, and would return to check if his master required anything else before retiring for the night.

"It's all right, Roberts," he called, not bothering to turn round in his chair. "I don't need anything tonight. Just take yourself to bed, man."

"It's...it's not Roberts, my lord."

Beth.

Rothsburgh sprang from his seat. He couldn't believe it. But there she was, coming slowly toward him, her cheeks flushed and her fair hair spilling in hopeless disarray from its fearsome bun, courtesy of his careless predation during their kiss.

"I...I thought... I didn't think you'd come back." His voice sounded cracked, broken. What did she want from him? He couldn't even allow himself to think she'd changed her mind. He wouldn't believe she had until she said the words.

She paused before him but an arm's length away, and he noticed then that she was just as breathless as he was. Her luminous gray gaze touched his. "I...I have considered your proposition, my lord."

"And?" He was on a knife's edge. The suspense was killing him. "What did you decide, Mrs. Eliott?"

She smiled softly and reached out her hand, placing it against his cheek. "I want to be your mistress," she murmured. "That is, if you still want me."

There was only one suitable response to her statement as far as Rothsburgh was concerned. He caught her against his chest and kissed her, his mouth laying claim to her so completely that she would not doubt his need for her, or that he did indeed, still want her.

She gasped against him but surrendered to the demands of his lips and questing tongue. She tasted delicious. More intoxicating and heady than wine or whisky could ever be.

Sweeter than honey.

He felt one of her hands, the one that had cupped his cheek, rise to tangle in his hair while the other pressed against his chest. But he wanted, needed her closer to him. He slid one of his hands from her elegant shoulder downward, mapping the curve of her full breast, her delicate ribs, her narrow waist, and then behind her to cup one cheek of her deliciously rounded derriere. He pulled her hips against him, so she would feel how she affected him so completely, and he was gratified to hear her moan as her hand twisted in the linen of his shirt.

He couldn't believe it. She wanted him just as much as he wanted her. But kisses were soon not enough. The thunder of his blood through his veins, in his heart, demanded more, so much more.

He dragged his head up for air. "Beth." He was panting, but he didn't care.

And so was she. She stared up at him through her long lashes, her beautiful mouth glistening and swollen from his kisses.

"Beth, I want you to do something for me."

Her lips tilted in a shy, yet almost coquettish smile. He'd never seen her smile like that before and he felt himself grow harder, if that were at all physically possible.

"Of course, my lord." She sounded deliciously breathless. "I suppose this is when a mistress should say, *whatever you desire*."

He smiled. There was plenty of time for him to make salacious requests, but his first one was quite simple and not salacious at all. "I want you to call me by my first name. James. Like you did when you first arrived. Will you do that for me, Beth?"

Her smile lit her eyes. "James," she murmured.

He didn't think he'd ever heard anything quite so beautiful. His gaze fell to her mouth again, and to his amazement, she appeared to quite deliberately press her perfect white teeth into her full lower lip.

That simple act was the equivalent of setting tinder to a fire. Rothsburgh groaned and hauled her against him, crushing her mouth with his, plundering her mercilessly with his tongue until she was moaning and frantically tugging his shirt from the waistband of his breeches. Her fingers slid beneath the linen to make contact with the bare skin of his stomach, and then she skimmed her hand upward to his chest. Her touch was like fire, a brand upon his already heated flesh.

She suddenly pulled away from the kiss to rasp against his throat. "James, will you take your shirt off for me?"

He was more than happy to oblige. He took a step back then ripped the garment over his head, tossing it onto the floor.

Beth stared at him with wide eyes. "Oh my," she whispered and closed the gap between them, one hand coming up to trace the line of his collarbone with her fingers before descending across his heaving pectorals to the ridges across his abdomen. "James...you are utterly beautiful."

He felt like a pagan god beneath her fascinated gaze. But one that was about to burst into flame if he didn't have her in his arms again. He reached for her and she didn't hesitate.

She crashed into his chest, propelling him backward, deliberately pulling him down to the hearthrug until she was lying on top of him, loose tresses of her hair falling about his face as she kissed him with equal ferocity. The strength of her ardor astonished him, thrilled him. Aroused him beyond all reason. But he wanted to touch her skin too.

He reached out a hand to fiddle with the buttons at the back of her gown, but she suddenly sat up, straddling him and his hand fell away.

"Not yet, my lord." She wriggled herself down his body until she was positioned over his thighs, and then her hand reached for the buttons fastening the fall front of his breeches. Her delicious pink tongue slid along her lower lip.

Surely she couldn't mean to pleasure him like that. Not the chaste Mrs. Eliott. He caught her wrist. "Beth? You don't need to do that for me."

She frowned slightly. "You don't like being pleasured that way?"

"Yes, but—"

"I want to." She smiled and placed her other hand against the rock-hard length of him, her fingers gently stroking him up and down through the fabric at his groin. He was a large man, and right at this moment, fit to burst. Whilst part of his brain screamed at him to stop her—he didn't want to scare her with the fierceness of his arousal—another part of him was intrigued that she would willingly want to do this. For him.

He let go of her wrist and rested back on his bent elbows. "All right."

Using both hands, she had him free in no time. His cock was so swollen, and his balls throbbed so much, he wasn't sure that he wouldn't lose himself before she even started.

He gritted his teeth and stopped breathing as she looked down at him. She was biting her lip again. Christ, what was she waiting for? He was in agony. He was in hell.

"Beth." His voice fell somewhere between a plea and a groan. He lifted his hips slightly, and then at long last, she wrapped her hand around his pulsating shaft, lowered her head, and then took him into her mouth.

He bucked and cried out from the pure, exquisite torture she inflicted on him as she slid her fist and hot wet mouth up and down, up and down in a perfect rhythmic counterpoint. Every now and again she paused to swirl her tongue around the head of his cock, or to lick the entire length of his shaft before returning to rhythmically suck him again. Where the devil had she learned how to do this? Her skill even surpassed that of any of his previous mistresses.

But thought was becoming too difficult as the pressure inside him began to build and build to catastrophic proportions. He should stop her before he erupted in her mouth.

Rothsburgh reached forward to bury one of his hands in Beth's hair to push her away, but then it was too late. With an agonized cry, he came with a great volcanic spurt, his body shuddering, every muscle tightening into rigidity as a titanic wave of pleasure surged through him. And somehow she was swallowing him, drinking him, sucking him dry until there was nothing left.

Gasping, he collapsed onto the rug. He couldn't move. He couldn't even open his eyes, although he badly wanted to look at Beth again. He felt her ease herself off his legs, and then after a moment, she was at his side. She lay a warm hand upon his forehead, then brushed a damp lock of hair away from his face. He looked up, but he still couldn't even drag in enough breath to speak.

She was smiling—perhaps even a little smugly—and holding a glass of Burgundy. She took a sip of the wine then tilted the glass slightly toward him. "Can I get you some, my lord?"

He grimaced and pushed himself up to a sitting position. "Beth...I can't believe you're still calling me, my lord...after pleasuring me like that."

Her smile grew wider. "James, then. Can I serve you some wine?"

He laughed and took the glass she had been sipping from —his glass—away from her. "I'm afraid we'll have to share this. Before you came back, I'd set about drinking myself into a stupor. This is probably the last glass. Unless you'd like me to ring for Roberts to fetch us some more." He immediately regretted his words.

"You wouldn't," she whispered, her face blanching.

He reached forward and twisted a lock of her silken hair around his finger. "No. I wouldn't. Considering what I'm going to do with you next, I wouldn't want there to be any interruptions."

CHAPTER 12

W hat *was* he going to do with her?

A shiver of nervous anticipation tingled over every inch of Elizabeth's skin as Lord Rothsburgh—James— let a lock of her hair slowly unravel and slide off one long finger. He offered her his glass, and she took it, taking another sip. The rich red wine mingled on her tongue with another taste—the delicious, salty taste of him.

Elizabeth was quietly pleased with his reaction to her love-making. She had wanted to please him, and this was the only act she knew that she was particularly adept at—according to Hugh at any rate. She hoped that the marquess would remember that she was good at something, even if she turned out to be a disappointment in all other respects.

And she also hoped and prayed that Lord Rothsburgh wouldn't disappoint her like Hugh always had. It was probably unfair of her to be placing such high expectations on one man. That he would be able to fulfill her when her husband had never been able to. But she so wanted to experience an orgasm when she was with a man. And given that Rothsburgh could arouse her so effortlessly—just being in the same room with him aroused her—she knew if she was actually physically capable of reaching that ultimate peak with someone, he would be the one to take her there.

She was risking everything—her very soul—to experience such a wondrous thing.

She glanced over at Lord Rothsburgh—*James*, she must remember to call him that—and let her eyes feast upon the glorious sight of his naked upper body. The long, lean lines and planes of rigid muscle, bone, and sinew, gilded by the firelight. The Prince of Darkness, the Great Tempter indeed.

Her gaze then drifted lower along the tantalizing line of black hair that ran from navel to groin, to the opening in his breeches where his spent cock still lay exposed in a nest of dark curls. Even in that state, she still marveled at the length and width of him. Had she really taken so much of him into her mouth?

He noticed where her gaze drifted, and his mouth tilted into a smile at one corner.

"Don't worry, Beth. I'll be ready again soon." And sure enough, within a second or two, his cock did indeed start to twitch and swell before her very eyes.

Oh. Elizabeth pushed a strand of hair away from her face with her free hand. And then shrieked as a sharp spike of panic speared through her. "Oh my God! My hair. There must be pins everywhere." She had to find her hairpins. She couldn't let the staff find them all over the floor. What would they think?

Elizabeth knew exactly what they'd think and as much as she didn't want it to matter, it still did.

She hastily placed the wine glass down on the hearth and began to crawl about the floor, looking and feeling for the pieces of thin wire. Rothsburgh was laughing. Aside from hearing his low chuckle, out of the corner of her eye she could also see him bending forward at the waist, his ridged stomach muscles contracting with mirth.

She shot him a glare. "Don't laugh. Help me, God damn you."

He immediately bit his lip, clearly trying to look contrite, but failing abysmally. Laughter still danced in his dark brown eyes. "I'm sorry, Beth. I'll help. It's just that after what you and I just did... Well, it's amusing to see you scrabbling about so." He roughly buttoned his breeches and then joined her on hands and knees, and within a few minutes, they had a small pile of a dozen hairpins.

She frowned then looked at Rothsburgh. "Thank you. But there were more, I think."

"They're probably in the drawing room near the piano. I did make a frightful mess of your hair when I kissed you the first time. I'll get them."

He returned within half a minute, brandishing the wayward pins and deposited them in her hand, amusement still tugging at the corner of his mouth. She slipped them into her gown's pocket along with the others, trying to think of something both witty and cutting to say, but in the end, she simply smiled back at him. She couldn't have explained why, but she suddenly felt uncommonly happy.

Rothsburgh's eyes suddenly softened, and he reached out to tuck another errant lock of hair behind her ear. "Beth, I would love to take out the rest of those pins. Would you let me?"

"Of course, my lord... I mean James," she said softly, quite mesmerized by his heavily muscled chest and arms as he moved a step closer. He gently pushed his fingers into the wild tumbling mass of her hair, searching for pins and releasing the snags, until her disheveled locks fell freely across her shoulders and down her back.

"Perfect," he murmured, then bent and placed a gentle, almost chaste kiss upon her lips.

Surprisingly, even though her earlier brazen behavior should preclude her from doing so, Elizabeth blushed. Perhaps because of his praise, perhaps because of the caring, more intimate sentiment with which he had bestowed the kiss. She wasn't sure, but she suddenly felt quite vulnerable being bathed by his warm regard. She was reminded of the time he had felt her forehead for fever, and it suddenly occurred to her why she found these more tender moments difficult to deal with. They reminded her of what she had been missing for so long in her life, and what she could never, ever contemplate sharing with James.

Love.

Elizabeth didn't know how long this affair would last, but if she had any sense at all, she would break it off and start again somewhere else, sooner rather than later, before she felt too much for this man.

That's where the real danger had lain all along.

"Why are you suddenly so sad, my angel?" James stroked her flushed cheek with the back of his hand, pulling her from her maudlin thoughts.

She summoned a smile. "It's nothing." She placed her right hand gently against the wide plane of his chest, then raked her fingernails lightly across his hot skin, watching his nipples pucker. He'd said that he was going to do something else with her... "I'm just wondering what is going to come next."

He grasped her hand and raised it to his lips. And then frowned. "Beth, your wedding ring..."

"I-I took it off," she explained, trying to keep her tone light, to minimize the significance of such an act. "After I made my decision—to be with you—it didn't seem right to wear it anymore. I mean, I don't *want* to wear it anymore."

"I'm honored," he said gravely, holding her gaze. Then quite deliberately he raised her ring finger to his mouth and drew it inside, sucking it gently and laving it with his tongue, his eyes never leaving hers. She gasped at the flagrant intimacy, the delicious wickedness of what he did as liquid warmth flooded her lower belly and made her slick between the legs.

Somehow, she managed to make her voice work. "I think it's time for whatever it is that you want to do next, my lord."

~

"I agree whole-heartedly, my dear lady. And I think we should retire to your bedchamber so I can show you exactly what I have in mind."

Beth raised her delicately arched eyebrows a fraction. "My bedchamber?"

Rothsburgh grinned. "Well, I don't mind undressing you here..."

"All right, all right. My bedchamber then." Beth blushed again and looked more than a little flustered.

He decided he liked it when she blushed. And he intended to make her blush a whole lot more before the night was through.

He retrieved his shirt from the floor and tossed it on. Although most of the staff would have probably retired for the night by now, it wouldn't do to be seen striding around the castle in a shirtless state in the company of a disheveled Mrs. Eliott.

"Come," he said, taking her hand and tugging her toward the door. He knew he was being impatient and demanding, but he really didn't want to waste another minute of this precious night. Beth followed him willingly though, through the gallery, up the stairs and along the hall until they were in her room.

He locked the door and turned to face her, his beautiful Beth.

Her hand was still in his, but he felt her fingers imperceptibly stiffen, and he noticed she was breathing quickly. Was it from the exertion of rushing up the stairs?

Or nerves...?

Yes, she was looking nervous. Even by the low light cast by the fire and candles, Rothsburgh could see the shadows of worry behind her wide gray eyes. Confusion tugged at his brain. After everything she had done to him—she clearly wasn't a novice, and she'd been married for Christ's sake—why was she suddenly looking so uneasy? Whatever the reason, he was clearly going to have to proceed cautiously, gently...slowly.

"Beth," he murmured, bringing her hand to his chest. And then he leaned forward and kissed her oh so softly. A brief, light touch only.

Her lips moved to return the kiss, but when he drew back, he could see she was still edgy.

Tilting her chin gently upward, he searched her eyes. "Are you having second thoughts about this...about us?" He couldn't hide the concern lacing through his voice. It would kill him if she pulled away now.

"No...I mean... I suppose I'm just a little nervous. I've never been with anyone else. And it's been such a long time... Months—in fact, practically forever—since I last..." A pink blush bloomed across Beth's cheeks as her voice trailed away.

"Ah." Why hadn't he thought of that himself? Rothsburgh carefully cradled Beth's face in his hands. He would kiss away her doubts and her resistance. He was certain he could. He had to. "We'll take it slowly then. I'll stop at any time...if you want me to. Although I might die in the process."

She smiled at that. "Well, we wouldn't want that, now."

Taking her response as an encouraging sign, Rothsburgh

stroked his thumbs along the sensitive flesh below her ears and was rewarded with a shiver. "I just want you to remember, Beth, that this time, my pleasure is your pleasure."

~

Elizabeth's breath caught at his words, and a deep thrill coursed through her, all the way to her very bones.

Her pleasure.

Hugh had never cared about her pleasure. Before he'd grown bored, he had taken from her, and had always left her wanting. But Rothsburgh—James—wanted her to experience pleasure.

"Show me," she whispered.

James did not hesitate. His mouth was on hers in the next instant, his lips and tongue caressing and teasing her gently. She tasted him back—the faint taste of Burgundy and the moist sliding heat of his mouth, the smell of his skin, all melded together and flooded her senses. When he pulled away she almost moaned with disappointment and she realized she had become hopelessly addicted to his kisses already.

He pulled her over toward the bed, his eyes dark and mysterious, locked on her face. "Turn around Beth," he said, his voice a deep, rich purr.

She immediately acquiesced. Sweeping her hair across one shoulder, he placed his lips on the nape of her neck, and she gasped at the feather-light contact. Her skin was so sensitive, she could feel goosebumps everywhere, and her nipples contracted to hard aching points. He slid the jet buttons of her horrid, bombazine gown undone, kissing the length of her spine, down to the edge of her shift and stays. His large, warm hands then slid across her shoulders and down her arms, easing the stiff black fabric away from her body until the gown fell to the floor.

Then his clever mouth was back at her neck, tracing a line of kisses from there up to one ear, and then down along her shoulder whilst his hands floated lightly over the bare skin of her arms, creating tingles of exquisite sensation wherever he brushed. He was taking his time with her, but it was fast becoming torturous when her very core was throbbing with anticipation. She almost couldn't bear it. She needed more.

She turned her head to the side. "My stays...please..."

His lips spread into a smile upon her skin. "Now, now. Patience, my dear Beth." His breath was hot against her sensitized flesh. Who would have thought that words and breath could themselves be a caress?

Nevertheless, he heeded her plea, and she felt him pulling the laces undone until the lightly boned corset joined her gown on the floor. Before he could stop her—he was not having it all his own way—Elizabeth turned around and pulled his head down for another kiss. This time he wasn't so gentle with her, and she reveled in the knowledge that perhaps she was tempting him to lose his control just a little bit too.

His hands came to rest on her waist, then pressed up and over her ribs until his palms found her aching breasts at last. She moaned softly into his mouth as he pulled and rolled her nipples with his fingers and thumbs through the thin linen and lace of her shift. Was this pleasure or the sweetest of tortures? Whatever it was, she didn't want it to stop.

He fumbled with the ribbon at the front of her shift, and she raised her hands and tugged it loose for him, impatient for his hands to be on her. But he didn't push his hands beneath the sagging linen, he took a step back, then pulled the garment over her head before tossing it away.

Now she was naked except for her silk stockings and slippers. She blushed, holding her breath and stole a look at James's face. Would he think her beautiful? She so didn't want to see the desire fade from his eyes.

But she needn't have worried. He was gazing at her, his eyes tracing her curves and hollows with a potent combination of awe and hunger.

Yes. There was definitely hunger. His eyes were molten black. She shivered, her nipples pebbling.

And then he smiled, his wide, perfect lips stretching into a lazy, lopsided tilt. "I would say you were a vision straight from heaven, except for the fact that you are as tempting as sin, my love."

My love. Surely he didn't mean that. He'd only used the endearment in the heat of the moment. Elizabeth confirmed her supposition when she glanced at his eyes and saw they were still smoldering with unabashed lust. Indeed, the air around them was heavy with it.

It had never been like this with Hugh. But she didn't want to think about Hugh anymore.

All she wanted to think about was James. And that was proving very easy to do as he cupped her breasts, and then lowered his head to suckle on one achingly tense nipple then the other. His teeth, and tongue, and lips were working her into a frenzied agony that was coalescing into one throbbing point between her thighs. Head thrown back with her eyes closed, she could barely stand, and clung to his iron hard biceps lest her knees buckle beneath her.

As if attuned to the havoc he was so happily wreaking upon her, James suddenly wrapped an arm around her waist, and with the other cradling her buttocks, he lifted her and bore her backward onto the bed, all the way up to the pillows. She opened her eyes and saw that he was looming over her, smiling his slow, lazy smile again.

Damn him, he was enjoying this far too much.

"I think you are a tad over dressed for bed sport," she managed to say, although her voice was little more than a husky whisper. She wanted to touch him again, feel the steel and heat of him under her hands and against her body.

But he simply grinned. "Well, perhaps I shall dispense with my boots for now. I wouldn't want these bed clothes to get too dirty." He moved to the side of the bed, and she heard the clunk of heavy leather on the floor. Somehow, she had already managed to lose her slippers, but her stockings had stayed in placed.

It was something James noticed too, as soon as he returned to her side. He loosened the ribbon garters, and then slowly peeled off each stocking in turn, his hands running over her legs all the way down to the tips of her toes.

"Even your ankles and feet are beautiful, Beth." Cradling one foot in his hands, he then glanced up at her with a mischievous gleam in his eyes.

Oh no. Surely he wasn't going to—

But he did. *He was.* He trailed a path of kisses from her calf to the arch of her foot. She squirmed, but he had her firmly trapped in his grasp. With horrified fascination, she watched him kiss her toes in turn until he arrived at her big toe and sucked it into his mouth. She cried out and bucked, but he didn't let go. It was wrong, it was depraved.

It was delicious.

By the time he'd finished with her other foot, she was nothing but a quivering mass upon the bed.

"This is what you call pleasure?" she panted, looking at him dazedly through half-closed lids. She tried to look affronted, but she knew that she probably looked anything but that.

"Not even close," he whispered, shifting back up the bed toward her head. Lying alongside her, he propped himself up on one elbow before leisurely running a finger from the indentation between her collar bones, down the valley between her heaving breasts, then along her abdomen to her navel...where he stopped. She sensed his gaze on her face again, and she glanced up at him. He was studying her, and a lump formed in her throat. The look in his eyes...it was almost as if he cared for her.

She swallowed. She couldn't stand the intensity of his gaze. It hurt to see such naked emotion. Yes, that's what it was. He was looking at her as if his heart was in his eyes.

"James," she breathed, and brushed a lock of silky black hair back from his forehead. "What is it?"

The expression in his gaze immediately lightened and his mouth tipped into a rakish smile. "I'm just planning what I'm going to do next."

Before she could do or say anything else, he dipped his head and kissed her, and the poignant spell that had surrounded them both, instantly dissipated. He cradled her jaw with one hand while the other began to tease her breasts again, but it didn't stay there long. His fingers swept lower, and then he was cupping the aching mound of her sex. And then one long finger slid between her slick folds—she was so wet, she was almost embarrassed—and with a deftness she should have found quite shocking, he found the very center of her being and stroked, around and around. And with that one touch her world exploded.

She arched her back and cried out as a lightning bolt of absolute pleasure ignited her body from somewhere deep within and shot charge after charge through her until eventually she melted back against the covers of the bed, completely spent, floating on a still, black velvet sea.

The word "pleasure" did not even begin to describe what she had just experienced. She couldn't even think how to define what James had done for her. She felt as if she'd been tossed up to heaven. And given the blissful feeling that was still spreading through her entire body, she rather thought she was still there.

She wasn't sure how long she drifted in this state, but suddenly, she was aware of James stretching out beside her again. But something was different.

This time he was naked.

Her eyes flew open. The glorious vision stretched out beside her was enough to jolt her out of her languor. She rolled toward James so her skin was pressed to his, his long, fully erect cock pressing into her belly like a silken-sheathed rod of iron. He was so hot and hard all over, such a perfect specimen of masculine power and beauty, that her body began to thrum with anticipation again, and she felt a fresh rush of slick heat between her thighs.

She raised a hand and ran it lightly from one broad shoulder, down his heavily muscled arm, across one lean hip to his firm buttock—and paused when her fingers came into contact with a long raised ridge—a scar—that slashed downward across the back of his thigh. To her mortification, she couldn't suppress her gasp of surprise in time.

James's hand covered hers and his brow creased with concern. "I should have warned you about my battle scar, Beth. Although it's far from pretty, I was lucky compared to most."

She swallowed. "Does it still hurt? I'm sorry if I—"

"No, it doesn't hurt. It was mainly superficial damage from a bayonet that I didn't see coming." His mouth quirked into a wry smile. "Believe me, the Frenchman responsible for my injury looked a lot worse at the end of the altercation than I did."

She frowned. "You make light of it. I don't understand how you can do that."

James gently raised her hand from where it had been resting on the back of his leg and brought it to his lips. "You are helping me to forget," he said in a low voice, and his eyes revealed such a raw, emotional intensity that Elizabeth felt she

165

was really seeing him for the first time. "Since you came here, all I can think about is you, Beth. You are like a balm for my soul. It's not just wanting. I need you. And I just thought you should know that."

He gently pushed her down onto the mattress, covering her body with his, and kissed her with such gentle reverence, she had to close her eyes against the sudden sting of tears. A rising tide of conflicting emotions she hadn't bargained on feeling suddenly threatened to overwhelm her.

This relationship—if one could even call it that—it was only supposed to be about sexual gratification. About satisfying their mutual carnal urges. So why did it suddenly feel like it was more than that?

An acute longing surged through Elizabeth's foolish heart at the thought that James needed her for more than the use of her body. She had never been *needed* by anyone before, least of all Hugh. The knowledge was powerful yet humbling at the same time.

But overriding all of these sensations was the sharp stab of her guilty conscience. James seemed to be exposing his very soul to her, and he didn't even know her real name, let alone that she was married. He had been unexpectedly candid with her, and all she had done, and would continue to do, was lie to him.

Her duplicity threatened to rise up and choke her.

"Are you all right, Beth?" James had pulled away and was staring down at her with concern.

"Yes," she whispered, not able to meet his eyes.

He lifted her chin so she couldn't avoid his gaze. "I promise I won't get you with child, if that's what you're worried about. I should have mentioned it earlier. But even if it's not that, I'll stop if you want me too."

Elizabeth shook her head and placed a trembling hand on the expanse of his chest where his heart lay. "No, it's not that. I trust that you'll be careful. And I definitely don't want you to stop." She reached up and touched his jaw. "I need you too."

It wasn't much, but at least that wasn't a lie. It was all she had to offer.

James's mouth suddenly tipped into a sensual smile and one of his large hands closed over her breast. "I'm so glad you said that, my sweet."

He pushed his impressive erection against her belly, and she arched her back slightly, reveling in the feel of him sliding against her skin. How would it feel when he was inside her? She began to part her legs beneath him, suddenly impatient with the overpowering need for him to fill her.

"Soon, my angel, soon," he whispered against her ear. "I don't want to go too quickly in case I hurt you." He suddenly lowered his head and suckled her taut nipples in turn, whilst one of his hands slid between her legs. His fingers stroked her already dripping folds, teased her aching core, making her writhe and moan all over again. She opened her legs even more, and he slid two fingers deep within her to stroke her passage, and a desperate sound—something between a cry and a deep guttural groan—escaped her throat.

"James," she moaned. "Please... I want you—"

He covered her mouth with his, thrusting his tongue deeply as he pushed her legs slightly farther apart with his own. And then, at last, she felt the head of his cock nudging where his talented fingers had been only moments before.

He pushed into her with a long slow thrust, and despite her readiness and willingness, she cried out at the sudden unfamiliar incursion, the intense burning friction. It had been so long since she'd had sexual relations, and James was so big, much bigger than Hugh. She realized she was panting, her breath a frantic rasp against James's shoulder.

James immediately stopped and stroked her face. "Beth, do you want me to stop?"

"No..." She tried to smile through the discomfort. "As I said before, it's been a while. I just...need a moment. That's all." She secretly prayed that she was right. She couldn't bear it if she didn't enjoy this, and that her worst fears would be confirmed after all: that there was something wrong with her. Or that James was too big for her. That all this had been for naught.

"Of course." James stayed perfectly still, resting on his forearms so that he was suspended above her body. She could see how much this cessation of movement cost him. He was gritting his teeth, and the thick tendons of his neck stood out. She closed her eyes and deliberately tried to relax her protesting muscles. She adjusted the angle of her hips slightly and wrapped her legs around his. The intense pressure immediately began to ease.

James seemed to notice too. "Better?" he murmured against her temple.

"Much." She arched her back, encouraging him to move again, and with a shuddering groan he surged all the way into her to the hilt of his iron-hard shaft.

"Aaah." Her cry of agonized pleasure was loud even to her own ears. She gripped his shoulders as he buried his face in her neck.

"Beth," he panted. "Oh, God... You feel like heaven."

He flexed his hips backward, slowly withdrawing, and this time the sliding friction was exquisite. He thrust into her again, and her hips pushed back against him, the muscles of her inner sheath greedily clenching around his hot, hard flesh, not wanting to let him go.

Yes.

He started to stroke in and out of her with a surer, steadier rhythm, and for the first time ever, Elizabeth began to feel something—a deep coiling tension that pulled tighter and tighter as James thrust faster and harder. *Yes.* This was what she had been missing. *Yes.* This pleasure that almost bordered on pain. She clawed at James's back and her ragged gasps mingled with his equally frenzied breathing. This feeling couldn't go on much longer. She almost couldn't bear it, this white-hot whirlwind of sensation.

She screamed as her womb suddenly convulsed, and she was lost in a storm of blinding ecstasy, as wave after wave of spasmodic pleasure coursed through her. She was lost, yet she'd never felt more whole or alive in her life.

She was barely conscious of James tearing himself from her and calling her name as he shuddered with his own release on the bed beside her. One of his heavy arms was flung across her belly. The smell of his seed, her musk, and their sweat mingled to create the intoxicating scent of desire fulfilled.

She had to swallow past a sudden lump in her throat. James had shown her all that she had been missing. And it had been glorious. So why did she suddenly feel like crying?

Because he is everything you've ever wanted and this bliss cannot last, her conscience whispered.

And when the time came for this to be over, as it had to be, she rather suspected someone's heart would be broken. Perhaps hers had even started to crack a little already.

Rothsburgh lay face down beside Beth, gasping and sweating, and so damned replete, so beyond satisfied, he could barely think. In his long history of carnal indulgence, he'd had all types of amazing bed sport. But this, what he had just shared with Beth, had transcended every single one of his past experiences.

And the reason for that decided difference, he definitely didn't want to think about.

He turned his head to the side to steal a glance at her, this woman that affected him like no other. She was lying on her back, her blond hair spreading in tousled abandon over her naked breasts. His arm still lay possessively across her slender torso.

His.

Beth was his at last. Perhaps that was the reason—simple as it was—that he felt the way he did. He'd wanted this woman for weeks, and now that she'd agreed to be with him and he'd sampled her abundant delights, he felt like the richest, indeed the most blessed man alive.

Too spent to do anything else for the moment, he let his eyes drink in the sight of her. And he thought he'd never seen her look as beautiful as she did right now. His gaze wandered across her perfect face—her eyes were still closed and her cheeks were flushed—down to her luscious breasts, their rosy peaks rising and falling with her breathing, just beckoning him to take them into his mouth again. Despite his bone-deep satiation, he felt his cock begin to stiffen at the thought.

He knew it wouldn't be long before he had her again.

He had no doubt she had reached her peak more than once, and the base male in him was gratified no end that he had satisfied her so well. Indeed, he'd never known another lover to be so aroused and responsive. He was in awe of the fact that when he'd touched her sex for the very first time, she had come almost immediately. And then when he'd first pushed inside her, he had felt her clench so tightly, so forcefully about him, he'd nearly lost control straightaway.

Rothsburgh smiled to himself, thinking of all the other ways he would make her climax, again and again before the night was over.

He pushed himself up onto one elbow and reached out to caress her face. The back of his fingers touched her flawless skin and then he froze. There were tears on her cheek.

Horror gripped his heart. *Oh no, no, no. Have I done something wrong?*

"What is it, Beth?" His voice sounded strained with a panic he couldn't hide. He couldn't bear it if she hadn't enjoyed the experience. That she would not want to do this again. "Please, tell me I didn't hurt you."

He heard her sigh before she turned her head slightly and looked at him, her eyes shining like liquid pools of moonlight. "No. It's not that at all." She smiled then—a small, sad, almost broken smile that tore at his heart. "I...I have a confession to make..." Her voice was barely above a whisper.

Rothsburgh searched her eyes briefly, trying to find the answer in their solemn depths. What in God's name could she mean? Whatever it was, it was certainly bothering her. It occurred to him that she was about to reveal something deeply personal about herself, which meant perhaps she trusted him a little. And even though anxiety gnawed at him, he also found the idea that she would confide in him more than a little bit pleasing.

She was watching him with the type of expression that suggested she was summoning her courage to speak again. Perhaps it would help if he could lighten the moment. He forced himself to pull a crooked, nonchalant smile.

"Hmm, Mrs. Eliott, it would appear that you have a deep, dark secret." He leaned over her and kissed her lightly on the cheek, tasting her tears before he whispered against her ear. "I'm not sure if a confession sounds ominous or intriguing."

She sucked in a sharp breath, and he drew back just in time to catch a fleeting look of fear in her eyes before her eyelids fluttered downward. "It's about my relationship...with my husband..."

The image of her in the grip of one of her nightmares, calling out to someone to leave her alone, suddenly sprang into Rothsburgh's mind. *Had* her husband abused her? Was that what she was about to tell him? His jaw clenched and his hands fisted. If that was the case, he was sorry the bastard was dead because he'd really love to kill him slowly with his bare hands.

He sought her eyes and steeled himself to ask the question as gently as he could. He had to know. "Beth. Did your husband hurt you? I know you've had bad dreams—when you were unwell—and I've wondered..."

Her eyes widened a fraction and she shook her head. "No... No, it's not that. He never physically abused me if that's what you mean. You've misunderstood me. I've been very unclear. I'm sorry." She closed her eyes for a moment, clearly trying to reassemble her thoughts before she met his gaze again. A shy smile touched her lips and she reached out a hand to cradle his rigid jaw. "I just wanted to tell you that tonight was the first time in my life that I've ever felt...that I've ever had...I mean, you gave me the gift of my first ever truly satisfying sexual experience... and I just wanted to tell you that, James. And to say thank you."

"What?" Holy hell. His jaw dropped. It couldn't be true.

She'd been married for how long? He realized he really didn't know even that basic fact. But regardless of whether it had been a month or several years, how could her husband not have been able to satisfy such an innately sensual, responsive creature? It defied all logic. The man must have been a completely useless dunderhead in bed.

He cleared his throat. "Apologies for my bluntness, Beth, but just so I'm clear, you're actually telling me this is the first time you've ever come?"

"Yes," she said simply, her mouth curving into the same, small broken smile she had given him before. He searched her face and he could see she was utterly sincere.

His poor beautiful Beth. No wonder she had exploded under his touch.

"I'm truly astounded, Beth." But that wasn't quite true. He was more than astounded. He was humbled. His heart swelled with an unfamiliar feeling of tenderness. And for once he welcomed the feeling.

He lowered his mouth to hers and kissed her gently taking his time, savoring her sweetness.

His. Yes, she was undeniably his after a confession like that.

Forcing himself to break the kiss, he caught her gaze again. He needed to say more. He wanted to let her know how much her revelation meant to him. "You do me great honor, Beth, by telling me such a thing. That I am the man that has brought you to climax for the very first time."

She smiled, then rather surprisingly, blushed. "Well, it was twice actually."

He smiled back. "Even better."

He felt his cock stiffen and he gently pressed it against her hip. Her breathing quickened and he saw something spark to life in her eyes.

He had an idea. Instead of kissing her mouth again, he lowered his head and ran a trail of slow, teasing kisses across her flat belly, down to the thatch of blond curls concealing her sex.

"James," she gasped, and he felt her hand grip the back of his head. "You can't..."

He raised his head and smiled his deliberately rakish smile. "Why not?"

"Because..."

He stroked a finger along her cleft. It already glistened with moisture. It appeared she wasn't as perturbed as she seemed. He caught her gaze and licked his finger, pleased to see her blush again. "You tasted me. Now it's my turn." He gently spread her legs and she didn't resist.

"You are quite wicked, you know that, don't you?" she said, but to his relief, there was now laughter in her voice.

"Entirely." He grinned up at her from between her silken thighs, his mouth mere inches from her quivering center. "Now, my sweet angel, lie back and let me see if I can make you come a third time."

~

Elizabeth *almost* lost count of how many times she reached her peak as night turned into early morning. As she lay thoroughly sated in the circle of Lord Rothsburgh's muscular arms, breathing in his now familiar masculine scent, she marveled at the fact that her body was capable of feeling such exquisite sensations over and over again.

All thanks to James—she was almost used to calling him by his first name now. He was...a miracle. She couldn't think of any other way to describe him after what he'd done for her.

Equally amazing to her was the fact that she had been able to completely satisfy a man like him—the very epitome of masculine virility—in return. Her lips curved into a soft smile against the warm, smooth flesh of his bare chest as she recalled how he'd seemed more than happy with her efforts at love-making during the night. She hadn't known that it was possible for a man to be so aroused for so long. It seemed as if he couldn't get enough of her. He made her feel wanted. And powerful in a wholly feminine way, like she was the most desirable woman in the world.

Elizabeth felt like she had been made anew, that she truly was a different creature. That she was indeed deserving of the title "Lord Rothsburgh's mistress."

She'd managed to push away all of her troubled thoughts for the last few hours as she'd given herself over to the completely addictive pursuit of giving and receiving physical pleasure. And given that she could barely keep her eyes open, she was not likely to think about anything at all for a while longer.

The fire in her room was now no more than a pile of red glowing embers, and all but one of the candles had burnt out. Despite the coldness of the predawn, she was warm and content. She snuggled further into James's embrace and let delicious exhaustion begin to claim her.

"Beth." James kissed her temple. "As much as I'd love to stay with you all night, I really should go, my angel. Before the staff are up and about."

Elizabeth's eyes flew open, all traces of sleepiness gone. "Of course," she said, starting to disentangle her legs from his and push away from his side. It wouldn't do for Lord Rothsburgh to be seen exiting her chamber. As it was, there would undoubtedly be raised eyebrows about the injudicious use of candles. James had been able to save the sheets of her bed by catching his seed with his shirt. Though she really didn't want to think about what any of the servants would make of the garment's state.

Rothsburgh caught sight of her naked breasts as the gold damask counterpane fell away and he growled, pulling her on top of him. "On second thought, I don't think I can let you go just yet—"

Panic fluttered in her belly. "James, you're right. You can't stay."

He chuckled softly and brushed a loose strand of her hopelessly disheveled hair behind her ear. "I know, I know, sweet Beth." But he didn't let her go. The amusement in his gaze suddenly ebbed away to be replaced by some other emotion that was more serious, and intense. *Intimate.* "I want you to know that I don't want to leave this bed. I do it only because I know your reputation matters so much to you."

"Thank you," she whispered. "I don't want you to go either—"

He suddenly dragged her down for a ravenous, open mouthed, soul-searing kiss. When he pulled away, his gaze trapped hers. His eyes were a burning, ferocious black. "Then let's leave here, Beth. As soon as the tide is out, let me take you away from here, to Edinburgh or Bath or London. Wherever you want to go, my love. Then we needn't give a toss about what anyone else thinks. I will buy you a house, jewels. Whatever your heart desires. Let me worship you, Beth."

Terror seized Elizabeth. She couldn't leave here. Here was safe. Here she was hidden. Even though James was looking at her with such expectation and wonder, she just couldn't accede to his request. The risk of discovery was too great. If anyone from the *ton* caught a glimpse of her, Hugh would find out. And he would come for her.

But James wanted to treat her like a queen. A goddess...

No. No, matter how tempting his offer, she couldn't accept. Not when certain danger and ruin lay ahead.

Oh, but how hard it was to turn her back on the gateway to Paradise.

"Beth?" James caressed her cheek with gentle fingers.

Elizabeth felt breathless, as if there was a great weight upon her chest, but somehow she managed to drag in enough air to speak. "I-I am honored, my lord. I mean, James. But living like that...in such prominent splendor. That is not me. I don't think... I mean, I can't do it. I'm sorry... I just can't do it."

James frowned. He raised a hand and cradled her cheek. "Shhh, my sweet Beth. It's all right. If you want to stay here, we will...for now. And I promise we'll be careful around the castle staff." He gave her a crooked smile. "I'm afraid you'll soon realize that I'm a very selfish man though. When I want something, I set out to get it. And make no mistake, it won't be long before I'll want you in my bed every night, all night. Hell, to be perfectly honest I'm going to want you all day as well, bed or no bed." He ran his thumb over her bottom lip and his voice, when he spoke again, was husky with need. "I just want you, Beth."

He kissed her again, but tenderly this time, and rolled her body beneath his. Elizabeth felt his manhood harden against her belly, but he didn't press her for more. Even though she was grateful to him for being so solicitous, part of her—the wanton part—wanted him to stay.

"Goodnight, or should I say good morning, my beautiful mistress," James murmured against her cheek. He raised himself and rolled away from her, and she immediately noticed the absence of his warm lean body. It was as if a piece of herself had suddenly been detached.

The cold light of early dawn was already beginning to gild the edges around the curtains as she watched James pull on his breeches and boots.

"Stay in bed for as long as you like today," he said, retrieving his crumpled and well-used shirt from between the twisted sheets. "I'll tell the staff you've had a relapse." He then flashed her a wide grin. "I want you to regain your strength for tonight, my sweet Beth."

She pushed herself up and reached out to touch his jaw, enjoying the heat of his skin and prickle of stubble against her fingertips. She couldn't deny she was beginning to care for this man, far more than she should. And she suspected he felt the same way. It seemed as if there was nothing that either of them could do to stop themselves from slipping beneath a rising tide of uncontrollable emotion. And for her, despite all of the risks, the urge to dive in was irresistible.

She suddenly wanted James to know something about her that was true. She caught his gaze. "Elizabeth," she whispered. "My given name is actually Elizabeth."

James smiled with such tenderness, her breath hitched. "Hmm. Be that as it may, I think Beth suits you better, my love." He kissed her once more, with gentle swiftness, and then he was gone.

My love. How many times had he called her that tonight? That was something Elizabeth had definitely lost count of. As she curled up in the bedclothes still warm from where James's body had just lain, she suddenly wished with all her foolish heart that it really could be true.

That she could actually be his love.

CHAPTER 13

Over the next week, despite her nightly lack of sleep and subsequent exhaustion, Elizabeth knew that she glowed with a certain indefinable something. She saw it when she looked in the mirror every morning. Her eyes shone softy, as if lit from within, and she couldn't seem to stop smiling.

Others seemed to notice the change in her too. Mrs. Roberts smiled at her knowingly whenever Elizabeth went into the kitchen to discuss the day's menu. Roberts even winked at her when he passed her in the hallway one day. Of course, Elizabeth had blushed, but it truly did seem that Lord Rothsburgh had been correct when he had originally asserted that his staff would not condemn her. It felt quite bizarre that others would be so accepting of the fact she was the marquess's mistress, especially when she could hardly believe it herself.

Thankfully, James did not press her again on the subject of quitting Eilean Tor and installing her somewhere else as his mistress proper. Instead, they had fallen very quickly and easily into a mutually satisfying pattern of existence. James spent every night in her bed—although sleep was the furthest thing from their minds—until the morning light began to creep into her room. Then she would rise late and go through the charade of pretending to be just the housekeeper with only domestic matters on her mind, when really all she could think about was James and his lovemaking.

But then James gave her little time to think of anything else. Highly important and "confidential" discussions on household management behind locked doors invariably turned into something else entirely. She quickly learned that one didn't just make love in a bed, but that desks, dining room tables, window seats, battlements, and even piano stools could all be used in a number of unconventional ways to perform sexual feats that she had never dreamed of.

Elizabeth had also given up using a copious amount of hair pins to secure her coiffure. Braiding and twisting her hair into a tight knot at the nape of her neck with only the barest number of pins turned out be the only sensible way to ensure she didn't leave a trail of them all over the castle. Not that it really mattered, given it was obvious what James and she were up to. But the conservative side of her still wanted to pretend she was a decent woman.

One of the unexpected delights of this arrangement was that Elizabeth experienced—for the first time in her adult life—the simple pleasure of being with a man who obviously enjoyed her company. James regarded her as an intelligent equal in conversation. Her opinion mattered to him. Sharing banter, engaging in discussions about anything and everything, even trying to trounce James at chess—he was a formidable player—all were equally stimulating and enjoyable. Hugh had rarely even given her the time of day.

The only testing part of the whole scenario was taking care to avoid slips of the tongue about who she really was. She had manufactured a history for herself—that she was the well-educated, middle-class daughter of a university lecturer from

Oxford. When she came of age, she had then married the younger son—Lieutenant George Eliott—of an equally middle-class family. However, she needn't have worried. Despite James's pronouncement that he wanted to know everything about her, he never pressed her for information, and she never volunteered more than the barest and vaguest of details. And that suited her no end.

Her secrets were safe.

As for Lord Rothsburgh, he seemed...smitten. Elizabeth could think of no other word to describe the way James looked at her, although she tried to tell herself it was only ever lust she saw in his gaze. His appetite for her seemed insatiable, like he was a newly wedded groom. He was everything that she had once hoped Hugh would be—attentive, witty, teasing, tender...

Loving.

The irony that James was everything she'd ever wanted in a husband was indeed bittersweet.

If only these halcyon days could last.

That was the thought that drifted through Elizabeth's bliss-fogged mind as she lay spent and gasping upon one of the chaise lounges in the drawing room, her skirts pushed indecorously up around her waist. James's head lay upon her naked lower belly, his warm breath caressing her oh-so sensitive flesh. She pushed her fingers into his silky black hair and caressed the nape of his neck, enjoying the feel of bone, strong muscles and tendons beneath her fingertips.

It was early afternoon and their lunch lay cold and neglected upon the small dining table in the library. She rather doubted that it would get eaten at all.

Who needs food when one can feel like this?

But she shouldn't feel like this. Despite the untold, heady satisfaction she derived from being Lord Rothsburgh's mistress, her guilt—for forsaking her marriage vows and deceiving James—followed her like an ever-present shadow. She was able to push it aside temporarily whenever she and James made love. But in quiet moments such as this, after the ecstasy had ebbed away and sanity returned, it settled over her again like a heavy pall.

Before her troubled thoughts could envelope her completely, James sat up and leaned over her to place a lingering kiss upon her mouth. Raising his head, his eyes gleamed with mischievous intent, and she knew he had something else in mind to while away the afternoon.

"I think, my sweet Beth, that we should—"

An unexpected knock at the drawing room door made her start.

James scowled. "Damn," he muttered when the knocking continued.

Then Roberts's voice could be heard. "Forgive me, milord," called the butler. "I wouldna interrupt unless it 'twere of some importance."

With an exasperated sigh, James helped Elizabeth to stand and straighten her skirts. She then quickly adjusted his cravat and smoothed his rumpled hair.

"Thank goodness we didn't undress," she whispered with a smile, attempting to lighten James's mood.

"Humph. Roberts better have a good reason for this," he said gruffly. He kissed her cheek then called out. "I'll meet you in the library in a moment, Roberts." Clasping her face between his hands, James kissed her again, soundly. "Stay here, my love, while I sort this out. I promise I won't be long."

After the connecting door to the library clicked shut, Elizabeth wandered over to one of the windows to gaze at the vast, lonely expanse of sea and sky. It was a blowy, overcast afternoon and the sea's dull pewter surface was broken by choppy white-capped waves. The elements and the sea seemed as unsettled as her thoughts.

Pressing her hand to one of the smooth diamond panes, the biting cold of the day penetrated the glass and made Elizabeth shiver. She suspected it wouldn't be long before the first snows fell. It would undoubtedly be a bleak and cold existence here during the seemingly endless winter. Unless you had a lover to keep you occupied.

But how long should she stay? The question weighed heavily upon Elizabeth, perhaps even more heavily than her guilt.

When she'd impulsively given into the temptation to become James's mistress, she had told herself that this affair should only be short-lived. But now that winter was coming, she needed to seriously contemplate the question: how long should she remain at Eilean Tor? Or more to the point: how long should she continue to be James's lover?

Another week? Two weeks? Should she go before the castle became snowbound and it was impossible to leave for months? Months in which her entire existence would become so enmeshed with James's that when it was time for her to go, it would hurt both of them, deeply.

Perhaps she should go now, before the fallen woman she was fell any further in love.

There. She'd finally admitted it to herself.

She'd fallen in love with Lord Rothsburgh. Hopelessly, foolishly, madly.

She'd tried so hard to deny the emotion building up inside her since she'd arrived here almost a month ago. But now, she just couldn't. It suffused her being, had changed the very fabric of who she was. Although she'd become James's mistress to experience fulfilling sexual congress at least once in her life, it wasn't just about that anymore. And because she cared so deeply for this man, she suspected that was why her deceit bothered her more than ever.

Part of Elizabeth prayed that she would soon hear word of

another governess's situation from James's sister, Lady Maxwell, because then she would have no choice but to leave. Even though it would be difficult, she knew that ultimately it was best for her sake as well as James's if she did just that—go —sooner, rather than later.

Before James felt too much for her as well. Because nothing could come of this. Because she wasn't free. To wish for anything more was like wishing for the stars, the sun, and the moon to be laid at her feet.

It was, quite simply, impossible.

Tired of staring at the gray day with only her circling, troubled thoughts for company, Elizabeth abandoned the window seat and settled herself before the pianoforte. Closing her eyes, she emptied her mind and let her fingers find the notes for her favorite Mozart work—the second *andante* movement of his hauntingly lovely Piano Concerto No. 21.

She'd perhaps made her way through the first half of the piece when she was suddenly roused by the sound of unfamiliar voices—loud male voices—that carried through the closed library door. As Elizabeth paused to listen, the door burst open and a strange man virtually fell into the room. He grabbed the back of a chair to keep from falling, then eyed her with a peculiar mix of male appreciation and consternation.

"Good God, Rossburgh...Where'd the hell didshou find this beauty?"

James suddenly appeared in the doorway, looking like thunder. "Blaire," he growled and seized the obviously exceedingly drunk gentleman by the scruff of his neck like a stray cat before thrusting him back into the library.

The marquess then turned to Elizabeth and bowed his head. "I'm so sorry, Mrs. Eliott, for Lord Blaire's...interruption," he said quite loudly, then he mouthed, "Are you all right?" His gaze lingered on her face, assessing her, his brow furrowed with concern.

Elizabeth forced herself to appear outwardly calm, relieved that the piano shielded her white knuckled grip on the edge of the keyboard. "It's quite all right I assure you, Lord Rothsburgh," she said stiffly. Although, she was quietly amazed that she could speak at all given that panic had stolen her breath, and her heart had leapt into the vicinity of her mouth.

Were these men James's friends? Friends from the *ton*? Good Lord in heaven, did any of them know her?

The name Blaire seemed vaguely familiar. Elizabeth prayed he wasn't one of Hugh's cronies that she may have met before. She hadn't immediately recognized the inebriated, disheveled nobleman who had so unceremoniously burst in. Nor had he seemed to recognize her. But then he was horrendously drunk.

But what of the others?

Through the open doorway came the murmur of other voices again, but for the moment, no one else appeared, foxed or otherwise.

James nodded once, seemingly satisfied with her response. She must have hidden her fear well enough. "Perhaps you could prepare three of the guest rooms and see to tonight's menu, Mrs. Eliott. Lord Maxwell and Lord Markham have also decided to pay me a visit. It seems we have an impromptu hunting party on our hands."

Lord Maxwell. That must be James's brother-in-law. Elizabeth wondered if he had news of another situation for her. But would James even tell her now that he seemed so taken with her? And she wouldn't dare ask Lord Maxwell herself. That would be much too forward.

The name Markham she didn't know at all. Perhaps everything would be all right. If only she could be sure about Lord Blaire though...

James was frowning at her. Too caught up in her own tumultuous musings, Elizabeth hadn't acknowledged his request. She nodded slightly and dragged in a much-needed breath before she spoke again. "Yes...my lord. I will take care of everything."

James turned toward the library, but then paused on the threshold and glanced back at her.

"I'm sorry," he mouthed, his dark eyes shadowed with something akin to regret before he disappeared.

Elizabeth stared at the closed library door and tried to control the wave of panic rising within her. She had never anticipated anything like this happening—that James's *tonnish* acquaintances would venture to this far-flung place. She had foolishly thought she could disappear, become someone else. But was one of her worst nightmares about to come true? Would she be exposed and would Hugh find her and reclaim her? If her husband found her...

Elizabeth shuddered. She couldn't bear to think what he would do to her.

The only reality that could be worse than that horrific turn of events would be that James discovered her duplicity. And that his regard for her would then die and be replaced by censure. Being the sinner that she was, she could hardly pray that it wouldn't be so. Because when all was said and done, James's condemnation would be exactly what she deserved.

Perhaps she should leave Eilean Tor right now.

But where would she go? Even an offer of another situation via Lord Maxwell would do her no good if it was discovered she was the Countess of Beauchamp. The only thing that was clear to her right now was that her mind was awhirl and she couldn't think straight. Making rash decisions wasn't going to help. She needed to calm down.

Elizabeth rose from the stool, and with shaking hands, closed the pianoforte's lid. Maybe she was over-reacting. Maybe Lord Blaire had only been a passing acquaintance, a society buck she had once danced with as a debutante. Or someone from Hugh's club. In any case, he certainly wasn't someone well known to her. The only sensible thing she could feasibly do was to try and remain as unobtrusive as possible for the duration of the hunting party. Her self-preservation was paramount.

Aside from no more pianoforte playing, there mustn't be any more liaisons with James whatsoever. And—oh, God—she really must move rooms, straightaway.

Housekeepers didn't sleep only a few doors away from the lord of the castle. Even if James's friends never deduced that she was Lord Beauchamp's wife, they would soon know she was Lord Rothsburgh's mistress. And she couldn't abide that either.

As Elizabeth frantically checked all the buttons on her bodice and smoothed her hair, she realized that underneath her fear, another feeling lurked. A deep disappointment was settling within her like a sinking stone.

She was simply the housekeeper again. She knew it had to be this way whilst James was entertaining guests. And of course, the distance between them would be nothing but artifice. But nevertheless, it would hurt to see cool indifference in her lover's gaze when she had grown used to him looking at her with such desire and dare she say it, affection? But then, wasn't she going to hurt him anyway? And she would probably see a lot worse than indifference in James's eyes when the time came to desert him.

Elizabeth closed her eyes tightly for a long moment to stem the unexpected welling of tears. Her fear of being discovered combined with this emerging feeling of desolation, and the certain knowledge that she must leave—all of it was almost too much to bear.

You'd best get used to this, Elizabeth. This is how it will feel to be the hired help again.

And you don't have time to wallow in self-pity. You have things to do and plans to make. So just get on with it.

Elizabeth dashed away her tears then huffed out a determined breath. First of all, she'd need to secure help to relocate her things to the servants' quarters before she even thought about carrying out Lord Rothsburgh's instructions. She quit the drawing room to search for Roberts and Maisie...only to almost bump into the butler. Roberts had obviously been hovering by the door in the hall outside.

"Mrs. Eliott, I'm so verra sorry to have startled you." His face was bright red with an uncharacteristic flush and he couldn't quite meet her eyes. "I was just comin' to see you, to let you know tha' yer things are bein' taken to the servants' quarters as we speak. Maisie is settin' up a room fer you. I didna think you would mind given the change in...circumstances."

"That's quite all right, Roberts." Elizabeth tried very hard not to blush herself. "That is most sensible. I am most grateful for your...foresight."

"Verra good, Mrs. Eliott." The butler offered her a smile, and then at last met her gaze, his expression sincere. "Although it isna really my place to say so, I just wanted to let you know tha' it is verra good to have you here. His lordship... Let me just say tha' in all my time at the castle, I havena seen Lord Rothsburgh lookin' so weel. Ever. An' it's all thanks to you."

Before she could say anything else, the butler inclined his head then retreated down the corridor. No doubt he had countless other duties to attend to as well. Even now, the bustling sound of activity—booted footsteps on flagstones and voices and various bumps and thuds—echoed up the nearby stairs from the Great Hall below.

Elizabeth shook her head, overcome with gratitude. Who would've thought that she could have garnered such support in such a short space of time? It was unexpected and humbling, and made the prospect of leaving—as she must— even harder.

A boisterous laugh coming from the direction of the library roused her. She had things to do as well.

Squaring her shoulders and lifting her chin, she set off for the servants' stairs.

~

"Mrs. Eliott, isn't it? Might I have a word with you? It's about my room."

Elizabeth froze mid-step on the sweeping stone staircase leading down to the Great Hall, her blood turning to ice, her heart stuttering to a stop.

Lord Blaire was behind her. How absolutely stupid of her not to have taken the servants' stairs. Since the hunting party's arrival the day before, she had been extremely careful, and had managed to avoid any direct contact with James's friends during the rest of that afternoon and evening. She had assumed that it would be safe to use the main stairs this early in the morning when the sun had barely risen and breakfast was still being laid out in the dining room. How wrong she'd been.

But it was no use berating herself now. At least she looked the part of the nondescript, unassuming servant with her hair pulled back tightly in a severe bun, and her plain, dark gray widow's weeds on. She didn't look anything like the expensively attired and elaborately coiffured Countess of Beauchamp. If she kept her wits about her and acted demurely, everything would be fine.

Keep calm, keep calm. You don't know him. He doesn't know you.

Elizabeth turned carefully around to face the rakish, now entirely sober nobleman who was obviously about to head out for an early morning ride. He stood at the top of the stairs, looking down at her, his head cocked slightly to one side as he tapped his riding crop against his lean thigh. His hazel-brown gaze was decidedly speculative as it ran over her. Clenching her fists in her skirts, Elizabeth willed herself to remain impassive beneath his regard. She would not blush or show any sign of weakness.

"Of course, my lord." She dropped into a small curtsy then raised her eyes to his arrogantly handsome face. "What seems to be the problem?" She still couldn't recall if she had ever made his acquaintance before. He reminded her of so many men of his class with his fashionably cropped brown hair, lean hawkish features, and confident smile.

Perhaps...

Lord Blaire's gaze sharpened on her face and Elizabeth dropped her own gaze to the stone steps at her feet. It had been inappropriate to stare at him so. She really must remember how to behave like someone in service. She couldn't afford to draw undue interest. Now more than ever.

"I think it would be easier if I showed you," he replied, then turned on his heel to stride back down the corridor in the direction of the stairs that led to the guest rooms.

Fear prickled along Elizabeth's spine. She seriously doubted that there was anything wrong with the man's room. The way he had looked at her...

Although there'd been no light of recognition flickering in his eyes, there had been a spark of another kind of interest that was almost as dangerous. Male lust. She was certain of it.

Elizabeth didn't want to follow him. But she was the housekeeper and convention dictated that she must accede to the man's seemingly reasonable request, despite her reservations. Besides, James's room was nearby. Surely Lord Blaire wouldn't behave untowardly when his friend and host resided in the same wing.

"I haven't got all day, Mrs. Eliott." Lord Blaire had paused to wait for her at the bottom of the next set of stairs.

Heavens, now she'd made him cross. All senses on alert, Elizabeth picked up her skirts and hurried to catch up, which was not easy given the man's long-legged stride. By the time she'd followed him up the next staircase and along the hall to his already open door, she was quite breathless.

He frowned at her with a concern that was undoubtedly feigned. "Are you all right, Mrs. Eliott?" He turned slightly and placed a proprietorial hand upon the small of her back. "Perhaps you should come in and rest a moment."

"I'm truly...fine...Lord Blaire," she said, trying to regain both her breath and composure, especially now that it seemed she was about to be forcibly ushered into his room. "You still haven't told me what's wrong."

Although she knew she sounded quite blunt, her manner even bordering on rude, she really didn't want to enter this man's bedchamber. It was at the very end of the hall, six doors down from James's room. And the thick oak door and stone walls were so solid, she would never be heard if she needed to call for aid. And the way Lord Blaire was running his gaze over her right now, his attention lingering on her mouth and then her chest, Elizabeth's instincts screamed at her not to take another step forward.

"Well, there is a frightful draft coming in through a gap in the casement window for one thing," he said bending toward her ear. He slid his hand from her back to grip her firmly about the elbow and attempted to steer her across the threshold again. "And then, there's the bed—"

A nearby door clicked shut. "Milord, might I be of some assistance?"

Roberts. *Thank God*. He must have been attending Lord Maxwell across the hall.

Blaire cursed under his breath, and as he relinquished his hold on her arm, giddy relief swept through Elizabeth. She immediately stepped back into the hallway out of Blaire's reach and turned to face the advancing butler.

Roberts bowed stiffly to Lord Blaire before fixing him with a dour stare.

"Lord Blaire has concerns about his bedchamber," Elizabeth explained to her unexpected champion. "A draft as well as a problem with the bedding I believe."

Roberts glanced beyond Blaire's shoulder into the room before returning his poker-faced gaze to the bristling nobleman. "I'm sure his lordship willna mind if I see to it, Mrs. Eliott. Mrs. Roberts will be wantin' you in the kitchen no doubt."

Elizabeth curtsied to Lord Blaire. "My lord." She risked a glance at his face and noticed he was glaring at Roberts, his lips compressed into a thin line.

Lord Blaire's eyes darted to her and he inclined his head slightly. "Mrs. Eliott." She was dismissed... For now...

As Elizabeth walked away, she could feel the nobleman's gaze following her. Next time, he would not be put off so easily. So there must not be a next time.

Her only consolation was, he didn't know her. She was definitely a stranger to him. Lord Blaire had studied her face and had not recognized who she really was. She was still safe.

And that was all that really mattered.

"Bloody hell, Rothsburgh. Are you sure you're not doing over your housekeeper? I know I would."

Rothsburgh forced himself to smile urbanely at Rupert, Lord Blaire—one of his brother-in-law's erstwhile acquaintances from his long-ago Cambridge days—when all he really wanted to do was slam his fist into the man's inanely grinning face. At this particular moment, for the life of him, Rothsburgh couldn't fathom why Maxwell was still friends with the tosser.

He unclenched one hand from the handle of his knife and took a swig of the excellent claret that Beth had selected to serve with their main course of duck. He wondered if he'd ever get the chance to see her—make love to her—whilst his well-meaning friends hung about the castle like a trio of pesky vermin.

Phillip Latimer, Lord Maxwell, had instigated the surprise visit to pull him out of the fug of self-pity his sister had declared him to be in when he'd last visited Edinburgh. Rothsburgh would happily wring Helena's pretty neck when he saw her again.

They'd only been here for two and a half days—fifty-five hours and twenty-six minutes according to the ormolu clock on the mantel—and yet he couldn't wait for them to leave.

"She's in mourning," Rothsburgh said as off-handedly as he could. "And besides, it has never been my inclination to sleep with the staff."

Blaire smirked. "Why would you want to sleep with her when you could just bend her over the nearest chair and—"

"Wasn't she the governess that applied for the post here?" interjected Maxwell. "I'll concede she's uncommonly pretty, but she also seems very refined. Much more so than you'd expect from someone of her station. I imagine she'd make an excellent teacher."

Rothsburgh nodded, grateful Maxwell had interrupted Blaire's ribald commentary. A man of honor, his brother-in-law would not condone such callous and disrespectful treatment of a woman in his employ. It was a pity that their current governess, Miss Palmer, was so damned efficient, then perhaps Beth could have worked within his sister's and brother-in-law's household.

Not that it mattered now. All governess's positions be

damned. The delectable Mrs. Eliott was his, and she wasn't going anywhere as far as he was concerned.

"Yes, she did apply for the position," Rothsburgh replied neutrally to Maxwell. "She came highly recommended by the Countess of Beauchamp."

"What? Hugh Harcourt's wife?" asked Blaire. "I've only met her once or twice, but she's another priggish blonde I'd love to fu—"

"What time shall we go hunting tomorrow, gentlemen?" interrupted Rafe, Lord Markham. A quietly shrewd, steely-eyed man, he obviously wasn't keen on Blaire's current line of conversation either. "I must confess, I'm a trifle tired after skulking around the moors for deer at the crack of dawn."

Rothsburgh grinned. "Not going soft in your old age are you, Markham?" The man had only recently returned from the Continent and it was rumored in certain circles that he'd been a spy for the British Government in the campaign against Bonaparte.

Markham simply shrugged and smiled, not bothering to bite back. He didn't need to.

Rothsburgh admired the man's sang-froid. Markham probably knew ways to kill a man that he'd never even heard of. Perhaps he could quietly ask him to take care of Blaire if he stepped over the line with Beth. "Gentlemen's hours shall we say then, Markham? There'll still be plenty of grouse to be had a bit later in the morning."

Markham inclined his head. "Agreed."

Maxwell then steered the conversation toward horse flesh, and Rothsburgh breathed a silent sigh of relief. The coil of tension in his belly was as tight as ever. If he didn't have Beth to himself soon, he'd snap. There was no chance he could arrange a rendezvous tonight. Despite Markham's admission of tiredness, he knew it was likely that they would be up until the wee hours drinking and playing cards.

Besides, Beth was now sleeping in a tiny room, right next door to one of the maids. Any assignation would be noticed for certain. And it wasn't as if he could entice Beth back to his own bedchamber. The chance of her being spotted by one of his guests would be high also.

Any way Rothsburgh looked at the situation, it was hopeless. He reached for his claret again and eyed his companions over the rim of his glass.

As uncharitable as it sounded, the sooner they were gone, the better.

CHAPTER 14

To Rothsburgh's relief, his chance to catch Beth alone came the very next day. On his return from grouse shooting, he'd entered the Great Hall with his dogs at his heels and had spotted Roberts and Beth disappearing down the corridor that led to Eilean Tor's wine cellar. As luck would have it, Maxwell, Markham, and Blaire had already disappeared upstairs, obviously not caring to linger whilst he'd been outside in the courtyard talking to the head groom about the need to re-shoe his horse.

Rosencrantz whined and thumped his tail.

"I know boy, I want to see her too," Rothsburgh said quietly, ruffling the hound's head. He probably should go upstairs and change out of his hunting clothes before he approached Beth, but then again, if he didn't act now, he might not have another opportunity to see her alone for another day or two. To have but a brief exchange with her everyday about something completely mundane and inconsequential—to pretend she meant nothing to him—it was killing him.

He bid Rosencrantz and Guildenstern to stay, and then he

all but ran across the hall and down the corridor to the cellar. The door was ajar and he slipped inside, pausing at the top of the stairs for a moment to let his eyes adjust to the sudden gloom. The cold, cavernous space, hewn from the rock-bed beneath Eilean Tor, was barely lit by the soft glow of several lanterns.

"Milord?"

Rothsburgh smiled. "Roberts. I'd like to talk to Mrs. Eliott about tonight's wine selection."

Beth was standing just behind the butler, her face hidden in shadow, but nevertheless, Rothsburgh thought he detected the hint of a smile on her sweet lips. Lips that he would soon be tasting. His heart began to pound, hot lust rushing straight to his groin.

Roberts bowed and carefully placed the bottle he was holding back in the racks. "Of course, milord."

The clever man had taken the hint and quickly ascended the stairs without so much as a lift of his eyebrows, or a backward glance.

The door clicked shut and Rothsburgh smiled with a deliberately wicked tilt to his mouth. "So, what's on the menu, Mrs. Eliott?"

Elizabeth's pulse leapt and her cheeks flamed as James shot her a clearly calculated, rakish grin. He was no longer the indifferent master—the role he'd been forced to adopt since the arrival of the hunting party. Her lover—her thoroughly disarming, deliciously sinful James—had returned. Even dressed in his hunting clothes—tight-fitting buckskin breeches that showed off his muscular legs to perfection, Hussar boots, a simple linen shirt, and a dark brown hunting jacket—he was utterly mesmerizing. There was no doubt that what was on his mind, right at this moment, wasn't dinner or the wine that would accompany it.

Not after she'd glanced at the front of his breeches.

Elizabeth licked her lips. Her mouth was suddenly dry with nervous anticipation and her heart was fluttering like a trapped bird within her chest. Although, how she could be nervous after everything they had shared, she didn't know. Perhaps she still wasn't used to being the recipient of such focused sexual attention. Or maybe it was because she and James were about to make love in the middle of the day whilst there were house guests about.

Or maybe it was simply because she was still plagued by her conscience and her plans to leave this man...

Regardless of her qualms, it would not change what was about to happen between them. Despite Elizabeth's doubts and fears, she suddenly wanted James so very much. As much as he seemed to want her. She needed to enjoy these moments and live life to the full while she still could, because all too soon this would be over.

"What would you like, my lord?" she asked, her voice sounding breathless, even to her own ears. That wicked smile again and she felt a sweet ache begin to pulse within her sex.

James held her gaze steadily as he descended, no, almost prowled down the stone stairs. "Everything."

She gasped. "Everything?" *Here in the wine cellar?*

He laughed and on reaching her, caught her hand and brought it to his lips. His kiss seared her knuckles making her shiver. "Don't look so alarmed, my love. I know we won't have time for absolutely everything. We'll both be missed before too long."

He drew her in so that her hand rested against the hard wall of his chest. Even through the linen of his shirt, she could feel the heat of his flesh, the steady beat of his heart.

"Whatever we do, I promise I won't mess up your hair," he

murmured with a crooked smile as he tucked a loose strand behind her ear. His smoldering gaze then dropped to her mouth, and he brushed a thumb across her lower lip. Why was he waiting? She couldn't bear the suspense.

"James," she breathed, gripping his shirt. It was both a plea and a demand.

"God, I miss you, Beth," he groaned. And then his mouth was upon hers, his arms crushing her to the rock-hard length of his body. She opened for him willingly and tangled her tongue with his, desperately seeking the taste of him, rejoicing in the deep throaty growl he made as their kiss deepened, became wilder, more urgent. She'd missed him too, missed this raw intimacy. How was she to survive when this was all over?

All such thoughts soon fled, however, when one of James's hands slid from the nape of her neck around to the front of her black wool bodice, and his fingers deftly flicked open the buttons, before sliding beneath her stays and shift to find her breast. He rolled her already erect nipple between his thumb and fingers, and she arched toward his hot touch, a low moan escaping her lips. The banked fire of suppressed desire flared within her, releasing her abandoned, reckless self.

She wanted more, so much more. She reached downward to stroke the iron hard shaft of James's erection. It pressed insistently against her belly, even through all the layers of their clothing. She desperately wanted to taste him, pleasure him there, until he lost control and cried out her name.

As she fumbled for the opening to his breeches, he stilled her hand. "Not yet, my angel," he murmured against her kiss-bruised lips. "I have something else in mind first."

Elizabeth's pulse thrummed and the apex of her thighs was suddenly slippery with the dew of her increasing arousal. "Something else" could only mean one thing. "I can hardly wait," she confessed, her voice no more than a husky whisper.

When had she become so willingly and shockingly licentious? She was about to have sexual relations in a wine cellar in the middle of the day and she was breathless with anticipation.

James grasped her about the waist and then, before Elizabeth knew what he was about, he'd effortlessly lifted her onto one of the sizeable wine casks that lay securely in a rack against the wall behind her.

"What...?"

"Shhh," he whispered, placing a long finger against her lips. "Trust me."

"I do... Always," she murmured and caressed his jaw with trembling fingers, holding his gaze steadily.

I love you. The words Elizabeth could never say to him threatened to spill from her lips, so she leaned forward and kissed him gently, trying to show him how she felt even if she couldn't tell him.

His firm lips slid tantalizingly beneath hers. He seemed content to let her lead for a few moments...until she teasingly ran her tongue over his bottom lip. She wanted to drive him wild again. He responded to her invitation immediately. With a low growl, he claimed her mouth, his tongue grazing against hers, and the firestorm of desire rose up again to engulf them both.

He pushed up her skirts to her waist and the musky scent of her arousal rose up around them. Continuing to ravish her mouth, he slid a finger up and down between her slick innermost folds, as his thumb began to stroke her quivering, swollen center of pleasure. Leaning back against the rock wall behind her, she couldn't resist the urge to part her thighs to allow him greater access. It was so wicked, so wanton...so wonderful.

James dragged his mouth from hers. "Let me taste you, Beth," he rasped against her ear, his fingers and thumb continuing to drive her need even higher. She made an inarticulate whimpering sound, perhaps she even nodded as she opened her legs wider, straddling the barrel. Whatever she did, it was all the consent James needed. Bending forward, he dipped his dark head and alternately curled and flicked his tongue against her pulsating core. She began to shudder and gripped his shoulders with talon-like fingers as the exquisite tension began to build higher, tighter almost to the point of pain. An abandoned moan rose in her throat, and she mindlessly spread wider for him. He ruthlessly took advantage of her exposed sex. He slid his tongue deep into her inner passage, thrusting and retreating as her hips began to undulate back and forth, matching his rhythm.

But she couldn't take much more of this calculated torture. Her breath was coming in short, ragged bursts that she couldn't control. She was so close to her peak, so close it hurt. Perhaps James recognized she was at her extremity because his mouth suddenly returned to her core and he suckled her. Hard. And she shattered.

Incandescent light exploded behind her eyes and she bit her lip, attempting to stifle the hoarse scream that rose within her as her womb finally clenched, and spasms of blinding pleasure coursed through her entire being, rendering her senseless to everything else around her.

Until James began to nuzzle behind her ear. Sighing, she arched her neck to allow his clever mouth and tongue better access to the sensitive flesh. She was well satisfied, but what about him?

"James, I think it's time that I returned the favor, don't you?" Elizabeth reached forward to stroke his rigid cock through the leather of his breeches. He groaned and pushed his groin into her hand, his mouth seeking hers. She could taste her own, slightly salty essence on his lips and tongue. It fired her own desire again, the desire to please him as he had pleased her.

"I want to taste you too," she whispered and loosened the

ties of his breeches. He sprang free and she grasped his hot, pulsing length, running her hand from base to silky smooth head, squeezing gently.

"God help me. Yes." He lifted her down, and once she stood steadily, he released his hold about her waist and eased himself onto the barrel. Legs astride, he leaned back, his cock standing up proudly, whilst his eyes—now black as midnight —were completely focused on her. He was breathing hard, almost trembling with need, waiting for her to ease his agony, to pleasure him.

A deep thrill coursed through Elizabeth as she realized how much power she wielded. That at this moment, this virile, powerful male was completely hers, to do with as she wished. Yes, she would pleasure him. And she would savor every single minute of it.

She licked her lips slowly, deliberately, and ran a finger over the slit at the end of his cock, smiling when James jerked and a droplet of moisture appeared. Bending forward, she placed one hand on his heavily muscled thigh, whilst the other cupped his swollen balls. As she began to stroke his hot, iron-hard shaft from base to head, she glanced up at him through her lashes. He was holding his breath, waiting for her to take him. But she knew that making him wait would make this all the sweeter.

"Christ, Beth," he gritted out, and she capitulated. She didn't want to be cruel. She delicately flicked at the bead of moisture with the tip of her tongue, and he groaned. He tasted and smelled wonderful, the spicy scent of hot, aroused male filled her senses, and she could no longer resist the temptation to take him into her mouth.

He gripped her shoulders as she bent her head and slid up and down his throbbing shaft slowly, almost languidly at first, taking her time, occasionally swirling her tongue around the slippery engorged head of his cock before returning to plunge rhythmically up and down again. Teasing him. Building the pace, increasing the pulling, torturous suction. Driving him wild.

"I can't...hold back..." His voice was a ragged gasp, and he started to thrust his hips to match her rhythm. Her heart sang. This was what she wanted—to push him over the edge, to take him to the heights of ecstasy as he never failed to do for her. He started to swell, and she deliberately drew him in, as far as she could and sucked hard one last time...and as she'd anticipated, he erupted. His hot seed flooded her mouth and she swallowed again and again, until his shuddering eased and he was empty and spent.

Elizabeth released him and straightened, delighting in the glorious sight of him reclining upon the barrel, drowsy-eyed and loose-limbed. *Satisfied.*

She would store this memory away as she had all the other memories of their lovemaking. When she was gone from here —as she soon would be—memories would be all that she had to sustain herself over the long, lonely years ahead.

She reluctantly stepped back and began to adjust her shift and refasten her bodice.

"Beth." James pulled himself upright and slid to the floor, reaching for her. He pulled her to him, then cradled her face between his hands, capturing her gaze with his. His eyes, fiercely intent, searched hers. "This...what we have...we both deserve more than this. I don't know how you feel, Beth, but I'm going mad not being with you. Not being able to look at you, touch you, kiss you the way I want to every moment of every day...it's torture. As soon as I can send these friends of mine packing, I will." Then before she could do anything more than cover one of his hands with hers, he kissed her—a deep searing kiss, a possessive kiss that she felt all the way to her bones. A kiss that touched her very soul.

What we have... James's words echoed in her mind.

But what did James think they had? Was it more than just sexual congress to him? After a kiss like that, Elizabeth knew with all her being that this man had feelings for her, deep feelings. And very soon, she was going to crush him.

Earlier this morning—after she had finished assisting the other staff with clearing away the breakfast service—she had noticed an advertisement in one of the newspapers that had been left out on the dining table A dowager baroness, Lady Dunleven, was seeking the services of a companion. A young woman of good standing with suitable references etc., preferably aged between twenty-one and thirty years of age. Applicants were advised to apply directly to a Mr. Innes, Lady Dunleven's man of business in Dundee.

Elizabeth had surreptitiously removed the page and secreted it in the pocket of her gown—the gown she was wearing now. She touched her pocket and felt the paper crinkle. A paid companion... How could she contemplate leaving this man for that?

But it was the right thing to do. For herself and for James.

Drawing herself away from James's embrace, Elizabeth fought to control the sudden prick of hot tears behind her eyelids. Unable to speak lest she betray her emotions, she instead bent her head and helped James to fix his clothing. He likewise helped her to straighten her garments before stepping back to check her bun.

"Hardly a hair out of place, Mrs. Eliott," he said with a lop-sided smile and dark mischief glinting in his eyes. "No one will suspect a thing. I'll leave first, and you follow in a few minutes."

Elizabeth nodded and forced a smile in return. "I still need to choose the wine. Something to go with grouse, I believe." She prayed her voice sounded light to James's ears, not brittle and tight as it had sounded to her. But he was distracted now, glancing toward the door. One of the hounds was whining.

"Yes. I'll leave it in your more than capable hands, my love." He kissed her quickly, yet softly. And then he leapt up the steps, disappearing through the door without a backward glance.

Wine. Focus on that, Elizabeth. Not on the false reference you will write for yourself when you go back to your room.

She retrieved the basket she used to hold the wine, and randomly chose two bottles of Madeira to go with the entrée of goose-liver parfait, and several bottles of Burgundy to accompany the main course of roast grouse. She would send Roberts back down later for the Champagne to go with the oysters. She really couldn't carry anymore.

The sound of the door scraping open and latching shut again caught Elizabeth's attention, and she turned, expecting to see Roberts or James again.

But it wasn't.

It was Lord Blaire.

"Mrs. Eliott, fancy finding you down here." A study in nonchalance—except for the intent expression in his eyes— Lord Blaire sauntered down the stairs toward her.

Elizabeth swallowed past the sudden constriction in her throat and tried to keep her breathing even. *Be sensible, Elizabeth. You don't know what he really wants.*

From what she'd already seen of him since his arrival, Lord Blaire seemed to be a man who was clearly fond of a drink or two. Perhaps he had just come in search of another bottle of his favorite spirit. But there was always an ample supply of port, whisky and brandy in the library and dining room...

As the nobleman drew closer, his gaze lewdly raking over her, she couldn't ignore the icy stab of fear in her belly. Just as she couldn't ignore the fact that he had tried to inveigle her into his room two days ago on blatantly false pretenses. Roberts had later informed her that there was nothing at all wrong with the viscount's bed, and there was certainly no draft. As much as she didn't want it to be true, it was fast becoming apparent that Blaire was the type of aristocrat who did indeed like to harass the hired help for sexual favors.

The question was: how far would he press her?

She really didn't want to find out.

She started to move toward the stairs and the relative safety of the Great Hall above, but Lord Blaire was too quick for her, and within moments she found herself trapped up against a wine rack and a stack of port barrels.

Elizabeth cleared her throat. She needed to stay calm and talk her way out of this situation. Just as she had talked her way out of a potentially deadly situation with Hugh, the last time she'd seen him in her bedroom at Harcourt House.

But staying calm was proving difficult when Lord Blaire was standing far too close for comfort with a falsely casual smile on his wide mouth. A smile that didn't quite reach his hazel eyes, as hard as topaz. Tiger's eyes.

And he'd been drinking brandy. Elizabeth could smell it on his breath. It would be hard to reason with an inebriated man, especially one who was obviously so single-minded and egocentric. But the added problem was, she really didn't know Lord Blaire, didn't know what ploys would work on him. Fear of falling out with his host and friend perhaps? The threat of an untimely interruption?

She had to try something—now—before her rising fear rendered her incapable of anything.

"Can I help you with something, my lord?" she asked, failing to keep the telltale note of nervous breathiness from her voice. "I'm expecting Lord Rothsburgh at any moment to check on what Roberts and I have chosen to accompany tonight's dinner. And Roberts—"

"You are expecting him to come back as well? Really? I think not, madam. In fact, Roberts was attending to some matter for Lord Markham when I left my room. And I saw

Rothsburgh leave here not two minutes ago, heading for his chambers. I'm sure you won't be missed, my dear, if that's what you're intimating." He reached forward and brushed her bottom lip with the tip of one long finger. "You have a pretty mouth, but a lying, wicked tongue, Mrs. Eliott. Does your master know how naughty you are?"

"I-I must protest, Lord Blaire." Elizabeth tried to take a step back but was caught up against the wine rack. Bottles clanked and threatened to fall. "Lord Rothsburgh would not condone—"

Lord Blaire laughed and grasped her chin roughly, angling it upward to study her face. "You're just a trumped-up little bitch. Feisty too, I'd warrant. All icy hauteur on the outside, but ready and willing for a fuck at the drop of any man's trousers, aren't you, Mrs. Eliott?"

With the heavy basket of wine between them, Elizabeth hadn't noticed that Lord Blaire had been busy with his other hand, undoing the placket at the front of his breeches. Not until he seized one of her hands and pushed it against his exposed, alarmingly erect member.

Oh, God, no.

A wave of nausea rose up, burning Elizabeth's throat. She had to get away. She wasn't going to be this man's whore. But she had nowhere to go but forward. And Lord Blaire was barring her way. Hot anger lanced through her, replacing her terror, and with a guttural cry, she thrust her basket forward into the general vicinity of Lord Blaire's midriff and groin, as hard as she could.

"Oof." Blaire took a step backward, the momentum of the heavy basket driving him back just enough that there was sufficient space to push past him. The basket hit the floor and glass shattered around their ankles, wine gushing everywhere like blood.

"Fuck. You bitch." Blaire clutched his groin as she stumbled past, heading for the stairs. But she wasn't quite fast enough. He caught at her skirts and she was jerked backward.

With a scream, Elizabeth slipped on the broken bottles and the wine pooling on the stone floor, then fell onto her hands and knees. Glass sliced into her, but she barely noticed the pain as she struggled to wrench herself away from Lord Blaire's grasp.

Somewhere, as if from a great distance, she was vaguely aware of other noises above the sound of Lord Blaire's grunts and swearing, and her own sobs. A dog's frenzied barking. A man shouting.

Please, God, save me. Whatever my sins, I don't deserve this.

The door at the top of the wine cellar flew open, and in the next instant, Rosencrantz hurtled down the stairs past her. The hound knocked Lord Blaire flat onto his back, then growled and ripped at his cravat.

"Christ. Beth." James was beside her, gripping her shoulders. "Are you all right? What did the bastard do to you? Tell me."

She was going to be all right. James was here. Elizabeth opened her mouth to speak but the words wouldn't come.

"Fuck. Rothsburgh. Get this dog off me." Blaire scrabbled backward through the wine and shards of glass, trying to fend off Rosencrantz who was now firmly fastened to the sleeve of his jacket.

James ignored him, focusing only on her. "Beth, look at me. What did he do?"

Elizabeth's teeth had started to chatter, but somehow she managed to formulate words. "He- He...t-tried to f-f-force me to... But I...p-pushed him away. And then the b-bottles broke..."

James nodded, kissed her forehead, then stood. "Rosencrantz. Heel." The dog immediately released Blaire's arm and retreated to Beth's side. Crossing over to Blaire, James then seized him by the lapels and hauled him to his feet. "Give me one good reason why I shouldn't kill you right now."

"You've got it all wrong, Rothsburgh," spat out Blaire. "She offered to fu—"

James's fist connected with Blaire's jaw and the man stumbled backward into the stack of port barrels.

He doubled over at the waist, spitting blood. "Jesus. Whatever she told you, she's a lying bi—"

This time, when James's fist slammed into the middle of Blaire's torso, he slumped to his knees, gasping.

"Wrong answer, Blaire," growled James.

Blaire scowled as he gripped his belly. "What's...the matter...with you? Why...don't you just...call me out?"

James dragged Blaire to his feet again. "Because that privilege is reserved for gentlemen, Blaire. And the way I see it"— he landed another punch in Blaire's gut, winding him again— "doing so"—another blow thrown upward struck Blaire's nose —"will just deny me the pleasure"—James's knee connected with Blaire's groin—"of beating you to a pulp."

James wrenched Blaire up and landed another punch on his jaw with such force, Elizabeth clearly heard the crunch of bone, and she closed her eyes. When she looked again, Blaire lay groaning and barely conscious in a heap at James's feet.

"James?" Elizabeth pulled herself to her feet. Her legs felt as unsteady as a new-born foal's and she had to support herself against the side of the stairs. "Don't. P-Please stop... He's not worth it."

James whirled around. "Beth. I'm so sorry." He was immediately at her side, cradling her in his arms. "You shouldn't have to watch this. You shouldn't have been subjected to any of this."

She raised her head from his shoulder and sought his gaze, searching for the right words, to convince him he didn't have to do this for her. To put himself at risk. There was no doubt in her mind that if she didn't stop him, he could quite possibly kill Blaire. And the resultant scandal would not only be dire for him, but for her as well. "I-I don't want... I don't want you to do anything rash... I'm all right. Truly."

A muscle worked in James's jaw as he studied her face, contemplating what she'd said. "Beth—"

"Rothsburgh! What the deuce?" Maxwell appeared at the top of the stairs along with Markham. Roberts lurked close behind.

James tipped his head toward the wine racks where Blaire still lay sprawled and moaning, clutching at his jaw. "Blaire disgraced himself in more ways than one. Get rid of him before I do something others may regret." Then he muttered under his breath so only Elizabeth could hear. "But I certainly won't."

Maxwell and Markham descended into the cellar, collected Blaire, and then disappeared with him up the stairs.

Roberts cleared his throat. "Milord? Is there anythin' I can do other than arrange fer a cleanup of the accident down here?"

"Have Lord Maxwell's carriage sent around first. I want Blaire gone from here before the tide comes back in."

"Yes, milord."

The door to the wine cellar closed again and James hugged Elizabeth close, murmuring soothing words into her hair. There, in the circle of his arms, breathing in his familiar male essence, her trembling started to subside and she barely noticed the stinging of her palms and knee.

Until James reached for one of her hands. She gasped.

James swore. "Sweet Jesus, Beth. You're hurt." He uncurled her left hand and exposed a long jagged cut on her palm that extended from the base of her thumb to her wrist. Aside from a few cuts to her fingers, her right hand was relatively unscathed in comparison.

"It happened when I fell amongst the broken bottles," she said shakily. "I think my left knee is cut as well."

"Let me look. Sit down on the stairs." He helped to lower her down, then he knelt and lifted her skirts. And swore again.

"I'm sure half of what you're looking at is red wine and Madeira, not blood," she said, trying to make light of the situation as James carefully rolled down her hopelessly stained and torn stockings. Despite her attempt at levity, nausea swelled within Elizabeth again, and she felt giddy with light-headedness. She was suddenly glad she was sitting down.

"I think there's still a sliver of glass in the cut in your knee, Beth, but I'll have to take a better look at it upstairs. It's as dark as Hades down here. But before I move you, let's get this bleeding under control first."

He swiftly removed the cravat from his throat and deftly ripped it into two before gently yet firmly wrapping one length around her left hand, and then the other around her knee.

Elizabeth tried very hard not to make a sound during his ministrations, to smother her gasps of pain. To be strong. But it was the sight of James, tending to her injuries with such care, that was eventually her undoing. Yet again, she was reminded of the oceans of difference between this man and her husband. Hugh was supposed to be the man who loved and cherished her above all others. But he never had, and he never would.

Despite her best efforts not to cry, a tear escaped. And then another. Tucking her right hand into her cuff, Elizabeth raised her sleeve to her cheek to try to hide the evidence of her weakness. She didn't think she could bear any more of James's sympathy lest she turn into a blithering, sobbing mess. But the movement caught his attention.

James focused his all too perceptive gaze on her face. Even in the gloom of the cellar, she couldn't hide.

Reaching forward, he brushed a third tear away with his thumb. A look of inexpressible tenderness filled his dark eyes. "There'll be no more servants' quarters for you, Mrs. Eliott. I think it's about time you spent some time where you belong. With me in my chambers, my love."

CHAPTER 15

I gnoring the rage clawing at his gut at the sight of her injuries, Rothsburgh held out a tumbler of whisky to Beth. "Here, my love. Drink this."

"Thank you," she murmured as she carefully took it from him with her bandaged hands. She dutifully took a small sip then grimaced. "I really hate this stuff you know. I'd much rather have a cup of tea."

He forced himself to smile. "I know but this will help to ease the shaking."

Like him, Beth was not herself and he hated seeing her like this—in pain, with a haunted look in her beautiful eyes. Dressed in one of her virginal white night rails, tucked up in a Clan Huntly tartan wool blanket on a leather settee in front of the fireplace in his room, she looked small and fragile.

Vulnerable.

Yet Rothsburgh knew that she was made of sterner stuff. Aside from the fact that she had managed to fend off Blaire, she had been nothing but brave whilst he had removed the glass from the gash in her knee. She'd barely made a sound when he'd bathed and then bandaged all her cuts, both large and small. Thank God, they were all quite shallow and didn't require stitches. He suspected only the laceration on her knee would leave a scar.

If only her emotional scars would heal so cleanly. Rothsburgh wanted to hold her, bury his face in her soft golden hair. Kiss the graceful arch of her neck. Undo the buttons at her throat and lay bare her full breasts...

Hell, despite the fact that she'd nearly been raped, the male beast in him wanted to make love to her, possess her, until she forgot about everything else except for the reality of the rapture they shared whenever they were together.

But he wouldn't. It was too soon. He knew that. As much as it pained him not having her in his arms, he would wait. Because she was worth waiting for.

Sitting down beside her on an ottoman with his own whisky, Rothsburgh immediately noticed how Beth's hands trembled as she raised her glass to her lips again. Even though her ordeal was over, she was clearly still in shock.

And underneath his own misbegotten lust for her, Rothsburgh was still angry as hell. Angry enough to rip Blaire apart with his bare hands. He tossed back a sizeable mouthful of the fiery single malt, enjoying the scorch at the back of his throat. He knew it would take much more than a dram or two to quell the burning urge to call for his horse and give chase to the blackguard. However, now that it was late afternoon, he suspected that the tide had already flooded the causeway. If it weren't for the vicissitudes of the sea, and Beth's earlier plea to stay his hand, he would have whole-heartedly given into the dark impulse to seek bloody vengeance.

But for now, it seemed he would be denied the satisfaction. And that meant he would somehow have to deal with his own self-directed anger and loathing—a veritable tempest of emotions engendered by his failure to anticipate that Blaire would assault Beth in the most monstrous, despicable way.

His guilt sat like acid in his gut along with the whisky. He should have known from the moment Blaire had stumbled across Beth in the library that the bastard was too interested in her. And after Blaire's comments about her at dinner two nights ago, Rothsburgh should have thrown the craven cur out then and there. But he'd been too dismissive, too laissez-faire. And now his beautiful, sweet Beth was paying the price for his carelessness and stupidity.

His Beth.

"Beth..."

She'd been nursing her whisky, staring absently into the fire, but at the sound of his voice, she turned to regard him with solemn gray eyes. "Yes?"

"I... Beth, I owe you an apology. More than an apology, in fact. I should be on my knees right now begging for your forgiveness."

Confusion clouded her eyes. "I don't understand..."

He removed her tumbler of whisky, then carefully took her right hand between his, taking care not to brush the bandaged cuts on her fingers. He didn't want to add to her pain—physical or emotional—by dredging up what had happened earlier, but he needed to do this. Admit that he'd failed her.

His precious Beth.

Rothsburgh sought her gaze and swallowed past the bitter taste of self-recrimination in his throat. "What happened to you this afternoon. It shouldn't have. I knew that Blaire had his eye on you from the very beginning—"

"James. Stop this." Beth reached out with her heavily bandaged left hand and gently touched his cheek. Her eyes narrowed and her forehead dipped into a frown. "It's not your fault. So don't you dare feel guilty."

"But if I had turned him away at the start—"

"You weren't to know—"

"Or had stayed with you in the cellar—"

"You were trying to protect my reputation. Hide what I am..."

"Yes..." Rothsburgh stumbled to a halt and stared into Beth's beautiful eyes as comprehension struck him like a cannonball. *Hide what I am*, she'd said.

His mistress.

The unspoken words crashed into the silence between them.

Beth dropped her gaze from his, but in the moment before she did, the expression in her eyes changed imperceptibly. The clear gray had become clouded with shadows.

Beth was his mistress. *Only his mistress.*

Was that the reason she hid away from him now? As if she were ashamed?

Why hadn't he seen it before?

He was such a blind, selfish fool.

Right from the very beginning of this affair, he'd known that Beth had wrestled with the idea of becoming his mistress. Just as he'd also known that she'd been troubled about other things. Things that she still resisted being drawn into conversation about. The grief she felt for her deceased husband was the most obvious cause of her secret sorrow. And despite her avowals to the contrary, he knew that there must be much more to the story behind her nightmare of being pursued.

But until this moment—perhaps because he'd been so caught up in the all-consuming, passionate rapture of being with her—he'd never really considered that he was to blame. That perhaps the source of her ongoing disquiet was that she couldn't reconcile herself with what she had become. Something she had never really wanted to be—a kept woman.

And he was solely responsible for pushing her into this situation. He didn't want her to see herself as a whore. Didn't she know she had never been that?

Rothsburgh reached out and carefully took her right hand and raised it to his lips. He suddenly knew how he could make this right. Because what he had with Beth wasn't just about sex. And what he felt for her was more than just affection.

He'd tried damned hard to close his eyes and ignore this feeling that had been growing inside him—from the moment he'd first laid eyes on this woman if he was perfectly honest with himself—but right now, he knew he couldn't any longer. Not after today. Never before had he felt such a tumult of complex and powerful emotions—lust, tenderness, protectiveness, and out and out blind rage—when the woman he cared about had been not only threatened but hurt.

He had long ago sworn to himself that he would never fall in love again. Not after Isabelle.

But what he shared with Beth...this was different. It had always been different.

There was no escaping the truth. And he had to let her know.

"Beth. I need to tell you something..."

James was kissing her hand, the touch of his lips feather-light against her skin. And his intense gaze was filled with such undisguised longing, Elizabeth's heart clenched and her breath froze in her chest.

James was looking at her as though he loved her. Like he was about to tell her that he loved her.

Please Lord, no.

After what had happened this afternoon, Elizabeth didn't think she had the strength to face this. She needed to say something—anything—to distract James from the confession he was about to make. To put off this moment.

The moment when she had to break his heart.

"Beth. I need to tell you something..."

Oh no, no, no. Elizabeth broke away from James's gaze and pulled her hand from his. She was shaking, her mind in roiling chaos. Words escaped her. She wanted to get up and leave James's chamber, but her knee was bandaged almost to the point of immobility, and she was tucked up securely in a heavy blanket. And James was sitting directly in front of her, barring any escape. She couldn't look at his face. She despised herself for not only her deceit, but her cowardice. James deserved so much more than she could ever be.

"Beth, what's wrong?"

Obfuscate. Dissemble. These were the only tools Elizabeth could think to gather together, to keep James at arm's length. Until she could think of another way to distract him from making any type of declaration. A declaration that she could never reciprocate aloud because that would be too cruel. To tell him that she loved him before she walked away.

Somehow, she dragged in enough breath to speak. She forced herself to meet his eyes. "The whisky is not sitting well with me, I'm afraid. And the fire is so hot... I need some air..."

Oh Elizabeth. You lie so badly.

Nevertheless, to her relief, her weak ploy worked.

The expression of hurt confusion in James's eyes was immediately replaced with one of concern. "Of course." He rose and as he crossed the room to open one of the bay windows, she took the opportunity to free her legs from the confines of the blanket before shakily standing up.

What are you going to do, Elizabeth? Run away? Fly out the window?

A strange bubble of sound—something between a sob and a gasp of laughter—lodged in her throat. She must be going mad. Indeed, she did feel quite light-headed, not like herself at all. She reached for the back of the chair.

"Beth..." James was at her side again, his strong hands

grasping her upper arms. His touch burned through the thin cotton of her night rail, and she felt her nipples harden to throbbing points. This was worse, so much worse. She couldn't think if he touched her. She fastened her gaze on the strong column of his throat. She didn't want to meet his eyes.

James's voice was soft and low. "My love..." He gathered her into his arms and placed a gentle kiss at the side of her trembling mouth. "You're exhausted. And you shouldn't be on your feet. Let me take you to bed—"

"No!" Elizabeth couldn't bear the thought of being intimate with James right now. Not if it led to a confession of love. She placed her hands against his chest without thinking, to push him away, but her cut palm protested. She tried to bite back a gasp of pain, but she wasn't fast enough.

James noticed. He lifted her chin, studying her face, his dark eyes grave. "It's all right, Beth. I only meant that you need to rest. Please don't mistake my motives. After what happened this afternoon, I certainly don't expect... I mean, I wouldn't press you for..."

For sex...

Maybe she'd been wrong. Maybe that was the answer. She could use sex to distract James, to destroy this poignant, agonizing tenderness between them. If she asked him to take her to his bed. If she pleasured him until he couldn't see straight. Remind him that she *was* nothing more than his mistress. His plaything. A whore. Then surely he wouldn't want to tell her...

She reached up and kissed him, hard, desperately. Swept her tongue into his mouth and wrapped her forearms around his neck to drag him closer. To stop him talking. She didn't want his words. She just wanted him. She would always want him.

And she needed to take what she could because tomorrow she would be gone from here.

She'd stayed too long already.

James yielded at once and he kissed her back with equal fervor, his hands tangling in her hair. He tasted of whisky and passion and everything she'd ever wanted. She wanted to tear at his shirt, at his breeches. Wanted to touch all of the hot, hard planes and contours of his body. But her bound, clumsy, painful hands were useless as she slid them down to the fastenings at the neck of his shirt. She moaned in frustration.

He immediately broke the kiss and pulled away. "Maybe we shouldn't do this, Beth. You're hurt—"

"No. I'm fine. Really. I want this, James. I want you." She was mortified to hear the desperation in her voice, but she was beyond suppressing it. She reached down to place her hand over his erection. She had felt it pressing against her belly as soon as she'd started to kiss him, but again her cuts pained her. She winced and bit her lip, blinking away the hot tears that threatened to spill.

This isn't working.

"I want you too, my love. But not like this. I can wait. You mean so much more to me than this..."

Oh no. Don't say it.

"Haven't you guessed how I feel, Beth?" James's voice was husky with emotion. He caressed her cheek with the back of his fingers before cupping her jaw so she couldn't escape his gaze. The tender light in his eyes was unmistakable. "I love you. And I don't want you to be my mistress. I want you to be my wife."

What?

A confession of love was bad enough...but a proposal?

A choked sound of distress caught in Elizabeth's throat. She couldn't breathe.

She wrenched herself away and ignoring the pain in her knee, stumbled a few steps across the room toward the open window. She could clearly hear the waves pounding futilely against the cliffs below, and a biting, icy wind pulled at her night rail and hair.

This was worse, so much worse than she'd ever anticipated. The man she loved was laying his heart at her feet, offering her heaven. And she had to say no.

She was in hell and God help her—although a sinner like her truly had no right to call on heaven's help—she was dragging James down with her.

And it was all her fault.

"Beth." James took a step toward her, his hand outstretched, stark bewilderment in his eyes. "I don't understand..."

She wrapped her arms around herself and tried to swallow past the anguish that tightened her throat and constricted her chest. If nothing else, she could at least give him an answer. Her voice when it emerged was ragged, hoarse. "I'm sorry, James...I can't marry you."

"But..." He broke off, dropping his hand, his forehead creasing into a confused frown. "I thought..." He shook his head as if attempting to knock his thoughts into order. His chest swelled as he dragged in a breath. "I've surprised you, shocked you, even. I can see that. I know it hasn't been that long since you lost your husband but...if you need time to think on this, Beth—"

Elizabeth shook her head. "No. It won't make any difference." She had to convince him. She didn't want him to harbor false hope.

James paled, his skin pulling tight across the angular planes of his strikingly handsome face as he suddenly seemed to recognize her implacability. "Could you at least tell me why?" The rawness in his voice sliced her to the bone.

Her vision blurred with tears. Incapable of speech, she shook her head again and then closed her eyes. Her throat ached with the effort it took not to sob. She should leave.

Go back to the servants' quarters. Her trunk was still there. Pack.

The moment had come. This was over.

"Beth. This doesn't make sense..."

"I know... I'm sorry..." Her voice was no more than a ragged whisper. She couldn't manage any more. She turned away from him, toward the door.

But James wasn't going to let her off so easily. Within the space of a heartbeat, he closed the distance between them and seized her by the shoulders, his fingers digging into her like talons. "Beth, look at me. Tell me what's the matter. After all we've shared, can't you at least tell me why you are rejecting me?"

She bit her bottom lip, hard enough to draw blood, and tried to tear herself away. But she was no match for James's strength. Desperation made him rough, but she welcomed the pain.

He grasped her chin and tipped her head up, forcing her to look at him. His eyes were black and turbulent. Like storm clouds. Like the crashing sea below. "Don't go, Beth. I beg you...not like this. I love you. Do you understand me? I need you. More than air, more than anything. I thought you felt the same way..." His voice cracked.

"I... Please...you have to let me go. I'm not worth it."

"Of course you are. Just because you agreed to become my mistress doesn't mean you can't be my wife. Nobody will know, and besides, I don't give a toss about what anyone thinks—"

"That's not the reason."

"Then what is it?"

Elizabeth opened her mouth to speak but halted. She didn't want to confess her crimes. Her duplicity. But maybe it was the only way he would let her go. And didn't he deserve the truth? The man that she loved.

Her voice was a mere whisper. "I'm not widowed."

James's frown was almost a scowl as he struggled to make sense of what she'd said. "What, you mean you've never been married?"

"No. Just the opposite..."

∾

No. Just the opposite.

Comprehension crashed over Rothsburgh like a tidal wave. He dropped his hands away from Beth. "What? Do you mean that you..." He couldn't complete the horrendous thought.

Beth's already pale face became ashen. "Yes... I'm married."

"No..." Surely she must be joking. But she wasn't. He could see it in her very expression. The way her bottom lip trembled and her slender throat worked as if she was trying to stop herself from sobbing. The tears in her eyes.

Jesus Christ.

His beautiful, sweet, angelic Beth. The woman he loved beyond all understanding was married.

Rothsburgh shook his head, backing away from her, trying to deny the shocking truth. His mind was reeling. His world had been blown apart. Fragments of thought and half-formed questions lodged in his brain like shrapnel.

Why? Why would Beth do this? Pretend to be free when she wasn't?

He'd known she had secrets. He'd known she was troubled. But never in his wildest imaginings had he thought that she hid something as awful, as shocking, as damning as this. He had to make sense of it. Heaven help him, even though she was splitting his heart in two, tearing his world asunder, he still loved her.

He dragged in a shaky breath and desperately fought to

marshal his chaotic thoughts. "Your husband... You said he died at Waterloo, but obviously he didn't. Was he even at Waterloo?"

Beth met his gaze. "Yes...he was at Waterloo."

Something true at last. Insane hope flared within him for an instant. What if Beth was not quite a widow? Perhaps Lieutenant Eliott had been presumed dead because there had been no evidence left after the battle. No body. Dead, but not officially declared dead. Rothsburgh had seen men blown to pieces... "Is he...is he missing in action then?"

"No. He came home..." Beth was shivering, a pale ghost in her nightgown, but he couldn't afford to feel a shred of pity for her. Not when she was shredding his soul.

"So where is he now?" he demanded.

"James." Beth's voice cracked. "I can't do this. Please... It won't do either of us any good."

"Christ, Beth. I'm trying to understand. You turn up here, professing you're a widow. You become my lover. I just... After everything we've shared, don't you think that you owe me an explanation, now that you've ripped out my heart?"

Beth's whole body flinched as if he'd struck her, and her face paled to the color of parchment.

"I'm sorry," she whispered then took a step backward. Away from him. And another. She retreated behind a wing chair.

Rothsburgh didn't know whether he wanted to drag her back into his arms or order her to go. Either way she wasn't his. Had never been his.

And there was virtually nothing on earth, nothing in heaven or hell that could excuse what she had done.

Beth was as deceitful as Isabelle. In fact, she was no different to Isabelle.

He'd fallen in love with another faithless, lying whore.

An adulteress.

A sickening combination of black despair and bitter anger started to churn in his gut. Even though he felt as if he was being flayed alive, he still needed to know why. Why Beth had pretended to be something that she wasn't. Christ, did she even care for him at all, or was everything an act? Was she that good an actress?

He pushed his hands through his hair to stop himself reaching for her—to shake the truth from her, or to take her to his bed. Pound into her, possess her until...until what? It didn't matter what he did—railed, cried, pleaded—it wouldn't change the irrefutable fact that she was married.

Above all, right at this moment, all he could fairly demand from her was the truth. She at least owed him that much.

"Sorry isn't good enough, Beth. You still haven't told me why. Why did you leave him? Why did you come here? Why did you lie about being a widow?"

Why did you come here and break my heart? "You must have a bloody good reason."

Beth shook her head, tears glazing her gray eyes then spilling unheeded onto her cheeks. If she was acting he should applaud her stricken expression. Despite his own burning anguish, his stupid, foolish heart contracted with pain at seeing her apparent devastation. Why wouldn't she answer him?

Her nightmares. Did it have something to do with her nightmares? He suddenly felt like a drowning man reaching for something to hold onto, to save himself and save her. To absolve her of the heinous, treacherous act she had committed.

"Your husband. Did he abuse you? Neglect you? Abandon you?"

"No...no, he didn't." Her voice was thick with tears. He could barely make out what she was saying. "We grew apart... and then... It's complicated..." She used her wrists to roughly dash the tears from her cheeks, swallowed, and looked directly at him. Her beautiful eyes were as bleak as a winter's day at Eilean Tor. "It doesn't matter why... It won't change what I've done. How wrongly, how badly I've deceived you... I should go..."

Beth abandoned her defensive position behind the wing chair and headed for the door. She was limping, but Rothsburgh didn't follow to assist her. Neither did he go to her aid when she had trouble turning the doorhandle with her bandaged hands. He didn't think he could bear to look at her. And he certainly didn't have the right to touch her.

Would he ever touch her again?

Even though dark, angry despair penetrated his heart, he couldn't quite stem the futile longing to go after her, seize her, take her.

But he wouldn't.

She belonged with her husband, Lieutenant George Eliott. *Poor bloody cuckold.*

Rothsburgh turned away. The door clicked shut.

His broken voice was barely a whisper in the empty room. "Yes...go... It's probably for the best."

CHAPTER 16

E lizabeth wasn't sure what the hour was when she eventually rose from the narrow bed in her freezing room. It was fully night judging by the unrelenting blackness outside the high narrow window—the only one in this tiny servant's chamber. The light of her single candle did nothing to relieve the pervading gloom. Neither did the squalls of rain constantly battering at the windowpane. But the atmosphere perfectly matched her own state, and indeed what her future would be—cold and dark.

Bereft.

And it was no less than she deserved given the sins she had committed.

Now that her initial grief had ebbed, an odd numbness had begun to steal over her. If nothing else, at least she could think and function a little again. However, her mind still reeled with incredulity at the thought that James had actually proposed to her. It was the last thing she had expected him to do. Her heart would bleed forever at the memory of his devastated face, at the very moment she had rejected him.

In some ways, his bitter anger on discovering she had

single-mindedly duped him was easier to deal with than witnessing his despair. He was justified in hating her. It could be no more than she already hated herself.

Maisie had knocked on her door once in the early stages of the evening. No doubt her wracking sobs had been overheard. But Elizabeth had ignored the girl until she had at last given up and gone away. After that, no one else had approached her. She was thankful that James—she should probably refer to him as Lord Rothsburgh—had not thrown her out straightaway. She knew she didn't deserve anything from him, other than his condemnation, so she was immensely grateful for that concession.

Crossing to the small chest of drawers by the bed, she checked her pocket watch—ten o'clock. It wasn't too late to find Roberts and ask when it would be safe to cross the causeway in the morning, and to check when the mail coaches would pass through Torhaven. If she could have, she would have left without seeking assistance. Although Roberts and the other staff wouldn't know what had precipitated her sudden need to depart, she felt so ashamed of what she had done, she felt thoroughly undeserving of any kind of aid. But there was no feasible way to leave Eilean Tor without it.

Elizabeth splashed icy water from the pitcher into a bowl, and washed her sticky, tear-stained face before beginning the painful and laborious process of getting dressed with her bandaged hands. She could hardly leave in her night rail, and she refused to ask for any kind of help from Maisie or Mrs. Roberts. Besides, she was going to have to manage by herself from now on, so it was best that she started getting used to it.

Her plan remained the same. She would try her luck at securing the companion's position with Lady Dunleven of Dundee. However, it seemed she would have to rely on her memory for the contact details of the baroness's man of business. The newspaper advertisement that she had so carefully hidden in the pocket of her widow's weeds had probably been destroyed by now. After James had taken her to his chamber, he had carefully stripped off her torn, bloodied and wine-stained garments, and Maisie had later taken them away to have them burned.

After Elizabeth had dressed, and as she clumsily slid the last pins into hair, she realized there was hardly anything left for her to do. She would speak with Roberts, pack her trunk, and then write herself another reference letter from the astute Lady Beauchamp.

Then she would simply sit and wait through the long cold hours until dawn.

Alone. And that was how she would spend the rest of her nights until the end of her days.

When consciousness returned, Rothsburgh really wished it hadn't. It wasn't just because he was lying face down on the hearth rug in the library with a blinding headache and a churning stomach. It was because the stark reality of living without Beth slammed into him with renewed force.

She can never be mine.

She belongs to someone else.

Last night, after she'd left his room, he'd set about drinking himself into a stupor that he hoped never to wake from, just so he wouldn't have to deal with the agonizing truth.

He clearly hadn't drunk enough.

With a groan he rolled onto his back and cracked open his eyes. Morning. Someone—probably bloody Roberts—had drawn back the curtains, restoked the fire and had thought-fully thrown a tartan rug over him. Even the brandy decanter —the one he was sure he had drained last night after polishing off all the whisky in his room—had been refilled and was sitting on its tray with a fresh glass beside it on his desk.

As much as he wanted to suffuse his brain with the numbing fog of complete drunkenness again, he really didn't think his stomach could tolerate it right now. Water, plain toast, and maybe some coffee were all that he was really up to. The brandy would have to wait until later.

Rothsburgh lurched to his feet and managed to make it to the bellpull without losing the contents of whatever was left in his gut—which was probably mostly roiling despair and regret at how badly he'd treated Beth. Shock at her disclosure had clearly rendered him incapable of thinking straight, but it was a poor excuse for his blatantly self-indulgent, wounded dog behavior. Christ, she'd almost been raped, was injured and in pain. Even though she'd deceived him—played him for a fool—he shouldn't have driven her from the room without even offering to call on one of the staff to provide her with assistance. There was no doubt about it, he'd been a thoughtless brute.

He crossed over to his desk and collapsed into his chair, clutching his spinning, aching head in his hands. As much as it would pain both of them—in fact he'd much rather face the prospect of having a limb amputated (and maybe it should be his head, it throbbed like the very devil)—he knew he'd have to speak with Beth sometime today, if only to arrange an alternative situation for her. Despite what had transpired between them, he wasn't completely heartless. He would never throw her out with no means of support, and nowhere to go.

But where *would* she go?

Would she want to return to her husband?

His gut told him that she wouldn't.

In the long dark hours of the night as he'd single-mindedly worked his way through one of his strongest malt whiskies, he had gone through their last fraught conversation in his head, over and over again before his thoughts had become too addled. What he'd failed to grasp then, and still didn't understand now, was *why*. Why had Beth done what she'd done?

The question was like a burning bullet in his brain, and he wouldn't be satisfied until he knew the answer.

One thing was certain, there had to be more to Beth's "complicated" situation than she had cared to admit. But then, he hadn't given her a chance to explain anything. The more he thought about what she'd said—or hadn't said last night—the stronger his instinct became that the Beth he knew—sweet, caring, intelligent, loving—wouldn't have left her husband on a whim. She must have had a damn good reason. But after his behavior last night—he cringed at the memory of how he'd lashed out at her—would she share it with him?

And neither did he think that becoming his lover was an inconsequential matter for her.

Now, in the cold light of day, Rothsburgh realized he'd been wrong to think of Beth as some cruel, calculating jade. Beth was nothing like Isabelle. And fool that he was, he'd been too quick to judge. He hadn't been fair to her. No, not at all.

After everything they'd shared, he couldn't turn his back on Beth. However much it hurt to see her, he would help her in whatever way he could.

Rothsburgh was roused from his tumultuous thoughts by the arrival of Roberts—brilliant man that he was—bearing an already assembled tray of refreshments: a jug of water, a pot of coffee, and fresh warm baps with butter and marmalade.

"I didna think you would mind tha' I took the liberty of bringin' you a few things for breakfast, milord," he said with the quiet gravity befitting a reverend at a funeral. Roberts obviously knew he had a splitting head. "'Tis close to eleven o'clock, an' as you missed dinner last night..."

"It's quite all right, Roberts. I appreciate your thoughtfulness." Rothsburgh gestured at the desk. "No need to set up the dining table. I'll just have it here."

"Verra good, milord." Roberts carefully laid out each item, clearly taking care not to clatter the china or cutlery, but when he was done, he hesitated by the end of the desk, empty tray in hand, looking uncharacteristically uncertain. "Milord..."

Rothsburgh glanced up from buttering one of Mrs. Roberts's excellent baps. "Yes, my good man?" He wasn't sure why, but judging by the expression on Roberts's face, what his butler was about to say wasn't going to be something he wanted to hear. He put down his knife. "What is it?"

"I just thought ye should know that Mrs. Eliott..." The butler started to fidget and the sinking sensation in the pit of Rothsburgh's stomach only intensified. "Weel, she left this mornin', milord."

"What?" Rothsburgh surged to his feet and gripped the table, partly to support himself, but also to prevent himself from throttling Roberts. "When?"

"At first light, milord, as soon as the tide was far enough oot. Todd took her over in the carriage to The Black Barnacle wi' her trunk to wait fer the eight o'clock mail coach south. I'm sorry, milord. I verra much wanted to tell you, but Mrs. Eliott made me swear no' to. She said tha' she wasna' fit to be employed here any longer. Tha' she had to go. An' after the incident wi' Lord Blaire yesterday...weel, I didna know wha' to make of things. She seemed...no' herself. I didna like to pry..." He reached into the pocket of his jacket and pulled out a parchment envelope. "But she asked me to give you this, milord...when you awoke."

Rothsburgh took the letter, not able to hide the shaking of his hand. "Before you go, Roberts, do you know...did she mention to you or to Todd, where she might be headed, other than just south?"

"I dinna think so, milord. But I could ask Mrs. Roberts or

Maisie per'aps. Might I also add, milord, even though it's probably no' my place to say, we are all verra...surprised an' saddened to see Mrs. Eliott go. She is a bonnie woman, milord. We shall all miss her."

Rothsburgh cleared his throat but failed to conceal the hoarse emotion in his voice. "Yes. Indeed." *Bonnie* didn't even come close to summing up the rare diamond that was Beth, but he appreciated the sentiment behind what Roberts had just said all the same. "That will be all, Roberts."

As soon as the library door shut, Rothsburgh tore open the envelope.

Lord Rothsburgh,

God, she'd gone back to using his bloody title.

Although I am probably the last person you would ever want to hear from, now, at the hour of my leaving, I felt that I couldn't go without expressing my sincere and humble gratitude for your care and kindness.

I will remember you always.

B.

Fuck. He didn't want her sincere and humble gratitude. He wanted her love.

Rothsburgh flung the letter down onto the desk and pinched the bridge of his nose as biting despair threatened to take hold.

He was solely to blame for driving Beth away. If he had been able to rein in his anger. If he had shown some compassion and offered to help her, instead of turning his back on her...

When Beth had said that she would go last night, he didn't realize that she meant to abandon Eilean Tor—him —completely.

Despite everything, this couldn't be the end.

He had to find her.

He drew in a shuddering breath and picked up the letter again, tracing the finely executed, elegantly flowing letters with the tip of one finger as if they could provide him with some clue as to Beth's whereabouts.

He didn't even know where to forward her wages. Hell, the last thing he wanted to do was treat her like some common doxy by paying her for her "services rendered." He wanted to give her his name, indeed everything he had. But he couldn't, and if she wasn't going back to her husband—as he suspected she wouldn't—she would need a way to support herself. For that reason alone he had to locate her.

Christ, she probably didn't even have a reference now.

Rothsburgh started to rifle through the stack of papers on one corner of his desk, praying that Lady Beauchamp's letter hadn't been lost. If Roberts or the other staff could recall any detail of where Beth was headed, when the tide was out he could attempt to return her reference to her. Or provide her with one from himself for that matter—if she'd accept it.

He'd do anything she wanted.

He'd almost given up, when at last, he spied the single sheet of thick cream parchment embossed with the Countess of Beauchamp's own distinctive monogram on the very bottom of the pile. He scanned the page quickly, looking for any piece of information that might give him another clue about Beth, where she came from, any former employers whom he could contact that might have a better idea of her background. If he had to, he would go all the way to bloody London to speak with Lady Beauchamp herself.

But there was nothing in the letter that he didn't already know about Beth.

Releasing an exasperated sigh, he cast the reference down onto the desk beside Beth's all too brief goodbye letter. Then blinked. Ran a hand over his eyes and looked again, hardly daring to trust what he saw before him.

Beth's handwriting and Lady Beauchamp's were *exactly* the same.

What the hell?

He picked up both pieces of paper, his mind reeling from the implications. There were only two possibilities: either Beth had forged herself a reference from a peeress of the realm—a seemingly impossible feat given that it was written on Lady Beauchamp's own personal stationery, and the wax seal bore the imprint of the Beauchamp coat-of-arms, or, the woman professing to be Mrs. Beth Eliott was actually Elizabeth, the Countess of Beauchamp.

And he'd stake his life on the second scenario.

It was as if he'd suddenly found the key to the puzzle box. Everything that had both intrigued and mystified him about Beth suddenly made sense: her innate poise and elegance in everything she did and said; her natural knowledge of staff management and running such a large household as Eilean Tor—unusual skills for a woman from the middle classes to have, but natural for a countess who probably ran at least two households. Her intelligence and quiet confidence. Her superb skills as a pianist. He'd always sensed she was someone from his own class, not just the wife of a subaltern with no social connections to speak of.

Other things fell into place in his mind. Blaire had once crudely likened Beth to the blond Lady Beauchamp. And Beth had even admitted to him when they had first made love that her name was really Elizabeth. Not that her disclosure was overly surprising, but at the time Beth had told him, he'd had the feeling that she was revealing something quite close to her heart, a well-kept secret about herself.

But perhaps most importantly, this revelation also meant that he now knew exactly why Beth had left her devil of a husband.

She ran away to save her life.

And nothing on this earth would stop Rothsburgh from finding Beth to tell her that he understood. And to offer her assistance in whatever way he could.

Married or not—he loved her.

CHAPTER 17

Dundee, Tayside, Scotland

Through his carriage window, Rothsburgh noticed that the horizon over the North Sea had begun to grow imperceptibly lighter as he approached the outskirts of Dundee. He'd been traveling since three o'clock the previous afternoon—the earliest time that he'd been able to safely cross the causeway—and between the jolting of his carriage over the rough roads and his turbulent thoughts, he'd barely slept all night. But being exhausted hardly mattered if he soon had Beth in his arms again.

After quitting the library yesterday morning, Roberts had learned that the young maid, Maisie had found something telling in the pocket of Beth's ruined gown—a newspaper advertisement inviting suitably qualified young women to apply for a companion's position for a Lady Dunleven of Dundee. Rothsburgh was certain that was where Beth was headed, especially when Geddes confirmed that she had indeed caught the south-bound mail coach heading to Edinburgh, rather than the north-bound one that passed through Torhaven in the early afternoon.

According to Geddes, the mail coach would have arrived at the Fife and Drum, Dundee's largest coaching inn, at around ten o'clock last night. Rothsburgh guessed that Beth would have secured a room there. Given who she really was, she probably had some funds to spare for accommodation for a short while. And if she hadn't found lodgings there, or anywhere else nearby, he still had the advertisement containing the contact details of Lady Dunleven's man of business, Mr. Innes, the person whom Beth would approach for the post.

If Beth wasn't at the Fife and Drum, or didn't contact Mr. Innes, Rothsburgh would turn Dundee and every town and village between Torhaven and Edinburgh upside down until he found her.

There was only one needling doubt that pricked at him. Beth had found the advertisement for the companion's post before he had proposed to her.

So, she had already been thinking of leaving him. And that worried him.

He'd thought that she cared for him. The way she'd smiled at him, kissed him, made love with him... He knew the difference between what they'd shared and just plain fucking.

But what if he'd been wrong? What if she hadn't cared for him as much as he did for her. What if the intensity of his feelings—although unstated until a night ago—had frightened her away?

Rothsburgh glanced down at Beth's goodbye letter in his hand, the writing barely visible in the uncertain gray light of dawn. She had expressed her gratitude. And that was all. And when he'd told her that he loved her, she'd never admitted any tender feelings for him then, either.

Hopefully, within the next few hours he would find Beth. And after he had begged her to forgive him for judging her so harshly, he would ask her how she really felt about him. Selfish sinner that he was, he didn't care that she was married. He still wanted her with every fiber of his being, and he had to know if there was any chance at all that she could love him in return.

~

It was bitterly cold in the small room Elizabeth had hired at the Fife and Drum. The tiny fire in the grate had died overnight, and the wind blowing off the sea constantly rattled the shutters and whistled with irritating shrillness through a crack between the windowpane and the sill.

Between the noise, her physical discomforts and her over-whelming sense of wretchedness, Elizabeth had given up on sleep long ago. With nothing better to do than to toss and turn and shiver, she rose with the first light of dawn and rang for a maidservant to request a pitcher of warm water to wash.

The sooner she dressed and ate breakfast, the sooner she could set about tracking down Mr. Innes, Lady Dunleven's man of business.

Once the maid had been and gone, Elizabeth wrapped herself in her cashmere shawl, then curled herself up in a lumpy, shabbily covered armchair before the fireplace to wait for her water. Aside from freshening up, she needed to bathe and re-bandage her cuts. An infection was the last thing she needed.

As she watched the flames take purchase in the freshly stoked fire, she turned her thoughts to what she would tell Mr. Innes about herself, as well as wondering what Lady Dunleven would be like. Anything to stop herself thinking about the darkly handsome marquess who she'd foolishly fallen in love with, and the cruel reality of never being able to see him, let alone be with him again. He must despise her now, and rightly so.

These were the same painful thoughts that had pervaded her mind throughout the long journey to Dundee. She imagined they would torment her for a long time to come.

Her only comfort was that she was still a nobody. A shadow who could fade into obscurity again. Hidden from Hugh. That was all that should matter to her, being able to live safely.

If only her wayward heart would stop aching.

An abrupt, rather loud knock on the door made Elizabeth jump. The maid must have returned. Roughly wiping the mist of self-indulgent, useless tears away from her eyes, she rose and limped across the cold floorboards to admit her.

"Yes?" she called, not willing to open the door until the young girl identified herself. A woman traveling alone needed to be careful.

"'Tis Heather, ma'am, with yer water."

Satisfied, Elizabeth clumsily turned the key in the lock with her bandaged hands and stepped back a few paces behind the door to shield her body from view when it opened. There was no privacy screen in this room, and it wouldn't do to be caught *dishabille* by anyone else who might be passing by in the hallway. "You may enter."

The door swung half-open. But it wasn't the maid.

Lord Rothsburgh stepped into the room.

Elizabeth froze, unable to utter a thing other than an inarticulate cry, while her heart leapt wildly with an electrifying combination of shock and ill-founded joy.

How did he find me? And why? Why would he bother?

Compelling, intense, devastatingly handsome as always, even with ruffled hair, an unshaven jaw and rumpled coat, the very room seemed to vibrate with Rothsburgh's presence. He'd obviously bribed or charmed the young maid into gaining access to her room as he was bearing a jug of water, and a few towels were draped over his forearm. He swiftly raked his gaze over her, then turned his head and called over his shoulder into the hall. "Thank you, Heather. I shall look after the lady from here."

Then he kicked the door shut behind him and bowed. His eyes were as soft as dark brown velvet. "Good morning, Mrs. Eliott. Or should I say, Lady Beauchamp?"

Oh God, no. Elizabeth's hands flew to her mouth, and she stumbled backward a few steps, nearly tripping over the roughly bricked hearth. She couldn't believe it. *Lord Rothsburgh knows who I am.*

The protective wall she had painstakingly constructed around herself had come tumbling down like a house of cards.

How had he found out her true identity? But more importantly, would he tell anyone?

"Please." Her voice was no more than a choked whisper. "Please, I beg you. Don't call me that! Nobody can know..."

Dark spots suddenly peppered her vision, and there was a strange rushing sound in her ears as Rothsburgh's alarmed face started to fade behind a dark mist.

"Beth!"

There was a crash of china—the water pitcher striking the floorboards—and suddenly she felt Rothsburgh's arms about her, dragging her up from the black abyss she had started to tumble into.

"God, Beth. It's all right. I'm sorry I startled you. Your secret's safe." He swept her up into his arms, cradling her against the solid wall of his chest, his face buried in her hair. "I'm going to put you on the bed. I don't want you to faint on me again."

As he carried her across the room, she pressed her face to his shoulder and took a shuddering breath, inhaling his distinctive masculine scent. Despite her confusion and terror at being discovered, she was flooded with a longing so acute, it hurt.

Stupid, Elizabeth. Always wanting what you can't have.

When Rothsburgh released her from his hold and drew away, she bit her lip to stop herself whimpering aloud. *No, don't let me go. Not yet.*

Common sense had clearly deserted her.

But then to her relief, Rothsburgh—she daren't think of him as James again—sat down beside her and took one of her trembling hands between his. His dark, intent gaze traveled over her face—even lingered on her lips for a moment—before returning to search her eyes. As if he still cared for her, in spite of the fact she had deceived him, and that she was a fool who'd married a man he clearly reviled.

"Beth, I'm such an idiot. Please forgive me for surprising you like that. I promise you, I won't give you away. I assure you that's not why I came here."

She nodded, wanting so much to believe the sincerity in his voice and in his eyes. She swallowed, moistening her dry mouth, still desperate to know how he had discovered her secret and why he had sought her out. She had to know before treacherous hope took hold of her.

But of course, there was no hope for them at all.

She swallowed and forced herself to speak. "How...how did you discover who I am?" she asked, her voice little more than a hoarse, choked whisper. "How did you find me?"

Rothsburgh's wide, beautiful mouth tipped into a gentle smile as he brushed a lock of her hair away from her cheek. Dear Lord, a display of tenderness was the very thing she craved, yet the last thing she needed. "Finding you was the easy part," he said. "Maisie had discovered the advertisement for the companion's position in your ruined gown before she burnt it, and Geddes saw you board the mail coach that headed south. As for discovering that you were not Mrs. Eliott and really Lady Beauchamp...after I found out that you had gone, I wanted to make certain that you would be all right. But you had left your reference letter behind. Then, when I saw that the countess's handwriting was exactly the same as the writing in your letter of farewell, I realized the truth about who you really are. And I had to let you know that I understood your situation. More than you realize."

Elizabeth shook her head, still not understanding why Lord Rothsburgh would bother to look for her after all that she had done, or how his anger had melted as quickly as snow that had been exposed to the summer sun. "But it doesn't matter whether you know me as Mrs. Eliott, or the Countess of Beauchamp. Either way, I'm still married. A wicked adulteress. I left my husband, and I betrayed my marriage vows. I'm not...I'm not the woman you thought I was. I deceived you. I hurt you. I'm despicable—"

"Shhh." Rothsburgh touched her lips with his finger, compassion lighting his eyes. "Yes, you left your husband. But you are not despicable—"

Elizabeth jerked away from his touch, turning her head as tears of self-loathing threatened. She didn't deserve this kindness. "Yes. I am," she whispered. "What I did was wrong."

"It's not wrong to try to save yourself from becoming another one of Hugh's victims, my love."

What?

Her gaze flew back to Rothsburgh's. It was impossible that he would know the reason she had left Hugh. And what did he mean *another* victim?

"I don't understand—how could you know?" she asked shakily, confused yet intrigued by his canny intelligence that bordered on the preternatural.

"That your husband has syphilis?"

"Yes," she gasped. This didn't make sense. Nobody knew that Hugh had the disease except herself, Dr. Morton. And Hugh's mistress...

Rothsburgh's eyes suddenly hardened to the cold black of obsidian. "I know because he gave it to my wife."

～

Beth's already pale face blanched to the color of the linen sheets upon the bed, and her next question emerged as an almost inaudible whisper. "Isabelle had syphilis?"

Rothsburgh's throat was suddenly tight as he stared into Beth's wide gray eyes. It was hard to admit something so humiliating, so personal. That your wife had taken a lover and had then contracted the pox. He felt like he was scourging off a layer of flesh, leaving him raw and exposed, more vulnerable than he had ever been before in his life.

But Beth had a right to know the truth, no matter how ugly and painful it was. "Yes, she did."

Beth's eyes sparked with comprehension. "But that would mean that Hugh and Isabelle were—"

"Lovers. Yes, they were, Beth."

Beth suddenly grasped his arm tightly with her bandaged hand, and he winced for her—the cut beneath must sting like hell—but she seemed oblivious as she caught his gaze. When she spoke, her voice held a note of urgent sincerity. "I want you to know that even though Hugh has it, I don't...I don't have syphilis. When I agreed to become your mistress, I meant it when I told you that I hadn't been with my husband for months. In fact, it has been over a year since he last... demanded anything of me." Her eyes suddenly widened with a look of panic and her pale cheeks were marked with hectic color. "God, I hope you don't think that I was the kind of woman who would ignore something like that. You must know that I would never have had intimate relations with you if—"

Rothsburgh placed his fingers over her lips. "Hush now. I

know you don't have it, Beth. I've seen you, all of you, remember." He tried not to smile when her blush deepened. "But more than that, I know who you are inside, regardless of the name you bear. And you are not that sort of woman. Just as I am not that sort of man." He brushed her cheek with his fingers, his heart swelling with tenderness, wanting to reassure her that he was a different man to her husband. That she could trust him. "I don't have the pox either."

"Thank you for telling me that. And believing in me," she said on a shaky exhale, as if she had only just started to breathe again. "After all of the lies I've told, that you would still trust my word, even just a little... Well, it means a lot to me."

"You only lied to protect yourself, Beth. I could never condemn you for that," he said gravely. "We've both been betrayed by the people we loved."

"Yes, it seems we have." Beth suddenly shook her head. "It seems so bizarre though. I still don't understand how you know all this? How can you be sure that it was Hugh that gave your wife syphilis? I mean, I don't want to defend my husband, far from it. He's had mistresses aplenty. But what you are telling me... It's...incredible."

Rothsburgh sighed and ran a hand down his face. Beth was right. It was indeed incredible. And he'd never wanted to believe any of it either. But he'd lived with Isabelle's faithlessness for such a long time, and he'd seen things—things he'd much rather forget—that proved beyond any doubt the truth of the matter. Beth's husband had indeed infected Isabelle with syphilis. And syphilis was the reason Isabelle had died.

Rothsburgh carefully clasped Beth's hands between his. "Believe me. I know. It defies belief. But I will attempt to explain the truth as far as I know it. If you want me to. I will warn you though. There are things that I will disclose that will...shock you...more than you have been shocked already."

Beth squeezed his hands, and her gaze was clear and steady as she regarded him. "Tell me everything."

Rothsburgh took a steadying breath. He could do this—tell Beth what she needed to know because she had asked him to, and he would do anything for her. But where to start with this whole sad and sordid tale that had affected both of them so profoundly?

Damn. This was going to be harder than he thought.

It wasn't long before Beth prompted him with her own question, saving him from his agonized musings. "How exactly did you find out that Isabelle had syphilis? And that my husband had given it to her?" she asked quietly. "Did she tell you?"

"Yes, she did," he said, not able to suppress the note of grim weariness in his tone. "But...not directly... I didn't find out until after she'd died."

Beth's usually smooth brow dipped into a confused frown as she tried to make sense of what he'd just said, but she didn't comment. She simply watched his face and waited for him to continue.

Rothsburgh dragged in another fortifying breath, mentally preparing himself to reopen old wounds. "Forgive me. I'm not being very clear. I don't think I've told you this, but Isabelle had been in Belgium with me during the campaign. That's when she contracted the pox from Hugh. But as said, I didn't find out then. As you know, I was wounded at Waterloo and Isabelle...well, she left shortly after the battle was over and returned to Eilean Tor. The last time I saw her was at the Duchess of Richmond's ball, the evening before the Battle of Quatre-Bras."

"Oh, James. She left you there? Without seeing you when you were wounded?" Beth's eyes glimmered with tears.

He was deeply touched by her grief for him. It was a sign she still cared. And it was the first time she had uttered his

Christian name again. It felt like a blessing to hear her say his name. Like water in the desert for a dying man.

"It's of no consequence, Beth. My injuries weren't that bad. And to be honest, I didn't want to see her. Isabelle and I, we weren't on the best of terms then. In fact, we hadn't been for a long time, as you already know."

Beth's expression was puzzled again. "Then if you never saw her, or spoke to her, how did you find out about her and Hugh, and the pox?"

"Isabelle left a letter on my desk in the library at Eilean Tor, confessing all to me. That Hugh had given her the pox after she had...been with him in Brussels. And that she was sorry for not being the mother she should have been. I suspect that writing that letter was probably one of the last things she ever did, Beth...before she went down to the causeway when the tide was coming in."

Beth gasped and gripped his hands so tightly it hurt. "Oh my God. You mean... It sounds like her death... It wasn't an accident."

"No. I don't think it was."

"Oh, James."

"She wrote that she couldn't bear the shame of having the pox. Dr. Addison—the physician from Blackhaven who visited you—he confirmed that Isabelle had been suffering from the most virulent form of second stage syphilis he'd ever seen. He'd attended her sick bed at Eilean Tor—the day before she went down to the causeway—and he told me that aside from having a terrible fever, her body had been covered in a red rash and wart-like sores. Apparently her hair had also started to fall out in large clumps. Isabelle would have hated that. She'd always been so proud of her looks.

"Anyway, I suspect that what Isabelle told me in her letter was true—that Hugh had only just recently contracted the pox, and that neither of them knew he had it when they—"

Rothsburgh broke off, clamping his jaw shut. He'd almost said "fucked," but he didn't want to utter that profanity in front of Beth. "When they coupled," he said after a moment. "And that may have been the case. The surgeon attached to my regiment informed our commanding officer shortly after our arrival in mid-May, that some of the local prostitutes were spreading the pox to the soldiers. And by all reports it was also quite a nasty strain. Colonel Cameron ordered our men not to fraternize with the women, but perhaps not everyone—the men from the other regiments—knew that."

Beth shrugged. "Perhaps. But I suspect that even if Hugh heard the rumors he would have dismissed them. He's always been reckless and arrogant, thinking he knows better than everyone else. And as humiliating as it is to admit, James, I know that my husband has not only kept a mistress from time to time, but that he also has a penchant for prostitutes. It doesn't surprise me at all that he would have taken up with one of them." She glanced down at her hands, still clasped in his. "He didn't want me to go with him to Belgium as I knew some of the other officer's wives were doing," she said quietly. "Not to keep me safe. It was because—and this is hard to say —he just didn't want me at all. For anything. And that has been a Godsend in a way...considering everything that has happened." She raised her eyes again. "Given what you've told me about your relationship with Isabelle, I'm surprised she went with you."

Rothsburgh grimaced. "She didn't accompany me at my invitation, Beth. When the orders came for the regiment to join Wellington, I was in London and I asked Isabelle to return home to be with Annabelle at Eilean Tor. Looking back, that was stupid of me to do. Isabelle always hated the place, claiming it was no more than a pile of rocks. I should have known that she'd do exactly as she pleased, which was often the exact opposite to what I had suggested. From what I understand, after I'd departed for the Continent with the regiment in early May, she joined the Duke and Duchess of Richmond's entourage and traveled with them to Brussels. I had no idea what she was planning until she arrived on the doorstep of my billet. I was angry with her of course, but being angry with Isabelle was always a useless enterprise. She didn't give a damned fig about what I thought. Or what her daughter needed.

"But that was always her way. She craved drama, danger even. And she'd grown bored of London. All the interesting crowd was now on the Continent she told me when she turned up." Rothsburgh felt the muscles in his jaw tighten at the memory of her self-centered flippancy. "It was as if she was attending the *ton's* latest form of entertainment. It was a novelty for her, a grand adventure. It didn't enter into her head at all that this was a war against the French. That men were about go to their deaths, or at the very least get horrifically maimed."

"Like you." Beth placed a hand on the side of his damaged thigh and her touch seared Rothsburgh as though his leg was bare.

Blood immediately began to throb toward his cock, and he shifted slightly to ease the building ache in his balls. Sweet Jesus, how could she so effortlessly arouse him? But now was not the time to explore if anything could still exist between him and Beth. Perhaps later when all their revelations had been made, their secrets shared. If Beth still wanted him...

God help him, he prayed that she did, because he still wanted her, married or not.

With an effort, Rothsburgh forced himself to ignore the effects of her incendiary touch in order to respond to her comment. "'Twas no more than a scratch—a sizeable one to be certain, but not all that bad, all things considered. I sustained it during the second battle—Waterloo—when things were nearly over. And it didn't put me out of commission for too long. Only a week or two. I'm a tough old war horse."

Beth's lovely mouth quirked into a gentle smile. "Thirty is not old at all. And you can't fool me. I know you try to hide your battle scars by making light of all you endured. But I know they're still there, James. You are too noble and stalwart for your own good." Her smile suddenly changed, grew rueful, and her eyes hardened. "My husband has never been the noble sort. He may have fought with honor on the battlefield, but that is probably as far as it goes. He certainly never behaved in an honorable way toward me during our marriage." Her forehead suddenly creased into a frown again. "But now I'm wondering, James... When did Hugh and your wife begin their affair? Did Isabelle say in her letter?"

Rothsburgh sighed, rallying the will to continue. His next secret was going to be one of the hardest to reveal. It was a disclosure that would strike Beth deeply. He sought her gaze and held it steadily. "Beth, I knew my wife was unfaithful to me long before she made her confession. And as hard as this is to admit, the reason I didn't want to see Isabelle after I was wounded was that I actually saw her...with your husband...at the Duchess of Richmond's ball."

Beth's eyes widened and her cheeks flamed. "You saw Hugh and Isabelle...together? Do you mean that they were—"

"Yes, Beth. I caught them *in flagrante delicto* during the ball. They were outside, in the yard behind the stables. I'd had a bit too much brandy, and I'd gone to get some fresh air." He closed his eyes briefly as the obscene image of Hugh fucking his wife from behind as she leaned over a pile of crates—like she was some common whore—intruded into his mind. If it hadn't been for the tumultuous arrival of the messenger bringing word to Wellington of Bonaparte's advancement across the French-Belgian border, Rothsburgh was certain that he would've run the bastard through with his short sword on the spot.

"Oh, heavens..." Beth's fingers bit into his. "I've heard many a story of the Duchess of Richmond's ball. How grand it was before it came to such an abrupt end when all the troops and officers were called away." She shook her head. "I can scarcely believe that Hugh and your wife would do something like that, in such a public place, with the *ton* all around them. It's depraved. And you were there... You must have been so angry. How utterly shocking that you had to go into battle after having seen something like that."

Rothsburgh shrugged. "I was angry, yes, which ironically always helps when you are in the thick of things on the battle-field. But now, I just feel...saddened. It was the last time I ever saw Isabelle alive. Sometime during the following week, while I was recovering from my injury, she decamped back to England. I like to think that she felt ashamed and sorry for what she had done, but I'm not sure. She never apologized in her letter. She only admitted that Hugh had infected her...and that she couldn't live with it." He paused for a moment and blew out a breath, willing himself to continue. Now to deliver the next series of blows. "Beth, even when I saw Isabelle and Hugh together, I wasn't surprised."

Beth frowned in apparent confusion. "What do you mean? I know you've told me that you and Isabelle had grown apart. But to actually discover your wife—in the act of betraying you—how could you not be surprised. Or even shocked? Unless..." Her eyes widened with dawning horror.

Rothsburgh inclined his head as his mouth twisted into a wry smile. "Unless I already knew that Isabelle was unfaithful to me? That's right, Beth. My wife had never been true to me at any time throughout our six-year marriage. In fact, Isabelle and Hugh were lovers before she and I even met. I believe she took up with Hugh sometime during her first Season in

London. But although Hugh wouldn't marry her back then, it seems neither of them could give the other up, even after they both married. Their affair went on in secret for years."

Beth gasped. "That's appalling. I had no idea. At all." She shook her head, her voice now trembling with deep emotion —outrage and shock he guessed. The same acrid feelings that had coursed through his veins when Isabelle had first flaunted her grand affair in his face all those years ago.

"I always thought it was me—that there was something wrong with me—and that's why Hugh couldn't love me," Beth continued, her voice shaking. "I knew he had lovers, mistresses, whores aplenty. But I never considered that he might actually love another."

She pushed herself back against the headboard and closed her eyes for a moment, her face pale and strained. She was clearly struggling with all that he'd told her. And there was so much more she needed to know—even uglier truths about her husband and Isabelle. Rothsburgh hated doing this—being the bearer of such sick and twisted news—but as much as it would shock her, she had a right to know.

He placed a hand over hers and waited until she opened her eyes before he spoke again. "Love... I'm not sure if Hugh or Isabelle ever really felt such a fine emotion for each other, Beth. What I do know to be true is that Isabelle certainly never loved me. In fact, the only reason she married me was because she was pregnant...with someone else's child."

As he expected, Beth looked utterly horrified, her eyes widening as the import of what he'd just said struck her.

For a brief moment it seemed she was unable to formulate words. "Oh... Oh my God, James," she uttered eventually. "Does that mean...Annabelle...she's not yours? Don't tell me she's Hugh's."

Elizabeth could barely speak...could barely breathe. After everything James had disclosed, this...this was too diabolical. To think that her husband had conceived a child with another woman. And the man she loved had been forced to give his name to a daughter that wasn't his. She stared at James, her heart seizing with anguished horror as he nodded his head, confirming what she'd just asked him to deny.

"I'm sorry, Beth. But yes...Annabelle is Hugh's daughter."

"Oh, James. I don't know what to say," she whispered, her throat tightening with the effort it took not to cry—for James, for Annabelle, and for herself. "What a terrible burden you have had to bear." She dearly wanted to comfort him and holding his hand suddenly didn't seem like it was enough. But she was faithless, and a liar, like Isabelle. She should be satisfied that James tolerated her touch at all. Instead, she swallowed past the ache in her throat and forced out another question. "Do you...do you think Hugh knows?"

James met her gaze. "Yes, I believe he has always known," he said gravely. "Isabelle told him when she first became pregnant. In fact, she demanded that he marry her. But at the age of twenty-two your husband was a rakehell of the highest order, and definitely not in the market for a bride. So Isabelle had to settle for me to hide her indiscretion. Of course, I didn't know any of that at the time. Not until it was too late." James's shoulders suddenly heaved with a great sigh and he ran a hand down his face, but the action didn't dispel the tension within him. A muscle still flickered in his jaw as he appeared to gather his thoughts.

"You see, when I first met her, she was the incomparable Lady Isabelle March, granddaughter of the Duke of Sommersby, and in London for her second Season. She was extraordinary and thoroughly captivating...and I fell in love with her the moment I saw her, even though there were rumors about her having a wild streak. But besotted sap that I was, I ignored the whispers about her and Hugh. I suppose I just didn't want to believe any of it, and Isabelle denied everything when I asked her. Well, at least until after we were safely married."

He laughed then, a cold harsh sound like ice cracking. "It wasn't until a few months after Annabelle was born—she was an early baby, apparently—that I began to suspect she wasn't mine. But I was in denial at first. I didn't want to believe that Isabelle could have betrayed me so grievously, and I couldn't help but love Annabelle from the start. But as she grew into a golden-haired, blue-eyed child, I could see she was someone else's daughter. Hugh's daughter. And Isabelle—cruel witch that she was—didn't bat an eyelid when I confronted her about it."

James suddenly squeezed his eyes shut as if he were in terrible pain. "Isabelle laughed at me, taunted me in fact," he whispered hoarsely. "I will never forget her words, Beth—and please forgive my crude language—but it will give you an idea of the sort of woman she was. She said, 'What was I supposed to do, James? You were in love with me and wanted to marry me. And even though Hugh is a better fuck than you, and I'd rather have wed him, he doesn't give a toss that he's fathered a bastard. Needs must when the devil drives, my husband.'"

Elizabeth bit her lip to stop the tears that threatened to fall —for James and his emotional scars. And for how black and bleak all the years of his marriage must have been. She was about to throw caution to the wind and reach forward to touch his tightly clenched stubbled jaw, but he opened his eyes.

His mouth twisted into a cynical smile. "Needless to say, my love for Isabelle died the moment she uttered those words. In hindsight, that only made it easier for me to cope with everything else my wife did."

"Everything else?" Elizabeth whispered. *How much worse could it be?*

~

Rothsburgh debated for a moment whether he should divulge the rest of his wife's sordid history to Beth. It would be like baring his soul, to admit the most abhorrent secrets of all. It was something that he'd never talked about to anyone else before.

But he didn't want any secrets between himself and Beth. And perhaps if he shared this information with her, she might understand why he had been so quick to condemn her for being unfaithful when she had first confessed that she was married. If she understood even just a little of the hell Isabelle had put him through, then perhaps she would forgive him.

He searched Beth's face. Although she was still pale and clearly shaken by all that he had already told her, he could also see compassion lighting her eyes. As if attuned to his uncertainty, she squeezed his hand, silently giving him the strength he needed to continue.

"After Isabelle and I married, I found out very quickly that there was something not quite right about her. She had a dark, hedonistic and completely unprincipled side. I told you earlier she craved excitement and danger. Well, even having Hugh as her lover wasn't enough."

"You mean she had other lovers? James... That's... It's too horrible, what you've had to endure."

He dragged in a breath. Swallowed. And despite his resolve to be strong, his voice emerged with a hoarse edge. "I won't lie to you, Beth. It's probably worse than you or anyone else could even imagine. You see my wife, in some circles, was known as the 'whore of the *ton*.' She was, without a doubt, society's best kept secret."

Beth gasped. *"What?"*

He rushed on—now that he had opened the floodgate it seemed he couldn't hold back the last of his dark revelations. "Isabelle was mercenary in chasing her own pleasure, Beth. She was a connoisseur of sexual indulgence. I seriously doubt there wasn't anything she wouldn't do. And she didn't care that I was the laughingstock of the men she had hand-picked for her exclusive male harem—usually the most dissolute rakes of the *ton*—year after year. Hugh was one of them of course. She called her harem the Sapphire Club and you could tell who was in it, who she'd invited, because she gave them all gold and sapphire signet rings, or cravat pins to wear that were engraved with her initials, *IH*. She wore a sapphire and pearl brooch herself whenever she was inclined to indulge in...her excesses... to let her fellow club members know she was available. You would have seen it in her portrait.

"I never knew any of this during the first few years of our marriage. I knew about Hugh of course. But not the others. Not until a friend, Lord Markham in fact—he has uncanny intelligence that man—heard the rumors and told me. I confronted Isabelle, but she didn't deny the accusations I was making. Far from it. She thought it was amusing that I had taken so long to find out. But there was nothing I could do. Divorce wasn't an option—I certainly wasn't going to parade the sickening and sordid details of our private life through Parliament and the courts. And Isabelle was independently wealthy—a bequest from her ducal grandfather—so I couldn't control her by cutting off her income. So with precious little options open to me, to spare myself the ongoing humiliation, I simply decided to stay away—to withdraw from most social spheres and become a recluse for all intents and purposes. I didn't want to continue mixing with the men who were doing over my wife."

Beth raised a shaking hand to her throat. "Hugh has a

sapphire cravat pin and a signet ring. They're his favorite embellishments. I had no idea whatsoever what they signified. How...disgusting." She shook her head in apparent bewilderment. "I don't understand. How did Isabelle get away with it? Surely, if word got out, she would have been shunned."

Rothsburgh couldn't hide the bitterness from his voice. "I know it sounds incredible, but I suppose it was worth the while of all her male entourage to keep her debauchery a secret. I mean, why would they want to pass up the prospect of getting an impromptu service from her in a darkened hallway at a soiree, or in a deserted cloakroom at Lord and Lady Such-and-Such's ball? She was insatiable and would do anything, anywhere. Even at Eilean Tor. That's why I had the drawing room closed up. A year ago, while I was away in Edinburgh on business, she brought two young bucks there. Roberts caught her with both of them and my valet in the drawing room, in the middle of the day. I just thank God that Annabelle didn't burst in on them. My wife had no conscience at all."

Rothsburgh glanced at Beth, wanting to gauge her reaction to all that he had divulged. He was, in fact, surprised she hadn't run screaming from the room after hearing about the foulness and depravity that had been part of his life for so long. But she hadn't even drawn away. She still held his hand and watched him steadily.

As their eyes met, she gave him a small, sad smile. "I don't think Hugh has much of a conscience either, James. It seems we both married unwisely."

Rothsburgh nodded, wondering how it had really been for Beth during the three years of her marriage. He still wasn't convinced that she hadn't been mistreated by her cur of a husband.

"I'm guessing you were like me, Beth, and that you were

duped by Hugh," he said softly. "I imagine that you loved him at the start."

"Yes," she admitted, her expression wistful for a brief moment. "He was handsome and charming, and literally swept me off my feet. I was twenty-one and imagined myself in love. I'd done the rounds of the come-out balls for two Seasons running, but no one had piqued my interest until I met Hugh. But then our marriage...Well, it was not what I thought it would be."

"I know you've told me that he didn't hurt you. But did he, Beth?" Rothsburgh felt his muscles bunch beneath his coat, and his jaw tightened almost to the point of pain. He knew where Isabelle's tastes ran. The rougher and more perverse the sexual act was, the better. He could imagine that Hugh could be a sadistic bastard in the bedroom. He'd have to be, to satisfy Isabelle.

But Beth was shaking her head, thank God. "No... I mean he was never gentle, but neither was he physically cruel. He just never seemed overly interested in me. Especially after the first month or so of our marriage. I was like an afterthought most of the time. It was almost like he didn't see me. Or he just couldn't be bothered with me. It didn't matter what I did, I never seemed to please him. He told me once, after a year of our marriage, that I was pretty enough but far too dull. I bored him. I think the only reason he married me was because I had the right lineage and looked the part. I was like a brood-mare really—just waiting in the stable until he decided it was time for me to bear him pretty blond children. Ironically, that only seemed to be the case after he'd contracted syphilis."

"Sweet Jesus, Beth. Don't tell me he tried to force you."

"No. He might have, but I didn't give him the chance. The night that he suddenly showed an interest was, strangely enough, the last night that I intended to spend at Harcourt House in London. The nightmare I have—it's about that night. When Hugh came to my room and told me his intentions—that he wanted to get me with child—I thought at first he had discovered my plan to leave, and that perhaps he was punishing me, by ruining me. I tried to hide from him—in a spare room in the servants' quarters—but he quickly found me."

Rothsburgh's gut clenched and he fought the urge to slam his fist through a wall, imagining it was Hugh's face. "How did you get away?"

"Jenkins, our butler, was my knight in shining armor that night. He heard Hugh trying to break down the door. When he asked Hugh if he needed anything, Hugh swore at him and told him not to bother because he was going back to his club for the night. He called through the door and told me that he would deal with me in the morning. But Jenkins hired a cab for me, and I left Harcourt House before the sun had even risen.

"The other thing I remember clearly about that night is how oddly Hugh behaved before he told me he wanted to bed me again. When he first came to my room, he was melancholy. Not himself. He looked like a man about to face the gallows. And now I know why, James. He must have been mourning Isabelle. And from what you've told me, I rather suspect that Isabelle is the only reason I escaped unscathed."

What? Rothsburgh shook his head. "I don't understand."

"I know you said Isabelle didn't have a conscience, but I'm wondering if she did have a trace within her. The only reason I knew that Hugh suffered from syphilis was because his mistress sent me a letter, warning me to take precautions. It arrived in the post at Harcourt House, addressed to me, at the start of September."

"That was two weeks after Isabelle died," he whispered. *Could it be true?* Could Isabelle have saved Beth from the undeserved and cruel fate that would have been hers otherwise?

"Perhaps she didn't write a letter for you only, my love," Beth said softly. "Perhaps she also wrote one to me. I still have it." She leaned over to the stand beside the bed to retrieve her reticule, and after unfastening it, pulled out a rather creased and stained piece of plain parchment. She passed it to him. "It seems perverse I know, to keep something like this—a letter from my husband's mistress. I suppose any sane person would have burnt it. But whenever I start to have doubts about what I have done—running away—I look at it, and it reminds me that leaving Hugh was perhaps the only thing I could do, to stay safe."

Rothsburgh unfolded the parchment with shaking hands.

Dear Lady Beauchamp,

You won't believe me, but I write this missive with the best of intentions...

He glanced up at Beth, then swallowed past the lump of emotion jamming his throat. "Yes. It's from Isabelle." He drew a shuddering breath and dashed away a tear. "I'm sorry, Beth. You'll think me a fool for reacting this way."

Beth shook her head. "I would never think that, James."

He believed her. There was no judgment in her expression, only understanding. He put Isabelle's letter on the side table and turned back to the woman he loved more than anything.

"It's just that...I have hated Isabelle for so long. But now, despite all of the terrible things she did, to discover that she had a shred of decency within her...it means a lot to me." He lifted Beth's bandaged hand to his lips. "Especially because she saved you."

Beth's eyes were shining as she reached forward and caressed his cheek. "Yes, she did."

She was touching him. Such a simple gesture, but one that conveyed tenderness. *Caring*. Perhaps more. God, he prayed that it meant more.

Rothsburgh suddenly didn't want to speak about Hugh or Isabelle anymore. His desire to find out how Beth truly felt about him was so great, he ached.

He turned his face toward Beth's hand and kissed her palm before catching her gaze again. "Beth, although I might seem overwhelmed with emotion right now, I didn't miss that you called me, 'my love,' only a few moments ago." Placing his hand over hers, Rothsburgh searched her beautiful face and her soft gray eyes, trying to see through to her very soul. He drew another steadying breath. "So, did you mean it, Beth? Am I your love?"

CHAPTER 18

"*So, did you mean it, Beth? Am I your love?*"

Elizabeth's heart began to pound wildly in her chest, and her cheeks flamed under James's intense scrutiny. The unconcealed longing in his dark brown eyes was so clear, it stole her breath away. Made her very soul weep because she couldn't possibly tell him what was in her heart. Even though James now knew who she really was, and understood why she'd had to leave Hugh, admitting how she felt about him wouldn't change anything.

She couldn't be with him. Not the way he wanted. And certainly not the way he deserved. He deserved to have the love of a woman who could truly be his. She had to make him see that there was no point in hoping for a happily ever after.

She had to send him away.

She tried to withdraw her hand from his darkly stubbled cheek, but he wouldn't let her. His eyes narrowed, grew darker as his grip tightened imperceptibly, not enough to hurt, but enough to let her know he wouldn't let her escape. Not this time. Not until she confessed. Judging by the determined look in his eyes right at this moment, resisting him wasn't going to be easy.

Elizabeth blinked away tears. Drew in a shaky breath as she prepared to hurt him. *Again.* "James, it doesn't matter what I want or how I feel—"

"Of course it bloody matters," he said with such unexpected harshness, she winced. "You know how I feel about you. Despite everything you've told me, that hasn't changed, Beth. And if there's any chance at all that you care for me... that you love me... I need to know."

His voice had a desperate, raw edge to it and she felt a sharp stab of conscience. Now that she knew how deeply he'd been scarred by Isabelle, she understood why it was so important for him to know that he was loved.

But she couldn't ignore the cold stark fact that there could never be any real future for them. Not when she believed he still had a chance to meet and fall for someone else that would love him equally in return. Another woman who was free and who he could wed. Who could give him the children he must long for. An heir that was actually his.

And she couldn't be that woman.

She shook her head. This was so hard, denying him what he so wanted to hear, what she so wanted to tell him. "James. I'm Hugh's wife. No matter how much you or I wish it wasn't so, we can't overlook that. You deserve so much more than I can ever give you. I'm not worthy—"

Some potent emotion she couldn't quite name—perhaps it was desire, anger or despair or a combination of all three— flared in the dark depths of James's eyes, and he reached out to grasp her face between his large hands so she couldn't look away. "What rubbish, Beth. I know I reacted badly when you admitted that you were married. But I was shocked and hurt, and I said things that I shouldn't have..." His gaze fell to her mouth and for an instant she thought he was going to kiss her with bruising force. Stake his claim.

But the moment passed quickly and instead, his hands slid in a gentle caress to rest upon her shoulders. His dark scowl faded to be replaced with a look of contrition. "I'm truly sorry for how I behaved."

"You don't need to apologize, James—"

"But I do. You and Isabelle are nothing alike, and I had no right to compare your actions to hers. You are everything to me. And regardless of the fact that you are married, I still want you..." His eyes held hers, and when he spoke again his voice was deep and soft like a velvet sigh in the dark. "I can't help it. I love you, Beth."

His gaze dropped to her mouth as he ran his thumb along her lower lip, and she couldn't suppress the hot tremor of desire that shot through her, all the way to her very toes. Such a tender, coaxing, calculated caress. He was clearly trying to seduce her into an admission. "I've told you before I am a selfish man. I'll have you any way I can... Everyone and everything else be damned."

Oh, foolish heart. Foolish hope.

You must be strong and crush them, Elizabeth.

But that was becoming increasingly hard to do as the heat of James's touch and his gaze began to seep through to her core, melting her bones and her resolve into a molten puddle, as if she was as insubstantial as a beeswax candle that had been set too close to a furnace.

Damn him. Why couldn't he see that she was trying to send him away for his own good? That he was better off without her?

Elizabeth dragged the last remnants of her will together. "Being with you would be wrong."

He sighed and a wry smile tugged at the corner of his mouth. "What are you going to do then, Beth? I'm damn certain that you're not going back to Hugh. Are you really going to spend the next ten to fifteen years—however long Hugh lives—in hiding, as some poorly paid companion or lowly governess?" He tilted her chin up and searched her eyes. "Can you really face that? All those long, lonely years ahead? Now *that* would be wrong."

"What alternative do I have?" she whispered, unable to hide the traitorous, telling catch in her voice. She was so tired of fighting him. And herself.

He smiled slowly and trailed a finger along her jaw, down her neck until he encountered the neckline of her chaste flannel night rail. He flicked the top button open. "You could stay with me."

He undid the next button, his eyes never leaving hers. "If you wanted to."

The last button came undone. "If you loved me."

Such temptation.

Heaven help her.

"Tell me, Beth." His dark gaze fell to her mouth again, and he leaned forward and placed a feather-light, almost innocent kiss at the corner of her mouth. "Am I your love?" Another teasing kiss on her cheek, then on her jaw. "Or do you feel nothing for me?" His breath was warm against her skin, and she shivered as he mercilessly traced a line of kisses from her earlobe, down her now exposed neck to the exquisitely sensitive flesh just above her collarbone.

"James..." Her voice emerged as a husky moan.

"Yes, Beth?"

"I...I can't think when you kiss me."

"Good. I don't want you to think." She felt his lips curve in a smile against her heated skin before he placed another kiss on her throat where her pulse fluttered wildly like a trapped creature. "I want you to tell me how you feel."

"You're not being fair."

His gaze returned to hers. Hot, dark, compelling. "I know." Another kiss, this time on her mouth. Ever so soft like a whispered prayer.

"Tell me." He breathed against her lips. "For the love of God, Beth..."

A rake's ploys she could attempt to resist. But against this raw, naked need, Elizabeth was helpless. She summoned her voice and at last uttered the words he'd been longing to hear.

"I love you."

～

Rothsburgh groaned against Beth's mouth.

Yes. At last. Thank God and all his angels. Elation and desire flared inside him in equal measure. But hearing it once wasn't enough.

He leaned his forehead against Beth's. "Say it again," he demanded thickly, fighting back tears.

"I love you, James," she murmured huskily, a smile like the warmest sunshine in her voice as she wrapped her arms around his neck. Drew him closer until their noses touched and their breath mingled. "I love you."

He must have died and gone to heaven. He exhaled on a great shuddering sigh and placed his hand at the base of her throat, feeling the rise and fall of her chest, the frantic beating of her heart that echoed the thunder of his. "And you'll stay with me?"

She didn't hesitate to answer now. "Yes. I'm yours."

"Truly?"

"Yes," She reached for his cheek and touched his tears with trembling fingers. "Oh James..."

"I love you, Beth."

～

For the first time ever, Elizabeth allowed herself to feel the full force of James's words, to let the idea of "I love you" and everything that meant, penetrate her being. It was like being suffused with the purest delight, the essence of joy itself.

And it was all because of James. This powerful, charismatic, beautiful man who rested his head against hers and cried his joy simply because she'd told him she loved him in return. Tears welled in her eyes. It was almost too much happiness for her to bear.

"Kiss me," she whispered on a tremulous breath.

James drew back a little and his wide mouth tilted into a gentle, lop-sided smile. "With pleasure, my love."

One of his hands shifted to the nape of her neck whilst the other curled gently around her shoulder, pulling her closer as he ever so slowly angled his head lower, and then covered her mouth with his. His lips slid against hers, satiny soft, as gentle as spring rain, and she sagged against him, boneless and melting as a sweet warmth like slowly flowing honey spread throughout her entire body.

Her lips curved into a smile beneath his as she realized that this was what truly being in love felt like.

But this tender melding of mouths was soon not enough. Elizabeth could sense the rising heat and tension in James's body—in the way his lips firmed against hers, how the muscles of his shoulders tightened beneath her hands, the increased pace of his breathing. James's tongue teasingly flicked against her bottom lip and with a moan, she opened her mouth for him. He responded with his own deep, throaty sound of satisfaction before boldly stroking his tongue against hers, tasting her mouth with a thoroughness that made her nipples ache, and moisture well at the apex of her thighs.

It was hard to believe that moments ago she'd been contemplating a life without James, a life without these intoxicating kisses that so effortlessly aroused her. A life without this extraordinary bliss. It was unthinkable. She must have been mad.

Ignoring the protest of her cut hands, Elizabeth buried her fingers into the silky blackness of James's hair at the back of his head, dragging him closer. At the same time, she restlessly crushed her breasts against the hot hard wall of his chest, greedily seeking more of the feel and taste of him, this infinitely addictive man.

She broke the kiss. "You are wearing far too many clothes," she breathed raggedly, tugging futilely at his coat.

"Agreed," he growled. "As are you, my sweet." He hooked his hand into the opening of her night rail, and ignoring her gasp, rent the flannel from neckline to waist. "I really hate this thing you know," he said with a hint of satisfied amusement lurking beneath the huskiness of his voice. "I've been dying to do that since I walked in."

"Is it really that dreadful?" she asked with mock indignation even as excitement spiked within her, making her nipples peak and her sex throb with anticipation.

"Yes. You know it is. Now lie back so I can rip the rest from you."

She eagerly acquiesced to his demand, pushing herself back into the lumpy narrow mattress before James used both hands to swiftly tear the rest of the offending garment in two.

He gently parted both sides, and with fixed concentration, regarded her trembling naked body. She could feel his rapt visual ravishment of her, clean through to her very bones. It made her heart race and her blood pulse heavily, and she pressed her thighs together trying to the ease the needy pressure. But it was to no avail. She needed his hands on her.

As if in concert with her thoughts, James placed one large hand at the base of her throat, then with a light, teasing touch, ran it down the length of her body, across her breasts, over her belly, all the way to the tight thatch of curls between her thighs, raising goose bumps. She shivered and closed her eyes, waiting for him to touch her there, right where she craved it most.

But he didn't. *Damn him*. He was going to make her wait. She made a mew of frustration and heard him chuckle right before she heard the thud of his boots on the floor.

"Patience, my love."

Opening her eyes again, she watched James steadily, hungrily, as he undressed in front of her, his smoldering black gaze never leaving her face as he tugged at his cravat and stripped off his coat, waistcoat and shirt. She bit her lip to stop herself from gaping as her eyes traced over all of the broad planes, sharp angles and defined ridges of his lean, muscular body. His breeches quickly joined the heap of discarded clothing on the floor, and she swallowed, mesmerized at the sight of his rigid, proudly jutting cock, long and thick, and ready for her.

Her fingers itched to touch him, and she pulled her arms from the remnants of her night rail. "Come to bed, James, before I freeze to death," she whispered. *Or die of frustration.*

Before she could blink, James slid his large body over hers. He was like a furnace, radiating the heat of a thousand summer suns. "Christ, Beth, you're like ice." He enveloped her shivering body, and she wrapped her arms around his shoulders, and tangled her legs with his, relishing the sensation of his hot, hard length against her. Especially the impudent jut of his cock against her belly. She started to squirm beneath him and she felt him shake with laughter.

"Jesus, it's like being in bed with a cold, wriggly jellyfish."

She humphed into his ear, resisting the sudden and unfamiliar, yet highly appealing urge to slap him on the taut cheek of one his buttocks, only because she knew it would hurt her more than him. "Well, you have no one to blame but yourself.

You're the one who decided to get rid of my warm and completely sensible night rail."

James drew back and rested on his elbows to study her, wicked amusement glinting in his eyes. "Beth, you're just lucky I love and want you so much that I could see past that hideous thing to the treasures lying beneath." He pushed his hips against her, teasing her with the thrust of his cock. "Besides, all you need to keep warm is me."

She smiled. "I won't disagree with you there." She reached up and stroked his jaw with her bandaged fingers, and he pressed into her palm, like a large, satisfied lion. She fancied she could almost hear him purr. "I wish I could touch you, the way I want to," she whispered.

James kissed her palm. "In time. Your hands will heal, my love." Dark mischief sparked in his eyes, and he grasped her by both wrists, bringing them up above her head and holding them in place with one hand. His grip was uncompromising. "I could keep them out of the way though. Tie you up. So I don't inadvertently hurt you." He kissed her, his tongue dancing suggestively against hers for a moment before he withdrew. "What do you say?" He nuzzled the sensitive flesh behind her ear before kissing her mouth again, this time with deep, bone melting languor. "I'd be nothing but gentle."

Beth made herself frown. "And I'd be completely at your mercy." The idea was shocking yet she couldn't deny it was also highly arousing.

"Entirely. Would that be so bad?"

"Very bad. Wicked."

He gave her a devastatingly rakish grin. "My thoughts exactly."

He bent his head and bestowed another deeply ravishing kiss that soon had her moaning against his mouth and arching against him in an agony of unsatisfied need. "James…"

"Mhmm." He dropped a trail of nipping kisses along her jawline.

"I want..."

A longer kiss at the juncture of her collar bones. "I know what you want, my love," he murmured against her trembling skin. "Trust me...you'll enjoy what I have planned."

If I don't die first— She cried out as James suddenly took one of her aching, tightly furled nipples into his mouth and suckled hard. A bolt of heat lanced through her all the way to her wet sex, and she bucked against his firm hold on her wrists. But he didn't let go. Instead, he mercilessly teased her breasts with teeth and lips and tongue and fingers until she was incoherent and helpless with desire.

"Please, James..." This torture was too cruel.

He chuckled against the underside of one breast, his breath teasing her oh-so sensitive flesh before he raised his head and flashed her a devilish grin. "I'll make a deal with you, my love. If you promise to keep your hands above your head, I'll touch you here." At that precise moment, two of his fingers slid unerringly between her wet folds into her inner sheath and her whole body bowed upward as another shaft of sizzling pleasure seared through her.

"I promise," she gasped.

"Good girl."

He released his hold on her wrists, and whilst continuing to torment her breasts, he began to slide his long fingers in and out of her, stroking the front wall of her passage whilst the pad of his thumb circled around and around her center of pleasure. Such agony, such bliss.

She couldn't hold her arms straight above her head any longer, and she folded them around her head, biting her lip to stop herself crying out as James continued his pleasurable assault on her, the pressure in her sex spiraling higher and tighter, as tight as the tautened wire on a bow about to release its arrow, so close to climax it hurt. She teetered on the quivering edge. Surely she would come soon... She had to.

Oh, please.

James tugged one last time on her nipple with his teeth at the same time he pressed into her throbbing core and on a sobbing cry, she came apart beneath him.

Her womb seemed to convulse endlessly as she was tossed about on a tumultuous sea of powerful release. The only thing holding her steady and anchored to reality was James's warm embrace, his soft kiss at her temple, her fevered brow, the corner of her mouth.

"I told you that you'd enjoy it, didn't I?" he whispered against her lips before kissing her softly on the mouth.

Still largely insensible, Beth stretched languorously beneath James before encircling her arms about his neck. She opened sleepy eyes and looked up at him. Even though he was right, she narrowed her eyes and frowned. He looked entirely too smug for her liking.

"You think you're clever, don't you?" she teased, arching her back a little so her belly pressed into his still ramrod straight cock. She wanted to drive him as wild as he had driven her. Return pleasure to him ten-fold.

He groaned softly, but then flashed her a small, lopsided grin. "A little. But it was all for you."

She didn't doubt that for a moment. She softened her expression as she traced the line of his sculptured upper lip with one finger, then caught his gaze. "I know. And as usual you have taken care of me first."

How could she begrudge him feeling pleased about the fact that he had satisfied her so well? More than well, in fact. Her climax had been sublime. She purposely hooked her legs around his hips and pushed herself against him again, her wet aching cleft opening against his rigid length.

He closed his eyes and hissed in a sharp breath. "Careful,

my angel. I might just lose myself all over your belly like a randy youth."

"Then what are you waiting for?" she whispered and then kissed the column of his throat where his pulse throbbed just beneath the skin. She inhaled, the spicy scent of him and his hot arousal making her head spin like she had just consumed a glass of whisky all at once.

"Take me, James," she breathed. "I'm yours."

Beth's naked, blatant demand set Rothsburgh trembling with need. Confounded woman. He *would* come all over her if she kept this up.

He growled deeply in his throat as Beth's lips made hot contact with his neck again, and he ruthlessly positioned himself between her thighs, the head of his cock brushing her slick sex. God, how he loved how wet she was. For him. He couldn't wait to be inside her, to at last make the connection between them complete. To make them one in the most basic, primal of ways.

He slid in, to the hilt, in one long smooth movement, relishing her gasp against his neck and the hot welcoming clench of her inner passage around him. He gritted his teeth and prayed for the strength to make this experience last, to make it memorable for both of them. He loved this woman with every shuddering breath that he took, with every beat of his pounding heart, and now that he knew Beth loved him too, the sensation of joining with her was profound. He felt like he was communing with her very soul.

He rested on his forearms, holding still within her for a long moment and looked down at her beautiful face—the tousled halo of pale blond hair, her flushed cheeks and her slightly parted lips, swollen and slick from his earlier kisses.

Her eyes were closed, but as he continued to remain still, watching her, her eyelids fluttered open and she looked at him.

"What is it?" she whispered, the soft gray of her eyes darkening a little as she reached up to brush a lock of his hair away from his brow.

He locked eyes with her, wanting her to understand how much she meant to him. "I love you, Beth. With everything that I am. Now and always. Don't ever doubt that."

He wanted to say more, but all at once, he couldn't fight the overwhelmingly powerful urge to move within her. He slowly began to withdraw, prolonging the delicious agonizing friction.

Beth moaned and the greedy grasp of inner passage grew tighter around his shaft as if she couldn't bear him to leave her body.

He hovered for one brief, breathless moment at her entrance, and then plunged into her satiny heat again, reveling in the hot gasp of her breath against his chest. Drew out again with lingering slowness, then swiftly thrust into her once more, deeper, harder. Claiming her as his.

"You're mine," he groaned.

"Yes," Beth hissed and angled her hips upward to take more of him. "Yours."

His heart surged and he dipped his head, plundering her mouth with lips and tongue, feasting on the dark honeyed recess of her mouth as again he slid out before slamming back into her.

My Beth. My love. My life's blood.

She moaned into his mouth and seized his buttocks with her hands. "Again. Harder."

He couldn't resist. He clenched his jaw tightly, willing himself not to come too soon as he began to increase the exquisite rhythmic pace of thrust and withdrawal. He would give anything to do this all morning, all day, hell forever if he could, to sustain this deep connection as he plunged in and out of Beth, to gaze down on her flushed face, her eyes unfocused and heavy-lidded with deep arousal. To hear her short panting breaths and rhythmic moans as he steadily drove her higher and higher toward climax. He could feel her sheath beginning to quiver and clench. His balls were agony, his head dizzy with need as he continued to pound into her.

Selfish brute that he was though, he wanted her with him as they both reached their peak. "Look at me," he demanded on a ragged, hoarse breath.

Her eyes immediately focused on him, the gray becoming as clear and bright as moonlight on water, despite her frantic, agitated state. Her hands slid to his sweat-slick shoulders and her fingers dug into him, seeking purchase against the relentless rhythm he'd set as she strove to keep her gaze fastened to his.

He thrust harder, faster, hurtling them both toward the edge of the storm. "Tell me..." Another merciless thrust. "You're mine."

"Yes, James," she gasped, her eyes flashing like silver. She arched beneath him. "Yours!"

And then she came, clamping around him so hard, he couldn't hold back any longer. He cried out in fierce elation, his voice merging with her own exultant cry as together they soared through the passionate tempest of their own making, before descending into the waiting arms of pure, unadulterated release.

He collapsed on top of her, flesh to flesh, heart to heart, soul to soul. Inhaled Beth's heady essence deep into his lungs as he felt the gentle quakes within her womb subside. He'd found heaven with Beth. And he would never let her go again.

And then she moved a little beneath him and his mind jolted with shock at the realization that he was still inside her.

He'd forgotten himself and had pumped her womb full of his seed.

God, no.

When they'd started this affair, he'd promised Beth that he would take care, that he wouldn't get her with child. But just now he'd been so caught up in the moment, he hadn't been able to see past his own selfish need. And he'd failed her.

But underneath the self-recrimination, he also detected the emergence of a quiet wonder as he suddenly imagined Beth growing ripe and luscious with a swollen, pregnant belly. He could think of no greater gift than Beth bearing his child.

But would she see it that way?

He couldn't marry Beth. That meant he wouldn't be able to give their child his name. And he instinctively knew that Beth wouldn't want their baby to suffer the ignominy of bastardy.

Oh Christ. What have I done?

He raised himself onto his forearms and his eyes traced over her perfect features. Her eyes were closed and there was a gentle smile on her lips. Shattering her afterglow was the last thing he wanted to do. But he had to.

He forced himself to speak. "Beth…"

At the sound of her name, Elizabeth pried open her drowsy eyelids and smiled up at James. She could lie like this all day, in his warm embrace. It was absolute bliss.

Or it would be, if it wasn't for the tense expression on James's face. His dark eyes were troubled and a muscle flickered in his cheek as he stared down at her.

Her heart clenched. They'd just shared the most earth-shattering bout of lovemaking one could ever hope for. What could possibly be wrong?

"James?" she whispered, unable to mask the uncertainty in her voice. Whatever he was going to say, it clearly wasn't good. "Tell me what's the matter?"

He searched her eyes. Swallowed. "Beth, I wasn't careful... I forgot to withdraw... I'm so sorry, my love."

Oh...

He spoke the truth. He hadn't withdrawn. She could still feel him inside her and the stickiness of his seed between her legs. She had been so swept away and then so deeply satisfied by James's lovemaking, that she hadn't noticed at all.

James continued. "I understand if you're angry. I've broken my promise to you—"

"Shhh." She placed a finger on his lips. "I'm not angry. It will be all right. I never became pregnant during my marriage. Not that I ever had intercourse very much. But I've always suspected that I'm barren."

"But you don't know that for certain. What if I get you with child?"

How would she feel? Until this moment, Elizabeth had never really considered it. She stroked James's deliciously messy hair away from his damp, furrowed brow and studied his tense, handsome face. If she were truly honest with herself, the idea of bearing this wonderful man a son or daughter filled her with a strange poignant joy rather than horror.

"Then I will love our child, come what may," she replied softly. "Because it is yours and I love you. We will work out what to do...if such a miracle ever happens. I trust you, James."

James's eyes suddenly became bright with the sheen of tears. "God, you are an amazing woman, Beth." His voice was thick with emotion. "The angels were smiling on me the day you crossed my doorstep."

He lowered his head and kissed her softly until her toes curled.

When he broke the kiss, he sought her gaze again. His expression firmed. "Know this Beth, if we should have a child together, I will talk to the best legal minds in the land. I will do whatever I can to make sure our child is provided for, even if he or she can never bear my name." He took another breath. This time when he spoke, his voice shook a little. "And I swear that one day, I will marry you."

Elizabeth's heart swelled with so much love, she thought it might burst as she recognized the strength of James's conviction. He would stand by her, no matter what the future had in store. He must truly love her.

She swallowed and fought back sudden tears of joy. Her voice when it emerged was husky with emotion. "That sounds like another proposal of sorts."

James's dark eyes shone as he steadily held her gaze. "It's more than that, Beth. It's a vow."

CHAPTER 19

Edinburgh, Scotland
November 1815

"There she is. Helena assured me they would all be out for a walk today."

Elizabeth peered through the fine black netting shrouding her face, in the direction James had indicated, toward the eastern gate of the Queen Street Gardens. Even after a month of being in Edinburgh, she still didn't feel comfortable showing her face in public in case anyone that she knew from her former life recognized her. The *ton* had eyes and ears everywhere, even this far north, of that she was absolutely certain. And as much as she longed to throw back her veil so she could clearly see the little blond girl ahead, she just couldn't take the risk. Not when she'd found so much happiness in her new life with James.

He was everything to her.

James tucked her gloved hand into the crook of his arm, then gently urged her forward along the path strewn with dark sodden leaves, toward the group headed their way: three children, the youngest tucked into a pile of blankets in a small but elaborate "baby carriage" pulled by a Shetland pony; two plainly dressed women who were most likely nurse and governess; and trailing behind, a liveried footman carrying a doll in the crook of his arm.

Even though it was cold enough to make their breath turn to mist, the afternoon held fair; a rare occurrence for a late autumn day in Edinburgh, James had informed her, when they had first set out on foot from her newly rented, beautifully appointed townhouse in nearby Herriot Row. Indeed, over the last few weeks since they'd quit Dundee for the capital, it had rained nearly every day.

Not that Elizabeth had minded overly much, if at all. Not when she had spent long lazy days at home with James, talking, laughing, reading, and making love whenever they fancied.

Of course, they had braved the elements on occasions. Soon after their arrival in town, James had insisted on taking her to a series of private appointments with Edinburgh's finest modistes and milliners along the Royal Mile in the Old Town. But aside from all of the exquisite silk, satin, velvet and fine woolen gowns, and other fripperies he had lavished on her, and that she could only wear for him in the privacy of her townhouse, he'd also purchased her a new wardrobe of the finest black garments that guineas could buy. Although he was not overly happy that she still insisted on wearing widow's weeds and veiled bonnets in public, he could see the sense in her determination to remain incognito. For now.

Elizabeth suddenly shivered. Even though she was perfectly warm in her black merino dress and well-cut matching coat, black kid gloves and walking boots, it wasn't the icy bite in the air that caused the frisson. She was about to meet James's daughter.

Hugh's daughter.

James halted their progress beneath a gnarled oak, its bare branches casting strange black fingers of shadow across the strong planes of his face. "I know you're apprehensive, my love," he murmured close to her ear. "If you'd prefer to turn back—"

"No. It's fine, James," she said, endeavoring to keep a steady voice. "It's just that... I'm not sure how I feel, to be honest."

She paused and glanced up the path. The small party was getting closer. Annabelle was only fifty yards away now. "No, that's not quite true," she said turning back to him. "I feel strange." She tried to smile then, even though her veil must obscure her expression. "I'm also worried that I'll frighten Annabelle off. She might think I'm a frightful witch dressed like this, all in black."

James looked over her shoulder and quickly scanned the park. "There's no one else here, Beth. It's a private park. If it makes you feel better, I'm sure it will be safe to lift your veil."

"I suppose you're right." Elizabeth began to lift the netting, but James stilled her hands.

"Wait," he murmured. "Allow me."

He gently raised the veil over her black bonnet, and Elizabeth was so vividly reminded of a groom lifting the veil on his bride, her breath caught in her throat.

If only it could be so.

James caught her gaze and a smile lifted the corner of his mouth. "Remember my vow, Beth," he said in a low, velvet-soft tone. "One day—"

A squeal of delight pierced the air. "Papa!" Annabelle was hurtling along the path toward them, her golden blond curls flying out behind her, the color as bright as the first daffodils of spring.

James laughed and bent to catch the child who flew into his arms like a small, royal-blue wool clad cannonball, nearly knocking him off his feet. "Annabelle, my bonnie lassie." He swung her around in his arms and she squealed with laughter again.

What an extraordinarily beautiful child who looked nothing like James, but exactly like Hugh. Elizabeth blinked away tears, overwhelmed by the sharp pull and prick of conflicting emotions in her heart. Sadness for James and Annabelle, anger at Hugh. Sorrow for herself that if things between her and Hugh had been different, then perhaps she would have been the one to bear him such a lovely child. Not another man's wife.

"I'm so sorry, Lord Rothsburgh." One of the women had rushed over, her cheeks flushed with high color. Then she scowled in admonishment at the giggling child in his arms. "Lady Annabelle, where are your manners?"

"It's quite all right, Miss Palmer," replied James, smiling at the flustered young woman whose entire face then turned beet-red, undoubtedly due to being the recipient of such dazzling regard. "My Lady Annabelle hasn't seen as much of me as she ought. And such is the exuberance of the very young. I am willing to make allowances on this occasion if you will also."

"Yes, my lord." Miss Palmer curtsied, then cast Elizabeth a small, slightly speculative glance. "My lady."

My lady. The governess had assumed she was someone of consequence because of the company she was keeping. Ignoring the tightening knot of unease inside her, Elizabeth tried to keep her expression pleasantly neutral as she inclined her head in acknowledgement. How on earth *was* James going to introduce her to Annabelle, indeed anyone, in a way that would even sound vaguely acceptable? One didn't usually introduce one's mistress to one's family. And even though she'd been here a month, it wasn't until today that James had put forward the idea of meeting his daughter.

Elizabeth wondered if James had also informed his brother-in-law and sister, Lord and Lady Maxwell, of her presence in Edinburgh. Now that would be highly awkward. It would be better for all concerned if he hadn't.

The sound of James's voice cut through her tangled thoughts. He was addressing the curious governess again. "That will be all for now, Miss Palmer."

"Yes, my lord."

As Miss Palmer turned to go back to her other charges, Annabelle turned her bright, summer blue gaze on Elizabeth. "Papa, is this the lady you've been telling me about?"

James nodded and continued to smile warmly, obviously unperturbed that he was about to introduce his daughter to his mistress. "Indeed, she is."

He bent down and placed Annabelle onto the path beside him. "Annabelle, allow me to introduce my friend, Mrs. Eliott. Mrs. Eliott, may I present my daughter, Lady Annabelle Huntly."

Elizabeth swept into a polite curtsy. "It's a pleasure to meet you, Lady Annabelle."

Annabelle smiled back, a dimple in her cheek. "It's lovely to meet you as well, Mrs. Eliott." Tipping her head, she then looked up at James. "Papa. She is even prettier than you said. Can she come to visit us at Maxwell House this afternoon?"

Before he could respond, Annabelle grasped Elizabeth's hand and began to bounce up and down. "Would you like to share tea with me, Mrs. Eliott? Cook makes the most excellent teacake. And I'm sure Uncle Phillip and Aunt Helena wouldn't mind at all."

James ruffled her curls. "Mrs. Eliott is rather busy at present. Perhaps another time, my sweet."

Elizabeth sighed inwardly with relief. So, he hadn't mentioned her to his sister or brother-in-law. She cast him a grateful smile and he smiled back, his brown eyes warm with reassurance.

But Annabelle was pouting. She tugged on Elizabeth's hand. "Well, at least come and meet my cousins, Charlie and Phillipa, Mrs. Eliott. Although Phillipa is rather grumpy at the moment. Miss MacFarlane, that's our nurse—although we call her Nanny—she says Phillipa is cutting a tooth. And you must come and see my doll, Miss Miranda. Papa brought her all the way back from Bruges. Fergus is holding her for me."

Elizabeth summoned a smile, trying not to notice that Annabelle's eyes were the exact shade of blue as Hugh's. "That would be lovely, Lady Annabelle. But perhaps we could take a turn about the park first."

"A wonderful idea, Mrs. Eliott," agreed James. "I've heard there is a pair of mute swans in Farmer Wood's Cattle Pond. You and Annabelle go on ahead while I speak to Miss Palmer and Miss MacFarlane, and say hello to my niece and nephew. I won't be long."

"Ooh, mute swans. I do love swans don't you, Mrs. Eliott?" enthused Annabelle, pulling Elizabeth down the path in the direction of the pond.

"Yes, I do too." Elizabeth followed Annabelle's lead, quite bemused yet thoroughly enchanted as she listened to the young girl unselfconsciously prattle away about this and that. To think that she had originally traveled all the way to Eilean Tor on the off chance of becoming a governess to this lovely, spirited child. Hugh's child. A child that would one day be her daughter as well, God-willing. She could scarcely fathom it.

Within minutes they came across the pond, dark and still beneath the shadows of the surrounding oaks. And as James had predicted, there were the two swans, floating upon the glass-like surface of the water, their graceful necks arched toward each other like a pair of lovers.

"Aren't they beautiful?" whispered Annabelle.

"Yes, they are," Elizabeth agreed softly. Even though she knew she was being ridiculously mawkish, she was suddenly unaccountably envious of their quiet, simple solitude. "It's a shame that we haven't any bread to feed them."

Annabelle smiled. "I'm sure Nanny or Miss Palmer will have brought some."

A sudden movement amongst the bare trees on the far side of the pond caught Elizabeth's eye. A man, dressed in dark clothing emerged from the copse, and started to skirt the edge of the pond, heading their way. Although there was nothing overtly sinister about his appearance or purposeful stride, fear prickled beneath Elizabeth's skin. She gripped Annabelle's hand and pulled her a little closer.

The stranger smiled and raised a hand in greeting. "Pardon me, madam." He held her gaze as he approached. "If it's no' verra much trouble, would ye mind directin' me to Queen Street. I seem to ha' lost my way."

"It's behind you. You'll need to retrace your steps, sir."

The man glanced back over his shoulder toward the copse. "Och, so it is." He took a few steps closer and peered at the lapel on Elizabeth's coat. "I see ye have a watch there. Might I ask ye fer the time?"

God, was he a thief? Elizabeth didn't bother to glance down. She refused to take her eyes off the man for a moment. Although her rational mind told her she was overreacting, her instincts screamed that she was not. "I believe it's just past one o'clock, sir."

His craggy face broke into a gap-toothed grin, and Elizabeth instinctively recoiled backward, tugging Annabelle behind her skirts. Where in God's name was James? If she screamed would he hear her?

"Och. Yer English, are ye?" The man's gaze suddenly flickered to a point behind Elizabeth and then his bushy eyebrows plunged into a deep frown. "I'll bid ye a good day, madam. I

285

mustna' be late." He doffed his hat, took a few steps back, and then all but bolted back toward the copse.

"I didn't like that man," stated Annabelle as the stranger disappeared into the trees. "He had mean eyes and he smelt like Papa's dogs when they're wet."

"Beth?"

Elizabeth was so relieved to hear James's voice, she nearly sagged into the pile of wet autumn leaves at her feet.

"Are you and Annabelle all right? Who was that man?" The moment James reached her, he pulled her swiftly into his arms. "Sweet Lord, you're shaking, Beth."

"There was an ugly, smelly man who said he was lost, and then he asked Mrs. Eliott the time," said Annabelle. "But I think he was lying. He was probably a pickpocket. Miss Palmer and Nanny say you must always look out for pickpockets."

"We're fine," Elizabeth said shakily, wanting to stay within the circle of James's arms, but she drew back, acutely aware of Annabelle's curious gaze on them. She made an effort to steady her voice. "And I don't know who that man was, or what he really wanted. But there was something not quite right about him. He asked me directions to Queen Street."

James's eyes darkened and his mouth thinned to a grim line. "Wait here." He released his hold on her arms and took off toward the other side of the park.

Elizabeth knelt down and held Annabelle gently by the shoulders. For all her youthful courage, the child's wide blue eyes were clouded as they darted between her and the trees.

"You were very brave, Lady Annabelle," she said gently, catching her gaze. "Your father will be all right and back here before we know it."

"I know. He fought for the Duke of Wellington at Waterloo and has lots of medals. I'm not worried about him."

Her forehead dipped into a slight frown. "But I was just wondering. Are you going to be my new mother, Mrs. Eliott?"

Elizabeth bit back a gasp. She and James had both under-estimated the child's perceptiveness. She concentrated on taking a calming breath and cleared her throat. "Your father... Lord Rothsburgh and I, we are just good friends, Lady Annabelle."

Annabelle shook her head, her golden curls bouncing. "Papa loves you. I think he wants to marry you. He called you 'Beth' and hugged you." Her frowned deepened and a shadow of sadness darkened her eyes. "He and Mama never hugged. Mama didn't like it."

Before Elizabeth could draw another breath, Annabelle threw her arms about her neck and buried her small face in the black wool of her coat. "I'm glad you like hugs. And you smell nice. Like flowers. I want Papa to marry you too."

Elizabeth's heart contracted so painfully it took her breath away, and she tightened her hold about Annabelle. She knew that this sweet child had been through so much, and it was nothing more than innocent yearning for a maternal figure that caused her to make such an impulsive pronouncement. But still...Elizabeth also wished with her whole heart that she could be a mother to the little girl. She opened her mouth to speak, but truly didn't know what to say. She didn't want to give Annabelle false hope that James would marry her anytime soon. So she simply cradled the girl in her arms and tried to swallow past the hard lump in her throat as she blinked away her tears.

A loud boyish whoop in the distance burst the stillness around them, and Annabelle pulled away. "That's Charlie," she said with a moue of annoyance. "I'd better go and tell him to be quiet, otherwise he'll frighten the swans." She ran off and as Elizabeth stood, James emerged from the copse.

"There was no sign of him," James told her when he

reached her side. Although his hair was ruffled, he was barely out of breath, belying the fact that he'd just been racing through the park. "I think he scaled the fence. I certainly don't think he's one of the local residents by the way you and Annabelle described him."

"Who do you think he was then?"

James shrugged. "Probably just a chancer or a pickpocket like Annabelle suggested." He grasped her hand and held it against his chest. "I'm just glad that you and Annabelle are all right." He glanced around. "Where is she by the way?"

Before Elizabeth could reply, Annabelle, with Charlie only a step or two behind, hared past them toward the edge of the pond.

"We have bread. Nanny had some," called Annabelle back to them, waving a brown paper packet in the air which Charlie promptly snatched from her. Annabelle squawked and snatched it back.

James smiled at Elizabeth and took her arm. "Perhaps some supervision is in order, my dear Mrs. Eliott. I've already been for a run. I certainly don't fancy a swim to fish these two out of the pond."

They advanced to the edge of the water and Elizabeth smiled quietly to herself as she watched James with his daughter and nephew. It was obvious he loved children. And he so deserved a child of his own. But would she be the woman to bear him one?

What if she wasn't barren?

Since their reconciliation at the inn in Dundee, James hadn't been careful about taking precautions against pregnancy. And she hadn't wanted him too. Part of her knew she must be mad. Any other woman, a sane woman, would feel both mortification and dread at the idea of becoming pregnant to a man who wasn't her husband; of bearing an illegitimate child. But she didn't.

Oh, how she'd fallen, so, so deep. Despite all of the risks, all of the potential censure, she would love to be the mother of James's baby.

She placed her hand against the flat of her belly and let herself contemplate for one wild moment that perhaps she might already be carrying James's child. A joyous feeling fluttered within her heart, as fragile and delicate as a butterfly.

She glanced at James, and it was as though he felt her gaze. He immediately turned to look at her, over the heads of Annabelle and Charlie—who were now quietly throwing breadcrumbs to the swans—and gave her a slow, heart-stopping smile. The one that made her knees feel like butter and made her skin tingle with awareness.

She smiled back in helpless thrall. How could she not? If this was madness, it was the most beautiful, fulfilling feeling in the world. And she never wanted to lose it.

After they farewelled Annabelle and the two youngest Maxwells, James escorted Elizabeth back to Rothsburgh House in St Andrew's Square. As the afternoon was still clear, he'd suggested that perhaps she might like to see the Palace of Holyroodhouse, and its extensive park. But they needed his curricle to make the trip, hence their detour via Rothsburgh House.

It was the first time Elizabeth had set foot in James's townhouse since she'd arrived in Edinburgh. Not because James hadn't wanted to have her there, but because she had insisted that she needed to remain as inconspicuous as possible. Rothsburgh House wasn't a remote, isolated castle on the very edge of the North Sea, and it certainly wouldn't do for the marquess to be seen housing his latest mistress here, in full view of Edinburgh's *tonnish* society. It would be noticed and remarked upon. And Elizabeth couldn't countenance that at all.

As she hovered uncertainly in the vestibule watching James issue instructions to Malcolm, his butler, she knew without a doubt that her taking up residence in Herriot Row had been the right decision. Even though James had introduced her to Malcolm as Mrs. Eliott—the recently bereaved widow of one of his fellow comrades from the Gordon Highlanders—she didn't think the stony-faced butler believed a word of it. She'd caught the man's cold stare of appraisal when James offered his arm to escort her to the drawing room for a quick cup of tea while they waited for the curricle. The dour Malcolm would never be as accommodating as Roberts, of that she was certain.

It was nothing short of a relief when the curricle arrived and they departed for the Park.

The trip through the wide New Town streets to Calton Road, and then onto the lower end of the Royal Mile, the Canongate, took no time at all. As soon as it came into view, Elizabeth knew straightaway that she much preferred the Palace of Holyroodhouse compared to the gray brooding bulk of Edinburgh Castle at the top of the Mile. Even though the turreted, honey-stoned palace was smaller than she'd anticipated—it had once been the royal residence for the now deposed line of Scottish monarchs—it was elegant all the same. Rather like a refined lady basking in the pale autumn sunlight.

Elizabeth recalled from her long-ago childhood history lessons that the ill-fated "Bonnie Prince Charlie" had been the last of the Stuarts to reside there—albeit briefly—before he'd had to flee after the failed Jacobite rebellion of 1745. And there hadn't been a monarch in residence since.

"It's lovely," she said as James drove the curricle down the last stretch of the Canongate toward the Palace, and its surrounding parklands. "Is the Comte D'Artois still staying in the Royal Apartments?" It was well known that the exiled French nobleman had been offered a place of sanctuary at Holyrood after the French Revolution.

"I believe he left some years ago," replied James as he drew the curricle up in the Forecourt. "The Duke of Hamilton's staff still maintains Holyrood though. We'll just need to speak with the housekeeper to arrange a tour of Mary, Queen of Scots' old apartments, over there in the left tower." He jumped down then helped her to alight. "I thought you might like that, given you and Mary have something in common," he added, flashing her a smile.

Elizabeth raised her eyebrows, puzzled. "How so?"

James took her hand, and as he tucked it into his elbow, bent toward her ear. "Why, her second husband, Lord Darnley, was rumored to have the pox."

Elizabeth's jaw dropped. "No!" She had known that Mary and the nobleman had not had a happy marriage, and that the Earl of Bothwell, her lover and third husband, had been implicated in Darnley's murder. But her governess had certainly never taught her such an unsavory detail, that Darnley had syphilis.

James shrugged. "There are accounts that Darnley's body was covered in pockmarks when it was discovered outside of the tavern at Kirk o' Fields, which isn't far from here. Like Bothwell, Mary was also questioned about her husband's untimely demise, but no charges were ever laid. Not that it mattered in the end. Queen Elizabeth had Mary arrested shortly after that on suspicion of treason."

Elizabeth shivered. "Heavens. Queen Mary certainly led a tumultuous life."

James squeezed her hand. "But unlike Mary, you will have a happy ending, my love."

Elizabeth made herself hold James's warm gaze, and with

some effort, smiled back as they stepped into the dark shadows beneath the triumphal gateway where a footman from the Duke of Hamilton's retinue waited.

What if he was wrong?

A strange sense of foreboding suddenly settled over her. A certain feeling that this existence with James would have to end.

And it wouldn't leave her. Like the heart-broken ghosts of Holyrood itself, it clung to Elizabeth throughout the entire tour, even followed her into the pale, late afternoon sunshine when she and James emerged from the Palace an hour later to take a turn about the grounds and the adjacent ruins of the Abbey Church of Holyrood.

"What is it, Beth?" James halted in the middle of the nave, one of the arches from an aisle window casting a dark shadow across his face so Elizabeth couldn't see his eyes. "Have all the ghosts and tales of dastardly deeds made you melancholy, my love?"

She shrugged a shoulder and forced a smile. "Perhaps. This whole place is beautiful, but terribly sad. Especially in here. I don't think there's anything sadder than a ruined church, don't you agree?"

She released James's hand and stepped carefully over the uneven, stone slab floor to study the inscriptions on the grave plaques that remained in the south-eastern corner of the nave. She didn't want to talk about what was really bothering her, the real reason for her unease. The talk of Mary and Darnley's past had indeed resurrected her own guilt about leaving Hugh. She could try to bury it, but it was always there. James wouldn't want to hear that.

She felt him behind her, his body warm and solid against her back, his hands on her shoulders.

"Beth." He turned her to face him and lifted her veil, his

eyes studying hers. "You can't hide from me, my sweet. Tell me what's bothering you."

She felt her cheeks grow warm, but she didn't look away. He was right. He knew her too well. "It's just that..." She swallowed. No, she couldn't, *didn't* want to talk about Hugh and her own misgivings. It wasn't James's burden to bear. It was entirely her own.

She reached out and touched his cheek, suddenly wishing that she wasn't wearing gloves. "I was wondering how long we would stay in Edinburgh. I must confess, I grow a little weary getting about like a black crow, always wondering if someone I used to know will recognize me."

James clasped her hand and angled his head to kiss the sliver of bare skin between her sleeve and glove, making her shiver. "I understand entirely. And I've been thinking about that too. Perhaps, after Christmas and Hogmanay, we could travel further afield, to Italy or Austria. Or indeed wherever you would like to go—"

The scrape of a footstep on the flags was loud in the stillness. James looked back over his shoulder.

"Dinna mind me, guv." A rough male voice bounced off the broken stones around them.

Elizabeth glanced beyond James's broad shoulder and gasped, fear clogging her throat. "James," she whispered, her voice trembling. "It's the man from Queen's Park."

Rothsburgh immediately spun around, his whole body tense and senses battle wary. He eyed the plainly clothed Scotsman with suspicion. "This is a private tour," he stated in his best military voice as he pulled Beth directly behind him. "You have no business being here."

The stranger smiled and took a few more steps toward

them, palms spread upward in a gesture of apparent supplication. "Och, I hadna known tha'. My friends an' I mean you an' the lady no harm."

At his words, two more burly looking men filled the archway of the west-facing door, the only entrance and means of exit in the whole ruined abbey.

Bloody hell.

Whatever was going on, it was bad. Very bad.

Rothsburgh's jaw tightened, and he felt the muscles of his arms bunch beneath his coat. Without breaking eye contact with the first interloper, he spoke in a low voice over his shoulder. "Beth, when you can, make a run for it back to the main entrance."

Clenching his fists, he then took a few steps toward the chancer from Queen's Park. If he could engage all three men, distract them, then perhaps Beth would have a clear path to the door. "I'd suggest you be on your way, all three of you. The Duke of Hamilton is a personal friend of mine, as is Colonel Dixon, the Commanding Officer of the Scots Guard. And as I seriously doubt you have any legitimate reason to be here, I'd suggest you leave. Now."

The chancer shrugged. "It doesna matter who ye ken, master high an' mighty." His face suddenly split into a gapped tooth grin as he pulled a pistol from beneath his coat and aimed it straight at Rothsburgh's chest.

Fuck.

Rothsburgh took another step forward. If he could get close enough, he could knock the pistol out of the chancer's hand.

"James. Don't." He felt Beth's hand on his arm and she stepped forward so that she was beside him.

Christ, no.

"What do you want?" she demanded, addressing the

armed stranger. Her chin was raised and her eyes blazed with silver fire.

Despite his gut-clenching, marrow-deep fear for her, Rothsburgh couldn't help but admire her bravery, misplaced though it was.

The chancer inclined his head. "You, of course, Lady Beauchamp."

What? How in the devil's name had her bastard of a husband found her?

They'd been so careful...

Rothsburgh glanced at Beth. Except for two spots of high color on her cheeks, her face was ashen.

"My husband hired you," she stated flatly.

"Aye. Lord Beauchamp's carriage awaits fer ye in the Forecourt, milady."

Beth raised her chin a fraction higher. "And if I refuse to go?"

"Weel..." Beauchamp's hired thug shrugged. "Then yer *friend* gets a wee bullet in his rather wide chest."

Beth's eyes blazed. "How dare you threaten Lord Rothsburgh?"

"Beth. Don't take another step." Rothsburgh watched the chancer's face and a muscle tightened in the man's jaw. For all his outward bravado, the thug was tense, nervous. "He may be lying."

"I can't take that chance, James. Not when..." She turned to him, her eyes shining with tears. "Not when your life is at stake."

"No." Frustrated, impotent anger and despair tore at Rothsburgh's gut. He grabbed Beth by the arm. He knew he was rough, but he didn't care. He couldn't let her leave.

"I have to go. What else can I do?" she whispered. The stark expression on her face told him that this was tearing her apart as well.

"Verra touchin' you two. But I do no' have time fer this. Lady Beauchamp, come with me now, or I swear I will put a hole through his lordship's heart."

Rothsburgh forced his voice past the hard lump of anguish in his throat. "This isn't over."

"I love you, James." Beth stretched up and touched her trembling lips to his in a fleeting kiss. It was like being caressed by the breath of an angel.

And then she withdrew her arm from his and walked toward her captors. And out of his life.

For now.

Holyrood Abbey might be a ruin, and his heart so black with anger, it was like the sun in eclipse, but with God as his witness, he would take her back.

Every step Elizabeth took away from James felt like a stab in her heart. Like she was dying by degrees as her life's blood leached out of her.

Although James had misgivings, she didn't doubt for a moment that Hugh had found her.

The men filling the entrance to the Abbey were dressed similarly to the man with the pistol. Black coats, nondescript clothes beneath. But unlike the chancer—James's smiling would-be assassin—their expressions were flat and stony, like the flags beneath her feet.

On reaching them, one of the men grasped her upper arm tightly. She barely felt it. "This way, milady."

As he steered her through the arched doorway and along the path toward the Forecourt, she heard the chancer speak again, his voice clear as a death knell in the silence of the ruined church. "Lord Beauchamp said to make sure he doesna follow us, MacCrae."

No.

Elizabeth's blood froze and her heart stuttered to a halt as blind terror gripped. She twisted in the thug's grasp, sucked in a breath to scream. But the thug had anticipated her reaction, and before even a shred of sound escaped her, she found his large meaty hand had been firmly clamped over her mouth and nose.

She kicked and flailed. Screamed anyway and tried to bite her captor's hand. Even over the sounds of her own futile struggles, she could still hear scuffling and grunting. A crunch and a dull thud.

Nausea welled within her.

Please, God, please. Let James be all right.

"Enough," the thug growled in her ear, "or I will have to silence you, milady."

She stopped thrashing, but hot tears blurred her vision and her breath came in short ragged gasps, like she couldn't breathe. Like she was dying.

No more sounds emanated from the Abbey.

"That's better." The thug kept his hand over her mouth as he pulled her round the corner of Mary's Tower and into the Forecourt where a plain black carriage waited.

As they approached, another hired thug threw the door open and she was bundled inside by her captor. And then the door slammed.

Elizabeth could see little. Heavy blinds were drawn across the windows and her eyes had not yet adjusted to the dark interior. But as the carriage lumbered forward, and she all but fell onto a seat, she recognized her husband's voice all the same.

"My dear Elizabeth. So lovely to see you."

CHAPTER 20

"Call off your thugs, Hugh. If Rothsburgh is harmed—"

"Tsk, tsk, my dear. I really don't think you are in any position to be dictating terms about how I should treat your lover, do you? Not after the merry dance you've led me."

Hugh's face was in deep shadow making it impossible for Elizabeth to read his expression. He seemed to be wearing a cloak with a high collar, a wide-brimmed hat tilted at such an angle that his eyes were hidden, and a thick scarf that obscured the lower half of his face. But she couldn't mistake the heavy sarcasm in his voice. She imagined his lip curled into the aristocratic snarl she knew so well.

When she didn't immediately respond to his jibes, he continued—a cat playing with a mouse. "Besides, I promised Blaire that I would repay the bastard in kind. As a gesture of my...appreciation for his rather helpful information."

Although Elizabeth knew from experience that it was better not to react to Hugh's taunting, she couldn't help but gasp. So that's how he had found her so quickly. Blaire *had* recognized her at Eilean Tor after all. He must have returned to London and told Hugh.

But she couldn't let Hugh get away with having Roths-burgh beaten to a pulp. She swallowed past the sickness rising in her throat. "Hugh. For the love of God. Hurt me if you must. But don't hurt James."

"My God, Elizabeth. You *love* him? That sap?" Hugh chuckled. "And who'd have thought such a thing was possible from a cold fish like you."

Elizabeth felt her cheeks flame and her hands clenched into fists. She knew without a shadow of a doubt that had she been holding a weapon—a blade, a pistol, a cudgel, anything at all—she would have used it on Hugh then and there.

But her fury quickly abated as Hugh's laughter suddenly dissolved into a bout of coughing. He clutched the scarf to his mouth, and as the fit eased, she could hear him wheezing.

"Hugh. I know that you—"

"Shut it, Elizabeth...I don't...want...to talk about it." He paused, his shoulders heaving with the effort to suck in enough breath. When he spoke again, his voice was so breathy she could barely hear him. "But don't worry. I won't try to *fuck* you if that's what you're concerned about. Dr. Morton was very clear. I just... I want you to come home."

He knows why I left him.

His assertion was crude, but for once, Elizabeth believed him. Despite her anger, her heart compressed then expanded oddly in her chest. She'd never seen Hugh like this before. Here in the confines of the carriage, his fear was suddenly a palpable thing.

Isabelle had been struck down by a severe secondary attack of the pox. So severe she couldn't bear it. What if Hugh was in the throes of it right now? He must be, if he was at last acknowledging the fact that physical contact with him was dangerous.

Elizabeth fisted her hands in her skirts, resisting the unfamiliar urge to reach out to her husband. Dr. Morton had warned her about the disease, of its stages and when it was most contagious. If Hugh had a rash... Even though she had gloves on, she was reticent to touch him. And he would probably reject any physical demonstration of kindness from her anyway. She sifted through the snarled mess of her wildly conflicting thoughts and emotions, trying to think of something to say that would comfort him even just a little. That he would accept.

But at that moment, the carriage drew to a halt. They had barely traveled ten minutes from Holyrood. Hope surged. If she could slip away...

Hugh reached out with a large gloved hand and gripped her forearm surprisingly tightly for someone so obviously sick and breathless. "Don't even think about it, Elizabeth. You're my wife, and never again are you going anywhere, unless I say so."

Hugh had taken rooms at Boyd's Inn, a rather small but exclusive inn that had once been a Bishop's residence. With a stab of irony, Elizabeth realized it was not even half a mile to Holyroodhouse. If she'd been able to get past Hugh's small army of hired henchmen, and his other staff, she could so easily have gone back to James.

But Hugh was having her watched so closely. She would not even make it a few steps down the corridor before she would be seized again. She certainly hadn't a hope in heaven of making it down the Canongate.

If only she could discover how James was. No matter how hard she tried, she couldn't suppress the image of him lying broken and bleeding in a cold, dark corner of the abbey ruins.

And I haven't even said goodbye.

She surreptitiously brushed away the tears that had slipped

onto her cheeks and glanced over to Hugh who sat before the fire, drinking brandy. He still wore his scarf, but it couldn't hide the ravages of the pox. An angry red rash covered his exposed cheeks and forehead, and she could see a scattering of bald patches across his scalp where clumps of his golden hair had fallen out. He still wore his gloves.

What a shocking disease. Although the prick of her conscience was sharp, and the pull of long-neglected duty inexorable, Elizabeth couldn't suppress the urge to see James. To make sure he was all right.

To say goodbye. And to tell him to forget her.

She abandoned her seat in a far corner of the room and steeled herself to approach Hugh. She wasn't worried that he'd touch her—she still believed the declaration he'd made in the carriage. But since they'd arrived at the inn, he'd barely said a word to her, had not even glanced her way. He was withdrawn, still so unlike himself that she hardly recognized him. She had expected more derisive sarcasm at the very least. But this quiet brooding...it unnerved her.

She sat in the wing chair opposite him, and he flicked her the barest of looks.

"If you've come to beg me to let you go back to Rothsburgh, you can just forget about it," he said tersely before returning his attention back to the leaping flames in the grate.

She clasped her gloved hands in her lap and let the silence stretch, trying to work out what to say that would make him change his mind. To give a little for once. But she had never understood this man, or the way his mind worked. He was an enigma. And she imagined she was the same to him. Like a mismatched lock and key, they had never fit together.

She would never be able to work him out. But for her own piece of mind, she had to try.

"Hugh..." Her voice sounded raw, like her throat had been scraped out.

He took a sip of brandy and continued to stare into the fire, as if she wasn't there.

She took a deep breath, tried again. "Hugh. What I did... What I've done... I can't change it. Any of it. All I can do is offer you a promise that I won't abandon you again."

Hugh shrugged. "Your promises don't matter because I won't let you go."

"I just want to make sure Rothsburgh's all right, Hugh. And to say goodbye."

He gave a snort of laughter, the red livid rash standing out against the paleness of the skin beneath. "What, one last poke before you're ripped apart forever?"

"Stop it." Elizabeth stood abruptly, her voice shaking with barely contained anger. "Don't you dare laugh at me, Hugh. Not after everything you did with Isabelle. For years and years."

Hugh's blue eyes narrowed and he gave her a cool, speculative look. She couldn't be certain but perhaps there was also a hint of respect in his expression. "You've changed, Elizabeth," he said quietly, a smile suddenly lifting the corner of his mouth. "I think I like this version of you better."

Elizabeth opened her mouth to speak, then closed it again. Of all the things Hugh could have said, she had not expected that. "Do you know," she said at last, "that's the first time in our married life that you've said something to me that's even close to a compliment?"

Hugh lifted his brandy glass and studied the amber-brown liquid before taking another sip. "I know you've been unhappy," he said quietly. "But I've always been a sick bastard, Elizabeth. You should be pleased that I left you alone...for the most part."

Elizabeth sat again. This was also the first time that Hugh actually seemed to be engaging in something that approximated an honest conversation.

"You should have married Isabelle," she said softly, studying his face.

He looked back at her. "Yes. I should have. But I was too young and selfish and stupid at the time." He took a sip of brandy and she noticed the glint of a sapphire in the folds of his scarf. "How much did Rothsburgh tell you?"

She considered his question for a moment but there seemed no point in lying. "Everything."

"Hmm." His gaze returned to her. "So, you know about Annabelle?"

She swallowed. "Yes. I met her today. She looks just like you, Hugh."

"Well, that's something, isn't it?" There was a decided trace of bitterness in his voice. "There'll be someone on this earth who carries my blood, even if she can't bear my name."

He closed his eyes and Elizabeth fancied that she saw a glimmer of tears in the long lashes that fanned across his pock-marked cheeks.

Although she knew she was being unkind by pressing him for information when he was so clearly upset, there was something she needed to know. Something that had been plaguing her ever since she had left him. "Hugh, that last night when you came to my room...did...did you know you had syphilis?"

He put down his brandy and swiped at his eyes with his sleeve. "No... Maybe..." He drew in a shaky breath and lifted his gaze to hers. "I was an arrogant prick, Elizabeth, and I didn't want to know. I just never thought something like this could happen to me. It wasn't until I'd heard that Isabelle had died...and then you left...I started to feel unwell and I went to see Dr. Morton. That's when I found out for certain."

His face suddenly contorted into a rictus of anguish. "I killed her, didn't I, Elizabeth? Isabelle died because of me." He dropped his face into his gloved hands and his shoulders began to heave with wracking sobs.

Despite everything she'd endured during their marriage —his indifference, his cruel comments, his rampant infidelity—Elizabeth's heart ached to see her husband brought so low. And there was nothing she could say that would help to mitigate his culpability. Even so, she sank to her knees beside him and placed a gloved hand on his back, on his coat.

"No...stay away from me." Hugh shrugged her off. "The rash...it's contagious."

"I know," she said softly, replacing her hand. "But I'm sure it's all right to touch you like this."

They stayed that way for some time until Hugh's sobs eased and all that could be heard was the quiet crackle of logs in the grate.

Hugh was the first to break the almost companionable silence. "It was probably for the best that you got away, Elizabeth...before I took you to bed...because I would have, you know. With the shock of hearing that Isabelle had died, I wanted an heir. But you of all people...you don't deserve this. Any of this."

Elizabeth bit her lip hard, willing herself not to cry. What if she'd stayed? What if she'd tried harder to make him see reason? Insisted that he see the doctor. Shown him the letter. "I tried to talk to you about it, Hugh. After I found out—"

"I know." He suddenly frowned and shot her a searching look. "How *did* you find out, by the way? It couldn't just have been the sore on my hand that made you suspicious."

Her breath caught. Guilt felt like a heavy stone in her chest. How would he react to her disclosure? "I received a letter, warning me. The writer claimed to be your mistress. I only found out recently that it was penned by Isabelle. After I showed it to James."

A tense silence followed. Hugh bowed his head and his gloved hands clenched into fists on his thighs.

God, had she been too quick to judge her husband? "If I'd shown you—"

"I would have told you it was rubbish." He fixed his bloodshot eyes on her. "I told Isabelle the same thing when she accused me of having the pox, the last time I ever saw her. It was in London, just after we got back from the Continent, after Waterloo. We fought, and she went back to Scotland. Like I said, Elizabeth, I didn't want to know. I understand that you felt you had no other option but to leave. But what I don't understand"—his gaze suddenly became disdainful—"is what you see in that soft-cock Rothsburgh. It certainly didn't take you too long to lift your skirts for him."

Elizabeth winced. "You probably won't believe me, but when I left you, Hugh, I never set out to be unfaithful. I just wanted to be...safe. It was pure chance that led me to Scotland. I applied for the governess's post at Eilean Tor. I heard about it through the Trust."

Hugh ran his eyes over her. "Hence the guise of virtuous widow. I'm sure that appealed no end to Rothsburgh. I always thought he was a self-righteous prig."

Elizabeth stood up, her cheeks burning. "That's enough, Hugh," she bit out. "You have no right to judge him."

"Are you pregnant?" His gaze dropped to her belly.

Her cheeks grew even hotter. "I don't know... Perhaps."

Hugh's mouth twisted into a mirthless smile. "Now that would be ironic. Rothsburgh's by-blow as my heir."

"Hugh—"

"Don't worry, Elizabeth. If you are, I'll acknowledge the child as mine. It'd serve Rothsburgh bloody right, though, if his bastard child ended up with my name. That would piss him off no end, I would imagine. It would be poetic justice for both of us, don't you think?"

Tears pricked and Elizabeth turned away. She probably deserved Hugh's censure. And she should be grateful to him for his...consideration, crudely stated though it was. Nevertheless, it hurt to hear him talk so cruelly about the man she loved, especially because James had taken such wonderful care of Annabelle.

"For God's sake, Elizabeth, if I give you until dawn tomorrow to say goodbye to him, will you stop blubbering?"

She swung around to face him again, relief and fragile hope flickering within her. "So James is all right then?"

"As far as I know. Well, that's not strictly true." Hugh smirked. "I'm sure Rothsburgh's got more than a few bruises and a sore head." His eyes narrowed and he raised an eyebrow, his expression now cynical. "It may surprise you, but I'm not entirely stupid, Elizabeth. If I only have a decade or so left on this earth, I certainly don't want to cut it short by having Rothsburgh's murder on my hands. He's not worth swinging for, believe me."

Elizabeth frowned then shook her head. "I don't understand. Why would you do this?" She didn't trust him. He must have some other agenda. It was not like him to make concessions. Especially about something like this.

He gave her a mocking smile. "So distrustful, my dear wife. But you're right. I'm not giving you this opportunity out of the goodness of my heart."

"Then why?"

He cast her a flat look, his contempt clear. "Well, it's not like I'm in any fit state to get a healthy child on you now, am I? You said a moment ago you might be pregnant. Well, I intend to make sure that you are. I'll be buggered before I let the title go to some thin-blooded distant cousin of mine that I've never even met. I'd rather have a bastard for an heir than none at all."

So, there it was. She was nothing but a brood mare to him after all. It shouldn't surprise her that he was willing to do just about anything, or let her do anything, to ensure the

Beauchamp line continued on, even if the child she bore wasn't his.

Elizabeth bit her lip again with the effort it took to stem the sudden sting of bitter tears. She was relieved that he didn't want to take her to bed. She should be thankful that she was going to see James one last time. But Hugh was making her feel dirty...and worthless.

This was more like the man she knew. She had been foolish in the extreme to expect anything else from her husband.

He was right. He was nothing but a self-centered, arrogant prick.

Hugh sighed heavily, as if bored. "Devil take you, Elizabeth. Will nothing please you? I've given you permission to fuck yourself stupid all night, and still you're not happy."

"I will do as you bid, husband." Try as she might, she couldn't hide the note of sarcasm in her voice.

"Yes, you damn well will." He gave her a long look. "There will be terms, though. I won't have you running off again. You owe me. I won't be made the laughingstock of the *ton* like Rothsburgh."

"Of course, my lord. I wouldn't want to be the one to dishonor your family name, after all."

His cool blue gaze hardened. "Even though I said before that I preferred this feistier version of you, I'd watch my tongue if I were you." He picked up his brandy and eyed her over the glass. "Now go and summon a footman. There are things that need to be arranged."

Elizabeth inclined her head, then turned away. There was nothing left to say, because in the end, she couldn't turn down the only chance she would ever have to say goodbye to James. Whatever the terms. Whatever the reason.

She would seize happiness while she still could, because come tomorrow, it may never be hers again.

~

"I'm verra sorry to disturb you, milord, but there's a footman at the door, claimin' to be from the Earl of Beauchamp's household. An' he's most insistent tha' he hand delivers a message to you, and only you."

What the hell?

Rothsburgh cast aside the tumbler of whisky he'd been drinking in a pitiful attempt to deaden his physical, if not emotional pain, and leapt from his seat. Striding past Malcolm, he quit the library and made straight for the vestibule. Sure enough, just outside the door stood a poker-faced servant attired in the Beauchamp household livery.

"I'm Lord Rothsburgh. What do you want?" he demanded. It was eight o'clock at night, almost exactly four hours since he'd last seen Beth.

Four hours since his life had been ripped apart.

After he'd come to in the abbey—he suspected he'd only been unconscious for a short time—he'd spent the next few hours single-mindedly pouring as many resources as he possibly could, into locating Beth—only to be informed an hour ago by Colonel Dixon of the Scots Guard that Lord Beauchamp was indeed in Town and that he, Rothsburgh, didn't have a hope in hell of getting Beth back. She was another man's wife, and that's all there was to it. Dixon could do nothing.

His friend wouldn't even tell him where bloody Beauchamp was staying.

"I dinna want a duel, or any other crime of passion on my doorstep, Rothsburgh," he'd said sternly. "My advice to you, my friend, is to forget her. Go home an' drown yer sorrows. I'm afraid ye canna do anythin' else."

Despite what Dixon had decreed, Rothsburgh couldn't let it lie. He would find Beth, if it was the last thing he did. No matter the cost. Even if he could never see her again, he had to know that she was safe. He'd already sent his own spies out into the night to find her. But now, ironically, there was one of Beauchamp's lackeys at his very door.

So what the devil was Beauchamp up to now?

"My lord." The man bowed and offered him a sealed note.

Rothsburgh snatched it from him—he was beyond caring about appearances—and hastily scanned the parchment.

It was from Beth. *Thank God.* He dropped his head. He felt like he could breathe again.

He read the message again and then addressed the footman. "I agree to the terms," he said tersely.

"Very good, my lord."

Rothsburgh then turned to Malcolm, who'd been lurking at a discreet distance during the odd exchange. "I'm going out," he said in a voice loud enough for Beauchamp's footman to hear. "If I'm not back by seven o'clock tomorrow morning, you are to inform Colonel Dixon of the Scots Guard. And tell him it would be best to check with Lord Beauchamp about my whereabouts as the first port of call. Is that understood?"

"Yes, milord."

Ignoring the pain in his torso—Rothsburgh suspected he had at least one cracked rib—he threw on a coat, then raced out of the front door of his town house. At the bottom of the stairs waited a plain black carriage—a carriage that was quite possibly the same one that had spirited Beth away only hours before.

Seeing no sign of the thugs that had beaten him earlier, in or outside of the conveyance, he leapt in. The liveried footman slammed the door and Rothsburgh momentarily hoped to God this wasn't another trap. But then, for Beth, it was a risk he was more than willing to take.

For her, he would do anything.

CHAPTER 21

Hugh had permitted her to take a room at the White Horse Inn, Edinburgh's largest coaching inn at the bottom of the Royal Mile, but a stone's throw from Holyrood Palace itself. Too restless to sit, her body a mass of raw nerves and strange jitters, Elizabeth paced the relatively well-appointed room—ironically it was the inn's bridal suite—praying that James would come.

What if his injuries were worse than Hugh had let on? What if he hadn't been at home when Hugh's servants had delivered her message? What if he'd had enough of the whole sordid business and of her?

She could understand if James had. But to the depths of her bones, she knew that he would come for her. Try to rescue her.

But that was impossible.

There was no chance that she would be able to escape from this room, let alone this inn. Hugh had covered every contingency. All of the inn's exits, including the mews directly below the second-story window of this room, were being discreetly guarded by his henchmen, all of them armed. Unless James brought half the garrison of the Scots Guard with him, there was no way out for her.

But then, after receiving her note, James wouldn't have had time to assemble his own men anyway. And Hugh's staff were under strict instructions to abort the whole plan if they suspected that James had done so.

Hugh would not be duped again.

While she waited, she fell to contemplating just how she was to explain the real reason for this meeting. Her note had provided the scantest of details, and James would have questions. He was too canny to accept her written reason for the assignation—that Hugh had graciously permitted her a chance to bid him a final adieu—at face value. He knew Hugh too well to believe such a bald-faced lie.

Her gaze fell to the rather large four-poster bed in the center of the room where her discarded gloves, veiled bonnet, and cloak lay scattered across the scarlet counterpane. Could she actually tell James, *my husband wants to make sure you have impregnated me because he cannot?*

She shuddered just thinking about what James would make of that. Of the dark thunder that would appear in his eyes.

At that moment, her agonized musings were interrupted by the sound of male voices in the corridor. The lock was tumbled and as the door swung open, her breath hitched.

"Beth." James appeared in the doorway, his dark eyes grazing over her with unconcealed emotion. Relief, hope, hunger...

And then before she could draw another breath he was on her, his arms crushing her to his chest, one hand pushing into the loosely arranged bun at her nape as his mouth covered hers. Claimed her again.

He was all right.

Elizabeth sagged against him, relief and desire making her head spin. Her hands fisted into the lapels of his coat and she kissed him back, their meeting such a frantic tangle of tongues and mashing of lips, she was barely conscious of the door being closed behind them. Of the scrape of the key as Hugh's servant locked it from the outside.

But the noise seemed to rouse James. He dragged his head up and brushed the back of his bruised, split knuckles against her cheek. "I don't know what is going on right now. But I'm just so damned grateful to see you, at this very moment, I don't care."

"I feel the same way." She reached up and lightly traced the strong angles and planes of his face with trembling fingers, noting a cut through his left eyebrow and bruising beneath the stubble along his jaw. A split and slightly swollen lower lip. "I thought those men were going to kill you, James."

He closed his eyes and sighed, pressing his jaw into her hand. "So did I when I first saw that pistol pointed straight at my chest. But I've learned a thing or two on the battlefield, thank God."

"So it would seem," she said, continuing to catalogue his injuries. She pushed her fingers into his dark, silky hair, noting that he winced a little when she found a rather sizeable lump on the back of his head. "And considering what was done to you, you'll be pleased to know that MacSweeney—the man from the park—is now sporting a broken nose and his accomplice has two black eyes."

"Excellent." James's mouth tilted into a brief half-smile before he opened his eyes. His expression sobered. "Tell me what this is all about, Beth. None of it makes sense. That Hugh would permit this...this meeting, after going to the trouble of snatching you back like that. I don't understand."

"I know." It was difficult to hold James's gaze. She didn't want to tell him the truth. But she would.

James frowned, his eyes narrowing as he searched her face. "He hasn't hurt you, has he? Because if he has—"

"No. He hasn't," she said hastily, caressing his hand as his grip tightened on her shoulder. "And he's assured me that he won't. He's unwell. He knows he can't be...with me any longer."

A muscle worked in James's lean jaw. "I wish I could believe that. If I had my way, you'd never have to suffer his presence again."

"James—"

"It's all right. As much as I'd love to put down your cur of a husband, I won't..." His expression suddenly changed, his brow creasing with exasperation. "How did he find you, Beth? He must have been looking damned hard to locate you so quickly. You've only been gone a few months. And you've been so careful."

Elizabeth grimaced. "I'm afraid it was Blaire. When he first arrived at Eilean Tor, I wondered if we'd perhaps met at one time. I wasn't certain. But he obviously did recognize me and told Hugh when he returned to London."

James nodded, his mouth a grim line. "I should have called the bastard out."

"It's too late now," she said with a small shrug. "What's done is done."

"Yes. But what now, Beth? I still don't understand why Hugh has allowed this"—he flicked his gaze around the room before returning to her—"at all. What's the catch? You and I alone, under lock and key. What is your husband up to?" James suddenly released her and began to stalk about the room like a caged beast, testing the door handle, flicking the blood-red damask curtains aside to look out the window before turning back to her.

Elizabeth swallowed past a suddenly dry throat. Now for the hard part. If James decided to leave now—even though she would likely shatter into a thousand pieces as soon as the door closed behind him—she would understand.

"Hugh wants an heir...desperately," she admitted, her heart beating strangely, an erratic nervous stuttering in her chest. "And as you know, he can no longer produce a healthy child."

A muscle flickered in James's jaw again and his eyes darkened. "So your husband wants me to be the stud bull," he stated flatly.

Her voice was the faintest of whispers. "Yes..."

"Sweet Jesus." James ran a hand through his dark hair then sought her gaze. "I haven't asked you this before...but are you already with my child, Beth?"

And there it was, the question she had longed to be asked by him, and to answer, but now hid from. Elizabeth's hands fluttered involuntarily to her stomach, and James's gaze followed the movement. Admitting such a possibility felt like a betrayal of the worst kind now that she was returning to Hugh.

"I honestly don't know," she said as heat suffused her cheeks. This should be a joyous moment, this sharing of special, secret knowledge. But it wasn't. Hugh had twisted everything. Put a stain upon it. "There's a chance I might be. But I won't know for certain for another week or so."

James nodded once. Looked away. Swallowed.

God, why doesn't he say something?

"James..." Beth's voice trembled and the sound of it pierced his heart.

He was being an ass, letting her hang like this. None of

this was her fault. But to think that Beauchamp had stolen her back, simply to use her and the *perhaps* of a child—their child —for his own selfish purposes.

He wouldn't allow it.

James clenched and unclenched his fists, relishing the pain as the torn flesh across his knuckles protested. He wanted to hit something, break something. If he could find out where Beth's husband was staying, he would take great pleasure in eviscerating him. Slowly. Preferably with a blunt instrument.

"I will find a way to get you out of this," he grated out, hating the fact that he sounded so tense and angry. That he was hurting Beth. But he couldn't help it. There was a darkness in him that he couldn't suppress. It squeezed his chest, crushed the air from his lungs, turned his blood to hot acid.

Beth shook her head, her gray eyes as tormented as the sea beneath Eilean Tor, her mouth a sad, tight line. "How, James? There's no possibility of escape from this inn. Will you kidnap me on the road back to London? Snatch me from Harcourt House in the dead of night?"

"If I must." *God, I have to, or I'll die.*

"Hugh will have me watched and guarded night and day. Any plan you devise will end in certain disaster." She took a shaky breath and lifted her chin, her eyes shimmering with tears. "You must forget me, James. There is nowhere that we would be able to go that he wouldn't follow. Not Scotland, not France, not Italy. It was one thing to be your mistress...in secret. But Lady Beauchamp cannot run off with Lord Rothsburgh. Think of the scandal—"

"I don't care about the opinion of society—"

"But what about your family, James? Your sister and brother-in-law and their children? Annabelle? They would be subjected to untold censure by the *ton*. They don't deserve that."

Rothsburgh ran a hand down his face, fighting against a

rising tide of bitter anguish. She was right. He hadn't considered them before, but now that he did...

Damn her husband to hell.

"James, I understand that you're angry. And you have every right to be, given this new scheme of Hugh's is nothing short of diabolical." Beth's voice was low and breathless, her cheeks wet with tears that now spilled freely. She closed her eyes and her throat worked before she spoke again. "If you've had enough of this. If you want to leave now..."

"God in heaven, Beth. Of course I don't want to leave," he cried, lunging toward her, grasping her shoulders. "Don't you understand? I never want this to end."

For one fraught, suspended moment, he stared at her. Her grief was starkly etched across her face, mirroring his own emotions exactly...

And then he was kissing her, his mouth hungry and demanding, his entire body aching with need for her, this woman like no other who was being torn away from him. His hands grasped her head, his thumbs angling her jaw upward to better plunder her mouth. It was a hard, angry, uncompromising kiss, but she didn't seem to mind. He felt her grip the back of his head, dragging him closer as she moaned into him and lashed her tongue against his. Only when he needed to breathe did he break the rough, desperate clash of their mouths and instead rained kisses over her face—her eyes, her cheeks, her temple, her jaw—tasting her sweet alabaster skin, the salt of her tears.

It wasn't enough.

He drew back. "Before I say goodbye to you tonight, Beth —not forever because I will *never* concede defeat, my love— then I will have you, in every way I know."

"Yes." Her eyes flashed silver, the expression within fierce. "Whatever you want, James..." She began to pull at the knots of his cravat, her lips hot and demanding on his jaw, nipping down his throat as she exposed the sensitive flesh beneath. He shuddered beneath her onslaught. But he needed more. Of her.

"Wait…" He shrugged off his coat and hooked it over the doorhandle to the room, then pushed a rolled-up rug against the bottom of the door. He did not want the prying eyes or ears of Hugh's minions bearing witness to what he and Beth were about to do.

She'd clearly thought that he would be so disgusted by her husband's nefarious plan that he would walk away. He had to show her that he would never, ever do that. That his life began and ended with her. But he only had tonight.

Rothsburgh turned back to where she stood by the fireplace watching him with her beautiful eyes, arms clasped about herself as if she were already bereft. He couldn't bear it. He closed the distance between them and kissed her again, backing her toward the wall beside the hearth with his forward momentum. Pushed a leg between hers and was rewarded with the sound of her moaning again as he ravaged her neck with rough kisses. She would have a rash from his stubble and bruises from where he sucked and nipped at her. Good. The thought filled him with immense satisfaction, fueled his already rampant arousal. She was his and he wanted to leave his mark.

Her hands clawed at the front of his brocade waistcoat and linen shirt, fumbling with buttons and ties. When she pushed her hands beneath his shirt and raked her fingers across the bare skin of his abdomen, he hissed with pleasure. He wanted his flesh to be branded by her too.

More. Now.

The imperative to taste her, take her was so great, he dropped to his knees before her.

"Lift your skirts," he rasped, staring up at her. She immediately complied with shaking hands, revealing her neat ankles encased in black kid boots, her slender legs clad in white silk stockings, and a tantalizing glimpse of the dark blond curls covering her sex.

But it wasn't enough. "Higher," he demanded, impatience and pounding lust roughening his voice. "To your waist. Show me everything."

And she did, even moving her feet apart a little to give him a breathtaking view of her most intimate flesh. *Better*.

Ravenous with need, James's hands traced over Beth's shapely calves and her naked upper thighs. Splaying his hands across her hips to hold her steady, he circled and dipped into her navel with his tongue before running his nose down the center of her silky smooth, flat abdomen, to her curls, deeply inhaling the musky scent of her arousal. He groaned. He wanted her so badly his balls throbbed, but he would satisfy her this way first before he lost himself inside her.

"Hook your leg over my shoulder, my love."

She did as he bid, and he was immediately afforded with the irresistible, mouth-watering view of her exposed, deep-pink folds already slick and glistening, and her swollen clitoris. Ambrosia had never looked so fine.

He gently opened her further with his fingers, then licked the length of her cleft, savoring her juices before he began to circle and lap her quivering center with his tongue.

"James," she groaned hoarsely and gripped his head tightly with one hand, her hips swaying forward, her thigh muscles trembling. He loved it that she was so wanton with him. That she let him have his wicked, wicked way. Even though she was panting raggedly, he recognized that she was not yet at her peak. And he was determined to fling her heavenward.

He started to slide two of his fingers in and out of her in a calculated, merciless rhythm whilst he alternated quick, light tongue flicks with a deeper suckling at her core. She was almost there. Hot liquid rushed around his tormenting fingers and he felt her rise up as her muscles clenched. And then she came on a heart-wrenching cry that was almost a sob. Her supporting leg gave way and she slid down, collapsing into his arms, shuddering, shaking, moaning his name into his neck.

He gathered her to him and held her tight, drinking her in, savoring the knowledge that he'd devastated her with pleasure.

As she kissed his throat, he could feel that her face was wet with tears.

"We haven't finished yet, my angel," he murmured into the disheveled mess of her hair. "Remember we have all night."

Don't think about the fact that this may be the last time you get to do this. Any of this.

～

Undone.

That's how Elizabeth felt. Completely and utterly.

When James began to loosen her hair from whatever remained of the arrangement, aftershocks of pleasure were still rippling through her, at odds with the despair in her heart.

But she couldn't dwell on the fact that tonight would be full of "last times" for them both. If she did, she would dissolve into a useless, blithering mess. James was right. They hadn't finished. They both needed to enjoy what little time they had left together, whilst they still could.

With a shuddering sigh, Elizabeth lifted her head from James's shoulder and placed her palms flat on the hard planes of his chest, the heavily muscled pectorals rising and falling with every ragged breath he took. He looked close to unraveling as well. This wouldn't do.

"I want you inside me," she said, her voice husky with both tears and desire.

He ran a thumb along her lower lip, his gaze searing her, making her sex throb anew. "My thoughts exactly, my love."

With shaking hands, she peeled off his already unbuttoned waistcoat, then helped him to pull off his shirt. Then gasped in horror. "James, you're hurt more than I realized." Her fingers ran lightly over the right side of his lean ribcage, tracing the ugly black and purple bruises that had obviously flowered there after his beating. A peculiar mixture of white-hot anger and anguish lanced through her at the thought of him being subjected to anything that would cause this much damage and pain. Pain he'd endured for her.

"It's nothing," he said lifting her chin, forcing her to meet his gaze. "Nothing will stop me from having you, Beth." Then he dipped his head and kissed her with such focused intent, all coherent thought soon skittered away to be replaced again by fierce, aching need.

Need that was not hers alone. James's cock was like a rod of forged iron, insistently pushing against her. Blindly, with desperate trembling fingers, she attacked the buttons securing the fall of his breeches until he sprang free.

Yes. She wrapped her hand around the throbbing, hot shaft of him and he sucked in a sharp breath, his eyes darkening to volcanic black. A dark thrill shot through her.

"How do you want me?" she murmured, running her thumb across the silken head where moisture already bloomed. The rich, heady scent of his arousal rose about them, and she longed to take him in her mouth, but tonight, they couldn't afford to waste his seed.

"This way." He rose to his feet, pulling her with him before he pushed her against the wall. She could feel the oak wainscoting digging into her lower back but she didn't care. She wanted him to be rough, to obliterate everything else from her mind except for the reality of him entering her. Taking her.

"I've always wanted you this way. Lift your skirts with one hand. Then grab my shoulder with the other." Before Elizabeth knew what he was about—of all the positions they had tried, James had never shown her this—he grasped her about the waist with one arm, and under her behind with the other, then lifted her off her feet.

"Wrap your legs about me," he panted, and as soon as she did, he raised her higher until she could feel the head of his cock pushing against her slick entrance. Then with one smooth movement, he thrust upward, until he had hilted himself fully inside her.

Elizabeth gasped. The sensation of his deep penetration took her breath away. She was impaled on him, crushed between his naked torso and powerful hips and the wall behind her.

Then James began to move her. The bunched, rock-like muscles of his upper body flexed and rippled as he began to slide her up and down upon his iron-hard shaft. She gripped his wide shoulders already slick with sweat, her nails drawing blood. His black gaze drove into her as surely as his cock hammered in and out of her. Driving her higher and higher. Making her sheath clench tighter. Her breath saw raggedly.

"Come for me, Beth." His voice came out harsh and low, between gritted teeth. He was so close to the edge, she could feel it, his shaft began to swell and thicken within her. At last, he closed his burning eyes. Cried her name again.

And then she crashed over the precipice with him, falling head-long with dizzying speed into bliss. Her body convulsed about him and she bit into his shoulder to stifle her hoarse cry of ecstasy. Such infinite pleasure.

She would never forget this feeling for as long as she lived. She would take it into her, make it part of her. Not just a memory—it would be an imprint on her soul. Like her love for this man.

"I love you, James," she whispered. And then she wept.

~

Much later, in the quietest, coldest hours just before dawn, Elizabeth awoke from a light doze with a start. And then cursed herself inwardly for wasting precious moments of this night to sleep.

In the soft darkness, she felt James kiss her temple. "It's only an hour or so before sunrise, my love."

"I know..."

The candles had burnt low, and only a soft reddish glow emanated from the fire. The room was cold, but she certainly wasn't.

She and James were naked, curled about each other in the four-poster bed, and Elizabeth couldn't—no didn't—want to move a muscle. Not because she ached all over—which she most definitely did after having made love with James in just about every conceivable way—but because she didn't want to lose this perfect, intimate contact with his warm, hard body.

She pressed her lips to his collarbone and inhaled the exotic masculine scent that was all his own. She wanted to tell him so many things: the depth of her love for him; that even though she would never, ever forget him, he needed to forget her and move on and find happiness with someone else...

All these words had already been spoken during the night. But she didn't want to say them again because she just knew she would cry. And she didn't want to spend their last hour together weeping against him. There had been too many tears already.

Perhaps she could just show him, all that he was to her, before they had to part. Forever.

She kissed his neck again, in the place where his pulse beat hard and fast, then skimmed a hand lightly across his broad chest, down his lean, ridged torso, to his hip bone and flank. She felt his manhood twitch against her belly and despite her sorrow, she felt her lips curve into a smile. How bittersweet these last moments with James would be.

She enclosed her hand around the hot, hard length of him, taking pleasure in the sound of him breathing her name on a deep groan. She wanted to do something, just for him, that didn't have anything to do with pleasing her...or getting her with a child.

She slid her mouth in a series of gentle, lingering kisses along the same path her hand had just traveled until she reached his swollen cock. It amazed her that even after all they had done, he was still so effortlessly aroused. The musk of their coupling was rich and heavy in the air around them, enticing her to take him—all of his delicious, tempting hardness—into her mouth.

And she did. She swirled her tongue around the silken, engorged head of his cock, savoring the salty taste of both their essences before she plunged her whole mouth down and around him as far as she could before withdrawing, back up to the tip again. Down and up, down and up, her mouth mimicking the suck and slide of their earlier couplings.

James's hand was splayed over her head, his fingers gripping tighter and tighter. Then all of a sudden, he grasped her face between his hands and stilled her movements.

"Beth..."

What was wrong? She lifted her head, but before she could speak, he sat up then kissed her, deeply, tenderly. Heartbreakingly.

When he pulled away, she could only just make out the intent, harrowed expression on his face. "Beth...I want you with me...this time." The words were left unspoken.

Our last time.

James sat up, pulling her with him before he grasped her gently about the hips and positioned her so she was straddling him. She sucked in a breath as she felt the delicious, teasing pressure of the head of his cock nudging between her folds, pushing at her already drenched entrance. The wanting within her was suddenly so strong, she couldn't wait for James to enter her. With a great shuddering gasp, she slid downward, engulfed the whole steely length of him, all the way down to the very base of his cock. He filled her so completely, so deeply, it took her breath away.

James groaned then suddenly pressed his teeth against the sensitive tendon at the juncture of her neck and shoulder, sending a sharp blast of pleasure through her. She gasped again, panting hard as her inner muscles quivered and clenched around him. She willed herself not to climax too soon. She didn't want this to be over in a short, sharp blinding moment. She had to make this last for both of them.

Attuned to her verging crisis, James raised his head and kissed her gently, his hands cupping her face as his thumbs stroked along her jawline. She whimpered and parted her lips for him, her tongue caressing his as she fought for control.

"Slowly, my love," he whispered into her mouth as his hands slid from her face, skated lightly down her arms to her breasts. He then expertly flicked his thumbs backward and forward across her already peaked, throbbing nipples, sending another volley of sparks straight to her trembling sex.

Like her, he was breathing harshly now, his expression strained. "I want you too much this way," he grated out. "Forgive me, Beth."

～

Before she could respond, Rothsburgh tipped Beth back onto the bed, covering her with his body. Although it cost him dear —his balls throbbed like hell—he remained motionless, suspended on the edge of a sacred-like moment, as his gaze locked with Beth's. Memorizing her. Her remarkable eyes were so solemn, so filled with love. It was killing him to let her go back to her husband to play nursemaid, to be nothing but a broodmare.

And what hurt the most at this particular moment, was that he knew she was putting on a brave face for him—that inside she was falling apart just as much as he was. But before they were carried away on passion's sure tide again, he had to let her know something.

He dragged in a breath then spoke with deliberate soft-ness. "I will love you, Beth, until the end of my days. And although you don't want me to, I *will* wait for you. Nothing you can say will convince me to give you up."

"James..." She reached up and stroked his face. "You can't—"

"Yes. I can." Ruthless man that he was, he would not listen to any further protests. It didn't matter what she said. He lowered his head and kissed her as tenderly, as reverently as he could, his tongue gently sweeping into her mouth, his lips sliding with intentional, tantalizing slowness. A tribute to their love.

She moaned into him, a small sound somewhere between a sigh and a whimper as her hands came up to caress his neck, his shoulders, his arms. Then her hips tilted and she cradled him, wrapped her legs about him. And he penetrated deeper. So deep. It was like he connected with her very soul.

"James..." Her voice was a desperate plea and she rocked her hips. As much as his heart longed to stay in this moment, his body couldn't resist her blatant invitation to move any longer.

But he would make this last. As long as he possibly could. He began a relentless, agonizingly slow rhythm, holding her gaze, loving her with his eyes just as much as loving her with his body. Retreating and returning with long, deliberate strokes within her tight, clutching passage. Relishing all the small sounds she made. The sighs and pants. Cataloguing every expression that crossed her face in these last shared minutes.

But as surely as the sun was beginning to rise beyond this room, he couldn't sustain this exquisitely restrained pace. The inexorable pull of sexual bliss drove him to plunge harder and faster, steadily escalating the tension, spiraling them both higher and higher toward the zenith they both sought. Together.

And then Beth cried out, her fingernails clawing him, her sheath gripping him in a spasm so tight, so uncompromising, he had no hope of holding back. With an almighty, shuddering groan, he let go and joined her, his world exploding into blazing rapture, like a comet burning through the heavens. Bright, perfect, heavenly fire, consumed him, suffused him, like his love for this woman.

My love forever. My Beth.

Rothsburgh collapsed onto her, then rolled and gathered her to him, skin to skin, heart to heart. Waiting for the knock on the door that would end these last moments in paradise.

"I love you," he whispered against her sweet-smelling hair.

And then the summons came.

"Lady Beauchamp, ye have ten more minutes until this door is unlocked."

Elizabeth lifted her head from James's shoulder and reluctantly pulled away. James was breathing heavily, still overcome from their exertions. His dark brown gaze, glowing with satisfaction and love, rested upon her face. *Oh my.*

She didn't trust herself to speak so she just looked at him and traced the outline of his chiseled lips and his stubbled jaw, his nose and his brows with trembling fingertips. Such strength and beauty. *This is how I will remember him whenever I close my eyes.*

"We must get dressed, my sweet angel," James murmured softly before turning his face a little to feather a light kiss upon her wrist.

Elizabeth nodded. He was right. The time had come.

Wordlessly, they rose and collected their discarded garments, then helped each other to dress, both taking every opportunity to caress with gentle hands, to place another kiss on exposed flesh before it was covered over. To Elizabeth, it felt like they were dressing to meet the end of the world, not the start of a new day. They hadn't even parted yet and already she ached inside.

She would never stop aching.

It wasn't until she began to tie James's cravat that she at last felt strong enough to speak without risking tears. "James..." She focused on the activity of her fingers as she worked the linen into a series of knots. She couldn't meet his eyes, but she felt his gaze on her face. "I know that we've already been through this...and when all is said and done, we may need to agree to disagree about whether you wait for me or not. But you will be forty, if not older when I am a widow in truth..." She glanced up then, and saw James's mouth was compressed into a hard, determined line. She bit her lip. *Oh dear.* She shouldn't have brought the subject up again. She didn't want to part on a quarrel.

Swallowing past the tight feeling in her throat, Elizabeth tried to blink away the sudden mist clouding her vision. "I just want you to be happy," she whispered.

James reached out and cradled her face between his hands, brushing her tears away with his thumbs. "I know...but I will only be happy if there is the promise of *us* again," he said gently. "I won't give up the joy of being with you, Beth."

"But if you meet someone else—"

"Shh." James placed a finger against her lips. "As you said, we will agree to disagree, my love." He tucked a lock of hair behind her ear. "I want you to promise me something though."

"What is it?" If it was within her power, she would do anything for this man.

He swallowed and placed a hand on her belly. "If you bear my child, Beth, will you write to me to let me know if it's a boy or a girl?"

"Of course," she breathed, her sorrow now truly threatening to engulf her. Even if Hugh never let her pen another private letter again—she was certain he would scrutinize every piece of mail that entered or left their household from now on —she would get word to James, somehow.

He nodded, his dark eyes suddenly shining too brightly as they roved over her face, his gaze ending on her mouth. His head began to lower and her heart twisted in agony. This was it. His kiss goodbye.

His hand pushed into her tangled hair as his mouth met hers, his firm lips sliding, caressing, worshipping her with lingering, heart-wrenching slowness. When his tongue stroked against hers, she couldn't bite back a whimper of distress and she sagged against him, clutching at his shoulders, her hands fisting into his shirt. Helpless with grief and desire. And love.

The key suddenly rattled in the lock and James let her go, just as the door grated open to reveal one of Hugh's grimly scowling henchmen. A small pistol was trained on James. Hugh was obviously leaving nothing to chance.

"Time fer his lordship to go."

Elizabeth nodded. Somehow, she forced her hands to relinquish their grip on James, and she took a step back. "Goodbye, my love."

Through the blur of her tears, she saw James's mouth tilt into a small, lop-sided smile. "For now."

He suddenly reached for her, pulled her back into his arms and gave her a swift, hard kiss. A determined kiss. Not a goodbye kiss at all this time. Then, just as abruptly as the kiss had started, he released her, strode to the door and snatched his coat from the back of the handle.

And then he was gone.

Elizabeth pressed her fingers to her swollen, trembling lips. The end of the world had indeed come at last. But it hardly seemed fair that she was still breathing, that her heart was still beating. That sunlight still filtered through the grimy mullioned window onto the rumpled bedcovers and the rug at her feet. Not when she wanted the earth to split open and the sun to be extinguished. She wanted to lie down here and never wake.

"Lady Beauchamp, yer carriage is here."

She glanced up to find the chancer, MacSweeney, was standing in the doorway.

His brow was creased with something like concern. "Are ye all right?"

She bit her lip hard as she put on her bonnet and lowered her black veil. "I'm fine."

Holding her head high, she then marched past him, out the door.

Back to Hugh.

Hugh was still seated in the wing chair before the fire, brandy in hand, when she walked into the sitting room of his suite at

Boyd's Inn. With the exception of his scarf, which now lay discarded on the hearth rug, he was still clothed in the same outfit she had last seen him in.

Had he been up all night, waiting for her? Brooding? Despite the fact that he had organized her assignation, she couldn't help but think he would punish her in some way. That her penance for what she had done was only just about to begin.

A frisson of cold unease crept down her spine as he cast her a measured look. His gaze was hard and assessing as it traveled over her disheveled hair, lingered on her stubble-grazed cheeks, slid to the bruises on her neck left by James's passionate kisses. Thank God he couldn't see below her skirts to where James's seed still clung to her inner thighs.

"You look like a whore, Elizabeth," he sneered, his consonants slightly slurred. It seemed he had indeed, been drinking throughout the night.

She felt her cheeks grow hot, but nevertheless she lifted her chin. "Isn't that what you wanted, Hugh? For James to tumble me all night?"

He snorted and tipped back what remained of his brandy in one large swig. "You'd better hope that Rothsburgh got the job done," he said as he poured himself another drink, then dispensed a peculiar looking concoction of darkly colored drops from another small, dark brown bottle—she suspected it was laudanum—into the golden-brown liquid. He swirled the mixture around, then glanced at her again, his eyes narrowed. "And you'd also best pray that it's a boy you carry."

Fear, like nothing else Elizabeth had ever known, suddenly frosted her blood and twisted her gut. The cat and mouse game had begun again in earnest. A taut silence stretched between them as she struggled to make her numb lips and tongue work again. "What do you mean?" she eventually asked, knowing that Hugh would probably enjoy the fact that she was breathless with fear.

"Suffice it to say, that if you fail to produce a healthy male heir, I'll have to get someone else to do the deed. And after what Blaire told me about his stint at Eilean Tor, I'm sure that he'd be more than happy to offer his services. He always wanted to be in the Sapphire Club, you know."

Elizabeth nearly choked on the nausea that surged to her throat and dark spots appeared before her eyes. She clutched at the back of a nearby chair to keep herself from falling. "You bastard," she whispered. "You wouldn't. I'd rather die than have that man touch me."

Hugh smirked and shrugged. "I don't know why you are looking so shocked, my dear wife. You know I don't mind sharing. And despite your previous history, you now clearly have the morals of the commonest street doxy."

She closed her eyes against his mocking visage and attempted to control her breathing and roiling stomach. She would not faint. She would not vomit. If she was to survive this life with Hugh, she must not show any more weakness.

"I will be able to let you know within a week or two whether I am with child," she managed to grit out from between clenched teeth.

He nodded once. "Good girl. And I'm glad to see you have regained control of yourself. You know how I hate histrionics."

Ice cold anger, as hard and sharp as an iceberg in the Arctic, formed within Elizabeth. It suddenly occurred to her that she would need to hold onto this feeling to sustain her through the long, fraught years ahead. She dragged in a deep breath and made herself release her hold on the back of the armchair. Smoothed her skirts. Lifted her eyes to Hugh who was watching her with sardonically amused interest.

"Is there anything else, my lord?" she asked with pretended docility.

He sighed and raked her with a withering look, but she steadfastly resisted the urge to flinch this time. "Spare me the false sweetness, Elizabeth. But yes, there is something you can do. Go and clean yourself up. We leave for Scarwood Hall within the hour."

CHAPTER 22

Harcourt House, London
August 1816

"Excuse me, my lady."

Elizabeth lifted her gaze from the tapestry she was sewing—a cushion seat featuring a pair of swans for the nursery upstairs—to find Jenkins lingering uncertainly in the doorway to the drawing room.

That was not like the butler at all.

Her brow furrowed with concern. "What is it, Jenkins?" she asked, laying aside her sewing as unease prickled beneath her skin. Something was clearly wrong.

Jenkins's eyes flitted briefly to her swollen belly—an action that was also uncharacteristic of the man because as a rule he would never overtly acknowledge her advanced pregnancy—and then he swallowed and cleared his throat. "There is a Bow Street Runner at the door, a Constable Vickery, who wishes to speak to you, my lady, and a...colleague who will not identify himself. I did mention that you are not receiving visitors at present. But the constable is most insistent."

Elizabeth's frowned deepened as her disquiet grew. "It's all right, Jenkins. Did either of them mention what this is all about?"

Jenkins hesitated, his lips compressing into a thin line before he answered. "No, my lady. But at the risk of both disconcerting and displeasing you by stepping beyond the bounds of my station, I feel I should mention that Lord Beauchamp did not return home last night."

"Oh..." Elizabeth felt the blood drain from her face, and she placed a hand over her belly where the baby—James's baby—suddenly kicked. "I know he went out last night with Lord Blaire."

"Yes, my lady...but he hasn't yet returned."

"I see..." Elizabeth closed her eyes and didn't know what to think or feel. After Hugh had entered into a stage of apparent remission from the pox, they'd left Scarwood Hall in Gloucestershire and had returned to London in the middle of the Season. With the rash resolved and his full head of blond hair—and therefore vanity—restored, Hugh had again taken to frequenting his club, gaming hells, and whatever other dens of iniquity he cared to visit, usually with Blaire in tow. That meant she rarely saw him or the equally lascivious and odious Blaire—a circumstance that she was wholeheartedly grateful for.

Indeed, once Elizabeth had announced that she was unequivocally pregnant during the long journey from Edinburgh to Gloucestershire, Hugh had been content to leave her to her own devices. For the most part. Although largely ignored, she knew her movements and correspondence were constantly monitored by his staff that included several recently appointed, burly footmen and a pair of pernicious lady's maids.

At times, Jenkins and Dr. Morton seemed to be her only allies.

But despite her lonely existence, Hugh needn't have worried that she'd do anything rash during her pregnancy. As much as her body and heart—indeed her very being—longed for James, she wasn't going to run off and find him. She would rather throw herself off a cliff than disgrace the Marquess of Rothsburgh's name and ruin his whole family's reputation.

No, she still believed to the depths of her soul that James should forget her. And as much as it pained her, she was determined to give him the time he needed to do just that. She didn't doubt that he loved her, but he had a man's needs—strong needs. She was certain he would one day meet another pretty society miss and fall for her. Perhaps not this Season or the next. But sooner or later he would. He deserved a wife who loved him, and children he could claim as his own.

And that couldn't be her or this baby.

For better or worse, she would remain with Hugh.

Unless she gave birth to a baby girl...

Although Elizabeth encountered Blaire infrequently, she couldn't help but notice the way he looked at her whenever he caught sight of her. The glaze of lust in his eyes. In the last few weeks, Hugh and Blaire had even taken to joking about commencing a "Moonstone Club" in honor of Elizabeth's gray eyes if she failed to produce the male heir her husband craved.

The thought constantly made her feel sick, even though her morning sickness had long since passed.

If she did give birth to a female child, she would undoubtedly have to run away again. But not to James. Her former friends—the women of the Widows of Waterloo Trust—someone would help, and provide her and her child with sanctuary. They had to.

If she lost all hope, she would indeed want nothing more than to throw herself off a cliff.

"My lady?"

Elizabeth sighed and opened her eyes. So Hugh hadn't returned home last night. The Bow Street Runner had probably come to tell her that he'd been involved in a dust-up over the outcome of a cockfight, or a game of cards. Or he had been found drunk and disorderly in Covent Garden, or in a back alley of St Giles's when he'd tried to pick up a prostitute. It had already happened once before this Season, and she'd had to buy the Runner off to keep his silence to stop charges being pressed...but it hadn't been Constable Vickery.

She felt the baby kick again and she felt a sudden twinge in her lower back. It wasn't long before the baby was due, Dr. Morton had informed her during his visit to see her the day before. A week at most, by his estimate. He'd given her strict orders to rest, and that she was not to be subjected to anything that would cause nervous excitement.

But now Constable Vickery and an unnamed stranger were knocking on her door.

"Just send them in, Jenkins," Elizabeth said with another defeated sigh. As the butler disappeared into the hall, she idly wondered how much spare money she had in the house. Hugh sometimes hid some in a Chinese puzzle box locked in a curio cabinet in his study, along with his stash of laudanum. Jenkins usually knew where he'd hidden the key.

"Constable Vickery and...a gentleman, Lady Beauchamp."

Elizabeth smiled politely as the stern-faced Bow Street Runner and his dark-suited companion came to stand before her on the drawing room rug.

"Gentlemen," she said with a gracious inclination of her head. Although the constable had not had any qualms about running his gaze over her figure, the other gentleman—a man who looked to be from her own class given the exquisite tailoring of his suit and his bearing—looked nowhere but her eyes.

The well-mannered stranger inclined his head in return.

His expression was solemn. "Thank you for agreeing to see us, Lady Beauchamp. I hope you will forgive our intrusion at this time. But we have come to you about a matter of grave importance."

"And you are..."

"Sir Farnsworth Harrington-Smythe, my lady. I am a representative from the Magistrate's Office."

"Oh..." Elizabeth was suddenly glad she was sitting down. *What on earth could Hugh have done now?* As she strove to keep her expression calm, she clasped her ringless fingers together in her lap. She'd left her wedding band in her traveling trunk in Edinburgh, and neither Hugh nor she had bothered to replace it with a new one.

Sir Farnsworth's brow descended into an even deeper frown. "Is there anyone else from your family at home with you this morning, my lady? Or a close friend?"

Elizabeth swallowed nervously and shook her head. "No... There is only me, Sir Farnsworth. Wh-what is this all about?" She noticed that Constable Vickery was transferring his weight from foot to foot and staring at the rug rather than looking at her now.

Something bad had happened.

Elizabeth's heart began to pound furiously in her chest and a sharp stabbing pain knifed through her lower back again, momentarily taking her breath away. *The baby...*

Sir Farnsworth cleared his throat. "I'm afraid I must convey some rather distressing news, my lady. And there is no delicate way to tell you this... Your husband, Lord Beauchamp, was found dead in Lord Blaire's rooms in Curzon Street earlier this morning."

Hugh's dead? It was as if the world had suddenly tilted sideways and everything appeared strange...not quite real.

Elizabeth shook her head, struggling to breathe as another pain gripped her body. "No... You must be mistaken." Hugh couldn't be dead. He had syphilis, but he was supposed to live for a long time yet. She was supposed to play the role of dutiful wife for another decade or more. She couldn't let her hope for another life—a free and happy life—take hold unless it was really true...

Constable Vickery spoke then, his gaze firm yet compassionate. "I'm terribly sorry, my lady, but there is no mistake. Lord Blaire's staff and another acquaintance, a Lord Kendal, identified your husband's body."

"But how...how did this happen?" *Hugh's been so well lately. It doesn't seem possible. Am I really awake?*

"There will have to be an examination by the coroner, of course," said Sir Farnsworth. "But at this stage it would appear that your husband succumbed to an overdose of the drug opium. It seems Lord Blaire and your husband, along with Lord Kendal, left a—shall we say club—in St James's in the early hours of this morning, and returned to Lord Blaire's townhouse. It seems they all then indulged in a rather dangerous cocktail of overly potent laudanum and cognac. Lord Blaire is also gravely ill and it's doubtful he will survive either."

"Oh...I see." Elizabeth dropped her gaze to her lap as she was battered by a storm of powerful, conflicting emotions. A strange bitter sadness. Overwhelming relief. Hope...

Hugh was dead. Her vain, cruel, self-indulgent husband had at last gone too far with his excesses and had paid the ultimate price. She could scarcely believe it.

She was a widow.

But she wouldn't think about James. She mustn't. She must clip this tremulous, budding hope within her. It had been nine months since she'd last seen him. He'd most likely moved on like she'd asked him to.

But what if he hadn't?

Another sharp pain gripped Elizabeth's back and shot all

the way round to her belly like she was caught in a vice. She gasped and clutched the arms of her chair as warm liquid suddenly gushed between her legs.

"Lady Beauchamp?" Sir Farnsworth took a step toward her, but she held up a hand.

"I'm all right, good sir. It's just the baby..." She held her breath as another contraction hit. "I would greatly appreciate it though...if you could ask my butler to send my lady's maid to attend me. And summon my physician, Dr. Morton."

CHAPTER 23

One month later...

"It looks as though the rain has stopped at last, my lady. There will be a beautiful sunset for certain, later this afternoon."

Cradling James's beautiful and immeasurably precious daughter in her arms, Elizabeth moved to where Nanny Robinson—a young widow whose husband had not returned from the field in Belgium last year—stood by the nursery window and looked out onto the gray day outside. The nurse was indeed correct. Although the cobbles in the street below were still stained to a dark gray by the weeks and weeks of constant rain, and the lime trees dripped in the square beyond, the clouds had thinned a little and watery sunlight filtered through the veil.

Toward the direction of Hyde Park, she could even see a small patch of pale blue sky. It was mid-September and it seemed that summer had only just now decided to put in a very belated appearance.

Elizabeth's gaze drifted to her daughter's tiny face. Jane

was beginning to stir from sleep, her eyes crinkling and her sweet rosebud lips puckering as the light from the window drifted across them both. Her spirits lifting, Elizabeth smiled then glanced up at the nurse. She had an idea. "I think after Lady Jane has had her afternoon tea, we might be able to risk taking her for her first walk in the new baby carriage, don't you?"

Nanny Robinson clasped her hands in front of her white pinafore and smiled with barely suppressed glee. "Oh yes, my lady. That would indeed be a fine idea. I will make sure Lady Jane is well-rugged up mind you, and that the footman carries lots of umbrellas, just in case."

Finding it difficult to resist the infectious enthusiasm that radiated from the nurse, Elizabeth's smile widened. "Very good, then."

As she settled into a comfy armchair by the fire and began to feed Jane, Elizabeth's thoughts drifted, as they inevitably did, to where James was and what he might be doing right now. After Jane's arrival, she had written to him as she had promised, to inform him about the birth of their child. And Hugh's untimely death.

But that had been four weeks ago. It would have only taken two weeks at the very most for her letters to arrive in Scotland... To be on the safe side, she'd sent one to his Edinburgh address and one to Eilean Tor, and it was unlikely that both would have failed to arrive. But then, the weather had been very bad this year...

Elizabeth sighed and stroked the dark, silky hair on the back of Jane's tiny head as the baby suckled noisily at her breast. She prayed her missives hadn't gone astray. Of course, she'd assumed that if James had been in London at the time of Hugh's death, he would have heard the news and all of the rumors that were undoubtedly circulating throughout the *ton*, about the scandalous death of the Earl of Beauchamp. And the sudden arrival of Lady Jane Elizabeth Harcourt on the very day he died.

Even if James had met someone else, she thought he might have called on her by now, to at least meet their child.

But she'd heard nothing. Not a word.

You told him to forget you, Elizabeth. You can hardly blame him if he took you at your word.

Nevertheless, his silence stung.

In the immediate weeks following Hugh's death and Jane's momentous arrival, she had been so caught up in the tumult of events that she had not really had a chance to dwell on when James might make contact with her.

Arranging Hugh's funeral and attending to his affairs had claimed much of her attention at first. Indeed, she had been quite flagrant in ignoring Dr. Morton's advice for once and had traveled with a one-week-old Jane to Scarwood Hall, where Hugh was laid to rest in the Beauchamp family vault, located within the local parish church.

Despite Hugh's position and title, it had been a quiet and relatively small ceremony, attended only by herself, Hugh's solicitor, Mr. Beasley, a suitably mollified Lord Kendal— Lord Blaire was still indisposed—and the Scarwood estate's staff and tenants.

Like herself, Hugh had been an only child and his parents had both passed away during his adolescence. His heir—the distant cousin he had mentioned to her—was currently being tracked down by Mr. Beasley. The new Earl of Beauchamp was rumored to be an employee of the East India Company and was currently living and working somewhere in India.

That meant that Elizabeth would still have a little time to relocate to the unentailed residence Hugh had bequeathed to her, a small but elegant townhouse just off Berkley Square.

Jane pulled away from her breast, and Elizabeth lifted her warm, tiny body to rest against her shoulder, inhaling her sweet baby scent. It was the most beautiful smell in the world, other than the lingering memory of spicy sandalwood soap and the man who used it.

Stop torturing yourself, Elizabeth. If he still loves you and wants you, he will come.

And if not...

She had the blessing of their daughter. And James could never have given her a more precious gift than her.

Fortunately, it looked like the rain was going to continue to hold off as Elizabeth—with Nanny Robinson pulling Jane's miniature carriage and a footman bringing up the rear—walked the short distance from Grosvenor Square to the Park Lane entrance of Hyde Park.

As they wandered quietly down one of the wide meandering paths between sodden lawns, hedgerows and garden beds, Elizabeth glanced skyward every now and again, encouraged to see increasingly more patches of soft blue appearing between the clouds that seemed to have darkened the heavens for most of the year. She smiled, not caring a bit when she subsequently splashed through a puddle in her completely frivolous purple walking boots, and the hem of her smart lavender-gray walking gown became stained.

Although she was still supposed to be in deep mourning, she had decided to flout convention this afternoon, and had donned an outfit that was more suitable for the period of half-mourning. Aside from her new gown with its matching spencer, she'd also given into the whim of wearing a jaunty black bonnet trimmed with violet ribbons and a waving ostrich plume. She'd already received a censorious look from Lady Newbury—one of the prickliest of society's grand dames—as the countess had passed by in her fine barouche.

But after everything she'd endured, Elizabeth no longer gave a fig.

The *ton's* opinion be damned.

It wasn't until they paused beneath a large weeping willow beside the banks of the Serpentine that Elizabeth's buoyant spirits unexpectedly plummeted to earth again. Casting her gaze over the still gray water, she spied a pair of mute swans drifting toward them. The memory it invoked of another day in another park was so strong, her throat constricted and her eyes brimmed with tears.

Sometimes she missed James so much it hurt to breathe.

She surreptitiously dabbed at her eyes with her sleeve—she didn't want to invite questions from Nanny Robinson—then turned her back on the swans and the lake.

Only to see her whole world blown into a million, jagged pieces.

Bowling along the path at a cracking pace, in the direction from which they had just come, was a stylish black curricle. And the man driving the fine pair of matched grays was none other than James.

But he wasn't alone.

Seated beside him, clinging to his arm, was an exceptionally beautiful, dark-haired young woman, dressed in the height of fashion.

"Slow down, James," the woman admonished on a peal of breathless laughter as they flashed past her.

James. She'd called him James.

Elizabeth pushed her gloved fist against her mouth to stifle the involuntary sob that rose in her throat. Her worst nightmare had come true. James had moved on.

And she only had herself to blame.

Blindly, she stumbled onto the path and turned in the direction of home.

"Lady Beauchamp...my lady." Nanny Robinson called

after her, but she couldn't stop. She had to get away from here before she collapsed into a heap on the muddy ground.

It had been over ten months—almost a year really—since she and James had parted. She should be happy for him. This is what she'd wanted for him.

But that had been before Hugh had died.

She was not far from the main gates when she heard the thunder of hooves drawing closer and the whicker of a horse.

"Beth. Beth, stop...wait..."

At the sound of that deep voice, the most loved voice in the world, she stumbled to a halt by an oak tree and grabbed hold of its trunk, her heart pounding in her ears, her breathing ragged and uneven.

Foolish, Elizabeth. Why are you doing this to yourself?

She really had no idea. It was as if her body had a will apart from hers. Her feet seemed to be rooted to the spot like the oak she clutched, her body unable to resist the powerful, magnetic pull of the man whom she now sensed close behind her.

"Beth..."

She felt his hand on her arm; the contact burned through the wool of her sleeve and her whole body shivered. Trembled, like the leaves above her. But she couldn't, wouldn't turn around. Seeing him again, with that other woman would just kill her.

Squeezing her eyes shut, she somehow dragged in enough air to speak. "I...I'm sure the woman you're with...your companion is quite lovely, James, and I should wish you every happiness...but please..." She choked back a sob. "Please, just let me go..."

James's grip on her firmed. "Never again, you beautiful ninnyhammer."

Ninnyhammer?

Elizabeth whirled around to face James. Even though the

corner of his wide mouth had tipped into a smile, there was the unmistakable sheen of tears in his dark brown eyes.

"I'm sorry I took so long to get to London, my love," he murmured, reaching forward to stroke her wet cheek with the back of his fingers. "But with all the rain we've had, the roads were an absolute quagmire. I actually didn't receive the letter you sent to Edinburgh until a week ago, and I didn't see anything about Beauchamp's death in the papers. And then my sister, Helena"—he inclined his head back toward the woman still seated in the curricle on the opposite side of the path—"slowed proceedings down by insisting on dragging the whole family along to London as well. But I must say, her presence did help immensely when I arrived at Harcourt House. Your butler wouldn't say where you were, or when you were expected back until my dear sister unleashed her charms on him."

Elizabeth swallowed, hardly daring to believe what her ears had just heard. "That's...the lady with you...she's your sister?"

James ran a long finger down her nose then lifted her chin, forcing her to meet his dark, soft-as-velvet gaze. "Yes, just my sister... Surely you know that my heart belongs to you. And only you."

Elizabeth bit her lip and heat crept into her cheeks. As he stood before her, his gaze drinking in her features like she was the only thing in the world that could sustain him, she realized how truly foolish she'd been to doubt him. *A ninnyhammer indeed.*

Nevertheless, she felt compelled to defend herself, even just a little. "I told you to forget me," she said, her voice no more than a husky whisper of sound.

He smiled gently and brushed his thumb across her trembling lower lip. "As if I ever could."

Apparently indifferent to the more than curious glances of passers-by on the path behind them, James suddenly pulled loose the violet ribbons beneath her chin, and then cast her bonnet to the ground. "I hope you're not terribly fond of that hat," he murmured as one of his hands slid into the artfully arranged curls at the nape of her neck. "Because I think it just landed in a puddle."

"What hat?" James could have thrown *her* into the puddle right at this moment and Elizabeth wouldn't have minded.

Without conscious thought her gaze flitted to his wide, oh-so tempting mouth, and in an instant, James's amused expression changed.

His gaze darkened and became entirely focused on her lips. "My beautiful Beth," he groaned, his voice hoarse with longing. He raised his other hand and caressed her tear-stained cheek. "God, how I've missed you." And then, at long last, he kissed her.

The instant James's lips touched hers, luscious warmth washed through Elizabeth's entire body, curling her toes, and rendering her boneless.

Such a perfect, rapturous, delicious kiss.

With sinuous slowness his mouth glided over hers, soft as silk, while his tongue languidly explored the recesses of her mouth. When his teeth pulled gently on her lower lip she was unable to suppress a moan.

Yes. She didn't care they were in the middle of Hyde Park, in the middle of the afternoon making a spectacle of themselves for all the world to see. Because this was true and this was real. And this was what she'd craved all of those long, lonely nights she'd lain awake just aching for James. The intoxicating taste of him. The dark spicy scent of him. The feel of his strong, lean body beneath her hands.

Her pulse raced and her heart sparked to life. It was as if the sun had come out again.

"Lady Beauchamp?"

James broke the kiss and they both turned to find Nanny

Robinson, mouth agape, standing a few feet away with the baby carriage. The sage footman, an older man who had been in the employ of the Beauchamp household for an eon, stood further behind, intently studying the wet grass beneath his feet.

The obviously horrified nurse glanced at James, blushed furiously, then focused on her mistress again. "My lady...I'm...I'm so terribly sorry to have...interrupted..."

Despite the fact that she knew she looked like a woman who had been flagrantly well-kissed, Elizabeth summoned a smile. "That's quite all right, Nanny Robinson. I expect you were just concerned about me."

The nurse nodded furiously. "If you w-would like, my lady," she stammered, her gaze flickering to James again before returning to her, "I could take Lady Jane for a turn about the rose garden..."

"Soon, Nanny Robinson." Suddenly feeling breathlessly shy, but bubbling with happiness at the same time, Elizabeth turned to James. She was delighted to see that he looked almost boyishly anxious with anticipation as well. She took his hand. "Come and meet Lady Jane Elizabeth, Lord Rothsburgh."

James followed her over to the baby carriage and looked down at his sleeping daughter. She saw him swallow and heard his breath catch as he gently touched one of Jane's rosy baby cheeks with the tip of a finger.

"She's as beautiful as her mother," he murmured. When he looked up at Elizabeth, she noticed his eyes were unnaturally bright. It was suddenly difficult for her to see clearly through the sudden mist that had appeared in her eyes as well.

Behind the shield of the baby carriage, one of James's hands suddenly slid to the plane of her belly. "Next time, my love," he whispered against her ear, "I will take great delight in watching your belly grow large and round, and I will not miss a single thing."

Next time... Oh my... She felt her cheeks grow warm, but she did not have time to dwell on the implications of what he'd just said as his sister, Lady Maxwell, called out.

"All right, James, you've had first look. Please come and help me down from this wickedly high curricle. I don't wish to break my neck before I get to see the baby."

James laughed and after dodging a passing barouche, crossed over to his sister and helped her to alight.

Helena, tall and graceful as a willow, approached Elizabeth and grasped her hand between hers. "Lady Beauchamp. I'm Helena, James's sister," she said smiling. "It's such a pleasure to meet you at long last. I've heard so much about you from my dear brother."

"Oh...it's lovely to meet you as well, Helena. And please, call me Beth." She wondered how much James had told Helena about their...situation. Probably everything, knowing James.

But Helena was smiling at her with such warm sincerity, it was obvious that she didn't give a farthing about their far-from-conventional history. And now she wanted to meet Jane.

"Thank you, Beth." Helena's wide elegant mouth, not dissimilar to James's, curved into another smile. "I must confess, since James told me about Jane's arrival, I've been dying to meet her. Would you mind if I take a peek at her too?"

"Of course you can," Beth said smiling back at the lovely woman. "And when she wakes, you are more than welcome to a hold."

Helena's eyes glowed. "Oh, I'd love that."

"Not before me you won't," James growled playfully at his sister.

Helena poked her tongue at him then dropped her gaze to

Jane. As they all looked into the baby carriage, the still sleeping baby grimaced a little, then pushed her tiny baby thumb into her mouth and began to suck.

"Oh heavens. She's gorgeous," whispered Helena. She looked up and gave Beth a dazzling smile, her brown eyes, a shade or two lighter than James's, twinkling with merriment. "I know this may sound awfully presumptuous, even wicked —and I wouldn't suggest this at all except I suspect that you and James have a bit of catching up to do—but would you mind terribly if I stole Jane and your nurse, and took a turn about the rose garden over there?"

Beth smiled. "Not at all. Take as much time as you like."

James pointed an admonishing finger at his sister and gave a mock frown. "Remember I get first hold."

Helena rolled her eyes but continued smiling. "So bossy. I really don't know what you see in him, Beth."

As the nurse, the footman, and Helena wandered away, James grasped Beth's hand and led her over to the side of the path again, beneath the shade of the oak but on the other side of the trunk this time, away from the prying eyes of passers-by.

Beth's heart began to pound in earnest when he next stripped off her gloves, stuffed them in his pocket, and then took her hands in his again.

"That's better," James said, his deep voice a caress in itself. "I've missed holding your hands." He stroked his thumbs along the underside of her wrists, sending hot shivers through her, then raised her fingertips to his lips.

"Only my hands?" she replied on an oddly choked voice as a strange combination of laughter, tears and breathless desire bubbled in her throat.

Fire sparked in his eyes. "No. But if I start describing to you now everything that I've missed, we'd be standing under this tree for the rest of the day and all night. It would probably be better if I just showed you afterward."

Afterward? After what?

Still holding her hands and her gaze, James descended to one knee before her.

Beth's breath caught as a heady thrill of anticipation flared inside her.

James's eyes were shining as he looked up at her. He swallowed, took a deep breath, and his voice, when he spoke, was uncharacteristically unsteady. "Beth, do you recall that I made a vow to you once?"

She nodded, breathless. "Of course."

He smiled, his dark eyes fixed intently on hers. "I think it's about time that I made good on that promise. Beth, love of my heart, light of my life. Will you do me the untold honor of consenting to marry me?"

Beth swallowed, and then drew in a shaky breath as she prepared to respond, not even bothering to blink away the tears of joy that suddenly brimmed in her eyes. There was no reason in the world that she couldn't at last answer James with the one precious word she'd always longed to say to him.

"Yes."

EPILOGUE

Eilean Tor, Scotland
Five years later...

"Mama! Mama! Wosy-cwantz stole my ball again!"

Beth put down her novel and pushed herself up from the tartan wool blanket to focus her attention on the flushed and endearingly disgruntled face of her three-year-old son, Jamie.

She'd been picnicking on the hillside beside Eilean Tor Castle with all her children. Now that their luncheon was over, Annabelle, now eleven, and five-year-old Jane were seated farther down the grassy slope, making daisy chains with the assistance of their governess, Miss Chisholm. Meanwhile, Nanny Robinson was attempting to coax a playfully defiant Rosencrantz to bring Jamie's ball back. Guildenstern, ears flapping and tail wagging, was loping about after seagulls.

"Well, that's a shame, my little Lord Torhaven," Beth said, addressing Jamie by his courtesy title (which she often used as his nickname) as she pulled him in for a hug. "You know he just wants you to chase him." Which was true. While Rosencrantz was obedient in every other way, unlike his brother Guildenstern, he steadfastly refused to abide by the rules of fetch.

Jamie nestled into her arms then pouted. "He wuns too fast. Even Papa cannot catch him."

Beth laughed. "That's very true. He cannot." She buried her nose in Jamie's tumbling ebony locks that were the same hue as his father's, then suppressed a small sigh.

James had been in Edinburgh attending to business matters for the past week, but he was due back any day. And Beth could hardly wait.

In actual fact, since they'd wed five years ago, they'd barely spent any time apart. Which was just the way they both liked it. She and the children often accompanied James to Edinburgh and London. But it was the beginning of the summer and the weather had been so lovely, James had suggested the family wait for him at Eilean Tor to take advantage of the fine warm days.

Here by the walled garden, the one Beth had started when she'd first arrived at the castle, all sorts of sea-hardy shrubs and flowers—golden-eyed daises and pink sea thrift and purple sea holly and white yarrow—thrived. Even the ancient rosemary bush she'd had replanted still held court. Bees and butterflies busily flittered around its tiny lavender-hued blooms and the light breeze carried the pleasantly astringent scent her way.

It was a poignant reminder of that unforgettable day when Beth had fully acknowledged her undeniable burning want for James. If she closed her eyes, she could see him as he strode up this very slope toward her. How he'd avidly studied her face beneath the shade of her bonnet, and how she'd blushed beneath his focused regard.

How she'd ached for him to kiss her.

That intense wanting, their all-consuming love for each other, had not yet waned over time. The longing to be with her Lord Rothsburgh was ever present in Beth's heart. To talk and laugh and share whatever experiences life offered them. Indeed, their life together was like a beautiful song she would never get tired of listening to, or a sublime bottle of wine she never wished to finish. A wonderful book she never wanted to end.

In her heart of hearts, Beth knew that James was just as deeply content as she was. He adored their children and loved being a father, and for her part, she was so happy that she'd been able to give him both a son and a daughter. And with heaven's blessing, there would be more children...

When Jamie scampered off to help Nanny Robinson in her ongoing quest to catch the unrepentant Rosencrantz, Beth rose to her feet. As she wandered down the slope to see how Annabelle and Jane were getting on, the long grass and golden heads of the buttercups brushed the skirts of her light-blue muslin gown. The girls had settled by a small hedgerow of whin bushes and had made great progress with their daisy chains. Jane's hair—now a light flaxen hue rather than the dark down she was born with—was adorned with a circlet of flowers, just like Annabelle's. Both girls looked up and beamed as Beth approached. Miss Chisholm made to rise and curtsy, but Beth bade her to remain seated with a smile and wave of her hand.

"Mama, we made this for you." Jane offered her a circlet of daisies. "You'll have to take off your bonnet."

"Indeed, I will." Beth loosened the blue ribbons of her straw leghorn bonnet and replaced it with the daisy crown.

"You look like Titania, Queen of the Fairies, Mama," proclaimed Annabelle with a bright smile. "Beautiful."

"Yes, you do, Mama," added Jane.

"Thank you." Beth touched Jane's bright hair and then Annabelle's. "And so do you, my darlings. You're my fairy princesses."

"Come and join our seelie court—" began Annabelle but then Guildenstern barked, drawing Beth's attention and she turned toward the sound.

James was back and Beth's heart leapt. His mount was cantering over the causeway toward Eilean Tor's keep and as she watched, James raised an arm and waved at them all.

Not ten minutes later, he was making his way toward their small party, his long- legged strides effortlessly devouring up the grassy slope between them. He was clearly so impatient to see them, he hadn't bothered to change out of his riding clothes. Rosencrantz and Guildenstern bounded toward their master, but James didn't slow his pace.

With a squeal, young Jamie rushed toward his father and James scooped him up and settled him on his hip as he began to traverse the remaining ground. Annabelle and Jane couldn't wait to greet their much beloved papa either. They flew down the incline before throwing their arms about his waist, at last halting his determined progress.

Beth laughed and joined them. "How was your trip, my darling husband?" she asked when James had answered all of the children's myriad questions and they'd at last let go of him and wandered off with Nanny Robinson. The nursemaid had thoughtfully suggested that they throw leftover bread crusts to the seagulls, so Jamie, Jane, and Annabelle were presently digging around in the wicker picnic baskets while Rosencrantz and Guildenstern watched avidly, tongues lolling, in case any scraps ended up on the grass.

"Successful in terms of sorting out a few things. But otherwise, horrendous," James said with a heavy sigh.

"Oh?" Beth could see he was jesting thanks to the gleam in his dark brown eyes.

He gently captured her chin between his fingers. "Because you weren't with me." His voice lowered and grew rough with longing. "I was a fool to insist that you travel home without me. I've missed you so much."

And then James was kissing her, deeply, and Beth was enveloped in perfect bliss.

She twined her arms around James's neck and rejoiced in her husband's taste and touch. The groan that spilled from his throat as her tongue danced with his. The press of his big hard body against hers. She would never grow tired of this feeling of belonging. Of this surging passion. Of this fierce yet exquisitely tender love.

A love that had only grown deeper over time. It was as warm and steady and strong as the sunlight caressing Beth's face. The joy that suffused her entire being whenever she was in James's arms was as bright and scintillating as the diamonds of light glancing off the deep blue sea behind them.

When James at last drew back, he was smiling down at her. Now was the moment to share her own news with her husband.

She cupped his beloved face between her hands. There might be deeper laughter lines etched around James's eyes, and a scattering of silver in the dark hair at his temples now, but those subtle changes only made him more irresistibly handsome, adding an unmistakable air of noble gravitas to his appearance. "I have something to tell you," she murmured. "Something special."

He cocked a black brow as his hands settled around her waist. "Oh yes? I'm all ears."

Beth bit her lip as sweet anticipation tripped through her heart. "I think I'm with child again," she whispered.

James's brown eyes glowed with the warmth of his smile. "Really? Truly?"

She nodded and her vision misted with happy tears. "Yes. Really. Truly. I'm three weeks late and my breasts are tender, and I've been feeling a little out of sorts first thing in the morning. But otherwise, I'm perfectly well."

James gave a wild whoop as he tightened his hold then lifted her and spun her around. When she landed on her feet, he bent his head and bestowed a sweetly tender kiss on her lips. "Beth, my love," he murmured huskily as he touched his forehead to hers while gently pressing one of his large hands to her belly, "you and our children bring me untold joy every single day. I never thought I could be so happy. It's more than I deserve."

"You deserve all of this and heaven too, my darling man," Beth returned.

James brushed away a tear that had slipped onto her cheek with his thumb. "I have heaven right here in my arms," he whispered, and Beth would readily own to feeling exactly the same way.

The End

AUTHOR'S NOTE TO READERS

Thank you so much for reading **Lady Beauchamp's Proposal**! If you have the time and inclination, please do consider leaving a review wherever you bought the book. I would greatly appreciate it!

Read on for an excerpt from Chapter One of the **The Ice Duchess**, Book 2 in the Scandalous Regency Widows series...

ENJOY A SAMPLE OF THE ICE DUCHESS

BOOK 2 IN THE SCANDALOUS REGENCY WIDOWS SERIES...

CHAPTER 1

Latimer House, Mayfair, London
18ᵗʰ October 1816

"Jonathon, I can't believe that you and Helena have managed to talk me into this hare-brained scheme." Georgiana, the widowed Duchess of Darby, turned her back on the crush in the ballroom of Latimer House and threw a baleful glance at her twin brother. *He should at least have the decency to look a little shamefaced.*

But Jonathon merely smiled broadly at her, setting her on edge even more. "Come now, Georgie dearest," he cajoled in the exact tone that always made her want to poke him in the ribs. "You know very well why Helena and I have embarked on this mission. You have been holed up in the Wolds for far too long." His expression altered slightly, his smile taking on a melancholy tilt, his blue eyes so like her own, softening. "Your mourning period was officially over a month ago. Allow yourself to have a little fun for once. Teddy would have wanted you to." Jonathon didn't need to add that life was far too short. The last year had definitely shown them both that it was indeed the case.

Georgie closed her eyes as a sharp bite of grief pierced her heart. She was more than just a little relieved to be lurking in a secluded alcove behind an elaborate floral arrangement on the edge of the ballroom. She really didn't think she could bear the prying eyes of the *ton* upon her right now. Thank the Lord her acquaintances were keeping their distance, obviously out of respect for her widowed status.

Poor Teddy. A husband in name only, but my best friend.

The love of Jonathon's life.

"I know, Georgie-bean," Jonathon said in a low voice, squeezing her arm gently. "I miss him desperately too. But life must go on. And twenty-eight is far too young to be acting the part of a dowager."

"Humph. Yet I'm far too old for this nonsense," she replied, her voice starch-stiff with an annoyance that bordered on resentment. She knew she sounded ungracious—not at all like a duchess—but she couldn't help it. She wasn't ready for this return to society. Heavens, after ten years, she'd truly had enough of this tired old parade. The false gaiety. The appraising glances and facile flirting. The ceaseless whispering of the *ton*. She really didn't want to don her social mask again. The famous Ice Duchess. Poised, remote, unshakable.

Untouchable.

But she must. Especially since matchmaking seemed to be high on the agenda of both Jonathon and Helena, Georgie's dearest female friend.

Jonathon raised a dark eyebrow. "Speak for yourself, Georgie. I certainly don't intend to spend the rest of my days as a monk." Reinforcing his point, he threw a calculated smile toward a beautiful young dandy with an elaborate cravat Beau Brummel himself would have been proud of.

"Be that as it may, I seriously doubt that Teddy would have wanted you to procure a lover for me." She caught her brother's startled gaze and narrowed her eyes. "Because that's exactly what your intention is this evening. And Helena's. You can't deny it."

This time Jonathon did squirm beneath her penetrating stare. His cheeks reddened and he cast his gaze downward as he pulled at his cuffs. "Hey ho, that's a bit strong, sis." Apparently finished with adjusting his apparel, he slid a glance her way again. "Teddy did ask me to make sure that you were happy. You know that as well as I."

Georgie barely suppressed the unladylike urge to roll her eyes. "How many times do I have to tell you that taking a lover —or indeed, finding another husband—will *not* make me happy, Jonathon?"

Her brother reached forward and stilled her hand that had been busily flicking her fan against her azure silk skirts. "But maybe it will."

Georgie made a moue of displeasure, deciding then and there she was going to summon her carriage and leave. No matter that she had only arrived ten minutes ago. No matter that Helena and her husband Phillip Latimer, the Earl of Maxwell, had gone to such pains to throw such a grand ball even though it was October. No matter that both her friends and Jonathon had engineered the evening so that several of the *ton's* most eligible bachelors were here for her delectation. They could deny it all they liked, but Georgie knew the truth.

Jonathon's grip tightened on her gloved wrist. "You're not going to cut and run are you? That would be poor form. Especially now that Helena is headed our way."

Oh heavens, no. Georgie followed her brother's gaze and spotted the dark-haired Countess of Maxwell weaving her way through the throng—her flame-red satin ball gown made her impossible to miss. Mercifully, she was by herself. No darkly handsome Lothario or Viking fair rake accompanied her. Georgie released the breath she'd been holding.

"Georgie, darling. There you are." Helena's wide smile lit her beautiful face before she turned her attention to Jonathon. "Why are you letting your sister hide away like this?" she admonished playfully. "I've been searching everywhere for her, Sir Jonathon."

Jonathon huffed out a sigh that was clearly affected. "She's taking her widowed duchess status far too seriously, I'm afraid. Before long we'll find her sipping tea or lemonade in the ladies' retiring room with a cold compress across her forehead, claiming her tired old bones ache far too much."

Helena laughed and touched Georgie's arm. "Surely not." But Georgie's attempt at a smile didn't fool her friend. After searching her face for a moment, a look of compassion replaced the twinkle in Helena's eyes. "Oh, my dear, there is a frightful crowd here tonight, isn't there? I completely understand if you are not quite ready for this. Phillip did warn me that this ball might be a bit too much too soon. If you *do* want to retire—"

Georgie shook her head, suddenly feeling guilty that she had planned to abscond. "It's all right, Helena. I can see how much effort you and Phillip have gone to this evening." She patted her friend's hand still resting upon her arm. "Just don't expect me to dance. You know how I loathe it."

Helena's dark eyes sparkled with mirth. "You're going to claim you're wearing the wrong sort of slippers again, aren't you? New ones that pinch?"

"She already mentioned her toes hurt on the way here," added Jonathon.

Georgie's mouth twitched with a reluctant smile. She clearly needed a new repertoire of excuses. "I'll stay for a little while," she conceded. "But both of you *must* promise not to introduce me to any remotely eligible gentlemen. I know what you are up to, no matter what you say."

Helena sighed dramatically. "As you wish. I promise I won't introduce you to anyone fitting that bill. But you can't stay hiding in the corner. Everyone will talk. Why don't you come and play cards? I know Phillip has been looking for a worthy piquet opponent. He's still smarting over the last time you trounced him."

Piquet. Georgie hadn't played cards since Teddy had died. He'd taught her everything there was to know about the game and she prided herself on her prowess. He'd also understood that to her, the cards were both a shield and a weapon during *ton* social events. And she wielded them well. It meant she didn't have to dance or cultivate mindless conversations with men who might have seduction on their minds. She could just play. But it hurt too much to think of the games she had played with Teddy. The challenge, the good-natured verbal sparring, the laughter...

But Helena wouldn't know that. Swallowing past a leaden lump in her throat, Georgie pasted a smile on her face and inclined her head. "That sounds absolutely perfect."

Helena's smile was as dazzling as the rubies and diamonds about her neck. "Wonderful. I'll go and find him."

As Jonathon claimed Georgie's arm and began to escort her out of her bolt hole and around the edge of the ballroom, he murmured in her ear. "As I've said before, dear sister, life goes on. Enjoy yourself. Win this game for Teddy."

Georgie nodded and squeezed Jonathon's hand. "I will. For Teddy."

Georgie took her seat at one of the piquet tables in the card room and removed her gloves, hoping that Phillip, Lord

Maxwell, wouldn't notice her slightly trembling fingers when he joined her. It seemed absurd to be so nervous. Where was her famous sang-froid?

It probably didn't help that a hush had descended over the card room as Jonathon had escorted her in, and at this very moment she could feel at least a dozen pairs of eyes, if not more, upon her. The unvanquished Ice Duchess—the woman who barely ever lost a game—was about to play cards again. Of course people were going to notice.

Curse her brother and Helena. She would have attracted much less notice if she had simply decided to dance after all. Lemonade in the ladies' retiring room seemed more appealing by the second. And where in heaven's name was Phillip? She glanced about the room but could not spy Helena's husband anywhere.

Not only that, she could see Jonathon disappearing out of the card room, no doubt chasing the dapper young buck he'd been making calf's eyes at earlier.

If Phillip didn't appear within the next thirty seconds, she *would* cut and run.

"May I join you, Your Grace?" A soft baritone drew Georgie's attention away from the ornately arched doorway of the card room and back to the table.

She glanced up. And it was all she could do not to gasp.

A dark-haired, lean-jawed rake was smiling down at her. Her dastardly brother and friends had set her up after all.

Blast them all to hell.

Drawing in a steadying breath, she summoned a slight smile. Her well-practiced, cool duchess's smile—a smile that had sustained her for almost a decade in the face of such obvious raw masculinity. Thank God she still had it.

"And you are?" she asked smoothly, arching an eyebrow. "I believe we've never been introduced." She thought she knew most rakes of the *ton* and she had only been away from

London for a year. But this tall, handsome man with smoke-gray eyes and a dark velvet voice she didn't know at all.

The corner of his wide, well-shaped mouth lifted into a smile. "Forgive my boldness, Your Grace. I am Rafe Landsbury, Lord Markham. Lord Maxwell has been...detained and offers his apologies. He asked me to stand in, in his stead." His eyes held hers—a question or perhaps it was a spark of challenge flared in their gray depths. "If you don't mind, of course."

As if she could refuse with everyone watching. She'd gleefully strangle Phillip, Helena, and Jonathon later for putting Lord Markham up to this. They probably thought she'd build up a rapport with the man over cards. Then he'd suggest they dance or perhaps peruse the supper table together. His large hand would touch her elbow, the small of her back. His fingers would brush against hers as he passed her a glass of champagne... She knew all the ploys he would use to try and get her hot and bothered. But she wouldn't fall for any of them. Never again. Just because she was a widow, it didn't mean she was fair game.

Lord Markham was still watching her expectantly so she affected a small tinkling laugh and shrugged a shoulder. "Of course I don't mind. Please, take a seat."

"Thank you, Your Grace."

Georgie tried not to stare as the nobleman folded his long, lean frame onto the damask covered Adams chair opposite her. *Markham, Markham.* No, not a memory of him stirred at all. *Where had such a man been hiding for the last decade?* He exuded such a quiet self-assurance as he watched her reach for the deck of cards, a completely unexpected and most disconcerting wave of heat swept over her face.

She hadn't blushed in years. *What is wrong with me?*

"Shall I cut first?" Her voice had a breathy edge to it and she forced herself to sit up straighter, praying that the extra air entering her lungs would fortify her for when she next spoke. But all the movement seemed to do was draw Lord Markham's gaze toward her sweeping neckline.

Why on earth had she dressed in such a frivolous, indecorous gown? So what that it was *à la mode* and the azure silk precisely matched the color of her eyes—or so Madame Dupuis, her modiste, had declared. What she wouldn't do for a fichu to hide the rise and fall of her bosom right now. Another blush scalded her cheeks.

Lord Markham's eyes returned to her face, his mouth tilting into another half-amused smile. The wretched man knew she was rattled, damn him. "By all means, cut away, Your Grace."

Georgie forced what she hoped would pass for a sophisticated smile on her face and managed to smoothly shuffle the deck. Placing the cards in the center of the table, she then made her cut. The queen of hearts was exposed.

Not the best card to start with but it would do.

She glanced at Markham and the rogue cocked an eyebrow at her, his mouth tipping into that decidedly irritating, knowing half-smile again.

Wonderful. The man was *going to flirt with her.* Probably for the entire card game. He obviously didn't give a fig that she'd just emerged from mourning. And he must know—the entire *ton* knew. Jonathon, if not the Maxwells, had probably told him that she was ripe for the plucking.

Unless flirting was just a ploy to put her off her game. Lord Markham struck her as a man who liked to play games in the true sense of the word. And to win. She would show him though. Georgiana, the Duchess of Darby, never lost. Ever.

Markham reached for the deck, his long fingers covering the cards before he took his turn to cut them. With a small jolt of surprise she realized the knuckles of his right hand were scarred, misshapen even. She stole a glance at his face and noticed further evidence of past physical altercations—a slight deviation to the bridge of his nose and the faint line of a scar running through one dark eyebrow. Was he a pugilist, or a military officer perhaps? But she had no more time to speculate on the man's recreational habits or profession.

Markham turned over the ace of hearts.

Oh, Lord no. She was already at a decided disadvantage, unsettled by Markham's good looks and devil-may-care manner. And now he'd claim all the subsequent advantages that came with being the younger hand during the first round.

"I'll deal." Markham flashed her such a confident grin, if Georgie had a drink at hand, she'd be tempted to throw it at him.

Instead, she simply smiled back and unclenched her teeth with an effort to reply, "Of course."

Markham reached for the cards. "What stakes shall we play for, Your Grace?" he said, his voice running over her like rich, thick treacle, making her shiver. His disconcerting gaze slid to her lips for the briefest of moments before returning to meet her eyes. "I am open to whatever you suggest."

Georgie blushed hotly again. Why did Markham make it sound as if they were playing something infinitely more dark and dangerous than cards? She would never be able to concentrate with his stare focused so intently on her, sexual innuendo lacing everything he said.

Provoking man. That's when Georgie had a premonition that she was in deep trouble. What if she, the Ice Duchess, lost? Oh, she would never live it down.

The Duchess of Darby never thought she'd meet a man who could melt the ice around her heart...until she crosses paths with Lord Markham. But will the past come back to burn them both?

Georgiana Dudley—the "Ice Duchess"—has just emerged from mourning after a nine-year marriage of convenience to the Duke of Darby, her twin brother's lover. Deeply hurt by a scoundrel a decade ago, Georgie swore she would never turn her head for any man, let alone another rakehell. But then she encounters the wickedly handsome and all too charming Rafe Landsbury, the Earl of Markham and against her better judgment, her interest is reluctantly aroused. An affair may be impossible to resist but dare she trust Lord Markham with her most intimate secrets...and her heart?

Society believes Rafe to be a diplomat but for many years he has been working on the Continent as a spy for the Crown. Leaving the shadowy world of espionage behind, he returns to London with the intention of finding a wife. When he is paired with the frosty yet fascinating Duchess of Darby at the piquet table during a ton ball, he is intrigued. Do-or-die man that he is, he's certainly not going to let her cool demeanor dissuade him from pursuing her.

When Rafe's dark past returns to endanger Georgie, he is determined to protect her at all costs, even if that means hiding who he once was. With the stakes so high, both Georgie and Rafe must decide if love is a risk worth taking...

How to Catch a Sinful Marquess, Book 3
How to Catch a Devilish Duke, Book 4

≈

STANDALONE TITLES

All She Wants for Christmas
Dashing Through the Snow
The Duke Who Came to Christmas Dinner
My Lady of Misrule
Long Gone Girl

≈

COMING SOON...

HIGHLAND ROGUES
The Master of Strathburn, Book 1
The Laird of Blackloch, Book 2

LADY MEETS ROGUE
The Lady and the Libertine (**FREE** for newsletter subscribers)
The Lady and the Privateer (Out July 2023)
The Lady and the Duke (Out January 2024)

ABOUT THE AUTHOR

Amy Rose Bennett is an Australian author who has a passion for penning emotion-packed historical romances. Of course, her strong-willed heroines and rakish heroes always find their happily ever after. A former speech pathologist, Amy is happily married to her very own romantic hero and has two lovely, very accomplished adult daughters. When she's not creating stories, Amy loves to cook up a storm in the kitchen, lose herself in a good book or a witty rom-com, and when she can afford it, travel to all the places she writes about.

Sign up for Amy Rose Bennett's newsletter via her website at www.amyrosebennett.com to receive all of her latest book news! When you subscribe, you'll also receive an exclusive FREE copy of her hot but sweet novella, *The Lady and the Libertine!*

When bluestocking Lady Angelina Pembroke decides the only way out of an impending but unwanted engagement is to ruin her reputation, she approaches London's most notorious libertine —a former naval officer dubbed the "Tattooed Viscount"—to ensure her plan is a resounding success. But sometimes, the road to ruination isn't all plain sailing...especially when love gets in the way...

Printed in the USA
CPSIA information can be obtained
at www.ICGtesting.com
LVHW090507010324
773216LV00038B/387